KU-496-024

SHAUN HUTSON

EXIT WOUNDS

PAN BOOKS

First published 2000 by Macmillan

This edition published 2001 by Pan Books
an imprint of Pan Macmillan Ltd
Pan Macmillan, 20 New Wharf Road, London N1 9RR
Basingstoke and Oxford
Associated companies throughout the world
www.panmacmillan.com

ISBN 0 330 37004 9

3 5 7 9 8 6 4

A CIP catalogue record for this book is available
from the British Library.

Typeset by SetSystems Ltd, Saffron Walden, Essex
Printed and bound in Great Britain by
Mackays of Chatham PLC, Chatham, Kent

*This book is dedicated to
Peter Lavery and Matt Smith.
They should know why.*

ACKNOWLEDGEMENTS

Here is, blah, blah, blah, some people and places who, blah, blah, blah. You know the drill by now, folks. While I was writing *Exit Wounds* there were several people, places and things who helped, hindered or were generally around while it was undergoing the sometimes painful process of creation. By the way, you might be interested to know that the original title was *Bastards*. Hands up who likes that title (hold on, I'm counting . . .). It was changed to *Exit Wounds* for various reasons, NONE of which had anything to do with me, but that's another story . . . (one I'll probably tell in another book . . .)

Anyway, down to the thank-yous:

Many thanks to my agent, Sara Fisher, for agreeing to represent me and then doing such a brilliant job of it (and I promise not to lower the tone of the place too much, Sara . . .).

Many, many thanks to everyone at my publishers for their continued faith and support, especially the sales team.

Huge thanks to Peter Nichols, Lesley Tebbs, Jack Taylor, Tom Sharp, Barbara Grant, Lewis Bloch and Stephen Luckman.

ACKNOWLEDGEMENTS

Nods in the direction of Dee, Zena, Jo Bolsom, Sanctuary Music, Iron Maiden and Wally Grove.

Many thanks to Martin 'gooner' Phillips. To Terri, Rachel and Rebecca. Also to Ian Austin. To Maurice, as ever, for the hot dogs and tea and also to Nicky Stinson (but keep your hands off my chocolates, right . . .?).

Special thanks to Hailey Owen, who is probably in a jungle by now, up to her armpits in diseased locals. Enjoy your break. Many thanks also to Tori at Centurion Card.

A very special thank-you to John Maloney and Tim, who wired me up, carried me around and generally made a very unpleasant experience almost bearable. For your expertise and your patience I am in your debt. The same goes for the doctors and nurses that night. A big thanks to Ted and Molly as well, who chose that one weekend *not* to be on holiday . . .

Indirect thanks, as ever, to Sam Peckinpah. There will never be another. Your genius is sorely missed, *compadre*. I hope this would have met with your approval.

Thanks to Aria guitars, Yamaha Drums and Nike football boots for helping to clear the mental blocks (even if sore fingers, blisters and pulled muscles were sometimes the result).

Many thanks to the Rhiga Royal Hotel in New York and Margaret in Lindy's, Times Square. It really does feel like coming home.

To Liverpool Football Club a huge thanks. Despite the occasional bout of raised blood pressure you continue to delight me. Thanks also to 'the Paisley Lounge boys', Steve 'Residents' Lucas (two pints before kick-off), Paul

ACKNOWLEDGEMENTS

'married now' Garner and Aaron 'eight holidays a year' Reynolds for still sharing the driving and jokes and tea at Keele.

I would say thanks to my mum and dad but, as ever, it seems too inadequate a word. I wish I could think of one to describe my gratitude.

Extra special thanks to my wife, Belinda, for absolutely, positively, everything. She knows what I'm thinking before I do. And I love her even more for that and so many other things (the chocolates are just a bonus . . .). Without her, I could not function. I can't put it more simply than that.

Of course there is someone else in my life too. The girl who lets me take her to the cinema when the mighty Reds haven't got a game on a Saturday, who has allowed me to learn the complete script of *The Lion King* (repeated viewings do that to you . . .), who actually believes Cartman is big-boned, who worships Metallica as I do, and who always says goodnight to Titi Camara . . . I am referring, of course, to my wonderful daughter. And, yes, we're still arguing about Barbie's most flattering outfit . . .

The last thank-you is always reserved for you lot. My readers. My toughest yet most appreciative and valued critics. My own 'Wild Bunch'. I can see a few bends coming up in the road and some of them lead to strange places.

Let's go.

Shaun Hutson

What is the worst of woes that wait on age?
What stamps the wrinkle deeper on the brow?
To view each loved one blotted from life's page.
And be alone on earth, as I am now.

Byron

SOUTHSIDE, KINGSTON, JAMAICA

THE BULLET HAD cut easily through muscle.

As he ran, Lestor Ford could feel a burning sensation spreading slowly from the wound at the top of his arm, enveloping the entire limb. Blood stained his shirt and splashed from the ends of his fingers, but the injury did little to slow his breakneck pace.

Ahead of him, feet pounding the potholed street, Ernie Codling also dashed along. Occasionally he would glance over his shoulder, but his eyes were looking beyond Ford.

He was scanning the narrow thoroughfares for their pursuers.

Onlookers watched them indifferently as they ran; they had no desire to become involved.

You kept your eyes open and your mouth shut when things didn't concern you.

There must be a reason why these two men were running frantically through the streets, sometimes clambering over the corrugated tin and zinc fences that bordered houses and roads.

No one asked these men if they needed help.

No one cared why one of them was bleeding.

Just mind your own business.

As Codling ran, his long dreads flapped around like so many angry serpents. He looked back again when he heard the fast-approaching roar of a motorbike engine.

They close.

He crashed into one of the untended heaps of rubbish that lined the street and tumbled over, rolling once, then springing up. The heaps were all along the pathway, like journey markers on a road to nowhere.

Ford followed close behind, bumping into a woman who was struggling with some groceries, the impact sending her flying, her provisions spilling into the street. Several children ran from a nearby house and snatched up some of the fallen food, dashing off before the woman could grab it. Her shrieks of indignation echoed in the ears of the fleeing men.

Codling wondered about heading further south, towards Kingston harbour itself. Using the mazelike streets as cover. Searching out somewhere to get his breath.

No point trying to hide; they would find him.

Nowhere to hide on the whole motherfucking island.

Just keep running.

Put some distance between himself and those who chased him.

He knew where he had to go, if only he could reach it.

There was a man he had to see – if he lived that long.

Twenty-eight years old.

Him a fucking old man.

For these parts.

Papa Ernie.

Codling continued to run. The breath was rasping in his lungs now. The heat from the blazing sun and the stink that filled these narrow, rubbish-choked streets was almost palpable.

His mouth was dry. His legs were aching. His heart hammered against his ribs.

Ford stumbled again and landed on his injured arm.

Codling heard his shout of pain.

He ran on.

Ahead, there was a crossroads.

The bike roared across, the rider slamming on the brakes when he saw his prey.

Codling saw him swing the Ingram M10 into view; saw his finger tighten on the trigger.

The stacatto rattle of sub-machine-gun fire filled the air. Bullets struck the ground close to his feet and drilled holes in the house behind him, blasting portions of the wooden window shutters away. Sickly yellow paint, already cracked and peeling, was stripped from the wall by the high-velocity impacts.

Ford was hit.

Two bullets in the chest; one in the face.

The 9mm shell shattered his cheekbone and erupted from the back of his head. It carried a sticky flux of pulverized bone and brain matter with it.

Codling realized Ford was beyond help.

Realized too that the rider would be forced to reload.

The thirty-two-round clip could be emptied in less than three seconds.

A crowd of children, the eldest no more than eight years old, looked on in fascination.

The driver slammed in a fresh magazine.

Codling ran at the bike and launched himself. He crashed into the rider; a youth in his late teens.

Fucking pussy.

Codling grabbed the youth by the throat, lifted his head a few inches, then smashed it back onto the concrete beneath.

Once, twice. Three times.

Blood began to spread out around the battered, riven skull.

Codling snatched the Ingram from the twitching fingers and slid it into his belt, then he hauled the 125 upright and swung his leg over the saddle.

He gunned the throttle and the bike shot off as if fired from a catapult.

One of the watching children walked across to the body and jabbed his small finger at it, thumb cocked. 'Bang, bang,' he chuckled.

Laughing, the others ran over and joined him, all of them pointing their make-believe guns at the dead youth.

Codling glanced behind him and saw another two bikes speeding after him.

He ducked low over the handlebars, guiding the machine with one powerful hand, pulling the Ingram from his belt with the other.

He fired short bursts behind him, spent cartridge cases flying into the air. One of the men was hit. He toppled sideways, the bike roaring on until it crashed into the wall of a bungalow.

The second rider hesitated, then merely sat and watched as Codling sped away.

You come for me now, pussy motherfuckers. You come for Papa Ernie.

Codling glanced down at the bike's fuel gauge: half full.

Plenty to get him where he wanted to go.

1

FUCK IT, THOUGHT Frank Newton.

Nothing else. Just fuck it.

He lay in bed for long moments, feeling the ache at the back of his neck and across his shoulders.

Neckache. Backache.

He swung himself gently out of bed and as he put pressure on his right leg his ankle ached too.

Everything fucking ached these days.

He sat on the edge of the bed and glanced across at the sleeping form opposite.

Paula's lips were slightly parted as she slumbered undisturbed.

Newton smiled, satisfied he hadn't woken her, then crossed to the window of the bedroom and looked out at the grey morning.

The house in Campdale Road overlooked Tufnell Park sports ground and he could see a man in a dark blue tracksuit jogging across the expanse of greenery surrounded by so much brickwork. Further up the road lay the Bush industrial estate. In the other direction was the gaunt edifice of Holloway Prison.

Two ends of the spectrum: work or jail.

There seemed to be very little in between as far as Newton was concerned.

Such was geography – such was life for many in this part of London.

He watched the jogger gradually slowing down. Saw him take a seat on a bench and light up a cigarette.

Newton grinned to himself and turned, heading for the bathroom.

He flicked on the shower, the water sputtering out reluctantly at first. It was as if it was as disinclined to face the new day as Newton himself.

While he waited for the streams of liquid to heat up, he studied his reflection in the full-length mirror.

Forty-two. In reasonable shape. The only thing that was worrying was the beginnings of a belly that bulged a little too prominently for his liking. He sucked in a breath. Drew in his muscles. Breathed out.

Fuck it.

Gravity was winning.

He inspected his visage in the shaving mirror.

Short brown hair. Pointed chin. A neck that wouldn't have looked out of place on a bulldog. There was still fire in those grey eyes, though. They sparkled with a lustre that seemed to have deserted the rest of his body.

He rubbed his protruding stomach, as if that simple gesture would make it disappear, then he stepped beneath the shower spray.

'Shit,' he muttered, wishing he'd waited a moment longer, but the water soon warmed up. He closed his eyes and allowed the jets to splash over him. They seemed to wash away the aches momentarily.

It had taken him more than an hour to drop off to sleep the previous night, something that had become more irritatingly commonplace during the past three or four years. Just once he'd like to get up in the morning and actually feel as if he'd enjoyed a good night's sleep.

He didn't waste any longer in the shower. He ran one hand over his chin and cheeks as he pulled on his towelling robe, saw the stubble on the face that stared back at him from the mirror.

He'd shave tomorrow.

As he left the bathroom he paused at the bedroom door, checking that his ablutions hadn't woken his wife.

She was still sleeping soundly.

He muttered to himself when he heard the noise from the hall.

Frank Newton padded downstairs.

2

As HE PICKED up the *Express*, he silently cursed the paperboy for making such a racket. He could still hear the little bastard fumbling around outside. Seconds later, a *Radio Times* came through the letterbox and Newton snatched at it, slipping his fingers into the flap to prevent it slamming down too loudly. He stood in the hall for a moment, listening for any sounds of movement from upstairs. Then, satisfied that Paula was still sleeping, he wandered into the kitchen.

The dull light of the morning wasn't strong enough to illuminate the room so Newton slapped on the fluorescents. One of them buzzed somnolently, then finally sputtered reluctantly into life.

He glanced at the back page of the paper: photos of one of the games from the previous night.

Some journalist rattling on about how great fucking Manchester United were, despite the fact they'd lost again.

Same shit, different day.

The front was no better.

Government scandal.

Inflation on the rise.

Some rich, talentless fucker marrying a mouthy tart who presented a show on TV.

Blah, blah, fucking blah.

He dropped the paper onto the kitchen table and prepared to make coffee.

On the fridge door, the white sand and clear azure water of Bermuda looked as inviting as ever.

Beneath it was another picture, also taken from a magazine, Blu-tacked into position on the cold metal.

The Hyatt Regency Hotel, Grand Cayman.

Newton looked at them both, as he did every morning, with a mixture of yearning and resentment.

In the photos, the glorious sunshine sparkled on the water and reflected off the pure white sands. Several tanned bodies were in view.

Lucky bastards.

He gazed at them for a moment longer, then retrieved the milk, sniffed the bottle to make sure its contents were still fresh, and set about making coffee.

What were they doing in Bermuda now, he mused. Soaking up the sun? Swimming in water so clear it was like liquid glass?

And in the Caymans? Dining on freshly cooked lobster? Washing it down with champagne that cost more per case than most poor cunts earned in a year?

And what was *he* doing? Waiting for a kettle with a dodgy element to boil so he could drink his instant fucking coffee?

He glanced at the pictures one more time, then flicked through the paper as he drank his Nescafé.

He didn't eat. He'd get something later. Newton merely scanned the paper for anything of interest but, as usual, found nothing.

He finished his coffee and rinsed the mug under the tap.

From one cupboard he took a packet of cornflakes, from another a bowl. Newton placed them both on the kitchen table along with a spoon and the sugar, ready for Paula when she came down. Then he headed back upstairs.

Paula stirred slightly as he pulled on black jeans and a dark sweatshirt, then stepped into a pair of trainers.

'Frank,' she murmured. 'You should have woken me up.'

'Do you want a cup of tea before I go?' Newton enquired, pulling on his jacket.

'I'll make it,' she told him, stifling a yawn. 'What's the weather like?'

'Shit. As usual. It's going to be cold today.'

'I hope the kids are wrapped up warm, then.'

Paula was gazing beyond him, as if her eyes were focused upon something he couldn't see.

'I'd better go,' Newton insisted.

He walked around to her side of the bed and kissed her on the forehead, then the lips. 'See you later, babe,' he whispered into her ear. He headed for the door, pausing to pick up a black holdall.

'I love you,' she told him as he reached the door.

'I love you too.'

At the bottom of the stairs he paused, unzipped the holdall and looked inside.

He locked the front door behind him and headed for the red Peugeot parked about halfway down the street. It was practically impossible to get a fucking space outside your own house. Everybody had a car in Campdale Road it seemed. He fumbled in his jacket pocket for the keys and headed for the vehicle.

Inside the holdall, the guns felt heavy.

3

THE ATHENA CAFÉ in the Holloway Road stayed open twenty-four hours a day.

The cracked and stained Formica-topped tables were usually occupied for most of that time too. Rarely, at any hour of the day or night, had Frank Newton been in when there wasn't at least one punter filling himself up with the various delights offered by the never-changing menu. Enormous breakfasts. Monumental lunches. It might not have been haute cuisine, but you got your fucking money's worth. And that was all people cared about.

He took a bite from his breakfast bun and wiped bacon fat from his chin.

Despite the early hour, there were half a dozen people in the café. Some preparing for a day's work in the nearby Nag's Head shopping centre. Some on the way home from a night shift.

Newton didn't know where they came from and he didn't know where they were going. Didn't care too much, either.

He sat at his usual table, close to the counter, his

back to the wall, a huge mug of tea on the table before him next to his plate.

The holdall was at his feet.

Best not leave it in the car. Knowing his luck, the fucking thing would get nicked. Not that anyone would be too keen to have a ten-year-old Peugeot away, but it wasn't the car Newton was concerned about. It was the holdall. Best keep it close.

An enormous man, dressed in a blue-and-white-striped overall, emerged from the kitchen at the rear of the café wiping his hands on a tea towel. He wandered towards the till, pressed a button and looked at the money laid out in the various compartments, then, after closing it again, he poured himself a mug of tea from the aluminium urn behind the counter and ambled towards the table where Newton sat.

He was, as usual, wearing a pair of carpet slippers on his large feet.

'Stan,' Newton said, through a mouthful of sausage, bacon and bread.

The big man sat down opposite him and swigged at his tea.

Stan Green was fully twenty-five stone. A mountain of a man, he could barely squeeze his massive bulk into the gap between table and chair.

'Diet still going well?' Newton said, grinning.

'Fuck you, Frank,' Green grunted. He pulled a piece of bacon from Newton's roll and pushed it into his mouth.

'How's business?' Newton wanted to know.

'Ticking over. What about you? Anything doing?'

Newton shook his head, took another bite of the bun and chewed contemplatively.

'I heard a tip yesterday,' Green said. '"Angel" in the three-forty at Ripon. Might be worth a punt.'

'Stan, you couldn't tip rubbish.' Newton smiled.

'Just trying to help, you miserable bastard. When was the last time *you* had a winner?'

'You stick to cooking, mate.'

'How's Paula?' the big man asked.

'She's fine.'

'Still working at that nursery?'

Newton nodded.

'It must be hard for her, being round kids all day, you know . . .'

Newton shot him a withering glance and Green allowed the sentence to trail off. He gazed down at the red-and-white-check lino for a moment, anxious to change the subject.

'Sorry, Frank,' he said as an afterthought. Then he added: 'I wondered where you were. You haven't been in for a few days.'

'I've had things to do. You know how it is, Stan.'

'Yeah, tell me about it. Always things to do. We had a fucking punch-up in here last night.'

Newton raised his eyebrows.

'Nothing worth a wank,' Green told him. 'Two kids about sixteen. Pissed. I threw them both out. One threatened to come back with his mates. I said I'd be waiting. Little cunt.'

Newton smiled.

'Sign of the times, Frank,' Green persisted. 'No fucking respect these days. I've had this place for thirty years now and I've seen things change around me.'

'I know how you feel. You know the real problem? We're all getting too old, too quick.'

Green sipped his tea. 'Do you remember Chris Park? Used to run a billiard hall in Primrose Hill,' the big man enquired.

Newton nodded.

'He died last week. Cancer. Poor cunt was only forty-two. Makes you think, doesn't it?'

Newton washed down a mouthful of food with some tea. As he glanced around the café it seemed that everyone else inside was younger than him except Green.

'Once you get past forty there isn't usually much to look forward to except fucking prostate trouble and rheumatism,' he observed.

Both men nodded.

'Like the man said, "Life's a bitch, then you die",' Green intoned.

'I'll drink to that,' Newton echoed, raising his mug of tea in salute.

As he crossed his leg, one foot brushed against the holdall.

4

UNDER PROTEST, LONDON was coming to life.

Beneath the banks of grey cloud and a watery morning light that did nothing to warm those heading for work, the city was heaving itself from its nocturnal slumber. Not, Frank Newton thought, that London ever truly slept. Somewhere within the confines of the capital, at any time of the day or night, something was happening.

This city where he'd been born, where he'd grown up, it never rested completely. Maybe sometimes, in the small hours, it moved down a gear or two, but its engine never stopped. Never puttered away into cold stillness. And some times, the quieter times, like those spent in darkness, saw the most feverish of activity.

As many were leaving for work in the mornings, some were returning from night shifts. His father had been a porter at Billingsgate for more than twenty years until his death a decade ago, and he had been one of those who had lived that peculiar, inverted lifestyle. Sleeping during the day and working at night, he would leave their small home at around one o'clock every morning and return at about eight. For many of those years he had worked with a drayman who delivered to more than a dozen pubs in the East End.

Hard work.

Newton could still see his father in his mind's eye. And he saw him, not as the wizened, skeletal form that had gasped out final rasping breaths in a hospital bed hooked up to drips and Christ-knows-what, but as that ruddy-cheeked man with bulging muscles and an easy smile. A man with calluses on his hands the size of pound coins.

He thought of him now as he sat waiting for the lights to turn green. Thought of how he had walked out of the hospital that night after his father's death clutching the old man's possessions. A pair of spectacles, a tobacco tin and six pounds in small change.

Not much to show for a fucking lifetime, was it?

There seemed to be more traffic that usual this particular morning and Newton guided the Peugeot along in the flow.

In the doorways of several shops lay bundles of rags he knew only too well were people.

They didn't have much to show either, did they?

A large yellow sign ahead informed him that a water main had burst in the Caledonian Road. That would explain the build-up of traffic.

Fortunately, he wasn't going that way.

His business lay elsewhere.

He glanced at his watch, then checked the timepiece against the dashboard clock of the Peugeot: 7.36 a.m.

Not that far now.

He switched on the radio and listened to the tail-end of the news. A couple of stories about a flood in India. A civil war in Rwanda.

Different fucking worlds.

Some football news.

Nothing much.

Paula would be up by now. She usually left the house about half-eight, once she'd finished getting herself sorted. He smiled as he thought about her.

A Corsa cut across his path, causing him to hit his brakes a little too hard.

Newton shook his fist angrily at the driver, who raised two fingers out of his side window.

'Prick,' Newton snarled, gesturing again at the man as he overtook him.

Fucking arsehole.

The man looked across, saw the fury in Newton's expression and sped off.

If only he'd known what was contained in the holdall on the passenger seat, Newton thought.

He smiled to himself.

Another fifteen minutes and he'd be there.

HANDSWORTH, BIRMINGHAM

TESSA RICHARDS CURSED as she inspected the tear in her stocking. It went from knee to thigh.

The fucking things were ruined.

As she made her way along the road, flanked on both sides by terraced houses of depressing similarity, she pulled her long leather coat more tightly around her. It was cold. She would be glad to get home.

She'd already been out longer than usual. Normally she left the house around ten at night and she was back by five the following morning, but business had been slow and she'd struggled to make her money the previous night.

And that last punter had cost her a new pair of stockings.

Stupid fucker.

And she was damned if she was going to give all of her earnings to Leroy this time. If she made a hundred in a night, then he took seventy: she did all the work, he took the rewards.

Like every other pimp she'd ever known.

But what was she going to do? A girl needed

protection on the streets. She'd seen what happened to those who tried to work alone.

Razor-slashes across the face and tits were not good for business.

She'd tell him she'd made a hundred. He'd never find the other thirty.

Tessa had already rolled the notes up and stuffed them into a condom. She had then carefully inserted the little package inside her vagina like an expensive tampon.

He wasn't getting his hands on *that*.

Tessa smiled to herself.

It was only thirty, she reasoned. Leroy had eight other girls in his stable, all of them bringing in over three hundred a night. Some even more. You could up your prices on most things if you did them bareback: another fifty quid on top of the usual twenty for a blow job without a rubber. Most of the girls had little choice but to work. They had family or habits to support.

And the habits were the most demanding.

Leroy also supplied the gear for his girls as well as dozens of other customers. She didn't know where he got it. Didn't really care. Some of it he cooked up himself.

Tessa shivered as she walked, the short nylon dress she wore beneath her coat offering little protection against the chill morning air.

Some of her trembling was due to the cold. Some to the fact that she needed some rocks.

Leroy would have them – he always did.

She loved him really. After all, one of her four children belonged to him.

She wasn't sure who the other three belonged to, but she loved them too.

Nearly home now.

She fumbled in her bag for the front-door key.

The kids would be asleep. Sasha, the eldest at twelve, always looked after them. She was a good girl; she helped her mother watch over the little ones.

She slowed her pace slightly as she approached the end of the street.

The car parked on the corner looked familiar.

It was Leroy's red TVR 450 convertible.

What the fuck was he doing here?

As she drew nearer, she thought it was empty, although it was difficult to see through the tinted windows.

No, there *was* someone inside.

A driver and passenger.

Perhaps he had one of the other girls with him.

As she drew nearer, the driver's door suddenly swung open and she looked inside.

Leroy Powell was behind the steering wheel, his eyes staring straight ahead.

The man next to him was holding a shotgun, the sawn-off barrels pressed against Leroy's head.

'Get in, bitch.'

The voice came from behind her. Part Jamaican, part

Brummie. She never even saw its source. Only felt rough hands pushing her towards the TVR and into the cramped space behind the front seats.

'And keep your fucking mouth shut,' the voice reminded her.

The shotgun was jabbed sharply against Leroy's head and he understood. He put the car in gear and drove off.

Only when the vehicle was moving did the passenger finally lower the weapon. He rested the yawning barrels against Leroy's thigh and groin.

The silence inside the car was almost palpable. Tessa could hear the sound of her own blood pounding in her ears. Her heart thudded so hard against her ribs it threatened to explode.

And, all the while, the car moved further and further away from her home. From Handsworth itself.

After what felt like hours, she began to see trees and expanses of greenery. She wondered how far from the city they were. Probably not that far – they probably hadn't even left its confines. In truth, they had only been driving for ten minutes.

Still no one had spoken.

When the silence was finally broken, she nearly screamed.

'Stop there.'

There was a lane cutting through a low hillside and the man carrying the shotgun pointed towards it with the sawn-off barrels of the weapon.

Leroy did as he was instructed, pulling the TVR onto a verge close to a water-filled ditch.

'Get out,' the same man said.

The other dragged Tessa out with him, shoving her roughly towards Leroy. They shared a glance, then looked back at the men who held them captive.

The first hefted the shotgun in his hands as the second reached inside his jacket and pulled out a Browning Hi-Power.

The sight of the automatic forced a muted whimper from Tessa. Tears began to flow down her cheeks.

She wanted to ask what was happening. Why she was being involved in this?

She wanted to tell the men that she had children. That they needed her.

If she'd had the time, she would have begged for her life.

Leroy was shaking uncontrollably.

From a distance of less than two feet, both men fired simultaneously.

The roar of the shotgun eclipsed the discharge of the Browning. The twin muzzles flamed, most of the savage eruption catching Leroy in the head. The right side of his face looked as if it had been caved in by a red-hot hammer. He dropped to his knees and then fell backwards, sliding down into the ditch.

Tessa was hit four times, the bullets slamming into her chest and stomach. She too fell backwards into the ditch, her face close to the pulverized remains of Leroy's head.

She was aware, for brief seconds, of dirty water washing over her, then she felt something warmer and realized it was her blood.

Three more bullets hit her, one of them blasting away a portion of her skull.

The man with the shotgun took fresh cartridges from his pocket, calmly reloaded, then discharged both barrels into Leroy's already motionless body. Some of the shot peppered Tessa, but she was beyond caring. Her body was shaking madly as the muscles spasmed and gave up their hold on life. Even the two gunmen heard the soft hiss as her sphincter loosened and they detected another stench to mingle with that of cordite and blood.

They stared down at the bodies for a moment longer before turning and walking back to the TVR, its engine still idling.

The first man slid behind the wheel of the vehicle and guided it onto the road.

They headed back towards the city.

5

Frank Newton hated being alone.

It gave him too much time to think.

Yeah, he'd been alone for periods of his life. Stretches inside, that kind of thing. But he had begun to feel uneasy during the last three or four years if he was forced to spend too much time outside the company of others.

It wasn't so much the desire for conversation he wanted; merely the proximity of other people seemed to be enough.

Anything that prevented him thinking too much.

And it was always the same thoughts; fearful thoughts.

Money problems. Medical problems.

Death.

Those little aches and pains that he'd not given a second thought to ten years earlier now seemed to plague him. A tightness in his chest these days seemed to give cause for worry. Headaches, too.

He'd have dismissed these ten or twelve years ago.

But not now.

He coughed hard and felt a slight pain behind his ribs.

Cancer?

He lit another cigarette and tried not to think about it.

He'd mentioned his fears to Paula, naturally. He told her everything. But he didn't go on about it too much. Why make *her* miserable with *his* fucking worries?

She had enough on her mind.

If he kept busy, then he could keep the unwanted thoughts at bay. He could forget what a wasted fucking life he'd had so far.

Perhaps that was the real root of his fear of death, he reasoned. If he'd done something important, something to make a mark, then perhaps he wouldn't be so fucking scared of death. But, as it stood, who the fuck would ever know he'd been here except his friends and what little family he had left? And in fifty years' time? He might have a headstone if he was lucky.

The thoughts had come upon him almost unexpectedly. They usually did.

He sat back from the table and looked around him, glancing at the interior of the lock-up.

He'd parked the Peugeot round the corner and walked the two hundred yards to the dark blue door. Selected a key for the padlock and let himself in.

The place always smelled of fresh paint, even though it hadn't had a lick of the stuff for more than three years. It was clean apart from some cobwebs in the corners. He sat watching a large spider picking its way across one of the gossamer creations, heading towards a crane fly that struggled helplessly in the glistening threads.

All *his* fucking worries would be over in a second, Newton mused, watching as the spider paralysed its prey, then began wrapping it in silk.

The lock-up was close to Finsbury Park station and every so often Newton heard the rumble of a train as it passed overhead. The ever-present roar of traffic from outside added to the background noise. But still it wasn't loud enough to prevent those thoughts intruding again.

There was a sink in one corner and he crossed to it and filled the kettle. Then he blew dust from four of the mugs that stood on the Formica worktop and splashed milk into them while he waited for the water to boil.

There was a *Mirror* laid out on the table and he returned to it, flipping it open to the racing pages.

Newton glanced at his watch, then concentrated on the runners and riders in the 1.30 at Lingfield.

The holdall lay at one end of the table.

6

James Carson had been watching the woman for the last couple of minutes.

Late seventies, he guessed. Grey hair. Skin like parchment stretched so thinly over swollen knuckles that it threatened to tear. She was gripping a small handkerchief that she periodically raised to her nose or eyes, sometimes wiping away a tear.

She had entered the waiting room of the Royal Free Hospital about an hour after him, accompanied by a nurse who had whispered something to her, patted her gnarled old hand, then left her, returning moments later with a styrofoam container of hot liquid.

It had remained untouched.

There was no longer steam rising from the contents.

Carson had been pacing back and forth prior to the arrival of the old woman, looking up anxiously each time he heard footsteps outside in the corridor. Wondering when someone was going to come and give him some news.

That had been more than four hours ago.

He'd spoken to a doctor when he arrived and a nurse had popped her head in once or twice to see if he was

OK, but, apart from that, he had seen no one except the old woman.

Carson had thought about kicking up a fuss.

Demand to know what's going on. Don't just let them stick you in a fucking waiting room and leave you to stew.

But that wasn't James Carson's way.

He'd never been one for complaining. In all his forty-eight years he'd rarely lost his temper. Could count the times on the fingers of one hand and then not need every finger.

People admired him for it. They marvelled at his temperament, even complimented him on it.

But now, at this precise moment, he wished that he could summon up a side of himself he had barely shown before.

He wanted to shout at someone; wanted to storm out into the corridor, grab the first doctor or nurse he ran into and *demand* answers to the questions that had been torturing him ever since he arrived.

Is my son going to die of this fucking overdose or not?

That should do it.

He got to his feet and began pacing once more, glancing occasionally at the posters that adorned the yellow walls.

AIDS

MENINGITIS

HEART DISEASE

Just the things you needed to look at when you were waiting to find out if one of your own flesh and blood was about to die.

He was aware of the old woman's eyes upon him and, as he drew close to her, he heard her sniffle quietly.

Carson wondered if he should stop and ask her what was wrong.

He thought better of it. Besides, what the fuck could he do except offer his sympathies and, at the moment, she wasn't the only one who needed help.

His son had been brought in to the Royal Free at around two a.m.

Carson had been informed roughly an hour later.

Phone calls at ungodly hours of the morning were nothing new in their house on the Golden Lane estate in Finsbury.

Carson had answered the call calmly.

He'd even told his wife to go back to bed – he would see to it. He'd ring her if he or Gary needed her.

It wasn't the first call.

It wasn't the first overdose.

Seventeen years old.

What a waste.

First time had been heroin.

They'd *both* gone along to the hospital and seen him hooked up to drips and machines like some kind of teenage Frankenstein's Monster.

Then it had been Ecstasy.

He'd been *very* lucky, the doctors had told them, that time.

Now it was heroin again.

Smack, H, whatever the fuck they called it. Him and his mates; the same mates who had left the flat where he'd been found. Left him to die. Called the ambulance, then fucked off for fear of getting caught.

Carson sucked in a deep breath that tasted of musty magazines and disinfectant.

And something else.

A cloying lilac perfume that he could only assume came from the old woman still seated in one corner.

He heard movement outside the door and turned, but the nurse who entered merely offered him a smile and headed for the old woman.

The smile was still there, but it was one of pity, Carson thought.

He saw fresh tears sliding down the old woman's cheeks as the nurse leaned close to her and whispered something, helping her to her feet and out of the room.

Carson thought about asking the nurse for news of his son.

He decided against it.

It didn't seem right.

Not now.

He'd wait another ten minutes.

Outside in the corridor he could hear the old woman crying.

7

FRANK NEWTON FLIPPED open his wallet and pulled out the notes inside.

Two tens and a five.

He fumbled in his jacket pocket and found another two quid in loose change.

Twenty-seven lousy sheets.

Fuck all.

More than some, less than most. But then again, he couldn't give a flying fuck about those who had less.

All his life he'd struggled with money; struggled to get it, struggled to keep it.

No problem spending it.

Oh no, no fucking problem at all.

It was all those years of passing shop windows, gazing in at stuff he knew he'd never be able to afford. Watching Paula try on dresses he knew he'd never have the cash to buy for her. Seeing people on TV raking it in. Reading in the papers about these fucking talentless cunts who passed for celebrities and how much their latest contracts were worth. How big their fucking houses were.

Blah, blah, fucking blah.

It hurt.

It hurt big-time.

And it angered him too.

The longer his life meandered aimlessly the way it had done for the past forty-two years, the more acute that hurt and anger became.

Was it too much to ask that he and Paula sample the good life just once?

The good life. What was that? Go on, define it.

No money worries ever again. Driving flash cars. Dressing in good clothes. Eating in top-class restaurants. Taking holidays when they felt like it. Two weeks in Bermuda. Two weeks in the Cayman Islands.

Fat chance. It might as well be the fucking moon.

And there were other considerations too, weren't there? Other things that money could buy apart from holidays, flash cars, good food, decent stereos, top of the range videos and TVs, designer clothes.

Etc., etc., etc.

It could buy the finest doctors too, couldn't it?

He swallowed hard.

The finest treatment.

He closed his eyes tightly for a moment, pushing the thoughts aside.

Don't even think about it. Not yet.

Whoever was responsible for that old phrase about money not buying happiness had obviously been rolling in it. Only *rich* bastards ever said things like that.

'Money's not the only thing in life.'

(It is when you've got none of it)

'I was happier when I had nothing.'

(Then give the money to someone who wants it)

'The pressure of earning so much money is unbear-able.'

(So get out, get a fucking job in Tesco's)

'What you've never had you never miss.'

(Doesn't stop you wanting it though, does it?)

The worst were the ones who had it dumped in their laps. The rich bitches and the fucking leeches who lived off Daddy's money. Swanned around at their society parties, sticking their workshy fucking faces at cameras. Smiling at journalists only too happy to snap away at them to fill magazines and papers with their stinking pictures.

And nearly as bad were the whining fuckers who won the lottery, then complained they couldn't cope with all the money.

Fuck them all.

Give it away. Give it to charity. Don't buy a ticket in the first place, but don't cry to the fucking media about how unhappy you are living with eight million in the bank.

You can't go down the pub and drink with your mates anymore.

(You can buy new ones, you pathetic, whining cunt)

You don't want to give up your job cleaning toilets.

(Then stick your fucking head down the pan and flush yourself and your Rolex and your brand new Mercedes that you never drive because you're scared of getting it scratched, flush it all away, you gutless, snivelling bastard)

Twenty-seven fucking, stinking, lousy quid.

Newton glared at it as if the money was mocking him.

A fiver on the favourite at Ripon. A fiver on a long shot at Lingfield.

A handy little double if it came in.

Paula would be upset if she knew. She'd asked him to cut down on his gambling so many times in the past.

Not stop, just cut down.

Was it too much to ask?

He pulled a Ladbrokes slip from his pocket and began scribbling down the details.

8

IN THE END, *they* came to *him*.

James Carson had paced the waiting room, flipped through the pile of fusty-smelling old magazines, more times than he could count. And he'd drunk enough of the black liquid that passed for coffee from the vending machine in the corridor that his bladder ached.

Then, just when his considerable patience seemed as if it had been stretched beyond breaking point, the door of the waiting room opened.

The doctor who walked in was a pretty young woman. Early twenties, Carson thought. Blonde hair pulled back so tight it appeared that the skin of her face was being stretched. Her long white coat was flapping open. Her complexion was pale. There were dark rings beneath her eyes.

She looked at him. First over, then through, the frames of her glasses. The clipboard she held looked too big for such small hands.

Carson was sure he could see blood beneath one nail.

He was on his feet the instant she entered the room.

'Mr Carson?' she said, not even attempting a smile. As if she knew the effort would be too great.

'Is Gary all right?' he wanted to know, taking a step towards her.

'Your son is stable,' she told him.

'Jesus,' he murmured and sat back down. It felt as if all the air had left him. As if that one, simple exclamation had emptied his lungs.

She stood looking at him as he sat with his head bowed. 'He's had problems with drugs before, hasn't he?' the doctor said.

Carson nodded. 'Can I see him?' he asked, suddenly raising his head and looking almost pleadingly at her.

'He's still unconscious.'

'I just want to see him.'

She glanced down at her clipboard, seemingly ignoring his request. 'We found evidence of heroin, cocaine *and* amphetamines in his blood. He's very lucky to be alive.'

Carson nodded again. 'That's what they usually tell us,' he said flatly.

'It's not to say he will be if it happens again.'

'If you're asking me to keep an eye on him in future, doctor, then all I can tell you is I'll try. Me and his mother would watch him twenty-four hours a day if we could. But even then he'd find some way to get hold of that stuff he takes.'

'Have you thought about trying to get professional help?'

'Like what?'

'There are clinics . . .'

'And they cost money.'

'NHS clinics.'

'He wouldn't go.'

'Mr Carson, I think it's worth looking into.'

'I know him. He's an addict. And the only way addicts can change is if they want to. That's right, isn't it?'

The doctor nodded slowly.

'He doesn't *want* to change,' Carson told her bitterly. 'Don't you think we've tried with him?'

'I was just offering a possible solution.'

'Well, I appreciate your professional concern, but it's wasted on him. If he won't take any notice of me or his mother, he's not going to give a toss what anyone else says, is he?'

'Sometimes speaking to strangers is more beneficial and all the counsellors are trained to—'

'Just let me see him, please.' Carson moved to the door, held it open and waited for the doctor to lead him to his son.

She hesitated a moment, then did as he wished.

There was a phone at the end of the corridor; he'd ring his wife, tell her that Gary was going to be OK.

Then he had another call to make.

9

ON A BAD day the smell was revolting.

And today was a bad day.

The wind was blowing strongly from the north, carrying with it an odour Jeffrey Hobbs had become familiar with during his years in the house.

He closed his bedroom window and looked through the sparkling glass in the direction of the gasworks that overlooked his house in Laburnum Street. Massive metal silos rose into the air, casting their shadows across this particular part of Haggerston like alien monoliths in some bizarre science-fiction picture.

Hobbs stood a moment longer gazing at the silos, then pulled the net curtains back into place, ensuring they were free of creases. He had washed and ironed them the previous day and didn't want the delicate material to become dirty again.

He glanced around the room, satisfied. From all four walls photographs stared back at him.

Dozens of them, all framed. Some faded or torn, some black and white, some colour, some cut from newspapers.

All were of him.

His favourite was above the bed. An action shot of him standing triumphantly over a beaten opponent. It was the night he had won the ABA Lightweight title at Alexandra Palace.

Beneath the photo hung his boxing gloves. The same ones he'd worn in nearly every fight.

He mimicked the pose in the photo, then made his way from the bedroom, closing the door behind him, just as he did with every room upstairs.

As he reached the top of the stairs he glanced at the handrail and noticed some specks of dust on the white paint. He took a perfectly white handkerchief from his pocket and wiped the dust away.

Hobbs hated dirt. He hated untidiness; always had, even when he was a child. Other kids he had played with would leave their rooms looking like bombsites, but not him. For as long as he could remember, he had always liked neatness.

A trainer had once told him even his boxing style was neat. Guard always high and tight. Footwork economical. He didn't waste energy throwing punches unless he was sure they would connect. Neat.

A place for everything and everything in its place.

Untidiness, to Hobbs, indicated a lack of discipline. And discipline had always figured strongly in his life. During both his training and the fights themselves.

If someone couldn't spare the time to organize their home and their belongings, then how could they expect to enjoy any order in their lives?

He wasn't compulsively neat, although Christ alone

knew enough people had accused him of that over the years.

Even inside, his cell had always been immaculate. Not just because the screws could find less to pick on, but because he himself enjoyed the order. He'd been like it every time he did a stretch.

And there'd been a few of those during his forty-two years.

He'd fought inside too: wing versus wing bouts. Him against some bruiser who fancied himself as a bit of a lad in the ring. Hobbs had dropped every one of them.

Except that fucking Welshman. It had been a lucky punch. Hobbs could still remember it to this day. He'd hammered the bastard, but then, just once, he'd shown an uncharacteristic lapse in concentration and dropped his guard. The right cross had caught him on the temple and sent him reeling. The world had gone hazy before him. In an angry flurry he'd broken the Welshman's jaw, split his eyebrow and flattened his nose. But the damage had been done.

He himself had sustained a detached retina in his left eye.

He'd never fought again.

Doctors had warned him that there was a very real possibility he could go blind.

Life had ceased to have any meaning from that day on.

All he strove for had been in the ring. It was the only place he had ever felt truly alive and in command.

And it had been snatched from him.

He'd lived in the house in Laburnum Street for the last four years and now, as he passed through the small sitting room, he wondered if it might be time to get out his overalls and paint brushes once again. The corn-coloured walls and white ceiling were in need of freshening up, possibly even changing. He'd think about it. Once he made up his mind the job would be finished in less than a week. After that, maybe the kitchen.

Probably the entire house.

He didn't have to consult anyone about his colour scheme; Hobbs had lived alone ever since he left home.

There had been relationships, but never anyone in his life whom he cared for enough to share it with. He'd been married to the ring.

As far as he was concerned, relationships brought nothing but complications. Besides, it took a special kind of woman to put up with the way he lived and, if she was out there somewhere, he had yet to find her.

There's a lid for every pot.

That may well be true. Hobbs just wasn't sure he wanted to search for his.

He wandered through into the kitchen and rinsed and dried the cereal bowl and spoon he had used earlier, putting them both back into their appointed cupboards. Then he took a dishcloth from a hook by the sink and wiped down the draining board and the worktop.

Hobbs opened the fridge and checked its contents. There were meals for each day of the week, all arranged in order. Some he had cooked and frozen himself the previous week, others were pre-packed; supermarket-bought. He'd do himself some rice with the ready-to-heat chilli on the top shelf for his dinner.

Perhaps even a small green salad on the side.

He smiled and headed towards the hallway, pausing to check that his black cowboy boots were clean. He'd polished them the previous day and left them to stand in the hall next to the large duffel bag that was propped beside the front door.

Hobbs reached for his jacket, brushing a speck of dust from the sleeve.

He studied his reflection in the hall mirror. The scars around his eyes and cheeks. The legacy.

He ducked down, raised his guard, then threw a left hook at the image in the mirror.

What might have been.

He picked up the duffel bag, pulling the drawstrings tightly together to seal it.

That done, he hoisted it onto one shoulder and stepped outside into the overcast morning.

As he locked his front door he wondered if the contents of the duffel bag might be visible to anyone who looked too closely, whether the outline of the object was discernible through the thick material.

He swung it before him and ran appraising eyes over the bag, shaking his head almost imperceptibly.

No one would be able to guess what the bag contained, despite its odd shape. Also, Hobbs was a powerful man; the weight didn't bother him.

After the door was locked, he pushed against it a couple of times to satisfy himself it was secure before setting off. Then he hooked both arms through the harness of the duffel bag and carried it as if it were a rucksack.

He could feel the chainsaw inside pressing against his back.

ST PAUL'S, BRISTOL

No ONE KNEW his real name. He was Tiger John on the posters outside the clubs where he worked as a DJ and he was Tiger John to all those who spoke to him.

It suited the big Jamaican.

Good name, Tiger John.

He carried the two heavy cases full of records back towards the waiting VW van, apparently untroubled by their weight.

He was a big man with huge hands and an easy smile.

The girls liked that smile; black girls *and* white girls.

There had been two the previous night. Both white, both in their early twenties, they had been hanging around close to the turntables while he worked and dancing energetically in an effort to attract his attention. It had worked. They had been fine-looking women: one blonde, one with a mane of auburn hair that had caught the multicoloured lights inside the club.

They had told him they shared a flat nearby. The blonde had slipped him the address and phone number and told him to call round when he'd finished work.

All he felt like doing now was going home and sleeping; it had been a long night.

But . . . they were fine women.

He smiled to himself and wondered about his best course of action. Go home, have a shower, freshen up, then pay them a visit.

Why not?

He headed back to the rear door of the club to collect the last of his records.

Inside, cleaners were already mopping the floor, sweeping up the dog-ends of both cigarettes and joints. The smell of ganja was still strong in the air. John stuck his head back inside and drew in a deep lungful of it.

One of the barmen was dropping cracked or broken glasses into a large plastic bin. The others he was rinsing in the sink beneath the bar.

John raised a large hand and waved farewell to the man, who nodded in his direction, then continued with his task.

The morning air was cold, a marked contrast to the stifling heat that had filled the club all night; a heat generated by so many gyrating bodies. John had watched the dancers as they weaved their patterns to the music he played. *He* made them dance. It was his choice of music that got them onto the floor.

It gave him a sense of power. He manipulated clubbers every night in different clubs all around Bristol. Work was plentiful when you were as good as he was and there were more than enough club owners happy to pay for his presence. He worked six nights a week, sometimes seven.

If the work was there he rarely refused. He enjoyed it and it paid well.

And it gave him the chance to sell his wares.

Just a few rocks here and there. Some ganja. Some charlie. There was always demand and he was usually able to satisfy that demand.

That was where the *real* money was.

And there were the other compensations too.

He fumbled in the pocket of his trousers for the piece of paper the blonde girl had given him, smiling as he reread the address.

He began loading the records into the back of the white van, pulling up the collar of his jacket against the early morning chill.

The metallic *swish-click* came from behind him.

He knew what it was without turning around. John had lived in St Paul's all his life; he knew the sound of a flick-knife.

He pushed the case of records into the back of the van, then slowly looked over his shoulder.

There were two of them: both in their late teens, both black.

One carried the flick. The other was holding what looked like a length of metal piping.

John had seen them before, in clubs in the area.

'You want something?' he asked.

'Get the fucking money, man,' said the one with the knife. 'Or I knife you up.'

'Get the drugs too,' demanded the other.

'If you run now, I pretend this never happen.'

'And if we don't?'

'I take that knife and stick it up your pussy arse.'

John glared at the two youths who opposed him. One lifted the blade so that the gleaming steel was level with John's chest.

The big man could see that the blade was wavering slightly. 'You shaking, man,' he said sharply. 'You drop your little toy in a minute. And when you do, I give it back to you. Right up your pussy arse. Now get the fuck away from me.'

The youths hesitated, then stepped back.

John took a giant stride after them.

As he moved from behind the open back doors of the VW van, he was aware of movement to his right.

Of a figure.

A much larger figure.

And that figure was holding something long, dark and metallic.

Tiger John turned to face the newcomer and saw the Franchi automatic shotgun the man held in his grip . . . saw him swing it up to his shoulder . . . saw the muzzle flame as he fired.

The noise was deafening. The roar of the blast reverberated in the still air.

The first discharge caught John in the left shoulder, pulverized bone and muscle and almost severed his arm.

He dropped to his knees, gasping in pain, and saw the figure work the slide, chambering another round.

The second blast caught him in the stomach, the shot ripping through his belly. He dug his right hand into the wound, trying to prevent his intestines spilling from the ragged rent.

The man holding the gun stepped closer, practically pressing the barrel to Tiger John's face.

When he fired, the blast tore away most of the left side of his head. A geyser of blood and splintered bone spattered the arm of the youth who held the knife.

John fell sideways, what was left of his skull at the centre of a spreading pool of liquidized brain matter. He knew nothing of the fourth and fifth shots that were fired into him.

Several curious faces had appeared at the door of the club as the sound of the shotgun blasts cut through the early morning quiet. They disappeared back inside rapidly when they saw the man with the gun pushing fresh cartridges into the Franchi. He worked the slide, then, holding the weapon level with his hip, fired two more rounds into the van itself. Each blast punched through the chassis. One exploded a box of records, scattering pieces of vinyl in all directions.

As the two youths ran in one direction, the man with the gun turned and walked unhurriedly back towards a blue BMW that was parked near the road.

When he climbed in, the occupant of the back seat patted his shoulder.

The car moved off.

10

THE FIRST OF the children arrived about eight o'clock.

The nursery in Brecknock Road catered for kids from six months right through to four years old.

Paula Newton usually arrived about half past eight, when most of the working mothers had dropped their charges off and disappeared for the day.

This day was no exception. She always walked to work; it only took her twenty minutes, sometimes less if the weather was cold.

She stood in the small kitchen where she and Lisa Bevan cooked meals for the kids and she watched as the little ones arrived. Watched as their parents helped them to hang up their coats on pegs that bore their names and kissed them goodbye.

She watched as some burst into tears and clung to their parents until members of staff coaxed them away with cuddles and the grateful parents made their escape.

It was the same every day.

The babies were taken into the Koala Room.

Those aged from two to three years into the Panda Room and the others into the Polar Room.

There were three workers for each group of kids, and each group contained no more than twenty faces registering every emotion from delight to downright fury.

The walls were festooned with paintings of children's favourites from TV, films and nursery rhymes.

The Teletubbies chased a big red ball around one door frame, pursued by the Wombles.

Kipper and Captain Pugwash vied for space on a wall with Bambi and Cinderella.

Hopper and Flik stared, wide eyed, at Woody and Buzz Lightyear.

Wallace and Gromit peered at a plate of cheese and crackers.

And then there were the drawings the kids themselves had done. Spidery scrawlings hung with pride on the walls, bright splashes of paint that looked as if someone had hurled a palette at the wall.

Paula knew which child had done each painting. She knew them all by name, even the babies.

Although her only duty was to cook the children's food, she occasionally helped out, particularly in the Koala Room. If the nursery was short-staffed, the workers were only too happy to receive her aid.

She worked there four days a week and had done so for the last five years. Paula had seen a succession of staff come and go because the wages were poor, but she loved the job. She loved being around the children.

A narrow corridor led from the kitchen to the nursery leader's office and Paula made her way along it, clutching the week's menu. It all had to be checked against dietary requirements and budget.

Paula glanced down at the little faces in the corridor as she passed.

A little boy wearing a Thomas the Tank Engine sweatshirt was brushing his hair out of his eyes as his mother hung up his coat.

Beside him a girl of three stood, head down, tugging at her Barbie jumper while her mother fastened the laces on her tiny Caterpillar boots.

There was another little boy crying, hanging onto his mother's arm as she tried to make her way to the exit. He was sobbing uncontrollably, but his mother seemed more concerned with getting away, relieved when one of the nursery workers scooped the boy up in her arms and hugged him. He was still crying when his mother slipped out of the door without looking round.

Paula paused beside the office door and knocked twice before stepping in.

'I'll be with you in a minute, Paula,' Andrea Braddock told her.

The nursery leader was sitting at her cluttered desk scribbling on a pile of newsletters. She was dressed in her usual tracksuit bottoms, sweatshirt and trainers. Her long auburn hair was tied back in a ponytail.

'It's just the menus for the week,' Paula told her, sliding the paper before her.

Andrea glanced at it, then nodded.

'That's fine,' she said, smiling as she handed it back. 'Just stick a copy on the noticeboard as usual so the parents can see, will you?' She returned to the pile of newsletters.

Paula hesitated a moment, then made her way back down the corridor towards the kitchen.

Most of the children were in their rooms now, doors closed.

There was a muted, almost unnaturally subdued atmosphere of peace inside the nursery, in marked contrast to the cacophony of sound that had swept the building during the last half an hour.

Paula saw that two coats had fallen off their pegs.

She hung Katie's pink mac back on its little hook, then did the same with Daniel's blue duffel coat.

There was a small woollen mitten lying on the floor too.

Paula picked it up, wondering which pocket it belonged in.

She checked the coats hanging above the fallen mitten; there was nothing that matched it.

It was an odd one.

Discarded.

Unwanted.

Paula looked around, cradling the mitten in her hand, then, carefully, almost lovingly, she slipped it into the pocket of her jeans.

11

'DAD, I'VE GOT to go now.'

Ray Gorman looked at his father and sought some kind of reaction in the blank eyes that stared back at him.

He placed one hand on the older man's arm and squeezed gently. It was like gripping a fucking skeleton. He dared not press too hard in case his fingers went straight through the flesh.

Colin Gorman looked at his son through eyes milky with cataracts and nodded.

How much of that was recognition?

How much was the Parkinson's disease?

The constant movement.

Gorman felt his father's body trembling. Saw the telltale quivering that sometimes developed into uncontrollable shaking and swaying.

He sat in the chair close to the small television set and peered at his son.

Gorman swallowed hard as he looked at his father. At the shuddering wreck that had once been his father.

This empty shell of a man was not the man who had

helped to raise him, who had carried him on his shoulders to matches at Upton Park when he was little.

This apparition was a shadow of that man.

It was almost too painful to look at him, but, Gorman reasoned, what choice did he have?

The old man was his flesh and blood. He couldn't just abandon him, could he?

And so they shared the small flat in Tower Hamlets. They put up with the dogshit on the landing outside. They tolerated the music that was played too loud in flats above and below. And they existed. Gorman got on with his life as best he could while his father slowly ended his.

Every day it seemed that a little more of him ebbed away. The old man seemed to shrink in that chair he occupied; barely strong enough to rise from it, he slept in it most nights, troubled, restless sleep that brought him bad dreams from the clouded recesses of his mind.

Dreams of when he had been able to walk around and look after himself. Dreams of the wife who had died eight years earlier of cancer.

Gorman himself often thought of his mother and, when he did, he felt a sting of guilt spear him.

He had always hoped

(*prayed was too strong a word and, besides, he wasn't sure if he believed in God*)

that his father would die first.

Forgive me for saying it.

Colin Gorman had always been reliant on his wife. Almost helpless without her.

During thirty-five years of marriage, she had paid the bills, done the shopping, the cooking, the decorating. Anything that had needed organizing, Molly Gorman had taken care of it. And now, with her gone, Colin Gorman had no one else to care for him but his son.

It was an intolerable burden for Gorman himself.

He was thirty-nine years old and, as much as he loved his father, he knew that this situation could not continue. It wasn't fair on *him* and it wasn't fair on the old man.

The Parkinson's disease was bad enough but, on Christmas Eve last year, the old man had been rushed into hospital with renal failure.

Gorman could see the catheter bag hanging beside the chair, half full of dark fluid.

He wondered if he should empty it before he left.

'The meals-on-wheels lady will be round about twelve, Dad,' Gorman said. 'She'll let herself in.'

The old man nodded again.

He kept on nodding.

The poor old fucker couldn't *stop* nodding.

Gorman sucked in a weary breath.

This couldn't go on.

And yet the alternative was almost as distasteful.

A home?

And if you do lock him away somewhere, those places aren't cheap. Looks like you're stuck with it.

Gorman placed the TV remote, an ashtray and a packet of Embassy on the small table beside his father's chair.

'If there's anything you want, tell the lady when she comes round, right?' he insisted.

'I-I-It's not th-th-th-the u-u-u-usual one,' the old man rasped.

'Well, tell her anyway. She'll get you what you need.'

Again the old man nodded.

And nodded.

Gorman leant forward and kissed the top of his head.

Felt the fine white hair and the wizened scalp.

'I'll see you later, Dad,' he said quietly, the knot of muscles at the side of his jaw pulsing.

When he turned away he did it quickly.

He didn't want his father to see the tears in his eyes.

12

FRANK NEWTON GLANCED at his watch, then looked irritably at the door of Ladbrokes.

10.09 a.m.

They should have been open at ten. On the fucking dot.

He cupped one hand to his eyes, attempting to peer through the glass door. The blinds were still down, but he could see movement through the slats.

He wondered about banging on the glass, then thought better of it and wheeled away, wandering back down the road in the direction he'd come.

There was a small café, a flower shop and a travel agent's close by.

He headed for the travel agent's, pausing at the window, looking in at the late bookings on offer.

THE ALGARVE – 7 NIGHTS SELF-CATERING £399 (including flights).

MIAMI – 2 WEEKS SELF-CATERING £435 (including flights).

Nothing about Bermuda or the Cayman Islands.

He pushed the door and went in.

Brochures everywhere: Greece, Spain, France.

Camping holidays, boating holidays.

Disneyland Paris.

Long weekends in New York.

Fuck that.

He glanced across at one of the red-uniformed young women behind the row of desks opposite.

She smiled perfunctorily at him, watching his progress along the shelves.

The brochure practically screamed at him.

THE CARIBBEAN

He took it down from the shelf and flipped through, aware of the young woman's unflinching gaze.

After a moment or two he turned and approached her. 'Bermuda or the Cayman Islands,' he said, sitting down opposite. 'I'd like some details please.' He dropped the brochure on her desk.

'When did you want to travel, sir?' she asked him and he noticed that the name badge she wore carried the legend: NATASHA STEEDEN.

Newton shrugged. 'I just wanted some prices,' he said flatly. 'Hotels, flights, that kind of thing.'

'Well, it depends what time of year you wanted to go.'

'Just give me the price of that hotel.' He jabbed an index finger at a picture in the brochure.

'Elbow Beach in Bermuda,' she said, as if telling him something he didn't know. 'You can fly direct from Heathrow.'

'How much are the rooms?'

She caught the edge to his voice and looked up.

However, she didn't hold his stare.

'They start at a hundred and twenty pounds a night, sir,' she told him.

'And the flights?'

'British Airways fly direct. Did you want Economy, Club or First Class?'

He wasn't slow to catch the disdain in her voice. 'First Class,' he said slowly.

She pressed several keys on her computer and then ran one false nail down the read-out on the screen.

'Three thousand, four hundred and sixty-five pounds return, sir.'

'What about the Cayman Islands?'

'Which one?'

'Grand Cayman.'

You smart-arse fucking bitch.

'Did you have any hotel in particular in mind, sir?'

'Yeah, the Hyatt Regency.'

'Their rooms begin at one hundred and ten pounds a night.'

'And the flights?'

Tap, tap, tap.

'First Class, I assume you want First Class?'

'That's right.'

'You have to fly to Miami, then get a connection to Grand Cayman. It'll be between three and four thousand pounds return.'

'Cheers.' He got to his feet.

'Do you want me to book it now, sir?' she asked without looking at him.

He snatched up the brochure. 'I'm thinking about it,' he told her. 'Do you get commission on the holidays you book?'

'Yes,' she replied, looking puzzled.

'Just curious,' he murmured and headed for the door. 'If I ever book it, I must remember to let someone else do it for me.'

And he was gone.

He spotted someone entering Ladbrokes.

'About fucking time,' Newton muttered.

He rolled the brochure and stuck it in the back pocket of his jeans.

From inside the travel agent's, Natasha watched him walk away.

13

THERE WAS BLOOD on the sheet.

Just a spot near the rumpled pillows, but Peter Morrissey leant forward and inspected the mark.

'You're a fucking animal,' he said, grinning. 'Look at that. You must have scratched my back again.'

Julie Cope stretched beneath the sheet, allowing the cotton to fall aside, exposing one shapely leg.

'I'll have to cut my nails,' she purred, flexing her fingers in his direction.

'Yeah, you will. It's like going to bed with a fucking cheese-grater.'

Morrissey stood beside the bed and buttoned his shirt. He was smiling down at her.

'Are you complaining?' she said quietly, pulling the cover aside to expose her nakedness more fully.

He ran appraising eyes over her body: tousled blonde hair; finely chiselled features; gravity-defying breasts and gloriously flat stomach; the fine triangle of downy hair nestling between those slim legs.

Julie grinned as she saw the expression on his face.

'Come back to bed,' she said, sliding one hand across her breasts, brushing the erect nipples.

'I've got things to do.'

'You didn't say that last night.'

'Anyway, you're supposed to be at school, aren't you?'

'I've got a double free. No lesson until after dinner.'

'Yeah, well, get dressed anyway.'

'You sound as if you're trying to get rid of me.' She pouted exaggeratedly.

He shook his head and turned away, grinning.

'My dad would kill me if he could see me now.' Julie chuckled. 'He's only a couple of years older than you.'

'Oi, watch it.'

'He's forty-eight.'

'Then he's more than a *couple* of years older than me, isn't he?'

'Oh, right, he's *four* years older.'

'Where did you tell your parents you were going last night?'

'They knew I was going to a club, then I told them I was staying with a mate. I always tell them that when I stay with you.'

'And they never check it out?'

'They couldn't give a fuck where I am.'

He regarded her impassively.

'They're too busy worrying about my fucking sister. How she's doing at college. They've always been more interested in her. The only time they ever talk to me is to have a go at me. I wish they *could* see me now. I'd like to tell them what you and me do together.'

'They'd throw you out, wouldn't they?'

'I could always come and live here.' She grinned at his expression of disapproval.

'Come on, get dressed,' Morrissey insisted.

'Well, why couldn't I?'

'Get real, babe. Fucking each other's brains out every night is one thing, but living together . . .' He allowed the sentence to trail off.

'I could cook for you. Do your ironing and all that shit.'

'I learnt how to do that in the army. I can look after myself.'

'You might need someone to collect your pension for you.' She laughed.

'You cheeky little cow,' he said, grinning. 'Now come on, move it. As much as I like looking at you, I want you to shift that lovely little arse.'

'Where are you going anyway?'

He tapped her nose gently. 'Keep that out,' he told her, smiling. 'It's business.'

'A job?'

'You could say that.'

'You're not leaving the club, are you? I'd never get in without you on the door.'

'Fuck off. You could pass for twenty-two when you've got all your slap on. You told *me* you were nineteen.'

'Only *two* years difference.'

'Three.'

'My birthday's in a month, you might as well *say* seventeen.'

He finished buttoning his shirt and pulled on a heavy leather jacket.

'Have you bought my birthday present yet?' she wanted to know.

'Yeah, a gag. Now stop fucking talking and get dressed.'

He turned and wandered out into the hall.

'Can I have a shower before I go?' she enquired.

'Yeah, but don't use all the fucking hot water.'

She padded, naked, into the hall.

'Lock up on your way out,' he told her. 'Leave the key in the usual place.'

'Will I see you tonight?' She snaked her arms around his neck.

'I'll be there. Just like I always am. In my monkey suit. Watching the door. Waiting for you.'

She kissed him and Morrissey responded, relishing the intensity. She slid one finger between her legs, then pressed it to his lips, allowing him to flick his tongue over the tip of the digit.

'See you later,' he said, licking his lips and smiling.

She closed the door behind him.

It was only a short walk from his flat to Harringey underground station.

He glanced at his watch. Thought about using his mobile to ring ahead and say he was on his way.

Fuck it.

Ten minutes and he'd be there.

STOKE NEWINGTON, NORTH LONDON

HE WAS GASPING for breath by the time he reached the tenth floor. Leon Green paused and glanced across at the doors of the lift and the sign that hung from them proclaiming: OUT OF ORDER.

Fucking things were always out of order.

Every time he came home it was like climbing Everest. Ten flights of concrete steps up to his flat. He was only twenty-three, but he was gasping and wheezing like some old bastard on forty a day. The fucking council should do something about those lifts. It was bad enough for *him*, but the old people who lived in the block suffered even more greatly.

Fucking council.

If it had been a white neighbourhood the fucking lifts would have been fixed quickly enough.

White bastards in charge of the council. What did *they* care if a few black people had to climb some stairs?

Motherfuckers.

He sucked in a few deep breaths, then fumbled in his jacket pocket for his key.

The flats on either side of him were empty; windows boarded up, doors locked and secured by two planks of wood nailed across. There was dogshit on the concrete walkway that led from the staircase.

Fucking dogs could get up high enough to shit here, couldn't they?

He let himself into the flat and closed the door behind him.

Even as he entered the small dwelling he could feel his stomach somersaulting. He broke wind; evil-smelling wind.

Leon dashed for the toilet, his insides churning.

As he slumped down on to the cracked plastic seat he wondered what he'd eaten that had given him the runs.

He opened his bowels and sat there, head bowed.

He had reached for some toilet roll and started cleaning himself when he heard the first of several thunderous bangs, impacts on the front door that were so loud they seemed to shake the entire flat.

'Oh, man, what the fuck . . .' he rasped irritably.

He continued wiping.

The door exploded inwards.

Leon felt his heart suddenly begin hammering hard against his ribs.

He heard movement in the hallway, was aware of several pairs of feet dashing about inside his flat.

His irritation had been replaced by fear.

What was going on?

Who was inside his flat?

Fucking law again? Ever since he'd been caught selling

charlie at a nightclub in Bermondsey over a year ago, they'd been on his arse.

Well, they wouldn't find anything *this* time. All his gear was hidden elsewhere.

The bathroom door crashed open and slammed back against the wall.

A tall man with a face as black as tar took one look at him, smiled crookedly, then grabbed him, dragging him from the toilet, his trousers still around his ankles.

There were two more men in the hall. Both black.

Then Leon saw they were carrying baseball bats.

The realization barely had time to register before the first of the blows caught him, a savage strike that almost shattered his right elbow.

He screamed in pain as more blows rained down upon him.

His back, his legs, his arms, even several on his naked buttocks.

He was trying to protect his head, but the men seemed intent on smashing the bones of his legs and torso.

Leon felt himself drifting into unconsciousness, into blessed oblivion, but a boot was driven into his side. He was rolled over onto his back.

Two blows shattered one testicle – burst it. The scrotum split like old leather.

He shrieked at this renewed agony.

His sphincter, already weakened, loosened again.

Blows to his chest broke ribs; one pulverized his larynx.

He could only gurgle in his own blood now and was finding it difficult to breathe.

Blood was spilling out of his mouth.

Through eyes clouded with pain he saw the men step back.

Saw another figure standing over him.

The fourth man bent low, pulled Leon to his feet and looked into his glazed eyes.

He said something, his voice so soft Leon barely heard it.

Besides, pain had blunted his hearing as surely as loud noise.

He was aware of the fourth man dragging him out of the flat. Onto the landing.

Towards the parapet.

Leon tried to struggle.

He looked down and saw the blood from his torn scrotum and burst testicle pouring down his legs. It left a trail from his front door across to the parapet.

As he realized what was happening he tried to fight back, but it was useless.

The fourth man lifted him bodily and tipped him over the edge.

Leon tried to scream, but no sound would come forth.

Blood ran freely over his fluttering lips.

He clutched at empty air for a second, then plummeted earthward.

The four men watched as his body hit the concrete ten floors below.

His head struck the hard surface first, the skull bursting open like an overripe melon.

The fourth man spat over the parapet in the direction of the pulped mess that had once been Leon Green.

14

FRANK NEWTON CHECKED his watch again. It felt as if he'd been at the lock-up for hours.

Where the hell were the others?

As if in answer to his question there was a loud knock on the door.

Whoever was outside waited only a second before stepping in.

James Carson raised a hand in greeting, then crossed to the table in the centre of the room and sat down wearily.

'I'm going to kill the little bastard, I swear to Christ,' the older man said, exhaling deeply.

'How is he?' Newton wanted to know. He flicked the electric kettle on. 'You said he was stable when you called.'

'He's all right. For now.'

'Did they tell you what it was?'

'The usual shit. Heroin. Coke.'

'You ought to keep him away from those useless cunts he hangs around with, Jim.'

'It's not that easy, Frankie. You can't watch your kids

twenty-four hours a day. If you had them . . .' He looked at Newton and allowed the words to fade.

'Yeah, I know,' Newton murmured, pouring hot water into the mug.

'It's not like he's a *kid* anyway,' Carson continued. 'He's nearly eighteen. He should know better, pissing about with drugs. He'll be dead before he's twenty.'

'Different generation, Jim. It was booze for us, wasn't it?'

'This is different, Frankie. There's a big difference between having a skinful and putting yourself in a bloody coma.'

Newton handed the older man his tea, watching as he prodded the tea bag with a spoon. 'What did Angie say?'

Carson shrugged. 'She was just relieved he was OK,' he confessed. 'If I'm honest, that was the main thing *I* was bothered about. He's not going to stop shoving that crap up his nose and into his veins, Frankie. Angie and I know that. But it doesn't make it any easier to cope with.' He sipped his tea. 'And neither of us are getting any younger.'

'Tell me about it.'

The two men sat in silence for a moment until Carson spoke again. 'I suppose you can't wonder at it really,' he murmured. 'I mean, I'm not exactly a great fucking role model, am I?'

Newton reached out and rested one hand gently on the older man's shoulder.

The door of the lock-up opened silently. It was the

sound of boot heels on the concrete floor that made both men look up.

Jeff Hobbs closed the door behind him, nodded in the direction of his two companions and laid the rucksack at one end of the table beside the holdall.

'Morning, "hoss",' Newton said, grinning, looking down at Hobbs's cowboy boots. 'Kettle's just boiled.'

'Two sugars while you're at it, Jeff.'

The other voice belonged to Ray Gorman.

The men exchanged greetings and Gorman sat down opposite Newton and Carson.

Newton thought how pale he looked.

'You all right, Ray?' Newton enquired.

'On top of the fucking world, Frank,' he answered acidly. 'What about you?'

'Is it your dad?' Newton wanted to know.

'It's always my fucking dad, isn't it? Poor old sod. I sometimes think he'd be better off dead.'

'You shouldn't say that, Ray,' Carson interjected. 'It's like tempting fate.'

'*He'd* be better off. *I'd* be better off. I don't know how much longer I can do it. I need some help. *He* needs some help.'

'Like who?' Newton asked.

'A professional. I'm no fucking male nurse, am I? He needs round-the-clock care and I can't give it to him. Not properly. I can't afford to pay for someone to come in to see to him. I can't afford to put him somewhere they'd be able to help him. So I'm fucked, aren't I?'

'It sounds like we've *all* got problems,' Hobbs offered, joining the men around the table.

'What fucking problems have you got, Jeff?' snapped Gorman. 'You live on your own. You haven't got to worry about anybody except yourself. You haven't got to clean out your old man's fucking colostomy bag when it overflows at three in the morning, have you?'

'You think I've got no problems, Ray? Why the fuck do you think I'm here? Would I be sitting here now if I didn't have any problems? Use it, will you?' He tapped his temple with one index finger.

'Leave it, both of you,' Newton said, glancing at each man in turn.

'Are we just waiting for Peter?' asked Carson.

Newton nodded.

'He's probably balls deep in that fucking schoolgirl he's seeing,' rasped Gorman. 'He's old enough to be her father. What's he playing at?'

'Jealous?' Hobbs said.

'Fuck off,' snapped Gorman. 'If I was looking for a shag, I'd make sure it was with somebody who didn't have to finish her *homework* first.'

The other men laughed.

'Have you seen her?' Newton asked.

'She looks a bit like the bird in that film *The Mask*,' Hobbs offered.

'What, you mean she looks like she's wearing a fucking mask?' Gorman muttered.

'No, she looks like the bird *in* it,' Hobbs corrected him.

76

'Cameron Diaz.'

'Yeah, she looks like *her*.'

'No wonder he's late,' chuckled Carson.

More laughter.

'Yeah, well I'm here *now*.'

They all turned to see Peter Morrissey standing in the doorway.

An uneasy silence descended for a moment as Morrissey stepped inside and closed the door behind him.

'What's so funny anyway?' he wanted to know.

'We were just talking about women,' Newton told him.

'*Young* women,' Hobbs added.

'Big fucking surprise,' Morrissey chided. 'You were talking about me and Julie, weren't you?'

Newton nodded.

'She got any friends who need a good seeing to?' grunted Gorman. 'You must have found a couple more behind the bike sheds.'

'They're out of *your* league, Ray.'

'Which fucking league would that be, Pete? Cradle-snatcher league?'

Morrissey shot him an angry glance.

'For fuck's sake, you must be desperate,' Gorman continued. 'Talk about mid-life crisis. Where did you meet her anyway? Were you working as a fucking lolli-pop man?'

Morrissey took a step towards his companion.

Gorman got to his feet.

'Leave it, both of you,' snapped Newton, getting

between them. He pushed one hand against Gorman's chest, one against Morrissey's.

They eyed each other angrily.

'You've got too much of that, Ray,' Morrissey hissed, tapping his lips. 'You want to keep it shut.'

'Or what?' Gorman challenged. 'You're not in the fucking army now, Pete. You don't give orders.'

'Shut it,' rasped Newton. 'We didn't come here to listen to you two silly bastards. We've got things to do and we've wasted enough time already. Got it?'

The two men continued to stare at each other, separated only by Newton.

He looked at each of them in turn.

'I said, have you got it?' he repeated.

Morrissey nodded slowly and took a step back.

'And you, Ray?' Newton insisted.

Gorman pulled away.

'Fucking dickheads,' snapped Newton.

He moved to the holdall and unzipped it.

'Now, if there's nothing else,' he said, looking at the other men seated around the table, 'we've got business to sort out.'

15

'ARE YOU HAVING a fucking laugh or what, Frank?'

Jeff Hobbs's words echoed around the lock-up like an accusation.

'Knock over a Securicor van?'

'We wouldn't be the first,' Newton said flatly.

The other men looked on with a mixture of bemusement and anxiety.

'It's not exactly our style, is it, Frankie?' Carson offered.

'And what is, Jim?' Newton wanted to know. 'Post offices? Corner shops? Factory payrolls?'

'We've always been small-time,' Carson insisted.

'Well, perhaps it's time we weren't,' Newton said irritably. 'Jesus, we've been fucking around with little jobs all our lives. When we were kids we did burglaries. We've moved stolen gear. We've nicked stuff from cars. All our fucking lives we've been scraping our way through. In and out of nick for minor offences. Never even anything *worth* doing the time for. And what have we got to show for it? We're all in our forties. Do you lot want to be doing stretches for receiving when you're in your fucking sixties? Because the way we're going that's how we're all going to end up.'

Morrissey took a drag on his cigarette.

Hobbs sipped at his tea and found it was cold.

Carson scratched his chin thoughtfully.

'I'm up for it, Frank,' Gorman said finally. 'I agree with you. It's about time we took something worth fucking taking.'

'It's not as easy as that,' Carson murmured.

'No one said it's going to be easy, but it can be done,' Newton insisted.

The other men looked on silently.

'If I'd thought it was going to be so hard to convince you bastards I wouldn't have bothered in the first place,' snapped Newton. 'What the fuck's wrong with you? This is a way out. After all these years of eating shit, doing time, pulling nothing jobs, am I the only one who wants to get out of this fucking game?'

'And if we do it?' Hobbs asked. 'If we get away with it and we get out. What then?'

'What do you mean, "What then"? Jeff, what do you want out of life?'

'I haven't given it a lot of thought.'

'Well, perhaps you should. Do you want to be inside when it's time to start drawing your pension? Or maybe you'd rather carry on doing what you're doing now. You *like* humping tins around fucking Sainsbury's, do you? Do you want to be doing that until they get rid of you because you're too old?' He turned his attention to Morrissey. 'And you, Pete, doorman at that club where you work. You think that's going to last for ever? There are plenty of younger blokes looking for jobs like yours. And when it's gone what will you have left? What have *any* of us got to look forward to? What have *any* of us got to show for forty-odd years? Fuck all, that's what. Well, I don't know about you lot, but I'm not breaking my back for the rest of my life. Scraping money together to pay bills. Wondering when the law are going to come knocking on my door.'

'It might be sooner than you think if we pull this Securicor job,' Carson mused.

'What exactly are *you* going to do if we hit it big, Frank?' Morrissey wanted to know. 'Run off to some fucking island in the sun?'

'That's *exactly* what I'm going to do.'

'And then what?' Morrissey persisted.

'I just want to get out. Get out of this business. Get out of London. Get out of the fucking country.'

'We've all lived within five miles of each other since we were kids,' Morrissey reminded him. 'We've been friends since we were this high.' He held the flat of his hand a foot above the table. 'We've done jobs together for as long as I can remember.'

'What are you saying, Pete?' Newton asked. 'That it has to stay like that? That things can never change? We deserve more. All of us.'

'I know that, but we've been in this business all our fucking lives.'

'So why not get out now?'

'Because it's the only thing we know.'

'Then let's *use* what we know and do this job. One big one and out for good.'

'But this is different,' Morrissey insisted.

'He's right, Frankie,' Carson interjected. 'If we pull this job and it goes wrong we're not looking at a two- or five-stretch. We're looking at life.'

16

'LOOK, FRANK. IF these bastards are too gutless to have a go, then fuck them. *I'll* do the job with you.'

Ray Gorman waved a dismissive hand in the direction of his three companions.

'Fuck you,' snarled Morrissey, lunging towards the younger man. 'I'll show you who's gutless, you little shit.'

Gorman raised his arm and saluted exaggeratedly. 'Yes, *sir*!' he snapped, his voice heavy with scorn.

Newton stepped between the two men.

Carson grabbed Morrissey's arm and pulled him back.

'You don't want to do it, that's fine, Pete,' Gorman rasped. 'You want to spend more time shagging your little schoolgirl, that's your business.'

Morrissey again made a grab for his companion and only the intervention of Hobbs prevented him achieving his objective.

'Fucking leave it, both of you,' bellowed Newton. His voice reverberated around the inside of the lock-up and both men froze, looking towards him.

'Jesus Christ, can't we even *talk* about the job without you two trying to kill each other?' hissed Hobbs.

'Then tell *him*,' Morrissey snarled, pointing an accusatory finger at Gorman.

Newton pushed the younger man back towards his chair.

An uneasy silence settled over the men.

Morrissey shook loose and wandered away from the table, hands clasped behind his head.

'Everybody just calm down,' Newton said quietly.

Hobbs reached into his jacket and pulled out a silver hipflask. He took a long swallow, then held it up. 'Anyone else?'

Newton managed a smile. 'Pete, sit down, will you?' he said, looking over in Morrissey's direction.

After a moment or two of pacing, the ex-army man finally did as he was asked, shooting Gorman a warning glance.

'Right,' Newton began, 'if everybody's finished . . .' He allowed the sentence to trail off.

The other men nodded.

'If anyone wants out, then say so now,' Newton muttered, his gaze moving slowly to each man in turn. 'If we're going to do this, we've *got* to do it right. Now. In or out. Ray, I already know what *you* think. What about it, Jim?'

Carson swallowed hard. 'I want to get out of the business as much as you, Frankie, you know that,' he said quietly.

'But?'

'No buts. I'm in.'

Newton looked at Hobbs. 'Jeff?'

He nodded.

'Pete? What about you?'

'You're right. We've been small-time for too long,' Morrissey offered. 'Let's do it.'

Newton smiled.

'What are we going to need?' Carson asked.

'Three cars. Two *during* the job. One after.'

Carson nodded.

Newton moved to the end of the table and unzipped the holdall. He lifted out three pistols and laid them on top of the paper.

Taurus PT–92.

Smith and Wesson .459.

Beretta 92F.

All 9mm automatics.

As the men watched he also removed two double-barrelled shotguns. Both twelve gauge Leland 210s. Both sawn-off so that the weapons were half their usual length.

'Say hello to the rest of the family.' Newton chuckled.

'Is that it?' Morrissey wanted to know.

'The hardware's *your* speciality, Pete. What else can you get?'

'How many guards in the van?' the former soldier asked.

'Two in the cab. Two in the back. The usual.'

'A couple of machine-guns wouldn't hurt,' Morrissey mused. 'Just in case we happen to have any fucking heroes on board. I'll sort it.'

'How do we get into the van?' Hobbs enquired.

'Blow it.'

'So why do we need this?' Hobbs picked up the duffel bag and pulled out the chainsaw.

'Fuck me, have you been watching those video nasties again, Frank?' Gorman chuckled.

'Learn how it works, Ray, because *you're* the one who's going to be using it,' Newton told him. He pushed the McCullough towards the younger man. 'Any boxes inside the van we cut through them with that.'

'What's the sp on the van itself?' Morrissey enquired.

'Every Friday afternoon at three, it collects from six betting shops in the Euston Road, the Edgware Road, Gower Street and Tottenham Court Road. It's an independent chain. It drops off at a bank in Bloomsbury Square around half past four. They always use a different route. We hit it before it reaches the bank.'

'Just cash?' Hobbs asked.

Newton nodded.

'How much are they likely to be carrying?' Gorman said.

'Not less than a million,' Newton replied quietly. 'That's two hundred grand each. Worth the risk?'

17

'How LONG HAVE you been working on this?'

Newton looked in the direction of the question and saw Carson watching him.

'All my fucking life,' Newton said wearily.

'How long, Frankie?'

Newton shrugged. 'Months,' he answered. 'I've been watching the van. Watching the shops, the bank, everything.'

'And the drill is the same every time?' Morrissey asked.

'Apart from the route to the drop, yeah.'

'Are the guards armed?' Hobbs enquired.

Newton shook his head. 'Not unless you count chemical Mace. It's all they're allowed to carry.'

'What about link-ups with the Old Bill?' Carson interjected. 'As soon as they get hit, they'll radio through and the bastards will be there like flies round shit.'

'We jam the frequency. Knock out the radio. It'll all happen so fast they won't have time to call.'

'And if they do?'

Hobbs's words hung ominously in the air.

'What do any of *us* know about jamming radio frequencies?' Carson said. 'Perhaps we *are* taking too much of a chance. This is big stuff, Frankie.'

'Big stakes, big rewards, Jim.'

'Come on, Jim,' Gorman insisted. 'Don't bottle it now. I thought you were in. Just think what kind of rehab clinic you could put your kid in for two hundred grand.' He smiled crookedly.

Carson shot him a furious glance.

'I know I'll be sorting out the best nursing home for my dad with my share,' Gorman continued.

'I wouldn't spend it until we've got it,' Hobbs murmured.

'So, what would you spend your cut on, Jeff?' Gorman wanted to know.

'I'll think about that when the job's done.'

'Miserable bastard. What about you, Pete?'

Morrissey shrugged. 'Maybe Jeff's right,' he said quietly. 'Best not spend it until we've got it.'

Gorman shook his head and waved a hand dismissively at his colleagues.

'So, when do we do it, Frank?' Morrissey enquired.

'Next Friday. That gives us ten days to prepare,' Newton explained. 'That should be plenty of time to make sure we've got all the equipment we need and run through the details. This one's got to run like clockwork.'

'What if one of the guards *does* decide to be a hero?' asked Carson.

All eyes turned to Newton as he picked up one of the

sawn-off shotguns and cradled it in his grip. 'Let's hope for their sakes that they don't,' he whispered.

'I'm not killing anyone,' Carson said. 'Not for two hundred grand. Not for twenty million.'

'Nobody's asking you to, Jim.' Newton met his gaze and held it.

'You don't have to kill them, even if one of the silly sods *does* try something,' Gorman reasoned.

'Put one in the leg,' Morrissey offered authoritatively. 'Anywhere below the thigh. It'll hurt like fuck, but it won't kill.'

'Are you telling me that if one of them fires at us you wouldn't shoot back?' Hobbs asked, turning to Carson. 'And you would?'

Hobbs reached for the Taurus and worked the slide. 'You're fucking right I would,' he snapped.

'With any luck it won't come to that,' Newton insisted. 'But if it *does*, then that's the way it's got to be. Anyone who's got problems with that, walk away now.'

'Jim, we've all used a little bit of muscle in our time,' Morrissey said. 'You cracked that geezer when we were in the Scrubs together. I saw you break his jaw.'

'That was different,' Carson rasped. 'He had it coming. The bastard was in there for rape anyway.'

'But you didn't smack him for that. You broke his jaw because he asked you if you'd suck his dick.'

The other men laughed.

Carson wasn't amused. 'He was a sex case,' he snarled.

'He was just nickbent,' Morrissey continued.

'Drop it, eh?'

'Ten days, then?' Hobbs said to Newton, steering the conversation back to the matter in hand.

Newton nodded. 'We'll run through the whole job in a couple of days,' he said. 'Who should be where, who's driving which car, that sort of thing.'

'And what do we do with the money once we've got it?' Gorman reminded him. 'Every copper in London will know those serial numbers by that Friday night. We'll need tongs to handle those fucking notes.'

'That's all sorted,' Newton assured him.

Hobbs raised his hipflask in salute. 'Here's to next Friday then,' he murmured.

The other men remained silent.

More than one of them was staring at the weapons lying on the table.

The fluorescents in the ceiling glinted on the polished metal.

18

It looked like a slaughterhouse. There were even droplets of blood on the bare lightbulb hanging from the ceiling.

Detective Inspector John Ridley stood motionless in the centre of the small sitting room gazing around.

To call it spartan would have been an understatement.

No carpet

(*there was none anywhere in the house apart from on the stairs and that was worn so badly the wood showed through*)

and no wallpaper.

A small sofa. A battered wooden chair with a leg broken off. A TV and a video recorder.

And two corpses.

Both black.

Both in their early twenties.

There were patches of mould in two of the ceiling corners where the damp had taken hold.

He could smell it, despite the other odours in the room.

The coppery smell of blood.

The more pungent stench of excrement.

The room was covered with the crimson fluid. Some of it had congealed to a deep rust colour, but most was still a vivid red.

Ridley continued gazing around the room for a moment longer, glancing at the huge vermilion sprays on the walls, floor and ceiling.

There was a severed thumb lying close to his right foot and he moved cautiously as he picked his way through the carnage.

For a big man (six-two and thirteen stone), he moved with an almost feline grace, careful not to disturb both the evidence and the other men who moved in and out of the room. They performed their specific duties with all the industry and speed of worker ants, swarming around the bodies; examining, measuring.

Every now and then the dazzling white of a flashbulb would illuminate the dingy room and the blood would appear to glow in the phosphorescent brilliance.

Ridley leaned closer to the first of the two bodies, running appraising eyes over it.

The face was disfigured by more than a dozen deep cuts, some exposing the cheekbones. Several teeth had been knocked loose and lay beside the corpse. One eye had been sliced in half by a savage blow and there was vitreous liquid on the cheek. The eye itself looked as if it had burst – popped like some opaque balloon. An ear had been hacked off.

Several huge gashes ran from shoulder to sternum and

there were eight or nine easily distinguishable cuts on the forearms of the unfortunate youth.

His rigored right hand had the fingers splayed; the palm had been split by another fierce cut.

'I think we can rule out suicide.'

The voice came from behind Ridley. He turned slightly to see William Nicholson crouching beside the second corpse.

The police surgeon was gazing raptly at the other body.

The machete was still embedded in the skull. Driven down with such force it had penetrated almost an inch into the bone.

The other injuries on the second corpse were mainly around the neck and Nicholson pointed to one particularly violent laceration that had almost severed the head.

'Have we got ID on them?' Ridley wanted to know.

His question was directed at a younger man who had entered the room carrying a small notepad.

He flipped it open.

'Winston Simpson and Rupert Hart,' the newcomer said, nodding at each corpse in turn.

At thirty-six, DS Darren Brown was twelve years Ridley's junior. The two men had worked together for the last eight months. Brown was something of an optimist; he thought that things might improve between them in time.

'Were they both killed with the same weapon?' Ridley asked.

Nicholson nodded. 'The machete,' he murmured. 'This one.' He pointed to the weapon protruding from Simpson's skull. 'Both men were beaten before they were killed and there's particularly heavy bruising on Hart's upper arms and striation marks on his neck.'

'Meaning?' Ridley said, his gaze still fixed on the two bodies.

'It looks as though Hart was made to watch while Simpson was killed.'

'Any prints?'

'All over the house, the weapon and the bodies,' Brown interjected. 'If the killers are in the index we shouldn't have too much trouble pinning them down. Hendon are checking the prints now.'

'So then all we've got to do is find them,' Ridley said, a note of scorn in his voice. 'Piece of piss.'

Brown and Nicholson looked at each other.

'Presumably no one in the houses next door heard or saw anything?' the DI continued. 'You know, like screams. No one heard that? No one saw somebody covered in blood leaving the house afterwards?'

'We're questioning everyone in the street,' Brown informed his superior.

'You're wasting your fucking time,' snapped Ridley. 'What's the saying around here, "See and blind, hear and deaf"? You won't get anything out of the neighbours.' He licked his lips. 'Did the victims have any form?'

'Both were known drug dealers,' Brown told him. 'Hart had done a three-stretch for GBH. Simpson had been away for eighteen months for living off immoral earnings.'

Ridley grunted.

'What do you reckon, John?' Nicholson asked, straightening up with some difficulty.

Ridley offered him a supportive hand. 'The machete's their trademark, isn't it?' said the DI. 'I'd lay good money it's the Yardies.'

19

THE INSIDE OF the Orion smelled of cigarette smoke and fried onions.

'How much money?'

Ridley looked around as he heard the words.

'You said in there you'd lay good money that the Yardies were behind those murders,' DS Brown continued, taking a bite from his hot dog.

Ridley wiped condensation from the inside of the side window and looked in the direction of the house.

Uniformed and plain-clothes men were still coming and going. The forensics team were currently giving the place the once over. He had decided to wait outside until they'd finished; give them some room. Give himself time to think.

He sipped his tea, wincing when he burned his fingertips on the plastic cup. He rapidly replaced it on the front parcel shelf. The windscreen was already sheathed with condensation too.

'Do you think they're linked to the other murders?' Brown persisted.

'Baseball bats. Machetes. They both get the job done,

don't they?' the older man mused, reaching for his hamburger and taking it from the greaseproof paper.

There was a small snack trailer at the end of the North London street, steam pouring from the vent in the roof. It was painted red and white and sported a Union Jack that fluttered in the gentle breeze.

As he watched, he saw the vendor wipe his nose on the dirty apron he was wearing.

Ridley suddenly didn't feel so hungry.

'I wonder when *he* last had a visit from the health inspector,' the DI muttered, pushing the burger back onto the parcel shelf and reaching for his tea instead.

He glanced around at the rows of houses on either side of them. There were faces at a number of the windows; some looking out warily, others carrying expressions closer to indignation.

'They don't want us here,' Ridley murmured. 'How many of them could give a toss if we find the killers or not?'

He sipped his tea.

'Somebody heard or saw *something*,' he continued. 'But they won't tell *us*.'

Brown glanced at his superior for a moment, then carried on stuffing the hot dog into his mouth.

'Hart and Simpson were both known drug dealers, right?' Ridley offered. 'So was Leon Green. Maybe they stepped on the wrong toes. Took business away from the wrong people.'

Brown nodded. 'Or it could just be pissed-off punters,' the DS added. 'Somebody bought some substandard gear from them and went back to complain.'

'With a baseball bat or a meat cleaver?'

'Depends how bad the stuff was they sold.'

Ridley shook his head. 'This is more than dissatisfied customers,' he said.

As he glanced in the direction of the house he saw two gurneys being wheeled out. On each one was a corpse, sealed in a black plastic body bag.

The two policemen watched as the grisly cargo was loaded into the back of a waiting ambulance.

A moment later, William Nicholson followed the bodies out.

Ridley wound down the window. 'Bill,' he called and the police surgeon headed towards the Orion. 'When can I have the autopsy reports?'

'Are you coming back to the Yard now?' Nicholson enquired.

'I'm going to have a root around in the house first,' the DI told him. 'See if anything's been missed.'

'I've already called Phil Barclay. We'll do the autopsies as soon as I get back. I'm not going to be able to tell you much more than you already know, John. Like I said inside, I think you can rule out suicide.'

Ridley nodded and raised a hand as Nicholson headed back towards his own car and slid behind the wheel. He pulled away close behind the ambulance and both vehicles moved off down the street.

'What do you think you're going to find in there?' Brown wanted to know. 'The forensic boys will have been over everything with a fine-tooth comb.'

Ridley shrugged. 'I just want to have a look,' he

explained. 'Things get missed sometimes. Little detail. They don't seem like much, but they could be important.'

'Are we going back in then?'

'*I'm* going back in. *You're* staying here. You can help with the house-to-house if you want.'

'I thought we were supposed to work *together* on this,' Brown protested. 'Like a team.'

'You've been watching too many films.'

'I'm trying to do my job.'

'Fine. Just don't get in *my* way while you're doing it.' As he spoke, he swung himself out of the Orion, taking the remains of the hamburger with him. He dropped it into a waste bin as he passed.

Brown watched as his superior headed back towards the house. 'Bastard,' he murmured under his breath.

20

FRANK NEWTON WAS always the last to leave.

The men had drifted away from the lock-up during the last twenty minutes. Each carried different thoughts with him now.

Newton himself sat at the table peering at the maps of Central London. The street maps. The specs of the Securicor van.

He reached across and gently brushed the barrel of the .459 with one index finger.

What would he do if he had to use the gun?

He knew that same thought was now embedded in the minds of his companions too.

A little muscle.

Putting a bullet in a man was a little different to smacking him with a hammer.

(*he'd done that*)

or breaking a chair over someone's head.

(*and that*)

No need to shoot to kill.

And what if the van's occupants *were* armed?

What if *they* had no compunction about opening fire?

He shook his head. They wouldn't be armed.

They wouldn't defend the money against those who sought to take it. Why should they risk their own lives for someone else's cash? They didn't get paid enough for that. They'd probably even help hand the fucking bags out.

Yeah, right.

If this was done right, then it would work.

One million pounds.

He thought about it.

Two hundred thousand each.

More than he'd earned in his entire, wasted, forty-two years. More than all the pissant little wage snatches, car robberies, fraud jobs and countless other blags he'd pulled in his time put together.

Enough to get out.

Enough to pay for the treatment.

The last hope.

IVF.

Him and Paula couldn't have kids. They'd tried unsuccessfully for the first ten years of their marriage before seeking medical help, only to be told that it was impossible.

Something else you can't have.

Newton could still remember a doctor telling them they could always try IVF. That it was expensive, but

(*and it was a big fucking 'but'*)

it was probably their only chance.

Paula couldn't sustain a pregnancy. Couldn't carry full-term. He'd forgotten the exact terminology.

What the fuck did the words matter? It added up to the same thing.

They would never have children.

Unless they could afford IVF treatment.

Even then it was a shot in the dark, but it offered them something that life had never offered before.

Hope.

It had been an all too rare commodity in both their lives until now.

Newton looked at the guns again.

He glanced at the road maps and the specs.

Two hundred thousand pounds each.

How many courses of treatment did that buy them?

No guarantee of success. She still might not conceive, might still fail to carry the child full-term.

No magical spell could be cast to ensure he and Paula were blessed with a child even after the treatment.

But at least the money from the job would enable them to try.

Was that too much to ask?

He picked up the .459 and hefted it before him.

Nothing was going to stop him taking that chance and God help any bastard who tried.

21

THE WARD WAS full.

All the wards were full. Not just in the Royal Free, but in most hospitals in the country.

James Carson stood at the entrance to Ward 5b and scanned the faces of those inside.

He saw one man roughly the same age as himself lying in a bed close by, propped up on a rampart of pillows. His chest and abdomen were heavily bandaged and his skin was the colour of rancid butter. As Carson moved through the ward he passed close to the bottom of the man's bed.

Same age. It could be you.

He wondered what had struck the unfortunate man down.

Stroke? Heart attack?

He paused for a moment, looking at the sleeping man. There were some wilting flowers in the small vase on his beside cabinet. Beside them a jug of water and a 'Get Well Soon' card. It seemed totally inappropriate.

It could be you.

The thought returned and remained, stuck in his mind like a needle in soft flesh.

He finally walked on towards the end of the ward. Towards the bed he sought.

Past the other concerned relatives and friends who had gathered around various beds during these visiting hours.

Gary Carson was sitting up, glancing disinterestedly at a copy of *Loaded*.

He was a tall, slim-built youth who looked as if he needed a few good meals to put some meat on his bones. His black hair was swept back behind his ears.

As Carson drew nearer, his son either failed to hear him or chose not to acknowledge his presence. He continued flicking through the magazine.

'Gary,' Carson said quietly.

Only then did his son turn to look at him. 'Have you come to take me home?' he said flatly. 'I'm bored out of my fucking skull in here.'

'The doctor says you've got to stay in for observation until tomorrow.'

He stood by the plastic chair beside the bed as if waiting for an invitation to sit down, but when none was forthcoming he slid the chair across and parked himself on it.

'Has your mum been in?' he asked.

'Yeah, she brought me those.' Gary motioned to a couple of newspapers, a crossword book and a copy of the *NME*. 'She didn't stay long.'

'She was probably upset.'

'Yeah, probably.' He was still staring blankly at the magazine.

Carson felt the knot of muscles at the side of his jaw pulsing angrily. He finally reached out and tugged the magazine from his son's grasp.

'What the hell were you playing at last night?' Carson snapped. 'You could have killed yourself.'

'I wondered when the fucking lecture was going to start.'

'The doctor said you were lucky to be alive.'

'Perhaps we should have a party, then. Celebrate.'

'What the hell is wrong with you? If it was the *first* time it'd be bad enough. Do you *want* to kill yourself?'

'Leave it out, will you? I know what I'm doing.'

'Is that why you're in here? Because you know what you're doing?'

'You don't understand.'

'Then *make* me understand,' Carson snarled.

The two people seated next to the adjacent bed turned and glanced at him when they heard the vehemence in his tone.

Carson met their gaze and held it.

He returned his attention to Gary, trying to keep his voice low. 'You know what these bloody drugs can do to you,' he said quietly. 'Why do you do it, Gary? Just tell me.'

'Do you really give a fuck? Either of you?'

'We're your parents. What do *you* think?'

'What have I got to look forward to in life?'

Carson had no answer.

'The dole? Prison? Scratching a living like you have ever since I can remember? I don't want that.'

'Well, these fucking drugs aren't going to help, are they?'

'When I take them, I forget about all the shit. I forget that my old man's a fucking loser.'

Carson looked at his son, but there was no anger in the stare. Only something akin to sorrow.

'If you keep taking drugs you'll kill yourself,' he said softly. 'If you don't care about yourself, at least think what you're doing to your mother.'

Gary shook his head and exhaled. 'They say that people who take drugs do it to run away,' he said. 'To hide from the world. Do you know the real reason I do it?' For the first time, he looked into Carson's eyes. 'I'm scared I'm going to end up like you. If I thought *that* was going to happen, I'd top myself tomorrow.'

22

JEFF HOBBS ENJOYED the silence inside the library in Appleby Street. It was like a haven amidst the bedlam that was the rest of the city.

He browsed the shelves slowly.

Fiction. Non-Fiction. Poetry.

There was nothing he wouldn't read.

It had been a pastime he had welcomed during his spells inside. During a six-month stretch in Wandsworth he'd managed to read both *Mein Kampf* and *War and Peace*.

He smiled at the recollection and continued perusing the volumes before him.

So many books – so many authors.

He thought what a wonderful life these writers must have; working alone every day, no one breathing down their necks. Responsible only to themselves, just them and their imaginations.

A bit like doing time.

He smiled once more and took down a book about the Crimean War, then another about Shaka Zulu; large tomes. They'd last him a week or two. He moved to the fiction section and saw one of the librarians replacing some newly returned books. Hobbs smiled sheepishly at her and she smiled back warmly.

She was in here most days.

Mid-thirties; dark hair; wonderful bone structure; slim; incredibly long fingers with immaculately manicured nails.

Wedding ring.

She could be a widow.

He moved closer and saw the badge pinned to her blouse: THERESA.

He thought about speaking to her, but decided against it.

Every time he saw her he thought about speaking. Just a simple hello or even mention the bloody weather.

It was a start, wasn't it?

The wedding ring was a thick band.

Hobbs had often wondered if the thickness of a wedding ring denoted the depth of feeling displayed by the wearer.

Did a thick band mean a greater love than a thin one?

Very philosophical.

THERESA's band was very broad.

He decided not to speak to her.

He collected a couple of volumes of fiction and a book about the 1938 Japanese invasion of Nanking, then he checked them all out and left.

THERESA was still tidying the shelves.

As he left the library he felt the first drops of rain and he quickened his pace.

The convenience store at the corner of the street was cramped, the aisles narrow.

Hobbs gathered what provisions he needed quickly; he knew where each of his requirements were. The shop smelled of spice and coffee.

He clutched his shopping basket, standing patiently behind a young woman with a small child. She counted out the exact amount of her £10.60 bill in ten- and twenty-pence pieces.

The child, a boy of four or five, kept turning and looking up at him.

Hobbs met the child's gaze, but his expression didn't change.

While he was waiting, Hobbs took a copy of the *Evening Standard* from the pile near the till and browsed through it.

His copies of *The Ring* were delivered to his door.

It was good to keep in touch with what was happening in the game.

The young woman was still slapping silver onto the counter.

Hobbs had time to read an article about a young boxer tipped to become a world champion

(*reminiscing? Thinking that should have been you?*)

before the young woman finished paying. Then he replaced the paper and placed his own goods on the counter.

The young woman began filling her carrier bags with her purchases.

The child was staring up at him again.

Hobbs paid, packed up his goods and left.

The child watched him go.

23

THE OLD MAN was crying when he got home. Ray Gorman could hear the pathetic sobs even as he put his key in the door.

'Dad,' he called as he entered.

Immediately the smell struck him. Acrid. Cloying.

'Dad, what's happened?'

As if he didn't know.

He hurried into the sitting room and the old man was sitting in his chair surrounded by a puddle of excreta that had soaked into the carpet and also stained part of the chair.

'Oh, Jesus,' Gorman murmured under his breath.

His father was still sobbing, clutching the ripped catheter bag in one shaking hand.

'When did this happen?' Gorman asked, wanting to put an arm around the old man, but recoiling from the foul odour.

His father tried to speak, his lips fluttering soundlessly. Tears rolled down his cheeks.

'It's all right, Dad, I'll clean it up. Come on, let's get you to the bathroom. Sort *you* out first.'

He slipped one strong arm around his father's waist and helped the old man struggle to his feet, trying not to wince at the vile stench.

They made their way through the flat to the bathroom and Gorman helped his father undress.

He spun the bath taps while the old man took off his reeking clothes.

'Did this happen long ago, Dad?' Gorman enquired, hurrying into the kitchen to find some bleach and disinfectant.

He threw some cloths into a basin full of water and headed first into the sitting room, then back into the bathroom.

His father was undressed. Steadying himself against the towel rail he shuddered uncontrollably.

A combination of the cold. The crying.

And the disease.

Always the fucking disease.

Gorman helped him into the bath.

'I'm going to clean up,' he told the old man. 'Don't you worry about it. It wasn't your fault. I'll be back in a bit.'

He retreated to the sitting room. To the basin of water and the cloths; the bleach and the disinfectant.

And the excrement.

This wasn't right. It wasn't fair on either of them.

He soaked a cloth in hot water and disinfectant and set to work on the carpet.

He'd get rid of the worst of it, then go back and check on his father.

There was some foam stuff he could get to remove the stain; he'd used it before.

The chair would be a different matter.

It was old, the covering almost threadbare. It'd be easier to bin the fucking thing.

He scrubbed away at the mess, leaning back occasionally to suck in a lungful of cleaner air.

The knees of his jeans were already soaked.

He could only guess at how long his father had been forced to sit in that fucking mess. Poor old sod. He'd go back and check on him in a minute. Change the bag. Put clean clothes on him.

Gorman remained on his knees for several moments, head bowed as if in prayer.

He couldn't carry on like this.

He wrung out the cloth and began scrubbing once more.

At least it looked as if the worst of it was coming out.

Until the next time.

Gorman sniffed and wiped his nose with the back of his hand.

'I won't be long, Dad,' he called. 'Nearly finished.'

This had to stop. Something had to be done.

He sat back on his haunches and wept softly.

24

As MORRISSEY GAZED at her across the table, Julie Cope ran a hand through her blonde hair. She was wearing just his bathrobe, the front open slightly to reveal her considerable cleavage.

Every now and then, Morrissey would feel her bare foot brush against his leg as he ate.

'This is good,' he said, pushing a forkful of lasagne into his mouth.

'Cooking isn't the only thing I'm good at,' she purred, licking her lips.

'I know that.'

'So, how did the job go?'

He looked straight at her.

'Your job, today. How did you get on?' she persisted.

'I didn't say anything about a job,' he reminded her.

'Then where have you been all day? You could have been here with me.'

Again he felt that bare foot against his calf, trailing up and down slowly. Morrissey reached down and grabbed it in his free hand, massaging slowly, pushing his index finger between her toes one at a time.

She squirmed slightly, giggled, then exhaled contentedly.

'More to the fucking point, what have *you* been doing all day?' he demanded. 'You were supposed to be on your way to school after I left this morning.'

'I didn't feel well,' she said dismissively. 'I'll go in tomorrow.'

'I *know* you will.'

'Now *you're* starting to sound like my dad.'

He tickled her foot, running his finger along the sole, but not letting go even when she squirmed and tried to pull away.

'If you keep having time off, your parents are going to want to know where you are and so are the school. It won't take them long to work out you're here and then we're *both* in trouble.'

'Don't you want me here then, Peter?'

'It's not that, babe, and you know it, but you'll be finished school soon. You've got to get a job.'

'Like you?'

He grinned sardonically. 'Bouncer at a local club four nights a week isn't exactly a job for a girl, is it?'

'I'm a young woman,' she reminded him, tossing her head exaggeratedly.

'Then you should be thinking about what you want to do, not fucking around with me all the time.'

'I *like* fucking around with you. I like being with you. I like everything about you. Especially your tongue and your cock.' She giggled.

Morrissey shook his head.

'Haven't they got any jobs at the dog track?' she asked. 'I could be a waitress or work in the betting offices. You know the boss there. You could put in a word for me.'

'Julie, I help out with security at Walthamstow when they ask me to. I've got no pull there. I can't get you a job.' He chewed more lasagne. 'Anyway, you should be aiming higher than just being a waitress,' Morrissey continued.

'One of my sister's friends is a waitress at Planet Hollywood. She does all right. She gets loads of tips.'

'I'm not saying there's anything wrong with waitressing. There isn't. I'm just saying that there must be something you always wanted to be. Something you wanted to do with your life.'

'Like what?'

'I don't know. Be a nurse or a nanny. That's what most girls of your age want to be, isn't it?'

'Get real, Pete. With the shit money *they* earn? Besides, I wouldn't want to look after *other* people's kids. My own, yeah. But not some snotty-nosed little bastard who belonged to someone else.'

'So what *do* you want to do with your life?'

'Something exciting. Like you have.'

He shook his head. 'What have I ever done?' he wanted to know.

'You were in the army.'

'And that's about it. I've pissed my life away, Julie. Don't you do the same. You only get one chance. I had mine and I fucked it up. If you *really* want to do something for me make me a promise now.'

She looked quizzically at him.

'When you get to forty-four, like me,' Morrissey said quietly, 'don't look back on your life and think of all the things you *didn't* do. Don't waste your one chance, babe. This fucking life is like a race. I got left at the starting blocks. And it was my fault. I've lost so much time, no matter how fast I run, I know I can never catch up. Don't let that happen to you.'

'Are you having a mid-life crisis, Pete?' She chuckled.

'This is no fucking joke,' he snapped, glaring at her. 'Don't end up like me. A waster. Sitting around wishing you'd done something more with your life. Instead of thinking about it, get out and *do* it. Promise me that.'

She nodded.

'Promise me,' he insisted.

'I promise not to waste my life,' she said, her voice almost a whisper.

They finished their meal in silence.

25

DI John Ridley heard the knock on his office door, but he didn't look up. His attention remained on the contents of the manilla file before him.

Even when the knocking became more insistent the detective barely lifted his head.

When he finally responded, DS Darren Brown stepped into the room. The younger man was also carrying files in one hand.

'Autopsy reports on Hart and Simpson,' he announced, brandishing the files before him.

'Any surprises?' Ridley wanted to know.

Brown shook his head. 'Traces of crack in Simpson's blood, but that's about it.'

Ridley continued looking at the file.

'Did you find anything in the house this afternoon?' Brown persisted, tiring of the silence.

'Nothing worthwhile.'

'Listen, guv,' said Brown wearily, 'I don't mean to sound pushy or anything, but if you did find something then I think you should tell me about it. I mean, we are supposed to be working *together* on this case, aren't we?'

Ridley finally looked up. 'I didn't find anything the forensic boys hadn't already turned up,' the DI told his companion.

'Then why did you want to go over the place without me?'

'It's just the way I work.'

'If you want to cut me out, then tell me, but—'

'If you've got a fucking complaint, take it to the commissioner. Ask to be re-assigned. Otherwise, get used to things the way they are.'

The two men glared at each other for long moments.

'Anything in *there* I should know about?' Brown said finally, nodding in the direction of the manilla file.

Ridley smiled humourlessly. 'Have a look,' he said, tossing the file at the younger man.

Brown opened it. 'Frank Newton,' he said quietly as he read the first page. 'Who is he? Is he linked with this case?'

'You must be joking. The nearest he's ever got to drug dealing is nicking aspirin from Boots.'

'Plenty of form.'

'It's all tuppenny-ha'penny stuff. He's made a career out of nothing jobs.'

'He's done time.'

'In and out like Mick Jagger's dick. But never for more than eighteen months at a time.'

'So what's *your* interest in him?'

'Call it a bit on the side. He's like a fucking gnat bite. I keep scratching at him, but he never goes away.'

Brown handed back the file.

'He's worked with more or less the same set of faces for the last twenty-five years,' Ridley explained.

'I still don't get it.'

'About sixteen, seventeen years ago, him and his boys pulled a wages job in Whitechapel. I'd just made DC. They gave it to me. I was full of enthusiasm. Like you are at the beginning.' He looked pointedly at the DS. 'One of the warehouse security men got in the way of the van Newton used to escape. Whoever was driving ran him down.'

'Killed him?'

'No. But the poor bastard lost a leg. Then he lost his job. Two years after that he topped himself. Left a wife and a little girl. He was twenty-eight. I *knew* that Newton was in that fucking van, but I could never prove it was *him* who was driving. The only witness was the security guard. By the time the case came to court he'd had a nervous breakdown. The whole case hinged on his evidence. Newton walked. Ever since, I've been trying to find something to nail the bastard for. If I could send him and his boys down for life I'd consider my time in the force completely fucking justified.'

'Why not let it go? Seventeen years is a long time.'

'Yeah, it is, and if it takes *another* seventeen I'll see Newton banged up and I'll personally throw away the key.'

'Why's it so important to you?'

'That security guard was my brother.'

TOTTENHAM, NORTH LONDON

So MANY OF the flats were boarded up it was difficult to tell which were occupied. The dwellings had a uniform look of neglect and disrepair.

That was why the location had been chosen.

The tower block on Meridian Walk was like every other in the area; anonymous and crumbling.

Those windows not boarded up were usually broken and most of the walkways were strewn with broken glass, rubbish and even discarded old clothes.

Number twenty-six Warwick House was no exception. From the outside, abandoned and vandalized. A shell.

Inside, however, was a different matter.

The men who worked inside the flat were shielded from prying eyes not just by boards but by sheets of steel at the door and windows. The outer door had a letter-box-sized hole in it. That door was secured from the inside by at least eight bolts.

All were currently in place.

The flat was more like a fortress than a former home.

The men who worked inside had no idea who used to live there.

They didn't care either.

Why should they?

Aston Thomas wiped perspiration from his face as he stood over the cooker looking down at the frying pan. It was hot inside the flat.

He adjusted the height of the flickering blue flame.

A cooker, a kitchen table and two battered plastic-backed chairs was all the room contained; leftovers from the previous inhabitants, gratefully accepted by those who now worked within.

Thomas and his colleague, Dudley Smith, rarely left the flat during the day.

After they entered, they would pull the eight bolts across, sealing themselves inside. Occasionally, one of them would leave to gather up food or drink, but, usually, they brought it in with them.

The fewer people who saw them come and go during the day the better.

Smith stood close to his companion and watched as he added ingredients to the hot frying pan.

Cocaine hydrochloride.

There were several bags of the white powder on the table.

Water from a milk bottle.

Bicarbonate of soda.

He shook the handle of the frying pan, mixing the ingredients, watching as they formed into rocks the size of his thumbnail.

When they cooled they would remove them and seal them in plastic bags.

Smith smiled broadly and patted his companion on the shoulder.

Thomas added more of each ingredient.

The banging on the door was loud, but both men were expecting it.

It was always the same knock.

The same code.

Even so, Smith lifted the steel flap on the letterbox and peered out.

There were three men standing outside.

One, the largest of the three Jamaicans, was cleaning his fingernails with the end of a cocktail stick.

Smith began sliding back the bolts.

When that was done, he unlocked the double dead-bolts and pulled the door open.

It groaned on its hinges.

The three men stepped inside, the largest of them passing straight into the kitchen.

Thomas turned as the big man entered.

From his jacket pockets he pulled three more bags of white powder and laid them on the kitchen table beside the others.

'Take care of that,' said the big man, gesturing towards the cocaine.

'I cook you up what you want.' Thomas chuckled.

'You cook me plenty money. Them rocks like gold.' He smiled broadly. He stuck the cocktail stick in his mouth and chewed on it. His dreadlocks hung like sleeping snakes.

The heat was intense and the big man unzipped his jacket.

As he did, Thomas saw the .357 calibre Desert Eagle in a holster beneath his left arm.

'You not thinking 'bout keeping any of them rocks for yourself?' the big man said quietly.

'I wouldn't fuck with you, man.'

''Cause you know what happen if you do.'

The big man pulled the Desert Eagle from its holster and worked the slide, chambering a round.

He pressed the pistol to the back of Thomas's head.

'I hear things,' he hissed. 'They no secrets from me. Remember that.'

Thomas swallowed hard.

The big man withdrew the pistol and replaced it in the holster.

'Toad be back tonight, pick up the rocks. He pay you.'

The big man nodded towards one of his companions. A thickset individual with a bald head and a bull neck.

'We have it for him, Papa,' Thomas said.

Ernie Codling smiled.

26

THE BLAZING RED flare exploded like a supernova.

Smoke drifted across the crowd, who were leaping up and down, grabbing each other and punching the air. One vast amoebic mass of humanity, shifting and swaying like a single multicoloured organism.

Frank Newton smiled and watched as the television cameras zoomed in on the burning flare and the ecstatic faces lit by its brilliant luminescence.

He reached for the remote and eased the sound down slightly.

His grin grew wider as he watched the dejected Manchester United goalkeeper grab the ball from the back of the net and kick it angrily away.

The third Juventus goal had finished them off.

Newton remained slumped in his chair in the sitting room.

'You're quiet tonight.'

He looked across at Paula, who was sitting on the sofa, a magazine open before her.

'What did you say?' Newton enquired.

'You. I said you're quiet tonight.' She nodded towards

the TV set. 'Usually when *that* lot are losing you're jumping around the room.'

Newton nodded almost imperceptibly. 'Sorry. I was miles away,' he confessed.

'Anywhere in particular?'

He managed another smile.

'Bermuda or the Cayman Islands?' she persisted.

'I was just thinking.'

'You've been thinking ever since I got home. You've hardly opened your mouth.'

'Be thankful for small mercies.'

She regarded him closely for a moment. 'What's wrong, Frank?' she said finally.

'Nothing.'

She raised her eyebrows quizzically. 'How long have we been married?' she asked him.

Newton looked puzzled. 'Fifteen years,' he told her.

'And how long have we been together?'

'Twenty.'

'So after all that time, I know when something's bothering you. And something's bothering you, isn't it?'

Newton jabbed the 'mute' button on the remote. 'I lost some money today,' he told her.

'Oh, Christ, Frank, how much?'

'Twenty quid.'

'You promised me you'd stop gambling.'

'It was twenty quid.'

'Twenty quid we can't afford,' she snapped. 'How many more times are you going to lie to me?'

'I never lied to you, Paula.'

'You said you'd stop gambling.'

'I said I'd *try*,' he rasped angrily.

'So that's it. You tried and you failed?'

'Along with most other things I do in life, yes. I fucking failed.'

'Don't give me your sob stories, Frank. I know them off by heart. I've been hearing them for long enough.'

'Sorry to burden you.' His voice was heavy with scorn.

They regarded each other silently for a moment longer.

'How much would you have won?' she asked.

'Eighty, ninety quid.'

'Is that all?'

'It's more than we've fucking got now,' Newton snapped. 'Paula, don't tell me you like living like this because I know you don't. You want to get out as much as I do.'

She swallowed hard, but didn't answer.

The long silence was finally broken by Newton. 'We had a meet today to discuss a job,' he said flatly.

'What kind of job?'

He sucked in a deep breath. 'Securicor van,' he told her.

'What did the others say?' Paula asked.

He managed a smile. 'What I expected. Jim wasn't keen. Pete went for it in the end. Ray couldn't wait to get started and Jeff thought it could be dangerous.'

'I think he's right.'

'So what else am I supposed to do? How am I supposed to get us out of this?'

'Out of what, Frank?'

'Out of this house. This city. This way of life.'

'We manage.'

'I don't want to just manage. I don't want to get by like every other bastard. I want more. And I thought *you* did too.'

'You know I do, but I don't want to see you back inside again. I've spent half my life waiting for visiting orders so I can come and see you in whichever bloody nick they put you. I don't want to be doing that when I'm sixty.'

'You won't be.'

'No, Frank, I won't.'

'What does that mean?'

'You know how much I love you and it hurts me to see you like this. All I'm asking you to do is be careful.'

'This job is worth the risk.'

'I hope to God you're right, Frank.'

27

'I know what I'm talking about,' Newton insisted.

'Just like you did on all those other jobs?' she mused and he thought he caught a hint of scorn in her voice. 'How much is the job worth?'

'Everything else I've ever pulled in my life has been peanuts compared to this. It's a way out. It's what we've always wanted.'

'How much, Frank?'

'A million or more.'

'Split five ways. It's not a fortune, is it? We couldn't live on it for the rest of our lives.'

'But we could get out. Start again. Somewhere where no one knows us. I could get a job. A *proper* job.'

'Doing what?'

'I don't know, I haven't thought about it. I never said it would set us up for life, but I just want to give us a fucking chance.'

They regarded each other silently for a moment.

'And we could pay for IVF treatment for you,' Newton said finally. 'The best doctors. The best hospitals.'

Paula got to her feet and brushed past him, heading for the kitchen. Newton followed.

'It's what you want, isn't it?' he insisted. 'What we both want.'

Paula filled the kettle and flicked it on. 'And if it doesn't work?' she said, her voice low. 'What if even the best doctors money can buy can't do anything for us, Frank? What then?'

'We won't know unless we try and we can't try unless I do this job.'

'So, you do the job. We get the money. We find the doctors. We have the child and sail off into the sunset. Is that the plan?'

'Yeah. Who says it can't work?'

'There's so much that could go wrong, Frank.'

'I've spent my whole fucking life being wrong. Not anymore. I'm sick of wondering what might have been. If I'd had the balls to pull a job like this twenty years ago we wouldn't be stuck here now.' He took a pace towards her. 'What do you see when you look at me, Paula? A failure. What have I ever given you except pain and worry? I haven't given you much of a life that's for sure. So, what *do* you see when you look at me?'

'I see the man I love. The man I want to spend the rest of my life with.'

'Then let me give you the life we've never had. If I could do that, then all of what's happened before would be wiped out.'

'I wouldn't change anything that's happened to us, Frank, because I wouldn't change *you*.'

They embraced.

For long moments they held each other as if afraid to let go.

'I love you,' Newton whispered.

When they finally parted, he turned and headed back towards the sitting room.

The door to the hall was partly open; the hinges needed fixing. Newton went to pull the door closed when he noticed something lying on the carpet beneath Paula's coat.

He crossed to it and picked it up.

He cradled the tiny mitten in his hand, his brow creasing.

'Frank.'

Newton heard her call him and, clutching the mitten, he wandered back into the sitting room.

'What's wrong?' she asked, setting his tea down.

'Where did you get this?' he wanted to know, extending his hand to reveal the mitten.

'One of the kids at the nursery dropped it,' Paula told him, lowering her gaze.

'Shouldn't you have handed it in, babe?'

'There's no name in it. No one claimed it. I think it belongs to a little boy called Daniel.'

Newton looked down at the mitten again, then handed it to Paula. She took it from him and pushed it into the pocket of her jeans.

'Why did you take it?' he asked.

When she met his gaze again he could see the tears in her eyes. 'When I picked it up, I tried to imagine what it would feel like to be his mother,' she told him, her voice cracking. 'When I see the parents arrive to pick their kids up I do the same. I see them run to their mums or dads and hug them. And I wonder what that's like. It's all I've got, Frank. All I can do is pretend.'

28

THE COCAINE FELT cold on his tongue.

Ernie Codling dipped his index finger into the white mound of powder on the back of his hand once again and smiled.

It was dark in the back seat of the Jag and the coke looked almost luminous on the end of the digit.

Codling pushed it towards the other occupant of the back seat, rubbing it against her lips, feeling her tongue flick out to warmly lick up the powder.

He watched through heavy-lidded eyes, allowing his gaze to wander over her body.

She was wearing a lilac blouse, open to reveal her shapely breasts. Other than that, she wore just a pair of white knickers. Her leather skirt lay on the floor of the car.

Codling tried to remember her name.

Caroline. Carol.

Something like that.

Brown hair that reached as far as her shoulders; finely chiselled features; large brown eyes that appeared black in the back of the Jag. One manicured hand rested on his thigh, working closer towards his groin. But her gaze was upon the mound of coke on the back of his hand.

Eventually he offered it to her, watching as she bent her head, pressed an index finger to one nostril and snorted. As she sat back she wiped the residue away with her thumb and forefinger.

The two men in the front of the Jag seemed relatively unmoved by what was happening behind them. Occasionally, the driver would tilt his rear-view mirror to one side and glance at the couple on the back seat, but otherwise he contented himself with driving.

'You pick up the money from Thomas and Smith?' Codling asked, feeling the girl's hand moving more urgently on his stiffening penis. She expertly unzipped his trousers and slid one hand inside, her fingers closing around his shaft.

The driver nodded.

'Toad. You hear me?' Codling persisted.

'I got it,' the driver said. 'They wouldn't hold out on us. They know better.'

'I don't trust them,' offered the man in the passenger seat.

'I don't trust no one, Skeng,' Codling added. 'But Toad is right. They know better than to fuck with us.' Codling let out a sigh of pleasure as the girl bent her head and enveloped the tip of his penis with her warm mouth. 'No one fuck with us now,' he continued, gently massaging the back of her neck, ensuring that she didn't lift her head. 'The word go around town that we in business. Everyone know we in control in them other places now. Our own people running Birmingham and Bristol for us and we had no trouble there since we take over. Chill, man. It all under control.'

'You know how many more operations we got to shut down before we have control here?' Skeng asked from the passenger seat.

'What we shut down so far is pussy, man,' Codling told him, feeling the pleasure building as the girl's mouth and tongue performed their magic upon him. 'There no big-time operations here we can't deal with. Everyone selling for themselves. No organization. We fix that. Soon we be running it all.'

'Whores sell the stuff,' Toad offered. 'Pimps sell it. Everyone sell it. How you going to control them all?'

'People got to know we have the power,' Codling said flatly. 'That how you control them. We already have that power in Birmingham and Bristol. We soon have it here.'

He grabbed the girl by the back of the neck and lifted her head. A string of saliva hung from her bottom lip to the top of his penis like some kind of liquid umbilicus.

Codling gazed into her eyes. 'That what it all about, isn't it, girl?' he hissed. 'About power. It power that turn you on.'

He slid a hand between her legs, pushing two fingers roughly into her vagina, probing deeper until he withdrew those two digits and held them up. They glistened in the half light.

Codling smeared her own moisture onto one of her cheeks, then pushed her head back down into his lap, grinning as he felt her mouth close over his penis again.

'When everyone know we have that power, then we run things here. We control everything. People don't want to work with us, then we wipe them out. London is like a big pussy, just waiting for us. And we going to fuck it 'til it raw.'

29

SHE WAS STANDING at the window when he parked the car. DI John Ridley saw the shadowy figure and exhaled deeply.

She was still watching as he locked the Cavalier and made his way to the front door.

'I know it's late,' Ridley said, raising a hand in supplication. 'I'm sorry.'

'You could have phoned.'

Patricia Ridley appeared briefly in the sitting-room doorway, then ducked back inside again.

Here we go.

'I lost track of the time,' Ridley said as he wandered into the room, slumping down in the nearest chair.

'That'll be your epitaph, John. "Here lies John Ridley. He lost track of the time."'

'I said sorry. What more do you want, Pat?'

They regarded each other in silence for a moment, then she crossed to the small drinks cabinet in one corner of the room and poured him a measure of Teachers.

Ridley accepted it and smiled as he brushed her hand.

'I bet you haven't eaten either, have you?' she said, although it sounded more like a statement than a question.

She sat down opposite him; on the small table beside her own chair there was a glass of wine.

Ridley raised his glass in salute, but she didn't join him.

He sipped the amber fluid, feeling it burn its way to his stomach. 'All right,' he said wearily. 'You're pissed off. You've made your point. Next time I'll phone. Next time I'll eat. Make me a list.'

She continued to gaze at him.

'You know how it is, Pat. You knew from the beginning.'

'Work comes first? Is that it? If you don't like it, then go? Just like your first two wives did?'

'I don't need this shit now.' He sipped at his drink.

'I'm not nagging you, John. I'm concerned about you. This job . . .' She allowed the sentence to trail off.

Ridley finished what was left in his glass, then poured himself another. 'What about it?' he wanted to know.

'It's more than that to you. You never leave it behind. Even when you're away from the Yard it's still with you. Twenty-four hours a day. I'm always wondering whether or not that phone is going to ring and you're going to go rushing off on some case.'

'I'm dedicated.' He laughed, but it had a hollow sound.

'You're obsessed.'

'It's what I do. And I do it well.'

'I know that. But why do you have to shut me out?'

'What do you want me to do? Come home and talk about it?'

'Did the others ask you?'

Ridley exhaled wearily. 'We've had this conversation before,' he said dismissively.

'*Did* they?'

'What I do and see when I'm working, it's *my* business.'

'Even if it destroys our relationship?'

'You know the rules, Pat.'

'Rules,' she snapped angrily. 'This isn't a bloody game, John. It's our marriage.'

'So what do you want to hear?' he rasped.

'I want to help.'

'And how are you going to do that?'

'I know when things are bothering you, when something's on your mind. Share it with me.'

'OK. Shall I start with today? The two guys hacked with a machete? You should have seen the blood. The fucking place was like an abbatoir. The coroner said one of them had sustained seventeen blows to the head alone. There were pieces of brain all over the fucking floor. Is that all right?'

She shook her head.

'Or would you like to hear about some of the other recent cases?' he persisted, his eyes blazing. 'A young girl, couldn't have been more than eighteen, she'd been tied up and raped. And when the three blokes had finished, one of them had stuck a beer bottle up her arse. Only problem was, it broke. They used the rest of it to cut her throat.'

Patricia lowered her gaze.

'You want me to come home every night and share things like *that* with you?'

There was a long silence, finally broken by Ridley.

'What I do every day,' he said quietly, 'what I see, it belongs here.' He tapped his forehead. 'It's not for sharing. Least of all with you.'

'So that's it, is it? We live separate lives. You get on with yours. I get on with mine?'

'When it comes to work, yes.'

'There *is* nothing else but work for you, John, and if I'm excluded from *that* then there's nothing between us.'

'Don't exaggerate.'

'When was the last time we went out together? For a meal or anything?'

He shrugged.

'I'm not surprised you can't remember,' she said bitterly. 'It's been so long.'

'I'm sorry. That's all I can say, but this is the way it has to be.'

She got to her feet and headed for the sitting-room door. 'I'll leave you alone then. You've obviously got things to think about.'

'I'll be up in a while,' he said without looking at her.

'I won't bother staying awake. You might get side-tracked by your work.'

He heard the door close behind her.

'Shit,' murmured Ridley.

He drained what was left in his glass and poured himself another.

30

THE CAR HAD been stolen three days earlier.

Frank Newton had struggled with the gears at first, but the red Corolla Estate was handling more easily now.

He lit another cigarette and fixed his gaze on the Securicor van.

He'd been following it for thirty minutes, never more than three car lengths behind, his eyes never leaving the other vehicle.

Traffic was heavy and had been ever since he'd begun his pursuit close to Lord's cricket ground. The van had led him down St John's Wood Road and now into the Edgware Road.

Newton felt warm and he adjusted the ventilation system inside the Corolla, blowing cool air.

On the passenger seat there was a small two-way Motorola radio, also stolen a few days earlier.

On the floor on the passenger side was a black canvas bag.

Newton would glance at it occasionally.

His heart was already thudding a little harder against

his ribs and every fresh look at the bag seemed to increase the rhythm.

Going to bottle it at the last minute?

The Securicor van slowed down as it approached some traffic lights and Newton did likewise, braking a little too sharply.

The driver behind him sounded his hooter and for a second Newton was tempted to turn and gesture to him.

Just get a fucking grip. Take it easy.

He gripped the wheel more tightly and waited for the dark blue van to move off.

His hands were wet on the plastic.

He wondered about switching the radio on, but decided against it.

Again he adjusted the temperature inside the car.

Take it easy.

For some reason, an image of Paula suddenly flashed into his mind.

Worried you're never going to see her again?

The lights ahead were changing.

The Securicor van moved off.

Newton followed.

'Do you have to do that?'

Jeff Hobbs spoke the words without looking at his companion.

Ray Gorman ignored him and continued fiddling with the radio of the stolen Montego.

Classical music. Pop. Country. Chat. As he found each new station, a different sound filled the car.

'Turn it off,' Hobbs snapped, finally looking at Gorman who continued twisting the dial.

'Fucking thing,' said the younger man irritably. 'Perhaps the cassette-player works.'

'And what are you going to put in it?'

There was a small selection of tapes in the glove compartment: the Corrs. Natalie Imbruglia. Blondie.

'Just leave it, will you?' Hobbs insisted, turning the key.

'Miserable bastard,' snapped Gorman, sitting back in his seat.

The car was parked in Gloucester Square.

It had been there just as James Carson had promised – waiting for them.

A young woman in her early twenties emerged from one of the buildings and Gorman ran appraising eyes over her shapely figure.

She glanced into the car, saw his penetrating gaze and looked away.

Hobbs wasn't sure exactly how long they'd been sitting there, but it felt like a long time. He looked at his watch again as if that simple action was going to cause the hands to move more quickly.

Gorman turned and looked at the Puma holdall on the back seat. He reached over and tugged at it.

'Leave it, for Christ's sake,' Hobbs snapped. 'What do you want to do, take the gear out and play with it?'

'I'm fed up of sitting around. I want to get moving.'

'Not until Frank gives us the shout.'

'This is fucking stupid. Just waiting.'

'All we *can* do is wait.'

It was Gorman's turn to look at his watch. 'Come on,' he whispered impatiently.

The two-way crackled and Hobbs snatched it up. 'Frank?' he asked into the mouthpiece.

There was a blast of static that made him hold the radio away from his ear for a second, then he heard Newton's voice.

'Get moving.'

'Got it,' Hobbs replied.

'About fucking time,' hissed Gorman.

Hobbs twisted the key in the ignition.

The car wouldn't start.

Again he turned the key.

The engine remained still.

'What the fuck is wrong with it?' Gorman said, a note of anxiety in his voice.

'Just take it easy,' Hobbs told him, turning the key a third time.

The engine groaned, then died.

'Jesus Christ,' Gorman snarled.

Hobbs tried again.

There was a spark.

He stepped on the accelerator too: a longer groan from the engine.

'The fucking battery's flat.'

'No it's not,' Hobbs insisted.

He turned the key savagely.

The engine caught.

He pressed on the right-hand pedal.

There was a comforting roar.

He allowed it to rev for a moment or two, then stuck it in gear.

Both men looked somewhat relievedly at each other.

The Montego moved off.

James Carson sighed as he was forced to brake.

The white Mercedes van came to a halt behind several other vehicles.

He peered out of the driver's side window in an attempt to see further down Regent Street, hoping to spot what had caused the latest delay.

He could see nothing.

He tapped agitatedly on the steering wheel.

'Take it easy, Jim,' Peter Morrissey said without looking round.

'It's this bloody traffic,' Carson replied, sucking in a deep breath.

Morrissey was still gazing out at the vast array of shops on either side and at the hordes of people who spilled in and out of them like some kind of tidal wave.

'It makes you wonder where everyone's going, doesn't it?' he murmured.

Carson didn't answer.

The traffic began to move slowly.

Morrissey glanced at the driver as they passed Hamleys. He could see the concern on the older man's face.

Morrissey reached for a cigarette and offered one to Carson, who merely shook his head.

'You look like you need it.'

'It's not a fucking fag I need,' snapped Carson, trying to control his breathing.

'Do you want *me* to drive?'

Carson shook his head.

They reached the next set of lights at a crawl.

Carson stepped on the brake again, glaring up at the red light.

As they sat waiting, Morrissey suddenly hauled himself through the gap between the front seats and fumbled around inside the holdall in the back.

As he slid his hand inside he felt it brush cold metal.

One of the 210s nestled within.

Next to it was a smaller, more compact weapon.

The Scorpion machine-pistol was less than three and a half pounds in weight, capable of spewing out 840 rounds of .380 calibre ammo every minute in the right hands.

'Are you really going to use that?' Carson said, glancing into the rear-view mirror to see his companion admiring the sub-machine-gun.

'Only if I have to,' Morrissey told him.

Carson sucked in another deep breath.

'Don't sweat it, Jim,' the former soldier said. 'I don't want to kill anybody either.'

'But what if you have to?'

His question hung in the air.

The two-way crackled and Carson reached for it.

'Go on, Frankie,' he said into the mouthpiece.

'The Securicor van's made its first pick-up,' Newton told him. 'It's just about to make the second.'

'Where are you?'

'Just turning into Marylebone Road. What about you? How are you doing for time?'

'Fucking traffic's heavy and it's getting worse.'

He stuck the van into gear as the lights changed.

'Well, just keep coming,' Newton told him.

The Mercedes van continued its tortuous journey.

31

The pick-ups took less than a minute.

Using a stopwatch, Newton timed every movement of the Securicor van and its crew.

He watched each time as two of them made their way unhurriedly from the vehicle to the betting shops, then returned a moment later holding large canvas bags. These they stored inside the van itself. The armour-plated truck would then pull off into traffic again.

Followed by Newton.

As he tailed it along Marylebone Road he was grateful for the efficiency of the guards.

It was becoming more difficult to stay close to the van, such was the volume of traffic, but he dared not try anything too extravagant in case he was spotted; either by the guards themselves or by a passing police car or a stray speed camera.

The first time the van collected, he had guided the Corolla up onto the pavement nearby, flicked on the hazard lights and waited, his eyes never leaving the van.

He had known that he would have to try another trick for the next pick-up.

When the time came, he pretended to stall the car until the van was moving again. He sat behind the wheel feigning helpless anger until the money was collected, then, as the van moved off, he followed, his car starting automatically.

As if by magic.

Third pick-up approaching.

He reached for the two-way radio.

'You should have gone down Oxford Street,' hissed Ray Gorman, looking at the cars that jammed the road ahead of them.

'It's taxis and buses only,' Hobbs reminded him, also gazing through the windscreen.

'What the fuck is the hold-up?'

Goodge Street traffic was nose to tail. It was as if the vehicles using it were building blocks, hammered into position by some huge, spiteful child.

Nothing was moving.

'Any suggestions?' Hobbs murmured, still not looking at his companion. He could feel his own heart beating that little bit faster.

Ahead of them, hooters sounded; as if that simple action was going to unblock the thoroughfare.

Gorman looked at his watch. 'I'm going to call Frank,' he said agitatedly.

'And tell him what?'

'That we're stuck in fucking traffic.'

'And what's *he* going to do about it? He's probably stuck in traffic himself.'

Gorman hesitated a moment, then reached for the two-way.

Hobbs finally shot him a glance. 'Leave it,' he rasped.

Gorman gripped the Motorola.

'Put it down, Ray,' Hobbs insisted, the knot of muscles at the side of his jaw pulsing.

The two men glared at each other, then Gorman dropped the two-way onto the back seat.

A gap appeared at last.

The traffic suddenly seemed to be moving.

Two car lengths opened up ahead of the Montego and Hobbs gratefully eased his foot down on the accelerator.

The pedestrian came from nowhere.

If Hobbs saw him he certainly had no time to react.

The man was in his early twenties. He stepped into the road without looking, ducking between two of the many parked vehicles at the roadside.

Hobbs stepped on the brake, jolting both men hard.

'You fucking idiot!' roared Gorman at the man who stood defiantly before the car, glaring in at the occupants.

'Leave it,' Hobbs murmured, his eyes never leaving the man who still stood there.

The pedestrian banged on the bonnet and pointed to the Belisha beacons on either side of the road.

'He's on a fucking zebra crossing,' Hobbs hissed.

Still the man stood motionless.

Behind, another impatient driver hit his hooter.

Gorman turned in his seat and drove two fingers angrily skyward, his face contorted in rage.

Finally, the pedestrian moved.

'You should have run the cunt over,' snarled Gorman.

He checked his watch again.

'Three more pick-ups and they're finished.'

Frank Newton's voice sounded almost robotic coming from the two-way.

'Where are you now?' he continued.

'Heading up towards New Oxford Street,' Morrissey told him.

'When the driver's made the last pick-up he'll more than likely double-back on himself,' Newton said. 'Check he's not being followed.'

'This traffic is getting worse, Frank. What if he decides to go straight to the bank?'

'He won't. It's standard procedure. Trust me.'

'Where are you now?'

'Just turning into Gordon Street, I can't be that far away from you.'

'You might as well be on the fucking moon looking at this traffic. How are the others doing?'

'I haven't heard from them yet. I'll check when I've finished talking to you.'

'Are we still going to hit the van where we said?' Morrissey wanted to know.

There was a harsh crackle of static.

'Frank, I said—'

'I heard you, Pete. Yes, we are.'

'I hope this traffic doesn't fuck us up.'

'They're stopping again. I'll call back in a bit.'

Morrissey put the two-way down and ran a hand through his hair. He glanced across at Carson, whose face was set in hard lines.

'They've probably got nearly two hundred grand with them already, Jim,' the former soldier said, forcing a smile.

Carson didn't answer.

32

HE WAS LOSING it. Frank Newton had slipped more than six car lengths behind the Securicor van and once or twice he'd lost sight of the fucking thing completely.

Come on. Come on.

The road ahead divided into two lanes.

If he could just overtake two of the other vehicles, slide the Corolla in closer to the van . . .

He checked his mirrors and indicated.

The traffic was slowing again.

Just nip in front of that fucking Astra.

He indicated, prepared to move back into the left-hand lane again.

The Astra driver realized what he was doing. He didn't intend letting him in.

Newton sucked in a breath and tried to nudge the bonnet of the Corolla into the small gap.

The Astra moved forward slightly.

A car in the right-hand lane sounded its hooter.

As the traffic crept forward again, Newton judged it perfectly.

He sped into the gap ahead of the Astra.

'Fuck you,' he murmured to himself, catching sight of the Astra driver's angry face in his rear-view mirror.

Four car lengths from the Securicor van now.

He had it in plain view.

Just take it easy now.

One more pick-up.

If the men inside the van were aware of his presence they had certainly given no indication of it.

Or had they already radioed through to the police? Told them they had spotted a car following them?

Newton tried to push the thoughts from his mind.

They had no reason to be suspicious; he'd done it by the book.

Bottle going again?

The two-way crackled. Newton snatched it up, his eyes never leaving the van.

'Frankie, it's Jim.'

'Go on,' he urged.

'We're just passing the British Museum now.'

Newton looked at his watch. 'Keep coming, Jim. We're bang on.'

'What about the others?'

'Coming into Tottenham Court Road. Won't be long now.'

There was a heavy silence at the other end of the line.

'This lot have got one more pick-up to make,' Newton said and tossed the radio onto the passenger seat.

There were traffic lights ahead.

All three vehicles between Newton and the Securicor van were signalling to turn left.

If he speeded up he'd be right behind it.

The other cars turned.

The traffic lights were coming closer.

Newton cursed as it appeared the Securicor van was speeding up.

Had they sussed him?

He swallowed hard.

The lights were on amber.

Fuck! Now what?

The van was going through. No problem.

Newton wondered if he would get through in time.

If he *dare*.

If the van got across he'd lose it.

If he sped up and raced across behind it, then they would see him for sure.

Come on! Think!

The lights were less than ten yards away.

Brake or keep going?

Newton tried to swallow, but his throat was dry.

Those fucking lights weren't going to hold forever.

The van shot across the junction.

Newton was no more than five yards behind it.

The lights flickered onto red.

Newton gripped the wheel.

Keep going.

They were on red when he swept through.

*

'What the fuck is this?' snarled Ray Gorman.

Tottenham Court Road was at a standstill; nothing was moving in either direction.

Hobbs couldn't even move the car out of Goodge Street.

He swallowed hard.

'We're fucked,' Gorman said angrily.

'Just wait,' Hobbs told him, looking around, trying to see what was causing the monumental jam.

He spotted it almost immediately.

'The traffic lights are out,' he said, gesturing ahead to the junction with Torrington Place.

'What do you mean?'

'The fucking things aren't working.'

'So we're stuck here?' Gorman blurted furiously. 'We're fucking stuck!'

Hobbs stroked his chin thoughtfully. 'They'll clear it,' he said, his voice catching slightly.

'Who? Who's going to fucking clear it?' Gorman looked at his watch, his heart thudding against his ribs. 'We're not going to make it,' he rasped.

33

'What do you mean you can't move?'

Frank Newton gripped the two-way radio in one hand as he drove, his eyes still fixed on the dark blue Securicor van ahead.

'There must have been some kind of power cut,' Hobbs told him, his voice breaking up slightly over the airwaves. 'The fucking traffic lights aren't working. Nothing's moving in either direction.'

Newton gritted his teeth. 'Any chance of turning round?' he wanted to know. 'Taking another route?'

'No way,' Hobbs informed him.

'The van's finished picking up. Their next stop is the bank.'

'We can't move, Frank.'

Newton swallowed hard.

Call it off now.

The road was beginning to dip sharply.

The mouth of the Euston underpass yawned before him, swallowing the traffic.

'Frank, wait a . . . I think . . .'

Newton could barely make out his companion's words.

'Say that again, Jeff.'

'Clear . . . traffic . . . coppers have . . .'

'Jeff!' he shouted at the two-way.

Static.

'I'm losing you,' he said, the signal breaking up into a prolonged hiss. 'Jeff?'

More static.

'Fuck,' snarled Newton, dropping the Motorola onto the passenger seat.

The Securicor van headed down into the underpass.

Newton followed.

He wound up his window as he entered the underpass, the stink of fumes filling his nostrils. The roar of engines was amplified by the subterranean cavern, the daylight momentarily replaced by the artificial glare of fluorescents embedded in the concrete all around him.

The road began to slope upwards again and Newton realized, with some relief, that they were leaving the underpass.

He reached for the two-way once more. 'Jeff,' he snapped. 'Talk to me.'

There was a loud crackle of static then he heard Hobbs's voice.

'. . . moving . . .'

'Say again?'

'We're moving,' Hobbs told his companion. 'The traffic's being directed by a motorbike copper.'

'Where are you?'

'I'm going to shoot up Gordon Street. We're close, Frank.'

Newton managed a thin smile.

It broadened as he caught sight of another, more familiar vehicle pulling out into the road ahead of him.

He recognized the white Mercedes van immediately.

Carson manoeuvred the vehicle into the flow of traffic, dropping back behind the Corolla.

Newton felt his pulse quicken.

Not long now.

The sweat on the palms of his hands made it difficult to grip the wheel, but he clung on, watching as the Securicor van's right-hand indicator flamed.

To the left was the monolithic edifice of Euston station.

'He's turning into Woburn Place now,' Newton said, his mouth pressed against the two-way.

'I can see him.' The voice belonged to Hobbs.

Newton glimpsed the black Montego in his wing mirror.

As he swung the Corolla across the lines of traffic he looked towards the holdall on the passenger seat.

It was already unzipped.

Ready.

'All right,' he said into the two-way, 'let's do it.'

34

THE MERCEDES ALMOST collided with an oncoming car as it overtook the Securicor van.

Frank Newton heard the sound of a hooter being banged angrily.

He guided the Corolla closer to the back of the van, aware that the driver had slowed down slightly.

There were cars parked on both sides of Woburn Place and he glanced at his own speedo: down to less than twenty miles an hour.

Behind him, the black Montego moved with similar purpose. Newton could see Jeff Hobbs's face quite clearly in his rear-view mirror.

If the crew in the security vehicle had any idea they were being followed they had given no indication of it.

Newton reached into the holdall and his hand closed over the woollen mask.

He looked again into his rear-view mirror, saw Hobbs and Gorman do the same. Saw them reach for their weapons.

The Securicor van was braking slightly.

Newton tugged on the mask, his breathing laboured through the material.

Sweat was pouring off him as it was; the mask just made it worse.

He knew that, up ahead, Carson and Morrissey must be ready.

The time had come.

The Securicor van braked hard and skidded slightly.

Newton heard a crash.

He floored the accelerator, gripped the wheel hard and gritted his teeth.

The needle on the speedo nudged twenty-five as he slammed into the back of the van.

The impact flung him against the wheel, his seatbelt snapping hard against his chest and shoulder, knocking the wind from him.

The Montego shot past. It scraped an oncoming Sierra and slammed into the side of the van.

The security vehicle was pinned on three sides, trapped by a parked car on the driver's side.

Newton flung open the door and practically fell out into the street. He was on his feet straight away, the Taurus 9mm gripped in one fist, one of the 210s in the other.

There was steam rising from the buckled bonnet of the Corolla.

From the Montego, Hobbs and Gorman were advancing towards the Securicor van. Gorman had the chainsaw gripped in both hands.

The vehicle was badly damaged by the impacts. The

back doors had been forced apart slightly and Newton could see two of the guards moving about inside.

As he stepped onto the pavement he could see that the rear doors of the Mercedes van were also open.

Morrissey was standing in the back, the Scorpion sub-machine-gun aimed at the uniformed men in the cab.

'Get out!' roared Newton, waving the weapons at the men inside. 'Get the fucking doors open!'

He fired one barrel of the 210 into the air as a warning, the discharge deafening.

He heard a scream from nearby, but didn't turn to find its source.

No time. This had to be done fast. Five minutes, tops.

Cars travelling in the opposite direction passed by as quickly as they could.

Some fucking do-gooder with a mobile could be calling the law even now. Got to hurry.

'Open the fucking doors!' Newton bellowed again.

Barely had his words died away than he heard the deafening roar of the McCullough.

With the razor-sharp blades spinning over 2,500 times a minute, Gorman advanced towards the stricken vehicle.

Newton looked at his watch.

Four minutes left.

The back doors swung open and the guards jumped out, one of them falling onto the tarmac. He was bleeding from a cut just below his hairline, presumably sustained in the collison.

The other man looked on blankly as Newton and the

others moved towards him. He was holding a nightstick in one shaking hand.

Hobbs pushed the barrel of the Beretta against the second man's cheek. 'Don't be a fucking hero,' he rasped, his voice muffled by the woollen mask.

'Please don't,' the guard blurted, his eyes bulging wide in their sockets.

His companion was on his knees, one hand clamped to his wound.

Gorman kicked at him as he passed, hauling himself up into the rear of the van.

He switched the chainsaw off, the sound dying away on the fume-choked air.

'Get the fucking money!' Newton shouted. 'Come on, move it!'

Three and a half minutes.

A dark blue canvas sack came flying out of the rear doors. It was closely followed by another. Then another.

'Come on, let's get this in the car,' Newton said, the 210 still aimed at the quivering guards.

From the front of the vehicle, Carson came hurrying into view.

'Get the car and let's load up,' Newton told him.

Carson ran as quickly as he could towards a grey Cosworth that was parked in Endsleigh Place. It had been there for more than a day, placed there by Carson himself.

The appointed spot.

As with all getaway cars, the headrest had been removed.

He unlocked the boot, then ran back towards the canvas bags that now littered the road behind the Securicor van. Moving as quickly as they could, he and Newton hurried back and forth to the Cosworth, hurling the bags into the boot.

'Get her started,' Newton snapped. Sweat was running into his eyes, making them sting.

Three minutes.

He'd barely finished speaking when they heard the first of the sirens.

35

'Shit,' snarled Newton as he heard the strident wail.

The other men looked at him, as if for guidance.

'Did you use your radio when we hit you?' Newton demanded, taking a step towards one of the guards.

He tried to shake his head, but the barrel of the Beretta pressed against his cheek prevented the movement.

Hobbs used his thumb to pull back the hammer, the sound seemingly deafening in the uniformed man's ear.

He closed his eyes, the colour draining from his face.

There was a monstrous roar from behind him. Gorman had started up the chainsaw again.

'Just move!' shouted Newton. 'We've got it all!'

Two and a half minutes.

He saw Gorman swinging the chainsaw blade close to the guard. 'They called the fucking law,' he snarled.

'No one called,' the guard blurted.

'Get in the car,' Newton urged, glancing at Hobbs and Gorman.

He looked behind him and noticed Carson struggling

with the driver's side door, trying to push the key into the lock.

The older man was visibly shaking, unable to push the metal home. He gritted his teeth, forced the key into the lock, turned it, then pulled it free again.

As he struggled behind the wheel he dropped the key.

For long seconds it seemed as if the world was moving in slow motion.

Carson saw the key fall to the ground.

Saw it hit the kerb.

Saw it spin across the tarmac.

Saw it drop through the grate of a drain.

'Oh, Jesus,' hissed Carson.

He knew what he had to do.

Stepping out of the car he drove one foot repeatedly against the steering column.

'What the fuck is he doing?' hissed Gorman, his voice barely audible above the roar of the chainsaw.

Carson continued kicking at the column, sweat pouring from him.

There was a loud crack as the cowling finally shattered.

He slid behind the wheel again, twisting the wheel. Wires hung like plastic veins from the pulverized steering lock.

Moving with a speed born of desperation, he slipped one hand inside his pocket and pulled out a small blade.

Newton ran across in time to see him strip the plastic sheaths from the wires.

Two minutes.

Carson twisted the ends of the battery and ignition feeds together, smiling inside the mask when the dashboard lights flared on.

He touched the exposed end of the starter feed to the join of the other two and the engine suddenly roared into life.

Jabbing the starter-feed wire against the other two he pumped the accelerator, careful never to hold all three wires together for too long for fear of burning out the starter motor.

As the engine revved, he allowed the starter-feed wire to drop away.

Through the eyeholes of their masks, Newton and Carson locked stares momentarily.

Then Newton spun away.

Ninety seconds.

The sirens were coming closer.

36

'WHERE ARE THEY?' James Carson shouted from the waiting Cosworth.

The sirens seemed to be deafening now.

Newton was looking frantically up and down the road.

So too was Gorman.

'I can't see any fucking police cars,' Gorman snapped.

'There,' Newton hissed, jabbing a finger towards Euston Road.

The sirens wailed loudly.

They could see blue and red lights spinning on top of the vehicles.

Three of them.

Moving fast.

Newton smiled inside his mask. 'Fucking fire engines,' he called triumphantly.

The trio of fire-fighting trucks swept past, the sound of their sirens gradually dying away.

Most eyes had turned in their direction.

Except for those of the younger Securicor guard.

Adam Heath saw that Hobbs had taken a step back; saw that the eyes of the men were elsewhere.

He had seconds and he used them well.

With lightning speed, he slid his nightstick from his belt and swung it at Hobbs. The hard wood caught him across the chin, knocking him off his feet, the Beretta skidding across the tarmac.

Heath struck again.

Gorman felt a thunderous impact across his shoulder, then his forearm.

He dropped the chainsaw. It hit the ground and spun like a ferocious top, smoke pouring from it.

'*Cunt!*' yelled Gorman, pulling the .459 from his belt with his free hand.

As Heath turned and tried to duck behind the Securicor van, Gorman fired twice, the recoil slamming the automatic back against the heel of his hand.

One shot screamed off the side of a parked car.

The second hit Heath in the back of the leg.

The heavy-grain bullet tore through the top part of his calf, splintering bone. It pulverized his cruciate ligaments and blasted the patella to atoms as it exited, practically severing his leg at the knee.

He toppled backwards.

As he did so he heard the roar beneath him and realized he was falling onto the spinning blades of the chainsaw.

The hand he put out to save himself was carved in two by the churning blade. Blood, fragments of bone and slivers of flesh flew into the air and the terrifying sound of the chainsaw was almost drowned by Heath's agonized screams.

He went over on the stump of his arm, unable to avoid the dozens of blades that scythed so easily through muscle and bone. It cut into his shoulder and the upper part of his chest, shredding his uniform as easily as it macerated his bones.

A large pool of blood began to spread out around him.

Newton pushed him away from the chainsaw with his foot, blood splashing onto his boot and jeans.

Hobbs was staggering to his feet, blood seeping through the mask. He lifted it above his mouth and spat a broken tooth free.

Carson rammed the Cosworth into reverse, the vehicle shooting backwards into the street where it almost collided with an oncoming Audi.

Gorman aimed the .459 at the head of the driver. 'Get out!' he bellowed.

The driver could only stare in terror at Gorman as he grabbed the door handle and wrenched it open.

'Get out, you cunt!' he screamed, throwing the terrified man from his seat, slamming the butt of the pistol against the base of his skull. He went flying across the road into the side of another parked car.

Gorman slid behind the wheel of the Audi.

'You and Jeff go now,' Newton told him, helping Hobbs into the vehicle. It shot away as if fired from a catapult, wheels spinning insanely on the tarmac.

The stench of burning rubber filled the air.

Newton heard the staccato rattle of sub-machine-gun fire and looked up to see Morrissey running towards him.

He looked down at the writhing body of Heath as he joined Newton.

'What the fuck was that?' Newton demanded.

'I told them to get down,' Morrissey snapped. 'And they wouldn't.'

The two men locked stares for a moment.

'I fired over their heads,' the former soldier said.

More sirens.

'They're coming!' Carson shouted from inside the Cosworth.

Newton pushed Morrissey towards the waiting vehicle, then allowed himself a final look at the battered Securicor van.

At the mutilated body of Heath.

The pool of blood.

The empty shell cases.

A big fucking mess.

The first police car nosed its way into Woburn Place.

37

THE BLUE AND red lights on top of the white Astra were spinning madly.

The police car moved as quickly as possible down the crowded thoroughfare, the two occupants running appraising eyes over the carnage before them.

The wrecked van.

Abandoned and damaged cars.

And the body – bloodied and still.

The Cosworth sped off, Carson weaving in and out of traffic as best he could.

The police car followed.

Looking out of the rear windscreen, Newton could see the passenger reaching for his radio. 'They'll have half the fucking Met here in a minute,' he hissed. 'Move it, Jim.'

Even as he spoke, he took another cartridge from his pocket and slipped it into the shotgun.

Morrissey, seated in the back with him, checked the magazine of the Scorpion.

'What are you going to do?' Carson demanded. 'Kill them?'

'Just fucking *drive*, will you?' spat Newton, his eyes never leaving the pursuing Astra.

The two cars continued down Southampton Row, moving as fast as the other traffic would allow.

Ahead of them, the Audi, driven by Gorman, was also trying to build up speed in the narrow confines of the street.

Carson looked ahead and saw the other vehicle mount the pavement to avoid several parked cars. Pedestrians scattered as the vehicle roared past.

Gorman swung the Audi back into the road, slamming into the side of another car. The vehicle shook, skidded, then tore onwards.

The two motorcycle policemen appeared from a side street like phantoms. They swung their bikes in behind the speeding Audi, the first of them accelerating alongside it.

Gorman glanced to his left and saw the bike.

He wrenched the wheel sharply, veering suddenly into the path of their pursuer.

The policeman reacted quickly and avoided the collision.

His companion roared up the other side of the car.

Gorman, gripping the wheel with one hand, dragged the .459 up and fired twice.

The sound was thunderous inside the car.

Both shots punched out the side window: cold air rushed in.

Neither bullet caught the policeman.

'Give me that,' snarled Hobbs, taking the automatic from him.

Gorman resisted for a second and took his eyes off the road.

'Jesus!' shrieked Hobbs.

A woman stepped in front of the Audi.

It was doing over fifty when it hit her.

There was a sickening crunch, then her body was flung skywards, slamming down on the roof of the vehicle before toppling onto the tarmc.

'You fucking idiot!' roared Hobbs, steadying himself.

He got off five shots in quick succession, empty shell cases spinning from the .459.

The blasts made their ears ring, muzzle flashes burning white on their retinas. The smell of cordite filled their nostrils.

Two bullets struck the nearest police bike.

One stove in part of the closest pannier, another exploded the front tyre.

The bike pitched madly, hurling its rider from the saddle. He hit the road hard as the bike cartwheeled away, crashing into the back of a dustcart.

There was a loud explosion as the fuel tank went up.

The bike disappeared in a ball of white, orange and red flame so intense that, as they swept past the inferno, Gorman and Hobbs felt the heat through the shattered side window.

The other bike dropped back, content to stay behind the fleeing Audi.

'Get *him* too!' Gorman screamed, seeing the bike in the rear-view mirror.

'Just keep your fucking eyes on the road,' Hobbs snapped. 'I'll worry about him.'

38

CARSON SAW THE red light approaching.

He pressed down hard on the accelerator and the Cosworth swept through the junction to a chorus of blasting hooters.

The police car followed, swerving to avoid a builder's van coming the other way.

'Hold on,' Carson warned his companions.

In the back of the car, Newton and Morrissey gripped the seat belts.

Newton could see the Astra drawing closer.

He could even make out the features of the driver.

Carson stepped on the brake, wrenching the wheel to one side.

The Cosworth spun around a corner, the back wheels screeching madly for interminable seconds, throwing up clouds of reeking smoke.

As he guided the vehicle down the side street, he checked a wing mirror and was satisfied to see the white Astra overshoot and career onwards.

He made another sharp left, then a right, the car slamming into a waste bin as it made the last turn.

Newton and Morrissey were tossed around like toys. Newton grunted in pain as he caught his shoulder on one of the car's side panels.

Morrissey fared no better: his head was snapped to one side and he felt a moment of dizziness as it struck a window.

Carson continued to manoeuvre the car with terrifying expertise, the needle occasionally touching forty as he sent them hurtling along narrow streets sometimes barely wide enough to take two cars.

One wing mirror was ripped away as the Cosworth collided with a parked car, but Carson drove on.

'We've got to switch cars,' Newton said, gazing out of the back window.

Sweat was pouring down his face. He tugged at his mask and pulled it free.

Morrissey did likewise.

'Every fucking copper in London will have the reg number of this one by now,' Newton continued. 'We've got to dump it.'

Carson kept driving.

'Are you listening to me, Jim?' Newton snarled, gripping his companion by the shoulder.

Carson took a hard left.

'Where the fuck are you going?' Newton demanded.

'Other side of the river,' Carson said, pulling his mask free. 'We'll dump it there.'

Morrissey and Newton looked at each other.

Carson guided the Cosworth along Lancaster Place, over Waterloo Bridge.

Newton looked out at the Thames flowing below them. Grey and stinking, it snaked through the city like a circuit cable.

'What about the others?' Carson asked.

'There's nothing we can do,' Newton said.

'So we just leave them?'

'What do you want to do, Jim? Go back and try to find them? They know the score. They know what to do. When they get clear of the Old Bill they separate and head for the lock-up. Just like us. We discussed it all. We planned it all. They know what they're supposed to do.'

'And what if they don't shake off the law?' Carson wanted to know.

The question hung in the air like the stench of gunpowder.

39

'HE'S STILL COMING,' snarled Gorman, peering into his rear-view mirror.

The motorbike policeman was keeping ten or twelve yards behind the Audi, weaving past cars when he had to.

And now both men in the Audi heard sirens drawing closer.

Two police cars pulled into view, one on either side.

'Move it!' Hobbs snapped.

He pressed the magazine-release button on the .459 and the slim metal rectangle dropped into his hand.

As the car thundered on he thumbed the shells into the palm of his hand and counted them.

Seven.

One extra mag in his pocket.

There was one chance.

'We've got to block the fucking street behind us,' he said breathlessly, his hair plastered to his scalp beneath the woollen mask.

Gorman swung the car into High Holborn.

The police followed.

There was a pedestrian-crossing ahead, people streaming across it.

'Get out the fucking way!' bellowed Gorman.

Those on the crossing heard the roar of the engine as it bore down upon them.

Screams; shouts; the squeal of brakes; the wail of sirens – all melted together in one discordant symphony.

The Audi sped through the mass of fleeing pedestrians, but missed them all.

Ahead, the road was narrowing again.

The leading police car was closing in.

Hobbs fired at the back windscreen.

Three, four, five shots.

It exploded outwards.

He could hear nothing for a moment, then he rested his arms on the parcel shelf and squeezed off two more rounds.

The slide flew back.

Empty.

He jammed in a fresh magazine and opened up, pumping the trigger, ignoring the numbing impacts of the recoil against his hand and the deafening eruptions as each 9mm slug was spewed from the weapon.

The front windscreen of the first police car shattered.

The vehicle skidded, slewed across the road.

He saw it slam sideways into a car coming in the opposite direction; saw the driver slump to one side.

The second police car overtook it and raced up to within feet of the Audi. The driver coaxed it forward and rammed the boot of his quarry.

'Bastards!' shouted Gorman, struggling to keep control of the vehicle. It clipped a lamppost and shuddered back onto the road.

Hobbs almost dropped the automatic when the second impact came. The Audi mounted the pavement, flattened a Belisha beacon, then sped on.

Hobbs fired lower this time, aiming for the tyres.

He knew that even a marksman with a rifle and scope would have trouble hitting anything at the speed they were moving.

This wasn't fucking Hollywood, was it?

He pumped six shots at the bonnet and front tyres of the pursuing police car.

Two found their target.

Bingo.

The police car sliced sideways across the tarmac, struck the kerb and flipped onto its roof, where it twisted gently until a van coming the other way smashed into it and set it spinning like a fucking roulette wheel.

The motorbike was still with them.

'Kill that cunt,' Gorman snarled, seeing the uniformed rider closing in.

More shots.

The hammer slammed down on an empty chamber.

'Fuck,' hissed Hobbs. 'I'm out.'

The police bike was within ten feet now.

Gorman hit the brakes.

The bike had no chance to stop.

It ploughed into the back of the Audi, hurling the rider into the air.

For interminable seconds he hung like a puppet with cut strings, then crashed down onto the bonnet of the Audi, rolling in front of the speeding vehicle.

There was a loud thump as his body was crushed beneath the wheels.

'*Fuck you!*' screamed Gorman triumphantly, seeing the pulped body in the rear-view mirror.

Ahead, Hobbs saw a familiar sign: the red circle with the blue legend across it.

CHANCERY LANE

'Stop the car,' he said, gripping Gorman's shoulder.

Gorman hesitated.

'Stop,' Hobbs insisted.

The Audi screeched to a halt and both men leapt out.

Some by-standers scattered, others merely looked on in bewilderment.

The two men ran into the tube station, vaulted the barriers and ran for the escalators. A guard shouted something at them, but they ignored him, clattering down the metal steps, knocking others aside, dragging the woollen masks off and jamming them into their pockets.

Gorman stumbled at the bottom, but hauled himself up.

There was a train waiting, its doors about to close.

Both men sprinted towards it.

The doors were sliding shut.

The train was preparing to move off.

Hobbs ran at it and crashed in through the narrow gap.

Gorman got his hands inside the sliding doors.

Puzzled onlookers on the platform watched the curious tableau.

Both men were pulling at the doors.

They slid open.

Gorman tumbled in.

The two men stood in the carriage gasping for breath.

Eyes turned in their direction, then returned to books or magazines.

It was a short ride to Holborn.

'We'll change there,' panted Hobbs, jabbing a finger at the underground map above the seats.

'What if they're waiting for us?' Gorman wanted to know.

Hobbs had no answer.

The train rumbled on, swallowed by the tunnel.

40

FIFTIES.

Twenties.

Tens.

The notes were scattered across the workbench like discarded sweet wrappers.

Some of the money had been sorted into piles, but the rest looked as if it had been emptied from the blue canvas sacks like rubbish delivered to a tip.

Frank Newton sucked on his cigarette and regarded the money impassively.

Carson was still counting it, a calculator beside him.

The other three men inside the lock-up were also watching him.

Hobbs sipped at a mug of coffee, massaging his chin with one hand, wincing every time he touched the cut there.

Gorman was pacing back and forth, occasionally glancing at his watch. It was 10.06 p.m.

Morrissey had a rolled copy of the *Evening Standard* in his hand, as if he was in pursuit of some troublesome fly.

The place smelled of sweat; and if tension had possessed an odour, it would have reeked of that too.

'Three hundred and twenty-six thousand,' Carson said finally, letting out a weary breath.

'What?' snarled Gorman. 'Where's the fucking million you promised us?' His words were directed at Newton.

Newton had no answer. He merely took a step towards the worktop and picked up a bundle of fifties.

'Three hundred and twenty-six grand,' Hobbs murmured.

'Plus loose change,' Carson added, jabbing at the buttons of the calculator. 'It's a bit more than sixty thousand pounds each.'

'Fucking great,' snarled Gorman. 'Only a hundred and forty short of what you promised us, Frank. Hardly worth doing fucking life for, is it?'

'If you hadn't shot that fucking guard we wouldn't be looking at life, you dozy bastard,' rasped Newton, rounding on him.

'I had no choice, he was trying to be a fucking hero. Anyway, I didn't kill him.'

'That's not what it says here,' snapped Morrissey, slamming the rolled-up newspaper down on the worktop.

He indicated the 'Stop Press' section in the margin of the back page.

'"Three killed, more than fourteen injured,"' Newton read aloud.

'Read the next bit,' Morrissey urged.

'"A spokesman for Winning Post bookmakers stated that just under one hundred and fifty thousand pounds had been stolen."' Newton looked at his companions. 'A hundred and fifty grand. What the fuck is he talking about?'

'Somebody's got their maths wrong,' Hobbs offered.

'It's an insurance scam,' Gorman said dismissively.

'How can it be a fucking insurance scam when they're claiming they lost *half* of what we've got here?' Newton retorted. 'If they were trying to screw the insurance they'd be saying they'd lost millions.'

He looked at Carson. 'You're sure, Jim?'

Carson nodded. 'Three hundred and twenty-six grand,' he said. 'Count it yourself if you want.'

'What the fuck is going on?' Hobbs wanted to know.

Newton threw the paper to one side. 'You tell me, Jeff,' he said flatly. 'We get over three hundred grand, the bookies claim they've only lost a hundred and fifty. What kind of fucking scam is that?' He looked at the money spread out on the worktop.

'Who cares?' Gorman grunted. 'It's still not enough. Shit. This was going to be a big fucking job. One to set us *all* up. It looks like you didn't do your homework properly, Frank.'

'Just shut it, Ray,' Morrissey said irritably.

'Don't tell me to shut it,' rasped Gorman. 'It might not matter to *you*. You can always put your little girl-friend on the fucking streets to earn you a few extra quid.'

Morrissey snatched up the Scorpion machine-pistol and pointed it at Gorman.

The other man pulled the .459 from his belt and

gripped it in both hands, the barrel aimed at his companion's head.

'Go on then, soldier boy,' hissed Gorman. 'Fucking do it.'

Morrissey pulled back the cocking lever on the Scorpion, the metallic sound reverberating inside the lock-up.

'Yeah, do it,' Hobbs said. 'Go on, kill yourselves. Three hundred and twenty-six grand split between three is better.'

'Fuck you,' snapped Gorman, not taking his eyes from his companion.

'Put the guns down,' Newton said evenly.

The two men hesitated.

'Do it!' he bellowed, the knot of muscles at the side of his jaw pulsing angrily.

Gorman and Morrissey slowly lowered their weapons.

'Right, girls, if you've finished,' Newton hissed, looking at each of them in turn. He sucked in a deep breath. 'The bookies say they lost a hundred and fifty. We've got three hundred and twenty-six.' He surveyed the money scattered on the worktop. 'That leaves a hundred and seventy-six grand unaccounted for. I'd like to know who it belongs to. Because I can guarantee you one thing – eventually, they're going to come looking for it.'

41

GARY CARSON KNEW he was being watched.

Despite the sea of faces and the endless barrage of sound inside the club, he was well aware of the sentinel who had been trailing him for the last hour.

Sometimes it was just the man: mid-twenties; short hair; shades; wiry.

Every now and then, the woman would join the watcher. She was also in her mid-twenties; shoulder-length mousy hair; round faced; dressed in a pair of jeans and a black crop-top and long cardigan.

Carson had seen this kind of thing before.

They had both watched him inside the club, anxious to approach him, but not quite gathering enough bottle to do it.

Perhaps they didn't know how to ask.

'Someone told us you had some stuff?'

Carson smiled to himself, sipped at his vodka and lemonade and continued chatting to the group of people around him.

The music raged on around them, the floor shaking as the bass thudded like some massive, overactive heart.

Carson finished his drink and headed for the Gents.

As he turned, he glanced in the direction of the two who'd been watching him from the other side of the bar.

Perhaps the bloke would approach him inside the bogs.

That was where most of his business was done.

He pushed the door open and walked in. The music sounded muffled inside the toilets.

There was a youth in his early twenties kneeling inside one of the cubicles, vomiting into the bowl.

Two other men stood at the row of urinals, happily chatting, oblivious to the retching noises coming from behind them.

A fourth man was feeding change into the contraceptive machine on the far wall.

Carson urinated gushingly.

He waited for the nervous cough, the light tap on the shoulder.

The bloke had seen him come in here.

He crossed to the sinks and inspected his reflection in the cracked mirror.

The door opened and two more lads roughly the same age as himself walked in, laughing loudly.

Carson washed his hands and left.

Still no sign of the watcher.

Perhaps he'd lost his bottle completely and gone home.

Carson returned to the bar.

No, he was still sitting there – sipping his drink. Waiting.

Fuck it.

Carson said his goodbyes and headed for the exit.

It was a short walk from the club to his home and, when he felt the cold wind nipping at his face, he was grateful for that.

He dug his hands into his jacket pockets and set off.

If the bloke and his girl were looking to buy now, then they weren't going to get much of a choice. All he had on him was half a gram of coke (reasonable shit, he thought. He'd chopped it himself with baby laxative), a few Es, some whizz and a little grass.

Business had been good.

He'd made over two hundred quid inside the club. People on the estate knew him, they knew he didn't fuck them around. He provided a good service and top gear.

He stopped to light a cigarette and heard footsteps behind him. Furtive, cautious footsteps that stopped when *he* stopped.

He waited a moment then carried on.

He heard the footsteps again.

Another hundred yards and he'd be home.

As he reached the gate he heard the footsteps quicken and turned to see two figures moving towards him.

As he'd suspected, it was the guy in shades and his girl.

'You took your fucking time, didn't you?' Gary said, grinning.

'Can you help us out?' said the man.

'What do you need? I haven't got much on me. Just some Es and a bit of whizz.'

'Are you Gary Carson?' the woman wanted to know, pulling her cardigan more tightly around her.

He sucked on his cigarette and nodded.

'Give us four Es,' the woman said, looking around anxiously.

Carson dug in his pocket and pulled out a small package of clingfilm. Inside it there were four white tablets the size of aspirins. 'Fifty,' he said.

She paid him and he handed it over.

The man reached into his pocket.

The woman into her cardigan.

They both produced slim leather wallets that they flipped open.

He could make out the ID even in the gloom.

'Gary Carson, you're under arrest for the supply and possession of illegal substances,' said the man flatly.

'Fucking coppers,' Carson snarled. 'How did you know?'

'It wasn't hard,' the man informed him. 'Besides, Claire's been on your arse for the last week.' He nodded in the direction of the policewoman.

She smiled.

42

'IT WASN'T YOUR fault, Frank.'

Paula Newton rested one hand on her husband's chest and gazed down at him.

He was looking at the ceiling above him, tracing the cracks in the plaster with his gaze. 'I let them down, Paula,' he said softly. 'All of them. They trusted me.'

'They still do.'

'I promised them two hundred grand each. They ended up with fuck all.' He looked at his wife. 'I let *you* down too. But then again I've been doing that for as long as I've known you, haven't I?'

She kissed him on the forehead. 'You didn't know,' she insisted.

'Know what? That the van was going to be carrying so little? That people were going to die? That we were going to be stuck with a hundred and seventy-six grand of fuck-knows-who's money?'

'Who *could* it belong to?'

'I wish I knew.'

There was a long silence, finally broken by Paula.

'We could get out anyway,' she whispered. 'If that's what you still want.'

'With what? Where are we going to go? Once the police figure this one out, they've got me for accessory to murder as well as armed robbery. And all for sixty poxy grand.'

'They've got no descriptions,' she reassured him. 'You've all got alibis. There's no reason for them to suspect any of you.'

He looked at her in the darkness and saw the tears in her eyes.

'If you left I'd understand,' he said finally, his voice cracking slightly. 'What have you got that's worth staying for?'

'I've got nothing *without* you, Frank. Sometimes I wish I had, but I haven't.'

She pulled herself closer to him, snaked her arms around his neck and drew him nearer.

'I read in the paper today that the security guard is still critical,' he said quietly. 'And that woman who was killed, she was married with two kids. What the fuck does that make me, Paula?'

'You didn't kill her, Frank. You weren't driving the car that hit her and you didn't shoot that guard.'

'No. But I would have.'

The phone rang.

Newton glanced at his watch. 12.36 a.m.

He and Paula exchanged anxious glances, then he swung himself upright and reached for the receiver.

'Hello,' he said quietly.

'Frankie, they've got Gary.'

He recognized Carson's voice immediately.

'Who's got him?'

'The fucking law. He was arrested tonight for possession of drugs. They've got him for selling too.'

'Where are they holding him?'

'Hackney. I should be with him, Frankie.'

'You stay away from there, Jim. There's nothing you can do. The last place *you* need to be at the moment is a fucking nick.'

'I can't leave him on his own, Frankie. It's not right. No matter what he's done, he's still my son.'

'Jim, you just stay where you are. Think about this.'

'He needs me.'

'The only thing *he* needs is another fix.'

'I thought you might understand. Obviously I was wrong.'

'Jim, for Christ's sake . . .'

He heard a click, then the buzz of a dead line.

Frank Newton sat on the edge of the bed staring at the receiver. He gently replaced it and looked around at Paula. When he spoke his voice was little more than a whisper.

'Now we *are* fucked,' he murmured.

43

THE INTERVIEW ROOM smelled of cigarette smoke and coffee.

It was barely twelve feet square and to call it spartan would have been an overstatement: three chairs; a wooden table; a cassette recorder; a clock on the wall facing him; and that was it.

One door.

One uniformed policeman.

One suspect.

Gary Carson stood the empty cigarette packet on the table in front of him, then flicked at it with his middle finger.

Stood it up. Flicked it over again.

Stood it up.

He reached for the styrofoam cup of coffee and sipped at it, wincing when he found it was cold. He dropped his cigarette butt into the black liquid and turned in his seat.

The policeman seated behind him, close to the door, was in his early thirties. He reminded Carson of a waxwork. He wasn't even sure if the uniformed man had blinked yet.

Carson glanced at the clock. 2.06 a.m.

How much fucking longer?

Anxiety had given way to irritation, his emotions changing the longer he sat in the small room.

They've got you this time.

He'd been made to empty his pockets on arrival at the police station and the evidence against him had been laid out before his eyes – his crime was there in plastic bags and wraps.

He'd seen the undercover policewoman who had helped arrest him just before he'd been ushered into the interview room.

Fucking bitch.

How long ago had that been? An hour? Two hours?

He looked again at the clock on the wall opposite.

It could have stopped for all he knew. It felt as if time had been suspended.

'I asked to see a brief,' he said finally, injecting as much bravado as possible into his voice.

The policeman didn't answer.

Carson swallowed hard.

From anger to uncertainty.

His emotions were riding that rollercoaster again.

'Any chance of another drink?' he asked, his tone more servile this time.

The policeman got to his feet and left the room, locking the door behind him.

'Black, no sugar,' Carson called after him and he managed a laugh, but it was hollow.

From uncertainty to fear.

He felt dirty; as if he needed a shower. He'd been wearing the same clothes since early that afternoon and there was a faint odour of sweat about him. He ran a hand through his hair and exhaled deeply.

From fear to despair?

He heard the key in the lock and turned to face the opposite wall again. He didn't recognize the man who entered the room this time.

A tall bastard with deep-set eyes, he was carrying two cups of coffee, one of which he set down in front of the youth.

He sat opposite Gary and flashed his ID.

'Detective Inspector John Ridley, Murder Squad,' he announced. 'I want a word with you.'

'What the fuck do the Murder Squad want with me?'

He felt the hairs at the back of his neck rise.

This was fear. No mistaking this emotion.

Ridley smiled and sipped at his coffee.

'If you're going to charge me with something, then do it, but I'm not saying a word until I've seen my brief.'

'I'm not going to charge you, Gary,' Ridley told him. 'I just want to talk. I think we might be able to help each other.'

44

'I DON'T KNOW anything about any murders,' Carson said, his voice cracking.

Ridley took another swallow of his coffee. 'Tastes like shit out of a machine, doesn't it?' he observed.

'What do you want?'

'I told you: a little chat. We've got something in common.'

'Like what?'

'A mutual acquaintance. I know your old man.'

'Good for you.'

'It might be good for *you* too if you can give me what I want.'

'Look, I don't have to speak to you without—'

'Without a fucking brief,' Ridley chided. 'I know the score, you little shit. I was hearing that crap before you were wiping your own arse.' He glared at the younger man.

'How do you know him?' Gary asked.

'Most coppers who've been in this game as long as I have know his name. Third-rate car thief, burglar. Any piece of shit job that comes along your old man is likely to be involved. He's like you, he's a fucking loser.'

'Tell me about it,' murmured Gary. 'So how did you know I was his son?'

'I'm a detective, remember. Word comes through that Gary Carson's being held at Hackney nick for drug dealing. Jim Carson's got a junkie kid. You don't have to be Inspector Morse to make the connection, do you?'

Ridley opened a fresh pack of cigarettes and pushed them across the table towards Gary. He hesitated, then took one, also accepting the light the DI offered.

'How did you find out I'd been arrested?' the younger man wanted to know.

'Word gets round,' Ridley said, also lighting a cigarette.

'So, what do you want from me?'

'Information.'

'About my old man? I hardly talk to the cunt.'

'You still live at home. You see him come and go. You know what he's up to. What jobs he's involved in.'

'We're not exactly close,' Gary said sardonically. 'I couldn't tell you from one day to the next what he's doing. I only go home if I have to. I usually crash with friends.'

'Has he been working lately?'

'What kind of work?'

'The only kind he knows.'

'I told you, I don't know. Even if he *was* going to do a job he wouldn't tell me.'

'Why not? Doesn't he trust you?'

'He couldn't give a flying fuck about me. And the feeling's mutual. I hate him. He hates me.'

'I understand he visited you in hospital when you od'd the other week. If he hated you that much he'd have slung you out before now. He's still your father.'

'Did you come in here to tell me how great he was?'

'No, you little shit, I came to make you a deal. At the moment you're looking at three to five *just* for possession and with your record, you'll get it. And no cushy young offenders home this time. You're going in with the big boys.'

When Gary raised the cup to his mouth, his hand was shaking slightly.

'And inside, you're the bottom of the fucking food chain,' Ridley continued. 'Fresh meat. Fair game to every nickbent shitstabber who can get their hands on you. By the time you come out there'll be pros in Bangkok who've been fucked less times than you. That's what you've got to look forward to, Gary.'

'What are you offering?'

'I want your old man. I want him sitting where you are now, but with thirty years hanging over his fucking head. But more than that I want a friend of his.'

'I don't know any of his friends.'

'Then steal his address book,' Ridley snarled, leaning forward towards Gary.

'Who are you looking for?' the younger man enquired.

'A geezer called Frank Newton. He's been a friend of your old man's for most of his life. They've worked together in the past. It's Newton I want.'

'And what if I help you get him?'

'You walk. All charges against you will be dropped.'

'What's this Newton bloke done?'

'None of your business. But I want him and I don't care what I have to do to get him. Doesn't it show you how desperate I am? I'm even prepared to accept the help of a fucking waster like you.'

'Has he been shagging your missus or something?' Gary chuckled.

Ridley shot out a hand and grabbed the younger man by the hair. With a movement combining speed and tremendous power, he slammed Gary's face against the tabletop, then pushed him backwards. As he slumped back in his chair, blood was pouring from his nose.

'You cunt,' he gasped, trying to stem the crimson flow with his fingers. 'It's fucking broken.' He looked at the blood that covered his hands. Tears were welling in his eyes.

Ridley got to his feet, standing close to Gary. 'You ring me once a week whether you've got anything or not,' he said, flipping his card onto the table. It landed in a small puddle of blood. 'If you hate your old man as much as you say you do, this should be easy for you.' He took a final drag on his cigarette, then dropped it into Gary's cup. 'And don't forget your coffee,' he said quietly.

Gary, fumbling for his handkerchief to staunch the blood from his smashed nose, heard the interview-room door close behind him.

When he turned round, Ridley was gone.

45

FRANK NEWTON SAT staring at the phone.

Seconds dragged on into minutes. He gazed at the device as if it were some kind of venomous serpent.

Paula wanted to say something.

But what?

Newton sucked in a deep breath and tried to compose himself.

So, Jim Carson's son had been arrested?

So fucking what?

It made no difference to their situation, brought the police no closer to them.

Even if Jim was crazy enough to go hairing off to Hackney nick, what difference did it make?

And yet, still he wondered if he should phone the others.

Warn them.

About what? What exactly are you going to warn them about?

'They'd be better off if the little shit went down,' he said quietly. 'He's caused them nothing but trouble ever since he could walk.'

'Kids, eh?' said Paula softly. 'Who'd have them?'

Newton turned and touched her cheek gently with one hand. She held that hand tightly for a moment, then lay back on the bed.

'There's nothing you can do, Frank,' she told him. 'It's Jim's problem.'

He nodded almost imperceptibly.

Still his gaze was fixed on the phone.

A moment later, he reached for it and began dialling.

Jeff Hobbs listened in silence as Newton recounted the events of that night.

Standing in his sitting room wearing just pyjama trousers, he nodded to himself as Newton spoke, but didn't attempt to open his mouth until his companion had finished.

'Anything I can do to help, Frank?' Hobbs said finally.

Newton said that there wasn't.

'They were never very close were they?' observed Hobbs quietly. He rubbed at his left eye, blinking hard. He wasn't sure whether the images before him were swimming because of his tiredness. Sometimes the old injury affected his sight. The doctors had warned him at the time that a detached retina could cause such problems.

The old injury.

He stood in the gloom listening to Newton.

'If there's anything I can do, call me back,' he murmured.

Newton said he was going to ring the others, perhaps ring Carson himself and find out what was happening.

'Leave it, Frank,' Hobbs insisted. 'There's nothing you can do.'

Newton apologized for waking him.

'Don't worry about it. I don't sleep that well anyway.'

Newton hung up.

Hobbs put down the receiver and wandered into the kitchen. Fuck it. He was awake now. Might as well have a hot drink, watch some TV until he felt tired enough to return to bed.

He boiled the kettle, then switched on the television, flicking through the channels.

Open University.

News 24.

An old black-and-white film.

He recognized it: Paul Newman in *Somebody Up There Likes Me*.

Fucking boxing film. Typical.

He switched it off.

'Let it ring.' Julie Cope gasped the words, arching her back as the pleasure intensified.

Peter Morrissey heard the phone and, for a second, he slowed his deep thrusts into her.

'Don't stop now,' she wailed, wrapping her slender legs around the small of his back.

The phone continued to ring.

Morrissey glanced at the clock beside the bed: 1.57 a.m.

Julie was raking her fingers up and down his back, urging him on.

Morrissey had almost stopped moving now.

'Pete, don't fucking stop, I'm nearly there,' she panted, trying to kiss him. 'Pete, please . . .'

He pulled out.

'You bastard,' she hissed at him, flopping back on the sodden sheets.

He raised a hand to silence her as he lifted the receiver.

He recognized the voice immediately.

'Frank, what's wrong?' Morrissey wanted to know.

Newton told him, as he'd told Hobbs.

Julie rolled over onto her stomach and edged towards Morrissey, stroking his glistening erection with one fingertip.

She was surprised when he swatted her hand away.

'Don't sweat it, Frank,' Morrissey said.

Julie prodded him in the back with one foot.

Newton said there was probably no reason to be concerned.

'I haven't even seen anything on the news about the job,' the former soldier said, grabbing Julie's probing foot with one powerful hand and pushing it away.

Newton told him there'd been a mention on the local news at 11.30.

'Forget about Jim's kid,' Morrissey insisted. 'He's got fuck all to do with us.'

Newton agreed and hung up.

'What was so important?' Julie said irritably.

'Business,' he said, without turning around.

'What kind of business?'

'It doesn't matter.'

'I thought it was my dad.' She chuckled.

'I can ring him if you want.' He reached for the phone.

She sat up, pressing her breasts against his back, feeling for his erection. She caressed it with her fingers and felt it grow harder still.

'Just come back to bed,' she whispered.

Ray Gorman wiped perspiration from his forehead as he held the phone to his ear.

'I've already been up for an hour, Frank,' he said wearily. 'My old man's not well. Some kind of stomach bug. I've changed his sheets twice . . .' He allowed the sentence to trail off.

Newton told Gorman about Carson's son.

'Useless little cunt,' Gorman rasped.

He listened as Newton told how Carson wanted to travel to Hackney nick to be with him.

'Let him go. What's the problem?'

Newton thought for a moment, then agreed it was nothing for them to worry about.

'Thanks for letting me know anyway.'

Somewhere behind Gorman there was a plaintive cry. He turned.

'Listen, Frank, I've got to go. I'm sorry,' Gorman said and hung up.

The flat smelled of excrement.

Gorman swallowed hard and wiped his face again. 'OK, Dad,' he called. 'I'm coming.'

46

No one noticed the red Saab parked beside the kerb in Dean Street.

Why should they?

Vehicles were nose to tail, jammed together like building blocks in an effort to find space anywhere along Soho's bustling streets.

The Saab was no more unusual than any other car.

Even at such a late hour parking space was at a premium.

The men inside the Saab watched people spilling from the doorways of clubs; some in couples, some in groups.

Some alone.

Neon lit the night, an electrically charged rainbow that cut through the gloom like a multicoloured blade.

It reflected off the wet pavements and streets, quite beautiful in places, as if an artist had spilled the contents of his pallet onto the concrete.

There was music playing too.

It drifted on the air from inside the clubs.

It was also playing on the Saab's cassette.

The men inside sat patiently. They'd already been there for over two hours.

Watching.

They'd drunk coffee. They'd smoked.

And they'd waited.

They would continue to wait for as long as they had to.

Another hour.

Longer if necessary.

People continued to leave the clubs, but it was one doorway in particular that the men watched.

One of them broke wind. The other two chuckled and complained, one slapping him lightly across the back of the head.

They joked.

Three figures left the club in one tightly knit group.

The driver of the Saab sat up, fingers drumming on the wheel. He gently turned the ignition key and the engine purred into life.

In the back, the other two men nodded to each other.

'There,' said Ernie Codling, pointing towards the huddle of figures near the doorway. 'That him.'

He was gesturing towards a tall, broadly built man in his early thirties. His ebony skin made him look like a part of the night.

The windows of the Saab were down. The air smelled of rain and exhaust fumes.

Codling lifted the M16 and pulled it in tight, readying himself for the fearsome recoil.

In the front seat, Toad worked the pump action of the Viking twelve-gauge shotgun, chambering a round.

Skeng pulled the collapsible butt of the Uzi into position and pressed it to his shoulder.

All three weapons opened up simultaneously.

The noise was staggering.

The air was suddenly filled with the staccato rattle of automatic fire. Muzzle flashes exploded from the barrels, blinding those who looked on with their brilliance.

But there were few who stood to watch the monstrous spectacle.

Everywhere, people were running, screaming and crying.

Codling held the Armalite tightly, feeling each thunderous recoil slam the weapon back against his shoulder. But he pumped the trigger, each heavy-grain bullet leaving the weapon travelling at over 3,000 feet per second.

Stray shots struck the pavement and blasted lumps of concrete free; others hit nearby vehicles and blew out windscreens and headlights. Tyres burst loudly as bullets cut into them.

The three men raked the doorway of the club, drawing dotted lines of death back and forth across the people leaving.

Their fire was concentrated on the three black men particularly, but others also went down in the furious fusillade.

A woman went sprawling, most of the left side of her face missing, while the man who tried to help her took two 9mm slugs in the chest.

Another was hit in the groin by a shotgun blast, his

testicles and most of his penis ripped away. He shrieked and jammed both hands into the raw wound, blood pouring down his legs.

The screams that filled the air were all but drowned out by the thunderous retort of the weapons.

Codling saw with delight that the big man had been hit.

Two bullets from the M16 had caught him in the chest and stomach. Portions of intestine had burst from the hideous rent, blood and lumps of reddish-pink lung tissue plastered onto the wall behind him, torn away by the exiting bullets.

Skeng reloaded, then continued firing, spent shell cases from the Uzi spraying into the air, some landing inside the car, others raining down onto the wet street.

Windows were blasted in, the sound of shattering glass mingling with the cacophony of shrieks and gunfire.

A man dropped to his knees, clutching at his throat. Blood was spurting from a wound, jetting fully three feet into the night air, spattering those nearby.

Codling drew a bead on the big man and fired off two more rounds.

Both head shots.

One blasted away part of the lower jaw. The second caught him squarely between the eyes, tore through bone and brain and exploded from the back of his skull, carrying away most of the contents. A semi-liquid flux of pulverized cranial matter splattered the wall. The bullets buried themselves in the brickwork, boring several inches into the stone.

'Go!' shouted Codling and Toad slipped the Saab out of its space with ease, driving it unhurriedly towards Soho Square.

A cloud of smoke still hung where it had been parked. It drifted on the reeking air like a filthy shroud.

47

GARY CARSON STOOD looking at the main entrance to Hackney police station and lit a cigarette. He blew the grey stream of smoke in the direction of the building.

He'd got a few bob on him; enough to get a taxi home. It was just a matter of finding one at this time of the morning.

Fuck it. Why not walk?

The air would clear his head. It might help him to think about what that fucking DI had said to him.

Grass up your old man and his mates. What was so difficult about that?

He touched his battered nose as he recalled the tall man.

There was still blood on his fingertips and his face felt sore.

Fucking coppers. They were all as bad.

He began walking, his hands dug deep into his pockets, collar turned up against the wind.

'Gary.'

The sound of his name made him turn. He stopped and looked in the direction of the voice.

The figure was gesturing to him from a Renault parked across the street.

He drew on the fag again, then headed towards the waiting vehicle.

'What are *you* doing here?' Gary asked the driver.

James Carson pushed open the passenger side door; an invitation for his son to climb in.

'I've been waiting for you,' Carson said. 'Get in.'

Gary hesitated a moment, then decided he was too cold and tired to dismiss the opportunity of a ride. He slid into the front seat beside his father and slammed the door behind him.

Carson guided the Renault away from the police station, passing a marked car that was just pulling in.

'How long have you been sitting out there?' Gary wanted to know.

'Since they brought you in.'

'If they'd charged me you could have been there a fucking long time.'

'How come they didn't?'

Because some big fucking DI who hates your guts as much as I do offered me a deal to fuck you and your mates over.

'They didn't have any evidence,' Gary said, looking out of the side window.

Carson glanced at him. 'You were carrying drugs,' said the older man and it sounded more like a declaration of fact than supposition.

'Would they have let me go if they'd found drugs on me?'

214

Carson looked again at his son.

'Just give me a fucking break, will you?' Gary persisted. 'What does it matter to you anyway?'

'How many times do I have to tell you? It matters because you're our son. Do you think we want to see you doing time?'

'So don't visit.'

'You ungrateful little bastard . . .'

'That's better. Drop the concerned father routine, will you? It doesn't suit you.'

'First it's an overdose. Then it's selling. You're going to wind up nicked or dead.'

'And it's my fucking choice. It's my life.'

'Well, as long as you live under my roof it's my concern too.'

'Yeah, yeah, yeah. You make it sound as if I'm the only fucking criminal in the family.'

'What's that supposed to mean?'

'Most of the gear in the house is nicked. Or it's been paid for with nicked money. I know what you've done. I know what you *still* do.'

Steady. Don't push too hard, too soon.

'Perhaps I could put up with your preaching a bit more easily if you weren't so fucking self-righteous about it,' Gary continued. 'What's that old saying about people who live in glass houses not throwing stones? Well, before you go into one about me selling some shit, perhaps you ought to remember that.'

'What do you want me to do? Take you on jobs with me?'

'Just don't make out you're so good and I'm so bad.'

Carson looked at his son briefly, then returned his attention to the road.

They drove the rest of the way in silence.

48

THE STENCH WAS appalling.

But the four men gathered around the body in the morgue barely reacted when the plastic sheet was lifted clear of the corpse.

'Say hello to Wendell Hadfield,' muttered William Nicholson. The police surgeon made an expansive gesture with his hand, sweeping it from head to toe above the body.

'Kong to his friends,' Ridley said flatly, gazing at the bullet-riddled corpse.

'I can see why,' DS Brown observed. 'Big bastard, wasn't he?'

'I hope you're talking about his stature,' Nicholson chuckled. 'And not his manly blessings.' He nodded towards the dead man's shrivelled, but still impressive, penis.

The other men smiled.

'Well, he's not going to need it anymore, is he?' Brown offered.

'You don't really need us to talk you through it, do you, John?' asked Phillip Barclay. The coroner was scratching at his cheek with one index finger.

'No. I think it's pretty obvious he died as a result of gunshots, Phil,' the DI said, his eyes never leaving the body.

'Eight of them to be exact,' Barclay told him.

'And his boys?'

'Both killed by the same weapons that took out Hadfield. We dug 9mm slugs and shotgun pellets out of both of them,' Barclay told him. 'With the shell cases we found at the scene I'd say somewhere close to two hundred rounds were fired. They're being checked for prints now.'

'Whoever hit him wasn't taking any chances, were they?' Nicholson mused.

'What's the body count?' Ridley asked.

'Including Hadfield and his boys, seven,' Brown told his superior. 'Another twelve were wounded. Two of those are still critical.'

Ridley walked slowly around the body, studying the savage wounds. One of Hadfield's eyes was open. It seemed to fix him in an unblinking stare.

'Any connection with that robbery near Euston the other day?' Brown wanted to know. 'I heard there were 9mms used there too.'

'Pistols, not sub-machine-guns,' Barclay told the DS.

'And that was a fuck-up,' said Ridley dismissively. 'This was professional. There's no doubt Hadfield was the target. Whoever did it just wasn't fussy about who they took with him.'

'We didn't get much in the way of witnesses,' Brown informed the older man. 'Somebody thought they saw two men in a car firing. Someone else said three, another said four. Take your pick.'

Ridley stroked his chin thoughtfully. 'Perhaps we should be as bothered about *where* he was killed as who pulled the trigger,' the DI offered.

The other men looked puzzled.

'What's the location got to do with it?' Nicholson wanted to know. 'It was just a club in Soho, John. They could have hit him anywhere around there.'

'That club he was leaving when he was shot was owned by Billy Parker,' Ridley said slowly, as if he wanted each word to register. 'It might be a coincidence; it probably is. It's just that the most powerful *black* gang leader in the city was murdered leaving a club owned by the most powerful *white* gang boss in London.'

'Do you think Parker had something to do with it?' Brown enquired.

'Hardly,' Ridley grunted. 'If he wanted Hadfield out of the way he's not going to do it on his own doorstep, is he? I'd just like to know what Hadfield was doing there in the first place.'

'It's a good club, perhaps he was having a night out,' Nicholson offered.

'Like I said, it's probably just a coincidence. After all, Parker owns half a dozen clubs in London,' Ridley mused. 'And Christ knows how much more property.'

'I thought hotels were his thing,' Brown interjected.

'He's been buying shares in top hotels for years now, but he started with the clubs like most of them do. His corporation's practically legit. We couldn't make a case against him if he bit the head off one of the Queen's corgis.'

'So what are you getting at?' Brown persisted.

'Perhaps Hadfield and Parker had something going together,' Ridley replied.

'Like what?'

'How do *I* know?' Ridley snapped. 'A business deal of some kind. Hadfield might have been able to get Parker into one of *his* scams. Perhaps he already had. Perhaps somebody didn't want them linking up. Who knows? We're pissing in the wind until we find out who killed Hadfield. Then we might have some idea *why* he was shot.' He pulled the plastic sheet back over Wendell Hadfield's body.

'It must be somebody pretty powerful to even *think* about taking on Hadfield,' Brown mused.

'And someone with access to that kind of firepower,' Barclay added. 'M16s, Uzis. Who's big enough to get hold of that kind of equipment?'

'It *is* a bit of a jump from machetes, isn't it?' Ridley offered, reaching for a cigarette.

Brown looked questioningly at him. 'What are you trying to say, guv?' he asked.

'For the last few months we've been scraping pimps off the pavement,' Ridley said flatly. 'Putting toe-tags on drug dealers and picking up pieces of small-time villains. But Hadfield was as big as they come in the black criminal set-up here in London. I reckon the boys we're looking for have finally moved into the Premier league. I think we've got a war on our hands.'

49

'HAVE YOU ANY idea what you're asking me to do?'

The words were spoken with a gentle Scottish accent, but the lilting tone of the question did little to disguise the vehemence of its delivery.

'Sir, I wouldn't be asking at all unless I thought it was necessary,' said DI John Ridley.

He regarded his superior warily. Noel Pritchard had held the post of Metropolitan Police Commissioner for three years. And during that time, Ridley had met him fleetingly just once before, when Pritchard had visited every department of New Scotland Yard not long after his appointment. Even during that first, brief introduction, Ridley had been aware of the power the man wielded; not merely because of his position, but in his very presence.

The Scot was a wiry man, a couple of years older than Ridley himself, but in that slight frame there was an atavism usually reserved for men twenty years younger. He had a handshake like a vice and eyes that pinned men as surely as lights mesmerized moths.

It was that gaze that now held Ridley captive.

The Scot sat back in his leather chair, clasping his hands on his stomach, tapping gently on his expensive shirt with his thumbs.

He reminded Ridley of a bank manager – albeit a very powerful and ruthless one.

'The media would scream police brutality,' said Pritchard quietly. 'Every bleeding-heart liberal in the country would cry racism and Christ alone knows how the black community itself would react. This is a bomb waiting to go off, John. And you're asking *me* to light the bloody fuse.'

'If we don't do something about this situation soon, sir, then the whole of London *will* explode.'

'So, you're convinced that there is a full-scale war about to break out between the two biggest Yardie factions in London?'

Ridley nodded.

'And putting four hundred extra men on the streets of Tottenham, Stoke Newington, Brixton and every other predominantly black area in the city is going to stop this war, is it?'

'It might make them think twice about blowing the shit out of each other if—'

The Scot cut him short. '"Might" isn't good enough, John,' he said flatly. 'I'm not committing that many men into such a potentially volatile situation on the strength of a bloody hunch.'

He pawed impatiently at the file before him.

'We've been following the progress of the Yardies for years now,' said Pritchard, tapping the file. 'Monitoring their activities as best we can. From what I've seen, I don't feel they constitute a big enough threat to warrant calling in so much extra manpower.'

'They've been fighting among themselves for the past ten years, sir. Perhaps they're more organized now.'

'Then show me some evidence of it.'

'Hadfield's assassination. The murders of Winston Simpson and Rupert Hart. The killing of Leon Green.'

'You think they're linked?'

'I think it's a hell of a coincidence that black dealers have been turning up dead all over London and now the leader of the most powerful black gang in the city gets blown away.'

'What makes you so sure the Yardies are behind it?'

'All the victims had Yardie connections. I think that one of the factions is trying to control the movement of drugs through the city. Hadfield was the last big obstacle.'

'The last big *black* obstacle. What about the other gangs operating in London? How strong are *they*?'

'As far as we know there are at least six criminal families working in the city. They've got interests in nightclubs, restaurants and pubs in North London, Soho, Middlesex and Chelsea. Supposedly they're linked directly with some of the South American drug cartels. They're into VAT fiddles, counterfeiting and fraud. That's north of the river. South of the river we've got an established family based in Woolwich and a big Turkish clan. Again, it's pubs and clubs.'

'And the most powerful?'

'None of them can touch Billy Parker. They wouldn't even try.'

'You said yourself that Hadfield was killed outside a club *owned* by Parker. He's not going to sit still while the Yardies take over his business. Why should you automatically think it's them when there are so many other organizations trying to get control?'

'If the Yardies could take out Parker, then they'd establish themselves as a genuine force in London. At the moment, we've got no way of knowing their strength. They might be in a position to challenge him.'

Pritchard stroked his chin thoughtfully. 'Are we looking at a race war here?' he said finally.

'No,' the DI answered flatly. 'No question.'

'Could it escalate into that?'

'I doubt it. The fact that the Yardies are black has got nothing to do with it. Not every black criminal is a Yardie. The Yardies are a criminal faction who happen to be black. Just like the Triads happen to be Chinese. It's as simple as that.'

'Even less reason to flood the streets of black areas with extra men then,' Pritchard declared.

Ridley exhaled wearily.

'Like I said, John,' the Scot continued, 'this is a very delicate issue. I don't want to cause problems if I can avoid it. If I sanction an increased police presence in black areas of London, this becomes a political matter as well as one of law and order. The politicians would have a field day. We're not exactly number one in black popularity polls at the best of times.'

'So what are you telling me, sir?'

'I'm telling you to get this problem sorted yourself. Find out who killed Hadfield and these other men. And if there *is* a Yardie war about to break out, then stop it.'

'Just like that, eh?' said Ridley, his voice edged with scorn.

Pritchard wasn't slow to pick it up. 'You do whatever you have to do,' he said, leaning forward across his desk. 'And do it quick.'

50

FRANK NEWTON KNEW he was being followed.

He'd clocked the black Laguna about twenty minutes ago; stopping when he stopped, occasionally cruising up to within a few yards of him as he walked.

He ducked inside a newsagent's on the corner of the street, his heart thudding hard against his ribs.

For long moments he stood scanning the racks of magazines, but he saw little. Faces smiled out at him from beneath each title, but Newton saw none of them.

He glanced in the direction of the street, waiting for the Laguna to move into view.

It didn't.

Why didn't they just confront him?

Whoever was driving the car must know that he was aware of their presence. They hadn't even attempted discretion.

Whoever was in the car couldn't give a fuck if he knew they were there or not.

It *had* to be the law. He'd convinced himself of that within five minutes of spotting the vehicle.

Fuck them. Let them stop him. They had nothing to link him to the Securicor job. Let them pull him in.

He swallowed hard, unconvinced by his own attempts at bravado.

There was a lad in his teens wandering back and forth in front of the magazines, his eyes seemingly fixed on the top shelf, but each time he got near Newton he dropped his gaze.

Newton finally picked up a *Star* and a packet of mints and headed for the counter.

Outside, the Laguna cruised past unseen.

Jeffs Hobbs smiled at the librarian as she handed him his chosen books.

A couple of novels and a biography of Angelo Dundee.

He'd be finished with the novels by the following day, but he'd take his time over the biography. He'd had to order it; had to wait a couple of weeks for them to acquire it. Hobbs was sure it would be worth the wait.

He made his way towards the main exit and out onto the street.

It was growing warmer, the sun forcing its way out from behind the clouds that had filled the sky since early morning.

It looked as if it was going to be a beautiful day.

He saw the two men walking towards him.

Both in their early thirties; well-built; smartly dressed.

There was something familiar about one of them.

A name began to roll around inside his head. He had a good memory for things like that.

Names. Faces.

As the men drew nearer it finally registered.

But, by then, it was too late.

Peter Morrissey splashed his face with water, rinsing the last of the shaving foam from his cheeks and chin.

He heard the knocking on the door as he dried his face.

'I'll go,' called Julie Cope and he heard her footsteps as she padded down the stairs and into the hall.

Morrissey pulled on a T-shirt and tucked it into his jeans.

He heard the front door being opened; heard voices.

It was probably the postman.

He made his way down the stairs towards the hall, still able to hear the voices. As he reached the bottom of the steps he saw the two figures standing inside; one on each side of Julie, who was looking at them alternately, then in his direction.

'They said they wanted to talk to you, Pete,' Julie told him, still wearing that bemused expression.

One of the men had his hand resting gently on Julie's shoulder.

Morrissey nodded slowly.

*

Ray Gorman hadn't slept well the previous night.

Nothing new there.

He looked across at his father.

Poor old bastard.

He'd been up half the night complaining about pains in his legs and arms.

Sometimes Gorman wondered if it would be a blessing if the pain was in his heart.

Just one big one. One merciful moment of pain, then peace.

He pushed the thought to the back of his mind.

The old man sat gazing blankly at the TV screen, head nodding incessantly. His gnarled hands were shaking too.

Gorman reached out and touched his father's arm, squeezing the painfully thin limb tenderly.

The old man looked at him and almost managed a smile.

Almost.

The doorbell sounded and Gorman got to his feet.

'That'll be the meals-on-wheels lady, Dad,' he said, crossing to the door of the flat. 'I hope you're hungry.'

As Gorman pulled the door open he prepared to welcome the visitor.

There were two figures standing there.

'Oh, Christ,' he whispered.

Frank Newton rolled the paper and stuffed it into the back pocket of his jeans.

He'd check the racing pages when he had a minute. If the three horses he'd backed had all come in then it should add up to a nice little accumulator.

He hadn't mentioned the bets to Paula.

Best not to.

As he left the paper shop, the teenager had finally managed to reach up and retrieve a copy of *Parade*. He was clutching it tightly to his chest, watching to ensure that there were no other customers at the counter or about to come in.

Newton smiled to himself as he left.

There was no sign of the Laguna.

Getting paranoid in your old age?

He checked across the road and scanned both ways. It looked clear.

Newton walked on.

The Laguna reversed from a small side street that appeared too narrow to accommodate it. It glided into view as if it had materialized from thin air.

The black vehicle blocked his path and he paused as the rear door was pushed open.

The man seated there was a little older than Newton himself.

Short hair. Heavily built.

His face was expressionless.

He patted the rear seat with a hand like a ham-hock. The other he slipped inside his jacket.

'Get in the car,' the man insisted.

Newton hesitated.

Then he saw the gun.

51

THIS WAS BULLSHIT.

That was all he could think of.

But it was true: it was pure fucking bullshit.

Gary Carson puffed agitatedly on the cigarette and glanced at his watch: 10.36 a.m.

He'd been here an hour already, waiting; watching.

Exactly *what* he was waiting and watching for he wasn't sure.

The garage he was watching was in Pindar Street, just behind Liverpool Street station. His father worked there now and then. When they had enough work, they called him in.

He could see him now in his oily overall, hunched over the bonnet of a car.

Gary exhaled deeply and thought what a waste of time all this was.

All this bullshit.

What kind of information could he find about his father for Ridley? The old bastard never did anything worth bothering about, and if he did he was hardly likely to tell his son, was he?

A son who hated him.

And yet, Gary knew he must find out something about his father. About this Frank Newton bloke

(*whoever the fuck* he *was*)

who Ridley seemed so interested in.

Perhaps he worked at the garage, Gary mused.

He dug a hand into the pocket of his jacket and felt the card that Ridley had given him. He studied it, running his gaze endlessly over the number the DI had written there.

He looked across at his father.

He paced back and forth for a moment.

Go home. You're not doing any good here.

He could go back to the house. Perhaps check through his father's belongings for

(*for what?*)

anything he could tell Ridley about.

He tossed the cigarette to the ground and prepared to turn away.

As he did he saw the car pull up close to the garage entrance.

Nice motor. Daimler or something like that.

He saw a man get out of the car and approach his father.

A well-dressed bloke in his fifties.

He saw his father wipe his hands on his overalls.

If only he could hear what they were saying.

As he watched, he was surprised to see James Carson move towards the car and clamber into the back seat.

There was another man waiting in the rear of the vehicle.

The car reversed out of the yard and disappeared into the traffic.

Gary pulled the card from his pocket and scurried around the corner towards the payphones that stood just inside the station entrance.

Five of the six were occupied. The last was out of order.

'Shit,' he snarled, glaring at a woman using one of them. She turned her back on him as she continued speaking.

Gary paced up and down the row of phones looking impatiently at their users.

There were other people waiting too.

A man in a pair of chinos and a white shirt was counting out coins into the palm of his hand, eager for one of the phones to be vacated.

When it was, Gary dashed forward, practically snatching the receiver from the hand of the young woman who had just finished her call.

The man in the chinos said something, but Gary ignored him.

He jabbed the buttons and waited.

The voice at the other end of the line barely had time to finish.

'I want to speak to Detective Inspector John Ridley,' Gary said breathlessly.

The voice at the other end wanted to know why.

'Because it's fucking important.'

52

THE ROOM WAS magnificent.

It reeked of good taste. Of wealth.

Of power.

Frank Newton sat on one of the trio of double-seater leather sofas and looked around.

Each time he moved, the fine leather beneath him creaked like the pages of some fantastically old book.

The walls were panelled; oak, he guessed. Paintings he didn't recognize, but which he guessed were worth a fortune, hung beneath angled lights.

The carpet was so thick it muffled all footsteps.

The furniture was antique. Dark wood to match the panelling.

One entire wall supported a cabinet filled with crystal. The light sparkled on it like the sun on scattered diamonds.

Ornaments as priceless as the paintings were dotted in strategic places around the room. The vase closest to him, Newton mused, was probably worth more money than he'd ever seen in his life.

The desk that he faced was a particularly superb piece. It looked as if it had been hewn from one enormous piece of oak. A massive, monolithic structure that was polished so brightly he could see his reflection in the wood. And behind it, in a fan shape, were half a dozen swords. All antique.

A razor-sharp samurai blade.

A three-foot-long, hatchet-ended *pallasch*, the chosen weapon of British cavalrymen in the nineteenth century.

He recognized a claymore.

A wickedly curved scimitar.

All were polished and gleaming.

The two men who had travelled with him in the car stood a couple of feet behind him, as motionless as the Lalique vases that adorned the room. Neither had spoken more than half a dozen words to him during the journey or since their arrival here.

Newton knew where they were. No attempts had been made to keep the destination secret from him.

The car had deposited him and his escorts in Mayfair, outside a Victorian townhouse complete with black metal railings and hanging baskets above the front door. Despite the façade, he knew that inside it was a highly exclusive casino.

He could only guess at the worth of the property in Hill Street. As he had clambered out of the vehicle, looking back down the street he'd caught a glimpse of Berkeley Square.

No fucking nightingales singing today, my son.

He'd been taken up three flights of stairs to the room where he now nervously sat.

There was a low droning noise coming from below

and it took Newton a moment to work out it was a vacuum cleaner.

The droning continued for several minutes, then stopped.

The silence that descended was even more unbearable.

It was broken only by the rumbling stomach of one of the two men with him.

He was tempted to turn in his seat, to ask the men who stood behind him why he was here, but he knew that wasn't an option.

Turn and you might find yourself looking down the barrel of the gun one of them had been carrying.

Newton could only guess at how long he'd been in the room. It felt like hours, but he guessed it was more like ten minutes.

He could watch the seconds ticking away on the antique grandfather clock near the window.

He finally heard the door behind him open.

'Frank Newton,' said the voice. 'Long time, no see.'

It was a voice he recognized. And, as he did, his heart began thudding that little bit faster against his ribs. It felt as if cold fingers were plucking at the hairs on the back of his neck.

The newcomer swept into the room and seated himself behind the desk, his eyes fixing Newton in an unblinking stare.

'How are you, Frank?' the other man said flatly.

Newton swallowed hard. 'I'm all right, Billy,' he answered quietly.

William Parker smiled.

53

For interminable seconds, Newton and Parker just looked at each other.

The silence that had seemed oppressive before Parker entered was now almost palpable.

Newton was aware of the other man's probing gaze, as if he was looking into him; searching.

William Parker was in his fifty-fourth year, but good living and plastic surgery had combined to make him look almost a decade younger. He was dressed in a dark blue Versace suit and a black Armani shirt; both were immaculate and fitted him perfectly. He looked every inch the successful businessman. Even the small crescent-shaped scar above his right eye couldn't spoil the image.

'Do you want a drink, Frank?' he asked, motioning to one of the men who stood behind Newton.

'No, thanks, Billy. I'm all right.'

'Go on, I insist. It's good stuff. Twelve-year-old Johnny Walker. I bought it on the way back from the States a couple of weeks ago. Go on. You're not driving, *are* you?' Parker chuckled and accepted his own drink from the tall man who appeared at his side with a crystal tumbler.

He lifted the glass and studied the amber fluid for a moment before sipping it.

Newton watched as another whiskey tumbler was set down on the desk before him.

'Cheers,' said Parker, raising his glass.

Newton nodded, picked up the drink and took a sip, feeling the liquid burn its way to his stomach.

'Use the coaster, will you, Frank,' Parker insisted as Newton prepared to set down his glass. 'Otherwise it marks the wood.' He patted the polished surface.

Newton did as he was instructed and Parker managed another smile.

'Are you a film fan, Frank?' he wanted to know.

Newton looked puzzled.

'I love the cinema,' the older man continued. 'Me and the wife go two or three times a week. I collect videos too. I must have five or six hundred films at home. I mean, the crap you get on TV these days, we just stick a video in. I was thinking of getting one of those DVD things. They reckon the picture quality's amazing. They said that about laser discs too, didn't they? You can't beat the cinema though, can you? Seeing it up there on the big screen. I used to love that when I was a kid. When the lights went down and you knew the film was going to start. I still get excited now, when the old curtains open and you think "here we go".' He sipped his drink.

Newton licked his lips. They felt dry.

What the fuck was going on here?

'Have you ever seen a film called *Charley Varrick*, Frank?' Parker continued.

Newton shook his head.

'Brilliant film,' Parker continued. 'Walter Matthau's in it. It's directed by the geezer who directed *Dirty Harry*. Anyway, old Walter Matthau robs this bank, right? Him and his gang. And they reckon they're going to get about two hundred and fifty thousand dollars, but when they count up they've got nearly three quarters of a million. The only trouble is, the extra money belongs to the fucking Mafia.' Parker laughed loudly.

The other two men in the room laughed too.

Newton looked around at them, then back at Parker.

'So, not only have they got the fucking law after them,' the older man continued, 'they've got this hitman called Molly chasing them too. Because, obviously, the Mafia want *their* money back as well. This fucking bloke who's chasing them is built like a brick shithouse and his name's Molly. Joe Don Baker took that part. He was very good. He's been in a few things lately. He was the private eye in the remake of *Cape Fear*.'

Newton reached for his glass, his hand shaking slightly. 'It sounds good,' he said, his voice cracking.

'Yeah, it was,' Parker told him, his smile fading. 'Sound familiar?'

'I'm not with you, Billy.'

'That Securicor job you pulled last week near Euston. How much did you get?'

The knot of muscles at the side of Newton's jaw

throbbed. 'What job?' he asked, a distinct lack of conviction in his voice.

'Don't fuck with me, Frank, it wouldn't be good for your health. How much?'

'Three hundred and twenty-six thousand.' Newton took another swallow from the fine crystal tumbler, his hand still cradling the glass.

'Three hundred and twenty-six thousand of *my* money, Frank,' hissed Parker, leaning forward across the desk.

He closed his hand around Newton's. Squeezing.

'It's a bit of a jump for you and your boys, isn't it?' Parker continued, the pressure on Newton's hand building. 'Out of your league.'

'The law don't even know. How do *you*?' Newton tried to pull his hand away from the glass, but Parker continued to grip hard.

'I've got more contacts on the street than New Scotland Yard,' Parker snarled. 'More faces on my payroll than the fucking Met. That's how I know. Where's the money, Frank?'

'Billy, I—'

He never finished the sentence.

Parker closed his hand hard around Newton's and the fine crystal shattered.

Newton shouted in pain as several shards of glass sheared into his palm and tore open the base of his thumb. Blood spurted from the wounds and he managed to pull his hand away, noticing that there was a shrapnel-like spear of crystal about three inches long protruding from the centre of his palm. He plucked it free and dropped it onto the desktop.

Parker tossed him a handkerchief. 'Don't bleed on the fucking carpet,' he snapped. 'It wasn't cheap.'

Newton swiftly wrapped the linen around his gashed hand, watching as blood soaked through the material.

'Now,' Parker said flatly. 'Let's talk.'

54

Frank Newton's hand throbbed like a bad tooth.

Every now and then he would look down at the blood drenched handkerchief and wince. Some of the crimson liquid had also splashed onto his jeans.

'Billy, I swear to Christ if I'd known that money was yours I wouldn't have gone near that fucking van,' he said quickly.

'Who planned it?' Parker wanted to know.

'I did.'

'How many others on the job?'

'You know everything else, Billy. You should know that too.'

Parker nodded. 'Fucking right I do,' he snapped. 'Carson, Morrissey, Hobbs and Gorman. Same faces you've been working with for twenty years. They were picked up the same time you were. I was going to speak to them later, but why bother with the oily rags when I can talk to the mechanic, eh?'

'Where are they?'

'Downstairs. Some of my lads are entertaining them.'

'We can give you the money back, Billy.'

'It's not just the money, Frank. It's a matter of pride. If word gets round that a bunch of fucking losers like you and your boys had a crack at me, then every prick with no brains and a bit of ambition is going to start sticking their oar into my business. And I can't have that. I've worked too hard and too long to get where I am now.'

'Like I said, if I'd known I would have steered clear.'

'You disappoint me, Frank. You've been in the business as long as I have. I thought you had it sussed. Who owned what. I thought you would have *known* those betting shops belonged to me. You can clean a lot of dosh through six shops in a week.'

'You use them to launder money?'

'Spot on,' the older man sneered. 'What did you think you were going to get?'

'A million,' Newton said quietly. 'Perhaps more.'

'Split five ways?'

Again Newton nodded.

'And what were you going to spend *your* cut on, Frank?'

Newton re-adjusted the makeshift bandage around his hand.

'Come on, I'm curious,' Parker persisted, a note of scorn in his voice. 'What were *you* going to spend *my* money on?' He glared at Newton.

The younger man lowered his gaze momentarily. 'My wife can't have kids,' he said quietly.

'Why? Are you firing blanks?'

The other three men in the room laughed.

Newton glared at Parker.

You fucking bastard.

'No, it's not that,' he murmured. 'She's got something wrong with her Fallopian tubes. Something like that. She can't carry full-term.'

Parker looked on impassively.

'We were going to use the money for IVF treatment,' Newton told him.

'How touching,' Parker said without a hint of emotion. 'Nice to know my money was going to be used for humanitarian reasons. Why the fuck do you want a kid, Frank? What could *you* offer it? What kind of life?'

'We'd have loved it,' Newton said angrily. 'We'd have got out of London. Started again.'

'You *can't* start again, Frank. This is the only kind of life you know. You belong here. It's all you're any good for.'

'You started the same way as me, Billy. Protection out of billiard halls. Moving stolen gear. The only difference between you and me now is that eight-hundred-quid suit. Underneath it, you're no better. Take away all the clubs, casinos, restaurants and expensive ornaments and we're no different.'

Parker regarded him impassively. 'For a man who's just stolen over three hundred grand from me, you've got a lot to say, Frank,' he said finally. 'You should be thanking me you're still breathing. Anybody else would have had your useless carcass dripping blood by now. Perhaps you ought to be a bit more fucking grateful.'

'If you're going to top me, then get it over with.'

'Use it, Frank,' Parker said, tapping his forehead with one index finger. 'If I'd wanted you and your boys dead you'd be floating in the Thames right now.'

'So what's the game, Billy? You know we knocked over that van. You know we took your money. Why *are* we still breathing?'

Parker got to his feet and crossed to the drinks cabinet where he poured himself another measure of Scotch.

Newton flexed the fingers of his injured hand, aware that the stiffness in the wounds was getting worse.

What the fuck was Parker playing at?

'Because I need your help, Frank,' the older man announced, a thin smile touching his lips.

'According to you I'm a loser. How can *I* help *you?*'

'It's *because* you're a loser that I need you. No one's going to miss you, Frank. No one cares about you.'

Newton clenched one fist in his lap. 'So tell me what you want,' he demanded.

'You stole from me, Frank. You owe me. I want that debt repaid,' Parker said, sipping his drink. 'It seems to me you've got three options. Number one, Steve or Ian there – ' he nodded towards the two men standing behind Newton ' – they can put a bullet through the back of your fucking head right here and now. You *and* those four arseholes you pulled the job with. Number two, the police receive an anonymous tip-off about that Securicor job. All five of you go down for life. And at your age, Frank, that means you die inside.'

'Third option?' Newton wanted to know.

'If you do as you're told and you do things right, you

walk away,' Parker told him. 'Not just that, you walk away a very rich man.'

'I still don't get it, Billy.'

'I want you to do a job for me, Frank.'

55

Newton shifted uneasily in his seat as Parker returned to his desk and sat opposite.

'What kind of job?' Newton enquired. 'What's wrong with some of your corporation boys doing it?'

'Because I need them. Every one of my employees has a specific task to do. In short, *you're* expendable. *They're* not.' The older man sipped his drink.

'So, what's the job?' Newton wanted to know.

'Have you ever heard of the Yardies, Frank?'

'Yeah. They're like a sort of Jamaican mafia.'

'Well, they're not just in Jamaica anymore. They're over here. They have been for the last nine or ten years. Getting stronger all the time. To start with they were just a bunch of drug dealers and pimps, but they've been expanding. Branching out.'

'Into what?'

'Gambling. Protection. Counterfeiting. They're getting ambitious. They're more organized too. They've got stables of girls working for them. They run a lot of the drugs business in London.' The older man lifted his glass and gazed at the amber fluid in it. 'They're young too,

Frank,' he continued. 'Perhaps they're the future, I don't know. Maybe we've all been in this game too long. Maybe it's time to get out the pipe and slippers. Perhaps we've all stayed too long. But I'm not ready to be pushed out yet. Especially by a bunch of fucking niggers.'

'And you reckon they're big enough to take *you* on?'

'One of their top men was killed outside a club of mine in Soho the other night. The law were round asking questions. Had I ever met him? Did I do business with him?'

'And did you?'

'I knew the geezer that was killed. Wendell Hadfield. He was all right. He knew his place. He didn't interfere with my business interests. But this new group are different. It was them who blew him away.'

Newton looked on with interest. 'Who's in charge?'

'His name's Codling. He calls himself Papa Ernie,' sneered Parker. 'Black bastard. He's been in London for a few months now. He's the one who's got them organ- ized. Before Codling arrived, they spent most of their time fighting amongst themselves over a few ounces of fucking smack. But this bastard fancies himself as one of the big boys. He doesn't just want to control Yardie operations. He's not content to do business in Brixton and Tottenham. He's trying to move in on more main- stream business. He wants to make a name for himself and he's willing to fight a war to do it.'

'A war with you? He must be off his head.'

'Like I said, Frank, he's young. Most of them are. They couldn't give a fuck about reputations. They've got no . . . what would you call it? No honour. No code. If they want to take somebody out they'll take his wife and kids with him. Blow away civilians. That's not right, is it? You don't do that.'

Behind Newton, Ian Milliner shook his head.

'They're fucking animals,' Parker continued. 'They've got no respect for any*body* or any*thing*.'

Stephen Milliner nodded.

'If they want a war, why not fight them, Billy?' Newton wanted to know.

'The last thing I need now is gang war,' the older man observed. 'It'd be expensive and it'd damage business. That's where *you* come in, Frank.'

Newton looked puzzled.

'I want Codling dead,' Parker said flatly. '*You're* going to kill him.'

56

'BILLY, I'M NO fucking hitman,' Newton protested. 'What's wrong with a couple of your boys doing it?' He looked towards the Milliner brothers behind him.

'I told you,' Parker informed him, 'I don't want anyone from my organization involved. Besides, Frank, you owe me. Look at this as a repayment of your debt.'

Newton sucked in a deep breath.

'You've used shooters before,' Parker continued. 'You used them on that Securicor job. I'll even supply them. I can't say fairer than that, can I?' He smiled.

The younger man looked down at his cut hand, the blood congealing in the deep gashes.

'It's up to you, Frank,' Parker insisted. 'It's a simple choice. Either you do this job or I'll put you and your missus, Gorman and his braindead old man, Morrissey and that little slag he's fucking, Carson and his junkie son *and* Hobbs all in the same hole in the ground. I'll bury the lot of you, Frank. I might even get a couple of the boys to fuck your missus first.' He glared at Newton. 'Still need time to think about it?'

Newton leapt to his feet, snaking a hand across the desk in Parker's direction. 'You touch Paula and—'

Parker cut him short. 'And *what*, Frank?' he chided.

Newton felt a strong hand on his shoulder. Ian Milliner pushed him back into his chair, then stepped away.

Newton shot the older man an angry glance and held his gaze.

'I'll say one thing for you, Frank,' Parker told him, 'you've got a lot of neck. The last bloke who threatened me ended up with most of his face missing. But just remember, *you're* in the wrong. *You* stole from *me*. And you're getting a good deal out of this. If you do the job properly you'll get paid too. Minus the three hundred and ninety grand you've already had of course. Let's call that a deposit.'

'You're going to pay us to kill Codling? It doesn't make any sense, Billy.'

'It makes *perfect* sense.'

'How much?'

'Two million.'

'Jesus Christ,' murmured Newton.

'Four hundred thousand each. Of course, the chances of all five of you coming out in one piece are slim so it might even be more.'

'When do you want it done?'

'I'll let you know. Dates. Times. Places. We'll supply the information. All *you* have to do is make sure you kill the cunt.'

'When do we get paid?'

'Fifty grand each up front. Let's say you can keep that out of the money you've stolen from me. The rest when Codling's dead.'

'But how can you be so sure killing him will stop the other Yardies?'

'He's the one with the know-how and the organization. Without *him* they'll all go back to nicking old ladies' purses and fighting over coke.' Parker drained what was left in his glass. 'Just a word of warning, Frank,' he said quietly. 'If any of your boys decide to do a runner, then I'll kill whoever's left. You're dependent on each other. One of you fucks up, the whole lot get it in the back of the head. Understand?'

Newton nodded.

'And now you can go,' Parker told him. 'Someone'll be in touch with the details.'

Newton hesitated a moment, then got to his feet. One of the Milliner brothers opened the door for him.

He was about to walk through when he heard Parker's voice again.

'Frank,' he called. 'There's something else.'

57

NEWTON TURNED SLOWLY.

'You can leave us alone, boys,' Parker said, waving his companions away. The two brothers left the room.

'What now, Billy?' Newton wanted to know. 'Do you want me to kidnap the fucking prime minister for you? Shoot the Queen?'

'Sit down.'

Newton did as he was instructed.

'How badly do you want a kid?' Parker asked.

'What's this got to do with anything, Billy?'

'Just tell me.'

'It'd mean everything to us. But with all due respect, what does it matter to you?'

'I've got a daughter, you probably know that. Kids are magic. There's something you can't describe between parents and their kids. They don't ask for anything except your love, Frank, and the love they give back is more powerful than any fucking drug. When my daughter puts her arms around me it's like nothing else in the world matters and she's twenty-six now. I can remember the first nappy I ever changed. Her first steps. Her first words. How her little hand used to fit inside mine. How she used to run up to me every time I walked through the door. And it just got better and better as she got older. I used to call her my little princess. She still is. She always will be.'

'I'm very happy for you, Billy, but what's this got to do with me? I'm never going to know what that feels like, am I? Is this part of the punishment for taking your money? You describe to me something I can never have?'

'Who says you can't have it?'

'Doctors. Specialists.'

'That's bullshit. You want a kid, I'll get you one.'

Newton looked at him aghast.

'It'll cost you ten grand,' Parker added.

The younger man's head was spinning.

'I've got dozens of girls working for me in the escort business,' Parker told him. 'They charge two or three grand a night. They make a good living. But the last thing they need is a kid. Every now and then one of them makes a mistake or she's unlucky. She gets pregnant. Most have them aborted. Some keep them. Some are prepared to do business.'

'You're telling me that for ten grand I can buy a kid off a pro who doesn't want it?'

'If you want a kid badly enough, then ten grand's a bargain.'

'But it wouldn't be our kid.'

'The kid doesn't know that. You turn up at the hospital, pay the money and you walk away parents. What's the problem? Nobody knows except you, your missus and the girl you bought the kid off. You get what *you* want. She gets shot of a kid she never wanted and the child gets parents who are going to love it.'

'Buying a kid? Jesus Christ.'

'Don't go all moral on me, Frank. You're going to pick up four hundred thousand for *killing* someone and suddenly you've got a conscience about paying ten grand for something you want more than anything else in the world.'

'We'd be buying it off a pro.'

'So what? It's not the kid's fault that's how its mother earns a living, is it? Now, are you interested or not?'

'Why are you doing this, Billy?'

'I grew up in a kids' home. I know what those places are like. Soulless, loveless fucking places. I wouldn't wish that on any kid. And that isn't me being sentimental, Frank. This is business. Pay your ten grand and all you have to do is specify your model. White or black. Boy or girl. Everything's for sale out there, you know that. I'm not doing you any favours, Frank. This is just another financial transaction, pure and simple. Take it or leave it.'

Newton swallowed hard. 'Can I think about it?' he muttered, almost guiltily.

'You do that. When you've decided, you give me a bell, right?'

Newton got to his feet. He hesitated, thought about saying something, but then made for the door, his shoes sinking into the plush carpet.

He paused at the door. 'Ten grand,' he said, without looking round.

'It's a bargain, Frank. You can take it out of that fifty thousand.'

Newton pulled open the door, waited a moment, then closed it gently behind him.

58

'THEY'LL KILL US.'

James Carson said the words flatly, without inflection. They sounded like a statement of fact; nothing more, nothing less.

The café in Shepherd's Market was busy. A constant babble of conversation mingled with the occasional buzz of the Insectocutor.

Jeff Hobbs watched a wasp fly into the fluorescent blue metal spirals, then drop to the floor behind the counter. One of the men making sandwiches stepped on the fallen insect almost gleefully, crushing it beneath his foot.

The clientele were mainly taxi drivers. They came in and out with dizzying frequency. Some took their coffee and sandwich and sat at one of the cluster of small tables or at the counter itself; others merely wandered in, picked up their order then returned to their cabs again, some to drive off, others to sit behind the wheel chewing on their food.

Frank Newton took a sip of his coffee and gazed across the table at Carson. 'And if we don't do it, Parker'll kill us,' he observed. 'It's not much of a choice, but it's all we've got.'

'We're lucky he didn't blow us away as soon as he found out we'd taken his money,' Morrissey offered, drawing on his cigarette.

'When does he want it done?' asked Ray Gorman.

Newton shook his head. 'I don't know,' he said.

'How many of them will there be?' Gorman persisted.

'I don't know that either.'

'What *do* you know, Frank?'

Newton wasn't slow to pick up the irritation in his companion's voice. 'I know what I've been told,' he said evenly, glaring at Gorman. 'Parker will give us the nod when and where he wants this Codling geezer hit.'

'And when he shouts, we jump,' Carson sighed.

'Fucking right we do if we want to stay alive,' Newton insisted.

'So, we just walk up to the bastard and shoot him?' Gorman continued. 'It's that simple, is it?'

'I told you, I don't know how it's going to work yet,' Newton rasped.

'And even if we get Codling, what about his men?' Gorman wanted to know.

'We take them with him if we have to,' Newton replied.

'How many of them?' Morrissey pondered.

'I don't know,' Newton told him, his tone almost apologetic.

'If you'd checked out those betting shops in the first

place we wouldn't be in this position,' Gorman hissed. 'Jesus, *you* of all people should know about *those*.'

Newton shot his companion a withering stare.

'And if you hadn't shot that fucking guard,' snarled Carson.

'What was I supposed to do? I didn't have a choice,' Gorman argued.

'Don't start that again,' Newton said angrily. 'What's done is done. The only thing that matters now is *this* fucking job.'

'What's to stop Parker killing *us* after we've shot Codling?' Morrissey enquired.

'Absolutely nothing,' Newton said flatly.

'I don't trust him,' Gorman added.

'Then *you* tell him we're not doing it.'

'Jesus, what a fucking mess,' Hobbs interjected.

'It could be worse.' Morrissey shrugged. 'At least this way we get the chance to make a bit of money.'

'A *lot* of money.' Gorman smiled. 'More than that fucking Securicor job anyway.'

James Carson merely sat staring into his coffee cup, as if seeking answers there. Newton saw the expression on the older man's face: the weariness, the anxiety.

'We just keep getting in deeper all the time,' Carson murmured.

'Once this is over, we really *can* get out for good,' Newton explained.

'After we've gunned down Christ-knows-how-many men for Billy Parker? Do you think the law are just going to ignore it, Frankie? We haven't got a chance of getting away with it. Even Parker knows that.'

'We've got to do it.' Newton sighed. 'If it gets Parker off our backs, it's worth it. I'd rather have the *law* chasing me than him.'

'If it gets us four hundred grand each it's worth it,' Gorman offered.

Morrissey raised his coffee cup in salute and smiled.

Hobbs also managed a grin.

James Carson looked at his companions impassively.

There was no emotion on his face; only the pain and concern that showed in his eyes.

'And after Codling,' he said quietly, 'who's he going to get us to kill next?'

The words hung in the air.

59

He wasn't there when she woke.

Paula Newton reached out sleepily, her hand groping across the sheet towards her husband, but the bed was empty.

She rolled over, blinking myopically.

The digits on the radio alarm glowed in the darkness: 2.06 a.m.

She waited a moment to see if she could hear him in the toilet, but there was no sound.

Finally, she swung herself out of bed, pulled on her housecoat, and padded down the stairs.

She found him in the living room.

He didn't turn as she entered. He merely sat staring ahead at the blank TV screen.

'I couldn't sleep,' he told her flatly.

'I guessed that. How long have you been down here?'

'An hour. Longer. I don't know.'

She sat down opposite him and, as she did, she noticed the glass of brandy beside the chair.

'Will *that* help you sleep?' she enquired, nodding in the direction of the liquor.

'I doubt if anything will,' he said, attempting a smile.

'What's wrong, Frank?' she asked him finally. 'Why are you getting drunk at two in the morning?'

He drew in a breath as if to say something, but then merely reached for his glass and took a sip.

'Is it this job you've got to do for Parker?' Paula continued.

He nodded. 'That and about a million other things,' he confessed.

Tell her the truth.

'The job that Parker wants us to do isn't what I told you earlier,' he said, draining the glass. 'He doesn't need me to torch some rival gang-leader's fucking club.'

'So what *is* the job? What kind of job takes half a bottle of brandy before you can talk about it?'

'He wants us to kill someone.'

She looked straight at him and, for fleeting seconds, he thought he saw tears welling up in her eyes. 'And you're going to do it?' she said.

'Yeah, I'm going to do it. I'm going to do whatever Billy Parker tells me to do. Because that's the way things are. In this business he's at the top of the food chain, I'm at the bottom. And I owe him.'

'You don't owe Billy Parker anything.'

'I took his money. By rights I should be dead now.'

'So, because you're not, you've got to kill someone? Because he says so?'

'Because that's the way it works. I don't want to go over it, I've been doing that all afternoon. This isn't a matter of right or wrong. It's a matter of survival. Mine. Ours. And there's something else too.'

She regarded him almost warily.

Newton got to his feet and retrieved the bottle of Hennessey. He poured himself another large measure and drank.

'Join me?' he said, thrusting the bottle towards her.

Paula shook her head. 'What else, Frank?' she asked evenly.

Newton chuckled. 'What would you say if I told you we could have a child?' he asked.

'I'd say you'd drunk too much of that.' She motioned towards the brandy. 'Perhaps I'd better go back to bed and leave you to it.' She got to her feet.

'I haven't finished,' he told her.

She turned and looked at him. 'No, you've got about half a bottle left,' she replied. 'Why don't you drink it all and then sleep it off in that chair?'

'Do you want a kid or not?'

'We'll talk in the morning.'

'No, we'll talk now.' He stood up and moved towards her, one hand reaching for her arm. 'Parker can get us a kid.'

'I thought he only ran pubs, clubs and restaurants. Has he moved into orphanages too? You're drunk, Frank,' she snapped, angrily shaking loose.

'For ten grand he can get us a kid. He told me. Just listen.'

She stood motionless.

Newton was breathing heavily.

'He can get us a kid,' he said finally, wiping his mouth with the back of his hand. 'Whatever we want.'

Newton explained falteringly.

Paula didn't utter a word, merely kept her gaze fixed on him as he rambled on about his conversation with the older man earlier in the day.

Only when he'd finished did she finally sit down opposite him.

'And you believe him?' she said flatly.

'Why would he lie? He's got me over a fucking barrel with this Securicor job. He doesn't need to bribe me when he can threaten me, does he? Why promise me a kid when all he has to do is put a gun to my head?'

Paula looked at him for a moment longer, then dropped her gaze.

'It might be our only chance,' he told her, his voice cracking. 'Our *last* chance.'

She shook her head almost imperceptibly. 'I don't know, Frank,' she said, still not looking up.

Newton moved closer, wanting to touch her, but not sure if he should. 'We can't have a child, we know that,' he said tenderly. 'According to the bloody rules we're too old to adopt. With my background and record we're never going to get a kid on the straight. We're not going to get another chance like this, Paula.'

'And in years to come, if that child wants to find its real mother? What then? If it runs off to be with her, does Parker give us back our ten thousand?' she asked cryptically.

'That won't happen. We'll be its parents. The only ones it'll ever know.'

When she finally raised her head he saw the tears coursing down her cheeks. Now he did move to her, enfolding her in his arms, feeling her body tremble.

'It'll be our child,' he whispered, stroking her hair. 'There's no need for it to ever know the truth. When this job is done the *three* of us will get out of London once and for all. Start again, like we always said we would. Only this time we'll start as a family.'

He lifted her head and kissed her on the forehead.

When she looked into his eyes, she saw that he too was crying.

60

'ARE YOU GOING to eat that?' Gary Carson looked at the cheeseburger.

'Help yourself,' DI John Ridley told him, watching as the young man reached for the burger and bit into it.

'So, did you recognize either of the blokes who picked your old man up yesterday?' the policeman asked.

Carson shook his head, chewing hungrily. 'Never seen them before,' he mumbled, wiping tomato sauce from one corner of his mouth. 'You said to ring whatever happened. I thought it was important.'

'It really doesn't bother you if I put your old man away, does it?'

Gary shrugged. 'As long as it gets *me* out of bother, I couldn't give a fuck,' he announced.

Ridley watched him for a moment, then stirred his tea with the plastic stick provided.

The Burger King at King's Cross station was busy. People queued at the counter, some taking their food away in brown bags, others struggling to find a vacant table inside. One man pushed a large holdall along the floor with his foot as he balanced a tray of food in his right hand and gripped a small suitcase in his left.

Two young girls, both in their late teens, were talking animatedly at a table near the window. One had removed her shoes and was rubbing her obviously aching feet on the tiled floor.

A puddle of Coke close to the counter presented another hazard to those making their way towards the tables laden down with food and luggage. Ridley watched as a gangling youth emerged from a door to the right of the counter dragging a mop and bucket.

A man in a white shirt and black jeans was sipping his coffee and reading a paperback, occasionally looking at his watch. Ridley assumed he was waiting for a train.

Logical enough as he was on a station. Full marks, Sherlock.

The DI smiled to himself as he noticed the man's elbow was in some spilled ketchup.

'I can't stay long,' Gary said.

'Sorry to have interrupted your busy social schedule,' Ridley chided.

'I mean, someone might see me with you and then we'd both be fucked, wouldn't we? I mean, if anyone saw me talking to a copper . . .' He allowed the sentence to trail off.

'Spoil your street cred, would it? Lower your standing among the other lowlife you mix with?'

Gary slurped his milkshake. 'I've got no information for you anyway,' he said, returning his attention to the cheeseburger.

'You keep those crafty little eyes peeled.'

'My old man couldn't nick car batteries without getting electrocuted. I don't know what the fuck you expect to get him on. Him or this Newton bloke.'

'Let me worry about that. You just worry about the fact you've given me nothing yet. Don't forget, Gary, three to five for possession. You underestimate your old man. There weren't many better getaway drivers in the business.'

Gary sniffed hard. 'I believe you,' he sneered.

'At least he never dealt in any of that shit you do.'

'Different generation, isn't it?' He stuffed more of the cheeseburger into his mouth.

'Who did you get your gear from when you were dealing?' Ridley wanted to know.

'I thought this was about my old man, not me.'

'Just answer the question.'

'I got it wherever I could.'

'Main supplier?'

'Why do you want to know?'

'Just tell me,' Ridley hissed, leaning forward slightly.

'Two of them usually.'

'Names.'

'Rohan Bovell or Winston Simpson.'

Bingo.

'The same Winston Simpson that was murdered two weeks ago,' said Ridley and it sounded more like a statement than a question.

'Yeah. How do you know?'

'Because I'm a fucking copper, dummy. We found him

and a mate of his called Rupert Hart in a flat in Stoke Newington. They'd both been killed with machetes.'

Gary chewed the end of his straw.

'This other guy, Bovell,' Ridley continued. 'Where does *he* live?'

'Look, I thought you were after my old man, what—'

'Give me an address, you little prick, or I'll arrest you right here and now or, better still, I'll get word to every fucking scumbag and lowlife on the street that you're helping me. Nobody likes a grass, do they, Gary?'

'He's got a place in Tottenham.'

'Write the address on there,' Ridley instructed, pushing a business card and pen towards the youth.

When he finished, the policeman snatched it away and got to his feet.

'If this is bullshit, I'll see you later,' he snapped.

'It's kosher, honest.'

Ridley was already heading for the exit.

61

SHE WATCHED HIM from the kitchen.

Paula Newton stood against the frame of the door, eyes fixed on her husband as he gripped the phone. He barely moved other than to nod occasionally, as if the caller could see him.

She'd called in sick that morning. There had been no complaints from the nursery. She'd told them she'd be in again the following day; it was just a cold. She didn't want to give it to any of the kids.

Sometimes lies were so easy, weren't they?

What kind of lies were they going to manufacture in the coming months?

Where had the baby come from?

She could hear the questions whirling around inside her head.

'We didn't even know you were pregnant.'

'How did you manage to keep it quiet?'

'So the doctors were wrong?'

Paula tried to push the thoughts to the back of her mind as she continued to watch her husband.

'Does she know we're coming?' Newton asked the voice at the other end of the line.

'It's all taken care of, Frank,' Billy Parker told him. 'Stop worrying.'

'What about the ten grand?'

'Give it to her when you see her. Her name's Stephanie Brownson. You give her the money, she'll give *you* the kid.'

'What's the kid's name?'

'As soon as you hand over the money it's yours, Frank. What you call it is down to you and your missus.'

'What if she changes her mind and doesn't want to hand it over?'

'She *won't* change her mind. Remember, Frank, this is business. Once the goods are paid for, they're yours.'

Newton looked in the direction of the kitchen and saw Paula watching him.

'Where do we have to go?' he wanted to know.

'The Abbott Clinic. It's a private place in Norland Square, Holland Park. You should be able to find it easily enough.'

Newton scribbled on the small pad beside the phone.

'She'll be waiting for you,' Parker continued. 'Don't be late. She's expecting you at eight.'

'What about the staff there? Aren't they going to be suspicious about what's going on? We turn up, take a baby off someone and bung her ten grand. It's not exactly common procedure, is it?'

'The nurse who'll let you in is on five per cent of the

selling price. She couldn't give a fuck. Just do as I've told you and you're sorted.'

'How old is the kid?'

'Three days.'

'Boy or girl?'

'What did you ask for?'

'A girl.'

'And that's what you've got. Now you know all the details, perhaps you should get down to Mothercare for some nappies. You're going to need them.'

Parker hung up.

Newton stood holding the receiver for a moment longer, then gently replaced it on the cradle.

He glanced in Paula's direction.

When he spoke, his voice was almost a whisper.

'Eight o'clock tonight,' he said softly.

62

'ARE YOU GOING to tell me what the hell is going on, guv?' DS Darren Brown looked at his superior as he swung the car into Jellicoe Road.

Ridley was peering out of the side window, searching for the address that Gary Carson had scribbled on the business card.

'We're following a lead,' Ridley said dismissively.

'Yeah, *your* lead. When are you going to let me in on what's happening?'

'Pull up here,' Ridley snapped, ignoring the question. He jabbed a finger towards a parking space and Brown swung the Orion into it. He hit the brakes a little too hard, jerking Ridley out of his seat.

The DI shot his companion a furious look.

'What did Carson tell you?' Brown demanded.

'I asked him where he got his gear. He told me. Satisfied?'

'No. What's Gary Carson got to do with this? Is he a suspect?'

'He used to buy drugs from a man killed by the Yardies. If we can find some links we might be closer to nailing whoever murdered Winston Simpson and Rupert Hart. I'd lay odds the same men killed Wendell Hadfield. Those same men are probably behind the rise in Yardie power we've seen during the past few months. Is that synopsis good enough for you?' Ridley glared at his companion.

He swung himself out of the car, followed by the DS.

'And Bovell's a dealer too?' he asked.

'According to Carson. Bovell might know something. He might even know who killed Simpson and Hart.'

'And you reckon he's going to tell us?'

'By the time I've finished with him, the bastard'll tell us who shot fucking Kennedy.'

There were half a dozen black youths standing around the entrance to the flats in Jellicoe Road. They looked on warily as the two policemen approached.

'Do any of you know Rohan Bovell?' asked Ridley.

'Who's asking?' said a tall youth in a puffa jacket and dark jeans.

Ridley flashed his ID.

'Never heard of him, mate,' the tall youth said, turning his back.

'Any of you?' Ridley persisted.

The others shook their heads or dropped their gaze.

'Nice car. You want to be careful leaving it round here,' one said, and the others laughed.

Ridley pushed past the tall youth.

Brown followed.

They made their way towards the lift and the DI jabbed the 'Call' button. The doors slid back enough to allow the men entry and Ridley checked the floor they wanted as the lift rose.

It moved slowly, threatening to stop at any moment.

Brown leant back against the wall, wrinkling his nose; it stank of piss.

In one corner there was a used condom and grafitti was all over the walls and the inside of the doors.

'Urban art,' said Brown, smiling and nodding towards the multicoloured spray-can murals.

Ridley ignored the comment, pushing his way through the lift doors when the car bumped to a halt. He made his way along the corridor to the flat he sought and banged hard on the door.

'Rohan Bovell!' he shouted.

'Can we do this without a warrant?' Brown enquired, watching as Ridley took a step back from the door and prepared to swing his foot at it.

'Do you want to stop me?' Ridley rasped and drove the sole of his shoe hard against the peeling paintwork.

The door groaned, but stood firm.

'Bovell!' Ridley bellowed and slammed another kick into the door. This time it flew back on its hinges, slamming against the wall behind.

Several curious faces appeared at the windows of the other flats on the landing. Ridley ignored them and strode into Bovell's home.

'Police!' Brown shouted, showing his ID to the perplexed onlookers.

Ridley quickly glanced round the small hallway, then pushed open the living-room door.

The heat was overpowering – the flat was like a greenhouse.

Brown joined him and both men halted, gazing at the contents of the room.

'Jesus Christ,' murmured the DS, his stomach contracting. He placed a hand over his mouth.

Ridley nodded towards the nearby phone. 'You'd better call forensics. And get an ambulance here too,' he said quietly. 'But tell them there's no need to rush.'

63

ROHAN BOVELL WAS naked.

His body was upright in one of the battered chairs in the living room of the flat, held in position by the lengths of nylon string and electric flex that had been wound around his wrists, ankles and neck.

His clothes had been found scattered across his bedroom. Most of the remainder of the flat was relatively untouched, although several drawers had been pulled out in the kitchen, their contents emptied onto the lino.

It was from the kitchen that the heat had emanated.

'That cooker must have been on for hours before you arrived,' said William Nicholson. 'That's what made it so hot in here.'

'That's where they heated the spoons,' Ridley said flatly. 'In the flames?'

Nicholson nodded, leaning close to the naked corpse and pointing the end of his biro in the direction of Bovell's groin.

'As far as I can tell they heated the spoons until they were red hot, then used them on his thighs, testicles, penis and backside,' the police surgeon said.

There were dozen of burns on Bovell's lower body. Huge welts had risen, only to burst and weep pus, then scabbed over before being seared away again. Purple sores and bright red blisters overlapped like some obscene jigsaw. Pieces of crusty, incinerated flesh hung from the extremities of some of the burns. What was left of the penis looked like an overcooked sausage. Even the pubic hair had been singed.

Several spoons, discoloured by flame and with tendrils of scorched skin still sticking to them, lay around the chair.

'What did they use on his face?' Ridley wanted to know.

The skin of the face, scalp and neck had been eaten away to the skull in places. What remained was a mass of oozing, liquescent slime that looked as if it might simply slide away from the bone at any moment. One eyeball had simply dissolved, leaving a fluid-filled cavity surrounded by shrivelled and scorched eyelids. The flesh had a tacky quality to it. As Ridley watched, Nicholson touched the end of his biro to a piece of mottled skin just below the remains of the bottom lip. As he withdrew the pen, strands of melted flesh came with it. They reminded the DI of slowly setting glue.

Even the teeth had been dissolved. Looking into a mouth twisted into a permanent wail of agony, Ridley saw that the enamel had been transformed into yellowish-white pulp. The tongue was almost completely gone.

'H_2SO_4,' Nicholson said flatly. 'Sulphuric. Battery acid to you and me. They poured some down his throat too.'

Nicholson indicated a large hole just below the larynx. Flaps of flesh hung all around it like the gills of a fish. 'It ate its way out just there.' He prodded the hole.

Ridley lit a cigarette and continued to stare at the body. 'How long's he been dead?' the DI enquired.

'Eight, nine hours?' Nicholson mused.

Brown wandered across to the scene of carnage. 'I just spoke to Barclay back at the Yard,' he said, glancing at Bovell's body, then deciding he'd rather stand with his back to it. 'The prints we found on the spoons and in the kitchen, Hendon have verified them as matching those on the machete that killed Rupert Hart and Winston Simpson.'

Ridley nodded.

'They also match the prints on the shell cases we found at the scene of Wendell Hadfield's shooting.'

64

Frank Newton brought the Peugeot to a halt and switched off the engine.

He glanced at the dashboard clock: 7.56 p.m.

Beside him, Paula sat looking straight ahead.

Newton reached over and gently touched her hand. 'Shall I go?' he asked quietly.

She didn't answer, merely continued to gaze out of the window, occasionally looking up at the evening sky. Thick banks of cloud were gathering above the capital. The threat of rain looked ready to reach fruition.

Norland Square was a peaceful backwater just off Holland Park Avenue. There was a park in the centre of it; surrounded by a high, black, wrought-iron fence, it was like a green oasis in the mass of grey concrete that enveloped it. Street lights burned with a dull, yellow, sodium glow. They reflected off the windows of the large houses all around the square. In many, curtains were drawn to shut out the night.

'Are you sure this is the right place?' Paula said, looking around.

Newton nodded. 'Have you got everything you need?' he asked, glancing into the back seat.

There was a Moses basket, several small blankets and a pack of Pampers.

Paula fumbled in her jacket pocket and retrieved a dummy. She looked at it. It had little yellow elephants on it.

'You OK?' Newton asked, squeezing her hand.

She nodded and swung herself out of the car.

He followed and together they crossed the pavement and made their way up the three stone steps to the large white front door of the building.

There was an intercom system with a button and name beside it: THE ABBOTT CLINIC.

Newton pressed the buzzer and waited, his heart thudding against his ribs.

They heard movement on the other side and a young woman dressed in a white uniform smiled welcomingly at them.

She beckoned them inside, into the well-lit hallway. There were paintings on the immaculately decorated walls: landscapes; portraits. A vase of fresh flowers formed the centrepiece on a table nearby. Newton could smell the delightful scent. Somewhere close he could hear a muted TV set. Doors led off from the corridor that snaked away from the hall.

He opened his mouth to speak, but the nurse merely nodded and they heard footsteps approaching.

The young woman facing them was in her early twenties, dressed in a long blue housecoat. Her shoulder-length blonde hair was pulled back in a ponytail. She wore no make-up.

Newton thought how young she looked.

Paula could see that she was carrying a tiny bundle in her arms. Wrapped in pink and white blankets and a shawl, the little bundle was making soft, rhythmic, gurgling noises.

The young woman looked at them indifferently, then passed the baby to Paula.

She turned her attention to Newton, who reached inside his jacket and pulled out an envelope that he handed to her.

She turned and walked back down the corridor.

The nurse motioned them towards the front door; out of the brightly lit hallway, away from the paintings and the scent of freshly cut flowers.

Back into the darkness of the street.

She smiled efficiently, then Newton heard the door close behind them.

They headed back to the car and he hurried round to the passenger side to let Paula in before sliding behind the wheel.

For long seconds they both sat motionless, then Paula pulled back the shawl slightly.

The baby was sleeping.

She reached out with one quivering index finger and touched its cheek.

So soft. So delicate. So perfect.

Newton looked at his wife, then at the sleeping child. He too reached out and, with infinite care, pressed a finger into the palm of one tiny hand. Instinctively, the baby clutched it for a second. It stirred slightly, but did not wake.

Paula smiled at him, her eyes full of tears. When she spoke, the words were barely audible.

'Let's go home.'

65

THE SOUND OF the drill was overpowering. The strident shriek of the spinning bit cut through the air like a blade.

It was joined a moment later by the buzz of a bandsaw.

Even the music thudding from the two large speakers on either side of the stage couldn't drown out the noise.

Billy Parker turned in the direction of the power tools and frowned, watching the workmen gathered there. He shook his head.

'I thought they were supposed to be finished before the club opened,' he snapped, reaching for his drink and trying to concentrate on the spectacle before him.

'They will be, Billy,' Mark Hatcher told him.

'It's supposed to open in two days and it still looks like a fucking bombsite,' Parker observed. 'Where did you find these builders anyway?'

'We've used them before, Billy,' Hatcher said.

'Well, don't use them again. Looking at what they've done so far I wouldn't trust them with fucking Lego.'

Hatcher nodded dutifully.

He was eight or nine years younger than Parker and had worked for him since he was twenty. He was a wiry man with a receding hairline and sad eyes. But Parker trusted his managerial skills. He had, at various times, been in charge of clubs, restaurants and casinos owned by the older man. He had been a natural choice for Parker's latest venture.

He'd bought the building in St Martin's Lane over a year ago and work had been going on constantly since then; first gutting, then renovating what had formerly been a tailor's and transforming it into a club Parker had named 'Sensations'.

Upstairs was a restaurant, downstairs a casino. The ground floor was equipped with one central stage and a dozen smaller podiums to accommodate the dancers, who would gyrate their way through the night, week-in week-out, from eight in the evening until two in the morning.

The club employed over seventy girls.

Four more were auditioning on the main stage as Parker and his associates watched.

He had their CVs in front of him. Each bore a couple of photos and details of previous jobs. He flipped through them, occasionally pausing to sip his Johnny Walker or to watch as the girls went through their routines. All to the accompaniment of thundering rock music that exploded from the large speakers flanking them.

'. . . *She was some kind of priestess, with a black dress on . . .*'

'The two on the right are sisters,' Parker mused,

glancing first at the CVs, then at the two brunettes dancing close together. 'Sue and Alix Byrne.'

'. . . *With her film star kind of features, she really turned me on . . .*'

Both were wearing PVC bikini bottoms and nothing else.

'They're handy little dancers,' Hatcher told him. 'The sister thing is a good angle too.'

Parker sipped at his drink and watched as one of the girls began sliding expertly up and down the pole in the middle of the podium, her long auburn hair flying all around her like serpents' tails.

'Nineteen years old,' he murmured. 'They grow up quicker these days, don't they?'

He and the men around him laughed, the sound swallowed up by the deafening combination of music and building work.

They were still laughing when Ian Milliner approached the table. He leant close to Parker, cupping one hand around his mouth both to amplify his words and also as a pretence to discretion.

'Someone here to see you, Billy,' he told his employer.

'Who knows I'm here at this time in the morning?' Parker wanted to know, glancing at his Rolex: 11.13 a.m.

'He says it's important,' Milliner continued.

'Tell him to wait. I'm busy.'

One of the other girls had rolled onto her stomach and was curving her shapely bottom up and down, moving snakelike across the stage, leaving a trail of perspiration behind her.

'Who is it anyway?' Parker asked.

'He says his name's Codling.'

66

'Do you think she's all right?' asked Frank Newton, concern in his voice. 'What's she crying for?'

He looked down at the little bundle in his arms and rocked the baby gently back and forth, trying to soothe her.

'She's just hungry,' Paula told him, grinning.

'She's *always* hungry.' Newton smiled.

He took the bottle of milk from Paula and pushed the teat towards the baby's mouth. It accepted the offering gratefully and began to drink.

Newton sat down at the kitchen table, looking down at the child as she fed.

'So,' Paula said wearily, 'what *do* we tell everyone when they ask where we've suddenly acquired a child?'

'We tell them to mind their own fucking business.'

'Frank, it's not going to be as easy as that and you know it.'

'Tell them we adopted. Tell them our application was finally accepted. Who cares, Paula? Once this job is done for Parker we'll be out of here anyway. No one will know us. No one will ask any fucking questions.'

She regarded him silently for a moment. 'And when it *is* done,' she said finally, 'am I still going to have a husband? Or am I going to have to tell people that my husband died and that I'm raising my daughter on my own?'

'It won't come to that.'

'Parker's hired you to kill someone, Frank. Do you really think it's going to be that easy?'

He gazed down at the baby as he adjusted the bottle.

'And even if you do get away alive,' Paula continued, 'there's the law to worry about. Am I supposed to bring our child to the prison where you're banged up every time I come to see you?'

'Stop worrying, Paula. It'll be all right.'

'I wish I was as confident as you, Frank. You've got even more to lose now.'

'You think I don't know that? So tell me, Paula, what am I supposed to do? Turn round to Parker and say, "By the way, Billy, I know I nicked a load of your money, but that's just the way it goes. I'm not killing this geezer for you so fuck off. Let's call it quits." That's a *sure* way of getting myself killed. He might just decide to take the baby back too.'

'So, when do we leave London?'

'As soon as the job's done. As soon as Codling's dead.'

'When will that be?'

'When we get the nod from Parker.'

'And where do we go?'

'The coast. The Midlands. Scotland. Ireland. Anywhere. Out of the country if we have to. That's what we always dreamed of, wasn't it? A fresh start in a new country. Just you, me and the baby.' He stroked the child's head with his free hand.

'We've got friends here, Frank,' she reminded him. 'How easy is it going to be to just leave them behind?'

'As long as I've got you and the baby, I can leave *anything* behind.'

She reached out and touched his arm.

The baby stirred, pawed gently at the bottle with one pudgy hand, then continued drinking.

'What are we going to call her?' Paula whispered, looking at the child. 'We never talked about names.'

'We never had any reason to.'

They both gazed down at the little girl.

'Natasha,' Paula offered.

'Michelle. After Michelle Pfeiffer.' He laughed.

She punched him playfully. 'Jane?' she said.

'No. The other kids would call her Plain Jane.'

'Laura.'

'Samantha.'

'Kelly.'

'Nicola.'

'Danielle.'

Newton looked at Paula, then down at the little girl. He smiled. 'Danielle. It's beautiful,' he said softly. 'Like her.'

She stirred in his arms.

He leaned closer and kissed her forehead.

Kissed his daughter's forehead.

My daughter.

'Hello, Danielle Newton,' he whispered.

67

BIG BASTARD.

That was Billy Parker's first thought when he saw Codling.

The Jamaican was dressed in a leather jacket, a white shirt

(*looked like Armani to Parker*)

black trousers and a pair of Caterpillar boots.

His dreadlocks hung past his broad shoulders and, as he looked slowly around the inside of the club, he smiled.

The two men with him were of similar build and age. Late twenties. They stood back slightly, hands tucked in their pockets.

Stephen Milliner got to his feet and stood behind Parker as the three black men approached the table.

Parker raised a hand in Milliner's direction as if to halt him.

The music was still thundering from the speakers.

'. . . *Love is a killer, a homicidal thing . . .*'

The girls on the podium continued their routines despite the fact their gyrations were being ignored.

'. . . I've got a target on my back, for a Cupid dressed in black . . .'

'Get them to turn that fucking music off,' Parker said, his eyes never leaving the trio of men facing him.

Adam Rawlings scuttled off and returned moments later as the club fell silent, the stillness punctuated occasionally by the noise from the builders.

For interminable seconds, the entire scene was frozen like some waxwork scene: Parker, Stephen and Ian Milliner, Rawlings, Paul Palmer and Mark Hatcher all faced the newcomers. Codling, Skeng and Toad stood like statues before them.

There was a smile on Codling's face. 'We all start shooting now or later?' he said.

Parker's eyes narrowed slightly.

The men were standing less than three feet from each other.

He knew his own men were tooled up; he assumed Codling's were.

If anyone did pull down now, there'd be a fucking bloodbath.

Codling held out both hands, palms up. 'I no John Wayne,' he announced, shaking his head, the grin still in place.

'What do you want?' Parker asked.

'I want talk to you. You the man.' He pointed one finger at Parker's chest, then held it to his lips and blew on the tip.

Still that grin.

'You know who I am?' Parker asked.

'Everyone know *you*, Mr Parker.' The grin slipped slightly for the first time. 'Everything that go down in London, you involved somehow.'

'Not everything. I didn't have anything to do with Wendell Hadfield's shooting.'

Codling's grin returned even more radiantly. He raised both hands. 'That was personal,' he said. 'Me and him, we had some business together.'

'You killed him outside one of *my* clubs.'

'How you know it was me?'

'I hear things. Word gets round.'

'And what's the word on me?'

'That you're ambitious. That Hadfield was in your way. That's why you took him out. You're taking control of the Yardies in London.'

Codling cracked out laughing, a great booming sound that seemed to fill the club.

Skeng and Toad also chuckled.

'Did I say something funny?' Parker wanted to know.

'Yardies.' Codling sniggered. 'What you know about Yardies, Mr Parker? You know nothing.'

Ian Milliner moved forward, but Parker shot out a hand to hold him back.

'Keep that dog on a tighter leash,' Codling chided. 'Or he get hurt. I get Skeng here to put that dog down.'

'You black cunt,' hissed Milliner, his right hand sliding towards the inside of his jacket.

The two men flanking Codling moved with incredible speed: hands dived inside coats . . . steel slid from leather . . . gun metal glinted beneath the lights.

Skeng had a .357 Desert Eagle aimed at Milliner's head.

Milliner himself had pulled a Glock automatic from his shoulder holster. He was holding it at arm's length. The barrel was no more than two feet from Skeng.

The barrel of an Ingram M10 sub-machine-gun, gripped by Toad, hovered before the other men.

Stephen Milliner held the 9mm Beretta Burst-fire in his large hands, the sights trained on Codling.

Time seemed to have frozen.

Seconds became minutes.

'Put them down,' Parker said quietly.

Codling nodded.

At first, the men on both sides hesitated, then, slowly, the weapons were lowered.

'Everyone need to chill,' Codling said, smiling. 'Your nice club nearly ruined.'

The men continued to face each other.

'So, Mr Parker,' Codling finally said, 'you think you know about me.'

'You're fed up with keeping stables of crack whores and letting the other spades fight over substandard drugs. You want to move up in the world.'

The grin finally left Codling's face. He glared at the older man. 'That's right,' he said softly. 'That's why I here this morning. I want to talk business with you.'

'I don't deal in the kind of business *you* deal in,' Parker said dismissively.

'Are you a stupid man, Mr Parker?' Codling enquired, the smile returning.

Parker took a pace towards him.

So did Palmer and Rawlings.

Skeng and Toad stepped forward alongside the Jamaican.

Here we go again.

'I don't think you are,' Codling continued. 'That's why I think you listen to my proposal. I think you do business with me.'

'What kind of business have *you* got that I could possibly be interested in?' Parker wanted to know.

'Twenty million,' Codling told him. 'Split right down the middle. What you think of *that* business, Mr Parker?'

68

'WHY SHOULD I believe you?'

Parker's words echoed around the office. He sipped at his Johnny Walker and looked across the desk at Codling.

The Jamaican was nursing a Jack Daniels in his large hand, sometimes lifting the Waterford glass to inspect the dark liquid, sometimes running the tip of one index finger around the delicate rim.

Behind him, Skeng stood motionless, sentrylike, beside the office door.

Adam Rawlings sat to Parker's right in the high-backed leather chair, fingertips pressed together to form a pyramid. He looked from Skeng to Codling and back again.

Below them, the sound of the building work seemed muffled, but it was still annoyingly audible.

'You walk into one of my clubs and tell me you've got a business deal for me,' Parker continued. 'That you're going to split twenty million with me. Why? What's the catch? It sounds like bullshit to me.'

Codling smiled broadly.

That fucking grin was beginning to get irritating.

'No catch,' Codling told him. 'And why I bother to find you if this deal is bullshit?'

'Then why cut *me* in? Twenty million's a lot of money. It opens lots of doors.'

'That's true,' Codling chuckled, lifting his glass in salute. 'It buys a lot of power.'

'So why share it?'

'I was showing you respect, Mr Parker. Respect mean a lot where I come from. You the man here in London, everyone know that. But what you said downstairs is true. I want the kind of power that you got. I want clubs like this.' He raised his hand and gestured expansively around. 'I want pretty ladies dancing for me, the way you have.'

'And that's why you had Wendell Hadfield killed. Because he was in your way.'

'He was a pussy. He had gone soft. He just a rich coconut. Now he a dead coconut.' Codling laughed. Skeng chuckled too.

'What the fuck is that supposed to mean?'

'Brown on the outside and white on the inside. He act like a big man, like a rudie, but he never see Jamaica. He wouldn't last two minutes in Kingston, man. I come from there. I know what it take to survive.'

'So what are you doing here?'

'This the land of opportunity for me.' Codling smiled. 'I gone as far as I could go back home. The money is here.'

'What's to stop *you* turning into a coconut?' Parker

grinned. 'Twenty million's a lot more than Hadfield ever saw.'

The smile slipped from Codling's lips. 'Pride,' he said flatly.

The two men regarded each other silently for a moment.

'All right,' Parker finally said. 'So what's the deal? Why are you here?'

'In a week from now, three couriers arriving at Heathrow,' the Jamaican said. 'Between them, they be carrying nearly three hundred kilos of coke.'

'How do you know that?'

'Like you, I hear things. Maybe just different things.' Codling smiled. 'One key fetch maybe thirty thousand here in London. That still good money. But when it turned into crack, you looking at forty pound a rock. Rocks only a fifth of an ounce each. There's a lot of rocks in three hundred keys. That where the money is. Twenty million in rocks. Street value even more. Probably thirty.'

'They'll never get it through customs,' Parker said dismissively. 'Not three hundred kilos. They'd need fork lifts to bring it in. Besides that, flights from the Caribbean are always the ones given the most thorough searches.'

'They not coming in from the Caribbean. They coming from America. From New York and Washington.'

'Who's the coke for?' Parker wanted to know.

'Some of it is being sent *back* to Jamaica to be sold.

Some is for the Far East. Some for other parts of Europe, The rest, who knows?' He shrugged. 'And who cares?'

Parker stroked his chin thoughtfully. 'And they're just going to walk through with three hundred kilos?' he mused.

'I'm not talking about mules here, Mr Parker,' Codling snapped. 'Not some fool with his belly full of coke-filled condoms that he swallowed before he got on the plane. Not some Rastaman with the stuff stuck up his arse or in his mouth. I'm talking about professional couriers. Men and women who do this for a living. Men and women with more contacts in customs and DEA than you can imagine. Anybody can be bought, you know that. They only buy the best.'

Again a heavy silence descended, finally broken by Codling.

'They arrive next week,' he continued. 'They spend the night in different hotels in London, then they fly out again. It the same way every time.'

'How can you be so sure?'

'Because I used to buy from them when I was in Jamaica. I know how this business works. I know these people.'

'Do you know what these couriers look like?'

'No, man. They change all the time, but I can get that information.'

'How?'

'Like I said, anybody can be bought. You let me worry about the couriers.'

'So what's your plan?'

'Take them out in their hotels.'

'Kill them?'

'If it come to that.' He grinned crookedly. 'For twenty million, I kill my own fucking mother.'

Parker regarded the Jamaican impassively. 'I still don't understand why you've come to *me* with this,' he said finally, sipping his drink. 'Like I said, why share it?'

'Maybe I need your help,' Codling replied. 'You got things I need to pull this job off right. I figure you be willing to lease them out for ten million.'

'What kind of things?'

'Men. Guns. Cars.'

'And you're telling me you can't get *those*?'

'I told you, I don't have what you have.' He waved a hand around him. 'Not yet.'

'Recruit a few pimps if you need some men, you must know plenty,' Parker sneered. 'Go and get a couple of spades to nick you some cars. How hard can *that* be?'

Codling glared at him and, when he smiled, the gesture never touched his eyes. 'I need reliable men,' he said quietly. 'The kind of men who work for you.'

'Fifteen million,' Parker said flatly. 'If I'm supplying services to you to do this job, then I want a bigger cut. You said yourself that the *street* value of that coke is over thirty million. By the time you've finished cutting it with laxative or baby powder or turning it into crack you'll make that back easily. Fifteen million's fair when you work out how much you'll make in the long run. What do you think of *that* business, Mr Codling.'

'Papa Ernie,' the Jamaican corrected him.
He was still smiling.

'Fucking old man, you should have let me kill him then,'
Skeng snarled as the Jag pulled away.

'It can wait,' Codling said, gazing out of the side
window towards the club. 'Anyway, when the time
come, I want to pull the trigger on that fuck myself. Mr
Billy motherfucker Parker. Before I kill him, I going to
let him find out what his own fucking balls taste like.'

'Twenty million quid,' sneered Adam Rawlings. 'Bullshit.'

Billy Parker poured himself another Johnny Walker
and returned to his seat behind the desk. 'There's a lot
of money in drugs, Adam, you know that,' the older man
said.

'And you believe what the black bastard said? Where
the fuck would he get information like that?'

'To be honest, I don't *care* where he got it. If it's
wrong, then we've lost nothing. If it's right, then we're
twenty million better off.' He raised the glass in salute.
'Twenty million *and* we get rid of that fucking zulu and
his boys once and for all. By the time we've finished
with them, it'll look like another Rourke's Drift.'

69

THE INCIDENT ROOM smelled of coffee and cigarettes.

DI John Ridley turned to face the policemen and women assembled before him. Some were in plain clothes, some in uniform. Huddled in groups or alone, some were seated, some standing. Without exception, they were watching him.

He had stuck two photos to the blackboard behind him and it was these that he now gestured towards.

'Aston Thomas and Dudley Smith,' he said, raising his voice slightly to ensure all in the room heard him. 'Forensics *and* Hendon have positively identified the prints on the machete that killed Hart and Simpson as belonging to these two men.' He hooked a thumb over his shoulder. 'Their prints were also found in Rohan Bovell's flat.'

'What about on the shell cases at Hadfield's shooting?' someone at the back of the room asked.

Ridley shook his head. 'Those remain unidentified,' he said, the disappointment evident in his voice. 'But, if we pull these two in –' he tapped the photos behind him ' – I'm pretty sure they'll be able to give us some pointers to who might have shot Hadfield *and* killed Leon Green.' He took a drag on his cigarette. 'Two sets of prints found on the shell cases also showed up at Leon Green's place *and* Bovell's flat. As with the third set of prints, there's no ID as yet.'

'Thomas, Smith and three unidentified men killed Leon Green, Rohan Bovell, Winston Simpson and Rupert Hart,' DS Brown interjected. 'The three unidentified men also murdered Wendell Hadfield.'

Ridley looked briefly at his partner, then turned dismissively away from him.

'So we know who used the blade and the battery acid,' a tall man in plain clothes observed.

'That's right,' Ridley echoed. 'Now we need to know who's handy with a baseball bat and an automatic.'

A ripple of laughter ran around the room.

'Any links between Hadfield and Billy Parker, guv?' another voice enquired.

'Parker's not part of this equation,' Ridley said flatly. 'This is a Yardie war. Whether or not it spills over into anyone else's concerns isn't the question at the moment.'

'No clues at all on the other three sets of prints?' the tall plain-clothes officer asked.

Ridley shook his head. 'Which means the killers haven't been printed because if they had then Hendon would have some record of it,' the DI mused. 'That means either no previous form, or they never got caught.'

'Contract men?' someone offered.

'It's possible, but I doubt it. Hadfield was a big noise,

but Green was just a two-bob dealer. No one's going to pay pros to beat a dealer to death with a baseball bat. Anyway, why waste all that energy whacking him around when they could have just blown his head off?'

Another chorus of laughter.

'Perhaps whoever killed him enjoyed it,' a voice nearby said.

Ridley nodded. 'You could be right,' he admitted. 'The same might apply to Bovell. Why use battery acid on him when a gun would have done the job more quickly? Even if the killers were torturing him, trying to find out information, they could have done it another way. Yet they took the time to heat up spoons and burn his wedding tackle, then dissolved his face. It's a hell of a way to pass the time, but it did the job.'

'Do you think they were trying to send a message?' a uniformed man near the back of the room asked.

'Without a doubt,' Ridley said. 'Once word got round about how Green, Hart, Simpson and Bovell died, then everyone would have been shitting themselves. Taking out Hadfield was the icing on the cake. Everyone knows there's a new boy in town now and, whoever he is, best not fuck around with him. The question is, exactly how ambitious is he? So far he's been content with taking over Yardie operations, but he's already got most of those in his pocket. Our biggest problem is finding out where he's going to hit next.'

'Whoever it is, guv, he can't be strong enough to challenge any of the established corporations in London,' a man in a leather jacket offered.

'Why not?' Ridley asked. 'Until we know who's behind this we haven't got a clue what he's capable of.'

'But Hadfield was still small-time,' the man in the leather jacket persisted. 'He was big with the other spades, but that was about it. Brothels, illegal gaming clubs in Brixton, drugs and porn. He was just a glorified pimp.'

'He had plenty working for him,' Ridley reminded the other man. 'He ran one of the biggest Yardie factions in the city.'

'So maybe one of his *own* men blew him away,' Leather Jacket insisted. 'Some pissed-off pimp or dealer who Hadfield was taking too big a cut off.'

'Whoever killed him did it with M16s, Mach 10s and brand-new automatics. How many pimps or dealers do you know with access to *that* kind of hardware?' Ridley shook his head. 'No, this was well organized, well planned and very efficient. Someone with that kind of firepower might just fancy his chances against the other organizations in London. Black *or* white. We've got to get him before he decides to make the crossover. Because if he does, this whole city'll go up in smoke.'

70

'I'M SICK OF hiding her away,' Frank Newton said irritably. He looked across the room at Paula, who was holding the baby in her arms. 'And how much longer can *you* stay away from the nursery before someone gets suspicious?' he persisted.

'I called them and said I'd be taking the rest of the week off,' Paula informed him. 'I thought that would give us time to sort some things out.'

'Like where to go? How to explain away a baby that everyone thought we couldn't have?'

'Then what do we do, Frank?' she asked quietly, stroking the child's cheek with one index finger, smiling down at her. 'You were the one who said we'd tell people to mind their own business if they asked about her.'

He nodded slowly. 'We got nearly two hundred grand each from that Securicor job,' Newton said.

'Half of which belongs to Billy Parker,' she reminded him.

'You think I'd forgotten? With what's to come from this other job, that gives us over half a million. It's enough to get out, Paula.'

'You mean once you've murdered this guy for Parker, then we'll be set up for life?' she said sardonically.

He met her gaze and held it. 'Yeah, that's what I mean,' he said flatly.

The baby shifted in Paula's grip, coughed and whimpered slightly. She rocked the little girl gently, holding her more closely.

'We could move now,' he offered. 'Buy a place outside London. We could be out of here before the end of the month. The three of us.'

'Then why *don't* we? Why don't we get out? Get away before you have to do this job for Parker.'

'I can't do that, Paula, you know that. I owe him.'

'You owe *me*, Frank. And now you owe Danielle too. You owe your daughter.'

Your daughter.

He ran a hand through his hair.

'You owe us a life together,' Paula continued. 'I don't want to be a widow at thirty-seven.'

'You will be if I try to run out on Billy Parker.'

'Is this how life's going to be from now on, Frank? Are you going to be looking over your shoulder every minute of every day?'

'I've spent my whole fucking life looking over my shoulder. And it hasn't *been* much of a life until now.'

'You're wanted by the police for an armed robbery. It's a miracle they haven't found you yet. The most powerful gang boss in London is forcing you to kill a man you've never met. If you don't do as he says *he'll* have you killed. Is *that* the life you wanted, Frank?'

'It's the way things are. It stinks, but it's all we've got.'

A heavy silence descended, finally broken by Paula.

'All right, then let's get out,' she said defiantly. 'We'll do as you say. We'll find somewhere outside London. If that's what you want.'

'I want you and the baby. That's what I want. But I need to know that you're with me, no matter what I do.'

'You shouldn't even have to *think* that, Frank, let alone ask it. Don't you know me after all these years?'

'We'll get things organized as soon as we can. Move out. Get away from here.'

Paula nodded.

He reached out and touched her cheek. 'I love you,' he whispered. 'And I'm not going to lose you.' He looked down at the little girl. 'Either of you.'

The phone rang.

Newton hesitated a moment, then wandered out of the living room into the hall and lifted the receiver.

He recognized the voice at the other end immediately.

71

'You're late.'

Billy Parker heard the door of his office open and looked up from the papers spread across the desk before him.

'Traffic was bad,' Frank Newton told him. He stood before the older man uneasily, feeling like a naughty child reporting to a headmaster.

'I phoned over an hour ago,' Parker reminded him.

Newton could feel sweat on his forehead and he wasn't sure that all of it was due to the heat of the day. The air conditioning inside the office above the Mayfair casino was on full blast; the constant drone sounded like angry wasps.

'Sit down, Frank,' Parker said.

Newton did as he was instructed.

He watched as the older man sipped at a glass of orange juice. There were droplets of condensation on the cool crystal. It served to remind Newton of his own raging thirst.

'This business with Codling,' Parker said. 'It's time to sort it.'

Newton swallowed hard.

You knew it was coming eventually.

'When do you want it done?' he murmured.

'Within the next week.'

'How will we find him?'

'That's the easy part. My boys will supply you with what you need: cars, weapons, stuff like that.'

Newton nodded.

'But there's something else,' Parker continued. 'Before you kill him, I want you to do a job with him.'

'Billy, what the fuck *is* this?'

'*This* is twenty million, Frank,' Parker snarled. 'And I'm offering you a piece of it on top of what I'm *already* paying you to kill Codling. Another million for you and your boys. Then we're even.'

Newton ran a hand through his hair. 'What's the job?' he wanted to know.

'Codling came to *me* with it. He needs help knocking over three drugs couriers. You're the help I'm going to give him. As far as he's concerned you work for me. You do the job with him, then you kill him. And then, Frank, you're set for life.'

The two men locked stares.

'Think about it,' Parker continued. 'A million for doing the job. A million for killing Codling. Plus what you've already had from me. More money than you could have made in your whole life, Frank.'

'You said we'd be even once Codling was dead.'

'I run the game, Frank, I can change the rules. Be grateful you're still alive. People who steal from me generally end up as fish food.'

'So what do you want me to do?' Newton asked wearily.

'Meet the black bastard. I'll set it up. Let him run the show. Let him organize it. You just do as he tells you. Once you've got the drugs in your hand, wipe that cunt off the face of the earth.'

'What kind of drugs?'

'Fucking aspirin, what do *you* think?' chided Parker. 'Cocaine, Frank, three hundred kilos of it.'

Drugs. Murder. Armed robbery. How much deeper do you want to go?

'I'm not *offering* you this job, Frank,' Parker said flatly. 'It isn't open to negotiation. This isn't a fucking union meeting. You're doing this to stay alive, remember? I'm *paying* you, when what I *should* be doing is redecorating this office with your fucking brains.'

Newton nodded almost imperceptibly.

'How's the kid?' Parker wanted to know.

'She's fine. Why?' There was a note of anxiety in Newton's voice.

'Just curious,' Parker murmured, his tone thick with menace. 'If you start having second thoughts, think about *her*. She can be taken away as easily as she was given, Frank. Like *everything* you've got.' He sipped his drink, the ice clinking against the glass. 'You've got a kid because of me. You're still alive because *I* decided you could be.' He leaned forward in his seat. 'I own you, Frank. I own the lease on your whole fucking life.'

Newton looked at the older man, his eyes narrowing slightly. The knot of muscles at the side of his jaw pulsed angrily.

'Now, you go and tell your boys the *new* deal,' Parker said. 'And if any of them want out, remind them that they're still alive because of me.' He looked down at his paperwork. 'I'll be in touch, Frank.'

Newton waited a moment, then got to his feet and moved towards the door. He glanced back in Parker's direction.

Fucking big shot.

'See you, Billy,' Newton muttered as he closed the door.

See you when all this is over.

72

HE COULD SMELL the fumes as he walked down the steps.

Frank Newton looked around the large amphitheatre that was Walthamstow racetrack.

Lost a few bob here in your time, eh?

The bowl-like construction seemed almost ghostly in the stillness of the afternoon. He thought how different it looked when it was full of people all shouting their dogs home, roaring delightedly or groaning dejectedly.

He knew both feelings; but his acquaintance with the latter was more intimate.

As he made his way down the steps towards the trackside, the smell of the fumes grew more powerful, as did the odour of wet sand from the track itself.

The fumes were coming from a small tractorlike contraption being driven round the track, dragging a large metal grid designed to flatten the sand. The driver, clad in white overalls, guided the machine carefully around the elliptical raceway.

Newton lit a cigarette and waited, watching as the carrier, fumes pumping from its overworked engine, turned into the home straight and began heading towards the winning post where he stood.

He waved.

Peter Morrissey waved back, switched off the engine and wandered across leaving footprints in the pristine sand.

'You're a bit early for the first meeting, Frank.' He chuckled.

Newton nodded.

'How'd you get in?' the former soldier asked.

'One of the side entrances was unlocked. That's *your* department, isn't it? Security?'

'And any other poxy job they can find for me.' He hooked a thumb over his shoulder in the direction of the small tractor.

Newton offered him a cigarette and he gratefully accepted.

'If you're looking for a tip, Frank – ' he grinned as he fished in his pocket for his lighter ' – try the three-dog in the second race tonight. I heard a couple of the kennel hands talking and—'

Newton cut him short. 'I spoke to Billy Parker this morning,' he said.

The grin slipped from Morrissey's face. 'What did he want?'

Newton explained.

'Shit.' Morrissey sighed when his companion had

finished. He lit the cigarette and drew hard on it. 'What did you tell him?'

'What the fuck do you think I told him? I said we'd do it.'

'Do the others know?'

'Not yet. I'm going to tell them now. And I think we should have a meet. Talk about it.'

'Why? We're doing the job, aren't we? If we all sit down to discuss it you know what'll happen. Jim'll shit himself. Ray'll jump at it and Jeff won't say fuck all.'

'You're probably right,' Newton agreed, managing a smile.

He wondered for a second if he should mention the baby.

Tell him about your daughter.

Then he thought better of it.

'When this is over, Pete, we're getting out,' he said. 'Me and Paula

(*and the baby*)

we're leaving London.'

'Where are you going?'

'Anywhere. Just away.'

'It sounds like a good idea. I don't blame you. But you've lived here all your life, Frank. Everything you've *got* is here.'

Newton grunted. 'Yeah. Perhaps that's why it won't be so hard to leave.'

'I'll talk to you later, Pete,' he said and headed back up the steps.

'Don't forget, Frank,' Morrissey called after him, his words echoing around the empty stadium. 'Tonight. The three-dog. Second race. It's a dead cert.'

But Newton was gone.

The drive to Laburnum Street took less time than he'd imagined. Traffic was fairly light and he reached the house in Haggerston just after three.

The huge gasworks silos towards the back of the houses rose like boils on contaminated flesh.

There was no answer at Jeff Hobbs's place.

Newton returned to the car and sat behind the wheel for a moment or two, wondering if he should simply sit and wait for his friend to return.

Finally, growing impatient with the vigil, he started the engine again.

He had an idea where Hobbs might be.

73

It WAS LIKE walking into an undertakers.

Newton was struck by the almost palpable silence inside the library on Appleby Street.

They're supposed to be quiet places, dummy.

There weren't more than three people visible and one of those was a woman who worked there. At least he assumed she did because of her name badge: THERESA.

He saw it as he passed.

The other two were wandering back and forth over the worn carpet; an old woman pulling a shopping trolley and a young lad in his late teens who was chewing the end of a biro as he walked.

Newton slowly wandered up and down the labyrinthine rows of books. Even his footsteps seemed intrusive in the stillness.

He turned a corner into the H–L fiction section and found a man in his sixties reading the blurb of a novel.

Newton passed him and headed towards non-fiction.

There was a number of tables set up in the reference part of the library. Daily newspapers were available for those who wished to read them.

It was at one of these tables he saw Jeff Hobbs.

He had a copy of the *Telegraph* spread out before him.

'I thought I might find you here,' Newton said quietly, pulling up a chair beside his friend.

Hobbs looked round. His expression of surprise gave way quickly to a smile. 'The books about racehorses are over there,' he said, nodding beyond Newton.

'Ha bloody ha,' Newton quipped. 'Next to the boxing books. But I suppose you've read all those, haven't you?'

Hobbs folded the paper.

'Can we talk in here?' Newton asked.

Hobbs pointed to a nearby sign: SILENCE PLEASE.

'Right, I'll talk quietly,' Newton told him.

Hobbs sat forward as his companion relayed the details of the meeting that morning with Parker.

Newton paused once when an old man ambled past the table and picked up one of the newspapers.

When he finally finished speaking, Hobbs was in the same position, arms folded before him.

'Well?' Newton said finally.

'Well what, Frank? You're not asking me if I *want* to do this job, you're telling me that you've agreed and we're *doing* it anyway.'

'We haven't got any choice.'

'I know that. I'm not arguing with you.'

'You know that, when this is all over, things are going to be different, Jeff.'

'If we're still alive,' Hobbs observed.

Newton shrugged. 'None of us should hang around here,' he murmured.

'That's what *I* was thinking. But then it's easier for me, I've got no responsibilities. No one to think about except myself. You've got Paula. Jim's got his wife and son. Jeff's got his dad to look after. Even Pete's got that young bird he's seeing. Perhaps I'm lucky being alone. I can up sticks and leave any time I want.'

'And will you?'

Hobbs looked in the direction of the raven-haired woman rearranging books on a shelf nearby, the woman with the badge that Newton had seen earlier.

'I come in here most days,' Hobbs said softly, his eyes never leaving the woman. 'I like the quiet. I love books. I always read a lot when I was inside. I see the same faces come in and out of here. I always see *her*.' He nodded towards Theresa. 'I usually speak to her. Just the usual bullshit, you know, "Nice morning." "How are you?" "Do you think it's going to rain?" "What kind of journey did you have today?" That kind of thing. When I first saw her wedding ring I thought that her husband was a lucky bastard.' He grinned. 'Then I found out that he'd left her. I was going to ask her if she wanted to go for a coffee. But then I thought, fuck it. *She* got hurt. If I get involved, *I* could get hurt. I'm better off alone, Frank. No one can hurt you when you're alone.'

Newton nodded almost imperceptibly.

'And, as far as the job goes,' Hobbs said, looking directly at his companion, 'I say, the sooner the better.'

74

'I CAN'T TAKE it any longer, Frank,' Ray Gorman said, head bowed. 'I know he's my dad, but he's got worse during the last couple of months. And no bastard wants to help him either.' The younger man clasped his hands together and rested them on the parapet. 'I call the social, but they couldn't give a shit,' he continued.

Frank Newton looked at his companion, then back at the half-open door of the flat.

'Once the job with Codling's done,' Gorman murmured, 'I can pay for Dad to be put somewhere they'll look after him properly.'

'And what will *you* do?' Newton wanted to know.

Gorman shook his head wearily. 'I haven't thought about it,' he answered. 'I don't want to leave London. I don't want to be too far away from the old man.'

'You might not have any choice, Ray. It'd make more sense to get as far away from here as possible. Until everything dies down.'

Gorman looked in the direction of the other blocks of flats that jabbed towards the sky like accusatory fingers. 'There's a girl in the flat underneath,' he began.

'She can't be more than seventeen. She's just had a kid.
I hear it crying some nights. Sometimes *all* night and I
hear her trying to keep it quiet. I heard her shouting at
it last night, about midnight. She went on for half an
hour. Just shouting, telling it to shut up. Then, it all
went quiet. No crying, no shouting, nothing.' He took a
drag on his cigarette. 'Christ knows what she did, Frank.
She could have killed the bloody kid for all I know. And
even if she had, no one would give a toss. Not the social
services. Not anyone who lives round here. Probably not
even the fucking law. The worse thing about it was I
understood how she felt. All she wanted was for the kid
to stop crying.' He looked at Newton. 'All I want is for
my dad to be where he'll be comfortable. And, yeah,
perhaps I am being selfish about it, but I want that
because I want *my* fucking life back. Not that I had
much of one before. I can't start living until he's gone.
Until he's not my responsibility anymore. Do you think
that's wrong, Frank?'

Newton shook his head.

'I'll steal drugs for Billy Parker and I'd kill Codling
and everyone with him to get out of here,' Gorman
confessed. 'This is the life I've got *left*.'

He took one final drag on his cigarette, then tossed
the butt over the parapet, watching as it hurtled towards
the ground below.

It was late afternoon by the time Frank Newton reached
the Golden Lane estate.

He found a parking space behind a beaten up old Mini and sat behind the Peugeot's wheel for a moment, the cassette still playing inside his own car.

'. . . *What a storm is threatening, my very life today . . .*'

Newton had a fairly good idea what James Carson's reaction to Parker's latest proposition would be.

'. . . *If I don't get some shelter, I'm going to fade away . . .*'

He turned off the engine and swung himself out of the car.

The house had a small but immaculately tended front garden. The little square of lawn resembled a piece of bowling green; not one single blade of stray grass intruded over the borders.

Newton smiled to himself.

Good old Jim.

He knocked and waited.

And waited.

Checked his watch and knocked again.

He was about to turn and head back to the car when he heard sounds of movement on the other side of the door.

It opened a crack and Gary Carson peered out at him; dressed in combat trousers and a Tommy Hilfiger T-shirt, he was sucking on a roll-up.

He ran appraising eyes over Newton, but didn't speak.

'Is your dad around, Gary?' Newton asked.

Gary shook his head, looking bemused that this stranger should know his name. 'Who are you?' he wanted to know.

'A friend of your dad's. I wanted to talk to him.'

'He's out. I don't know when he'll be back.'

'Do you know where he is?'

Gary shrugged.

Newton turned away. 'Get him to call me when he gets in, will you?' he asked. 'I need to talk to him about some work.'

'What's your name?'

'Frank Newton. He's got my number.'

Gary's eyes widened.

Newton. Frank fucking Newton.

No need to nudge. No need to hold. Three fucking bars.

Jackpot.

He watched as Newton walked back to the waiting Peugeot, then he closed the door, a grin spreading across his face.

75

DI JOHN RIDLEY heard the tapping on his office door and looked up. Detective Sergeant Darren Brown paused at the threshold before his superior beckoned him inside.

'What have you got?' Ridley said wearily. 'You've come to tell me you've arrested Thomas and Smith and they've identified the other three men?'

'Sorry, guv, no.'

'Fuck it, sit down anyway.'

Ridley massaged the back of his neck. He could feel the tightness there, creeping towards the base of his skull. In another half-hour he'd have a headache. He fumbled in his pocket for the strip of Nurofen he always carried, but came out with just empty foil.

'Shit,' he grunted and tossed it into his bin.

'I've been thinking,' Brown said.

Ridley applauded exaggeratedly and Brown eyed him irritably for a moment.

'Go on,' the DI said, reaching for a cigarette.

'Hendon have got no record of any prints that match the ones we're looking for, right?'

'Tell me something I *don't* know.'

'If there's no record, then the killers have never been done before, because if they *had*, then their prints would be on file.'

'Is there a punchline?'

'They've never been caught in *this* country, that's why Hendon haven't got them on file.'

Ridley regarded his companion silently this time.

'We're assuming that whoever killed Hadfield, Bovell and the others are Yardies. Now if we're right—'

'Then their prints could be on file somewhere else,' Ridley interrupted.

Brown nodded. 'Somewhere we know the Yardies are already established,' he mused.

'That could be anywhere in the world,' Ridley said dismissively.

'They're predominantly Jamaican, everybody knows that.'

'And there are posses in the States too,' Ridley replied. 'They've been linked with everyone from the Colombian drug cartels to the fucking IRA.'

'We've got to start somewhere. Let's start with Jamaica.'

Ridley didn't answer, merely stroked his chin thoughtfully.

'Let's at least give it a try,' Brown persisted. 'What can we lose?'

'It's not much to work with.'

'It's more than we've fucking got now,' Brown snarled.

The two men regarded each other warily for long moments.

'So what are you going to do?' the DI finally asked.

'Fax the three sets of unidentified prints to the Jamaica Constabulary Force. See what they send back.'

'OK, do it,' the DI instructed, watching as his companion got to his feet. 'What are you looking for out of this, Brown?'

The DS looked perplexed.

'A promotion?' Ridley wanted to know. 'Is that what you're after?'

'I'm just doing my job, guv.'

Ridley nodded. 'Are you sure it's not *my* job you'd like to be doing?' he asked.

Brown closed the door behind him as he left.

The phone rang. Ridley waited a moment before picking it up.

'Hello,' he said, still massaging the back of his neck.

The voice at the other end sounded excitable; Ridley had trouble recognizing it at first.

'Slow down,' he said. '*Who's* been to the house?'

'Frank Newton,' Gary Carson told him.

'Are you sure?'

'He left his name, told my old man to ring him. Something about work.'

Ridley sat forward in his seat, gripping the receiver so tightly it seemed he would snap it in two. 'How long ago?' he wanted to know.

'Two or three hours.'

'And you're sure it was him.'

'He said his name was Frank Newton. Why would he give a false name?'

'Describe him.'

'For fuck's sake, he—'

'*Now*,' rasped the policeman.

Carson did as he was told.

Ridley nodded to himself as he listened.

'Is that it now?' Carson wanted to know.

'What are you talking about?'

'Are we square now? You said you wanted to get to Newton. I've given him to you. That's the deal.'

'*I'll* tell you when I've finished with *you*, you little shit. Just keep your stinking ears and eyes open. And you let me know what*ever* you hear. Got it?'

He hung up.

76

'AND WE'RE SUPPOSED to trust this cunt?' Ray Gorman murmured, running appraising eyes over the front of the house.

'No one says we have to trust him,' Frank Newton reminded his colleague. 'Just work with him.'

'And then kill him,' James Carson added quietly.

Newton nodded. 'That's right, Jim. Then kill him,' he echoed.

The three of them clambered out of the Peugeot.

Newton looked a little further down the street and saw Peter Morrissey and Jeff Hobbs. The ex-army man was making sure the door of the Astra was firmly locked.

'Lots of criminals around these days.' He grinned and dropped the keys into his pocket.

Hobbs nodded. 'I know, that's how *I* started,' he said. 'Hubcaps first, then the whole car.'

Both men were smiling as they joined their three companions.

'What's so funny?' Gorman enquired.

'We were just reminiscing,' Morrissey told him. 'Is

that it, Frank?' He nodded towards the house across the street.

Newton took a drag on his cigarette and nodded. 'Let's go and talk to Mr Codling,' he murmured.

'Are you sure it's the right house?' Gorman wanted to know.

'It's the address Billy Parker gave me. Northern Avenue in Lower Edmonton,' Newton informed him.

'Shouldn't we have met them somewhere more ... neutral?' Gorman asked.

'Don't worry about it,' Morrissey assured his companion. He patted his jacket, pulling it aside slightly to reveal the Beretta 9mm nestling in the shoulder holster there.

'You take it easy, Pete,' Newton said to him. 'All we're going to do is talk. For the time being.'

'Five white boys coming,' Skeng announced, watching from one of the first-floor windows.

Codling joined him and peered out, running appraising eyes over the group crossing the street. 'Let's go see who Mr Billy Parker sent us,' he remarked, making his way towards the stairs.

His footsteps echoed on the bare floor as he walked – indeed, the entire house was without carpets. Like many along Northern Avenue, it had been boarded up when Codling had found it.

Perfect.

There were three large bedrooms, a bathroom and an

airing cupboard on the first floor. Downstairs, the lower level consisted of a large living room, a kitchen, a utility room and, even more convenient for the Jamaicans' purposes, a hatch that led down to a massive cellar.

They stored their weapons there: the '16s, the Ingrams, the 'machines'.

Tools of the trade.

Only the most rudimentary home comforts had been installed since Codling took charge of the building. After all, as far as he was concerned, this was only temporary. After the job was done, after his other business concerns were taken care of, then would be the time for luxury. Time to throw money around. Time to live like a king.

Everything was there for the taking. Nothing and no one was going to get in his way.

No God could help them if they did.

He passed Aston Thomas on the stairs and made his way into the living room.

Toad was stationed at the window too, watching Newton and his companions as they drew closer. He tapped the butt of the .357 Desert Eagle jammed into his belt. 'You should have asked Parker to come with them,' he said. 'We could have taken care of him now.'

'I got plenty time to deal with Mr Parker,' Codling assured him.

As he spoke he glanced over his shoulder in the direction of the door that led to the kitchen.

Dudley Smith stood there, the Viking SOS automatic shotgun gripped in his large hands. He worked the slide, chambering one of the lethal twelve-gauge shells.

'You wait.' Codling grinned. 'I call when I need you.'

Smith disappeared into the kitchen.

There was a loud knock on the front door.

Codling nodded to Toad.

As he heard the door being opened he allowed his hand to slip inside his jacket.

His fingers gently brushed against the cold metal of the 9mm Sig P220 automatic.

The safety catch was already off.

77

Frank Newton barely took his eyes off Codling as
he spoke.

*Not every day you get the chance to have a good look at
a man you're going to kill, is it?*

Peter Morrissey, leaning against the wall close to the
bay window, was more concerned with the layout of the
place. He studied every crack in the paintwork, every
chipped tile around the fireplace.

The location of the doors and windows.

Just in case.

His eyes were constantly scanning the room and its
occupants.

He was well aware that Toad was reciprocating. The
black man's gaze moving slowly from face to face as if
trying to memorize each of Morrissey's companions.

It was warm inside the room.

The heat of the day didn't help, but the sheer presence of eight men in such an enclosed space seemed to
increase the discomfort.

James Carson had wandered into the hall once or

twice, there to be confronted by either Skeng or Thomas.

Skeng had now joined the others in the living room. He sat on a chair behind the sofa upon which Codling was ensconced.

Carson and the others could hear Thomas moving about upstairs, walking from room to room on floorboards that creaked protestingly under his weight.

What was he doing up there?

'And you want to gamble everything that the couriers are coming in on these flights?' Newton said when Codling finally finished speaking.

'This is no gamble, man,' the Jamaican assured him. 'I *know*. The three of them will be on the flights I told you.'

'Assuming you're right . . .' Newton continued.

'You don't have to *assume* nothing,' Codling snapped. 'I telling you, that is the way it going to be.'

'He don't believe like his boss don't believe,' Skeng added and the three black men laughed.

Newton eyed them silently.

Maybe it won't be so hard to pull the trigger on you fuckers after all.

'Run through it again, from the beginning,' he said finally.

'You have trouble understanding English?' Codling chuckled. 'How many times you want me to tell you?'

'I want *your* boys to be sure what they're doing too,' Newton told him through clenched teeth. 'If they fuck up, we're not hanging around for them. I'm not getting caught because a bunch of fucking jungle bunnies can't handle themselves.'

Skeng sat forward on his chair, one hand sliding inside his jacket.

Toad took a step towards Newton.

Morrissey moved away from the window to block his advance.

Gorman slipped one hand into the pocket of his own jacket.

Codling and Newton continued to glare at each other, apparently oblivious to what was going on around them.

'Leave it,' said Newton finally.

Codling nodded.

'Now,' Newton continued, gesturing towards the Jamaican. 'From the beginning.'

'The first courier flies in from Chicago,' Codling began. 'The second from Washington. The third, she come in from New York.'

'You never said one of them was a woman,' Newton interjected.

'So what it matter to you?' Codling grinned. 'I take care of her, if you can't.'

'You really *don't* give a fuck, do you?' the older man observed, a note of distaste in his voice.

What had Parker said? 'No honour. No code. Animals.'

'We talking about twenty million. Is one more life. Is nothing,' Codling sneered. He blew on his fingertips. 'Gone like that for twenty million.'

'And then what?' Morrissey wanted to know.

'Once the couriers land,' Codling continued, 'they pick up their luggage. They travel to separate hotels. They plan to fly out again the next day.'

Newton listened in silence.

'We follow them to their hotels,' the big Jamaican said. 'Take the drugs. Split them up. Everyone happy.' He grinned.

'It sounds too easy,' Newton grunted.

'Everything easy when you know what you doing,' Codling told him.

'Do the couriers know each other?' Newton asked.

Codling shook his head.

'What if you miss the marks?' Morrissey said.

Codling looked bemused.

'The couriers. What if you're wrong about them?' Newton continued. 'What if we end up following the wrong three people? What if they're not even on those flights? What if they get stopped at customs?'

'I told you, let *me* worry about that.'

'Well, you make fucking sure you get it right,' Newton said, his voice thick with menace. 'If anything goes wrong, we're not going down with you.'

'Mr Billy Parker, he tell you to do as I say, right?' Codling mused.

Newton nodded.

'Then fucking do it,' the Jamaican rasped. 'I tell you that's the way it going down, then that's the way it going down. Understand?'

'Two days from now?' Newton said flatly.

'We all be rich men.' The Jamaican laughed.

And you'll be a fucking dead man.

Newton nodded. 'Two days,' he murmured.

78

'I THOUGHT I heard you come in.'

Patricia Ridley pulled her dressing gown more tightly around her and padded into the sitting room.

'Sorry, I didn't mean to wake you,' her husband apologized.

'I wasn't asleep.'

'You should have taken one of your tablets,' he offered.

'Now you're home I probably won't need them. It's when you're not here I find it difficult to sleep. Funny that, you'd have thought I'd have been used to it by now, wouldn't you? You not being here.'

As he turned away from her Ridley rolled his eyes. It was an anticipatory gesture; he knew what was coming next.

'You were gone before I woke up this morning,' she reminded him. 'What time did you leave?'

'About seven. I had some paperwork I wanted to clear.'

She nodded. 'Do you want to know what *I* did today?'

she asked. 'Do you want to hear about the exciting things *I* got up to?'

He regarded her impassively. 'Tell me,' he said dutifully.

'Only if you can spare the time, John. I know it's not as important as *your* work, but—'

He cut her short. 'For Christ's sake, Pat, just say what you want to say,' the DI snapped.

'I spoke to my mother.'

'How is she?'

'Oh, *she's* fine. The problem is my father.'

Ridley waited expectantly.

'He's been suffering from chest pains for the last couple of months on and off,' Patricia continued. 'They did some X-rays.'

'And?'

'There were shadows on both lungs. They think it's cancer.'

'Christ, I'm sorry, Pat.' He got to his feet and crossed to her, snaking an arm around her shoulder.

'They want to perform a biopsy,' she told him.

'When?'

'As soon as possible.'

'It might not be cancer, Pat, it—'

'I want to be with him, John,' she interrupted.

Ridley nodded.

'I thought we could stay for a few days, just until he's out of hospital.'

'That's a good idea. You go.'

'No. Not just me. *Us*.'

'I can't, Pat. It's impossible. Not now.'

'Then when, John? When would *anything* ever fit into your timetable that didn't involve work?'

Ridley sighed. 'I'm not going to get into this again,' he said dismissively. 'You go. Be with your parents. It's *you* they need, not me.'

'But *I* need you. Doesn't that matter?'

'If I could come, I would.'

She looked at him for long moments, then got to her feet. 'I'll leave in the morning,' she said quietly.

'Take as long as you need,' he intoned, attempting to inject a note of concern into his voice.

'Thanks,' she murmured bitterly. 'That's so good of you, John.'

'It might be best if we had a few days rest from each other,' Ridley offered, his smile forced and unconvincing.

'Best for who? At least you won't have me nagging you when you get home, will you? You could sleep at the Yard. I'm sure you'd feel more at home there.'

Ridley looked away from her.

'I don't know how long I'll be gone, John.'

'I told you, take as long as you need.'

'And when I come back? Are things going to be different between us?'

He looked at her warily for a moment.

'If I stay for two days, two weeks or two months, the job will still be there, won't it? Your obsession.'

He nodded.

'What are you going to do when it's all over, John? When there *is* no job? When you retire? What then?'

'I haven't thought about it.'

'Why? Because you're afraid? There isn't that long left for you. What is it now, seven or eight years until you retire? It'll soon pass. And then what will you have?'

He regarded her with something akin to anger.

'Is that why you love the job so much?' she asked venomously. 'Because you're afraid of what you'll be without it? Afraid how empty your life will be?'

Ridley didn't answer, merely watched as she made her way to the sitting-room door.

'Don't bother to wake me when you leave in the morning,' she told him. 'I'll leave a message on the answer-phone when I get to my parents. I wouldn't want to disturb you.'

And she was gone.

79

THE COLOURFUL FIGURES danced their mechanical dance on the mobile above the little girl's cot. Frank Newton stood watching as the Teletubbies moved slowly round in time to the strains of 'Twinkle Twinkle, Little Star'.

Beneath them, Danielle was sleeping soundly.

My girl.

He reached in, thought about touching the soft skin of her cheek, then feared he might wake her.

Newton retreated from the room, pulling the door closed behind him. He made his way downstairs to the living room, where Paula was gazing blankly at the TV.

'She's fine,' Newton announced, slumping in the chair opposite. 'Must have been dreaming.'

Paula regarded him silently for a moment, the only sounds in the room being the television and the steady buzz of the baby monitor.

'Do you think Codling was telling the truth?' she asked finally.

Newton nodded almost imperceptibly. 'He's a dead man either way,' he said flatly.

'Unless he gets you first, Frank.'

'He's not going to try and kill us *before* the job, is he? And, once it's done, that's it . . .' He allowed the sentence to trail off.

'As simple as that?'

'Hopefully.'

'What's the next step?'

'We meet with a couple of Billy Parker's men at the lock-up tomorrow. They'll supply us with the guns for the job. They'll hand over the car keys for the motors we'll use.'

'What if Parker's setting you up?'

'There's no need for him to. Why go round the houses rigging a set-up when he could have just blown us away the minute he found out *we* were the ones who nicked his money?'

Another heavy silence descended.

'In thirty-six hours all this'll be over,' Newton exclaimed. 'One way or another.'

'And then?'

The words hung in the air, like the last breaths of a dying man.

You could see your face in them.

Jeff Hobbs smiled as he inspected the sparkling leather.

He'd placed two pieces of newspaper carefully on the kitchen table to protect the surface while he cleaned the boots: the last of his tasks before he went to bed.

He'd ironed a white shirt and a pair of black jeans, sponged down one sleeve of his leather jacket.

All done.

Everything was ready.

He felt tired, but doubted if he'd be able to sleep.

There was a documentary on BBC2 about Sugar Ray Robinson he'd watch before retiring. Perhaps take a milky drink to bed too; it sometimes helped.

Sometimes.

If not, he would read until sleep overtook him.

Hobbs began clearing away the polish and the brushes, storing them carefully in the red plastic box reserved for them.

He blinked hard, his vision blurring slightly in his left eye.

The old injury.

Images swam in and out of focus and he kept his eyes closed.

He gently touched the eye, opened it carefully; still a little fuzzy, but the clarity was returning.

He waited a moment longer, then continued with his tidying.

The old man was asleep.

Ray Gorman was thankful for that.

He sat in his chair watching the steady rise and fall of his father's chest. The movement was occasionally interrupted by a shudder or a slight cough, but not enough to wake him.

Gorman reached for the remote control and eased the volume of the TV down.

Best not to wake him.

As he watched, his gaze strayed to the colostomy bag; it was three-quarters full with dark liquid.

Gorman knew he'd have to change it soon.

Soon.

He got to his feet, hearing his neck bones creak as he tilted his head, first to one side, then the other.

As he passed his father he reached out with one hand and touched the old man tenderly on the shoulder.

Colin Gorman stirred slightly, but did not wake.

There was blood everywhere.

As Peter Morrissey knelt beside the youth he could see that his shirt was soaked in the crimson fluid that was pouring from so many gashes in his face.

There was more on the wall, on the floor and on a table close by. There were even a few specks of it on Morrissey's black jacket.

He'd claim the dry-cleaning bill back from the club.

That was only fair.

Above the thudding bassline of the music inside the club he could hear nothing.

Not even the girl in the white dress screaming only feet from him – at least it had, at one time, been white. Large portions of it were now spattered with her boyfriend's blood.

He looked at the girl and it seemed as if she was screaming in silence.

Several of her friends were trying to comfort her. One was even pointing to the remains of the glass that had been rammed into her boyfriend's face.

The lethal weapon was on one end of the bar, the jagged edges stained red.

Morrissey had no idea why the glassing had happened. It just had.

Things like that were par for the course in clubs and pubs.

The former soldier was trying to tell the youth that there was an ambulance on the way, but he could barely hear himself speak. And the recipient of his concern was past caring anyway.

The younger man was slumped back against the bar, eyes half closed, a portion of glass protruding from his left cheek.

Morrissey exhaled deeply.

It looked like being a long fucking night.

The music hammered on.

The girl continued screaming soundlessly.

James Carson dried the crockery carefully and laid it on the kitchen table.

Then he took the cutlery from the drainer and began wiping the moisture from each knife, fork and spoon.

He was alone in the house.

Angie was at bingo.

Gary was . . .

Christ alone knew where Gary was.

He put each utensil into its appointed place in the drawer, placed each dried plate, cup and saucer back in the right cupboard.

It would save Angie a job when she got home.

It was the least he could do.

She'd be home in less than an hour. He'd try to look more cheerful when she arrived; he didn't want to burden her with his worries.

It wasn't his way – never had been.

As he placed the teatowel over the radiator to dry, he wondered whether or not to wander down to the local for a quick pint before last orders.

He decided against it. He wasn't very good company at the moment.

They both heard the crying through the monitor.

'I'll go,' Paula said, getting to her feet.

Newton touched her hand as she passed him on her way upstairs.

Through the monitor he could hear Danielle's mournful little cries, then Paula's soft, reassuring voice quietening her.

His wife and daughter.

His family.

He tried to convince himself that what he was preparing to do he was doing for them.

It didn't work.

80

IT LOOKED LIKE a fucking armoury.

Guns everywhere.

Frank Newton took a drag on his cigarette and stood gazing at the awesome array of firepower before him.

Both tables in the lock-up were covered with the instruments of destruction, on display as if on offer at some maniacal car-boot sale.

Pistols. Rifles. Sub-machine-guns. Shotguns.

The only thing missing was a howitzer.

He was sure that if Ian and Stephen Milliner could have found one they would have brought that too.

Ian was the youngest of the two brothers employed by Billy Parker, his closest and most trusted of bodyguards. Newton had known them, or at least known *of* them, for as long as he'd been in the business. Both had form, both had done time for everything ranging from GBH to attempted murder.

Neither had been brought to justice for the numerous killings they had *actually* carried out; some at the behest of their employer, others for their own reasons.

They didn't bear much of a resemblance to one

another considering they were blood-kin. Separated by just eighteen months, Ian was tall and thin faced with almost disproportionately large hands. His sibling, Stephen, was shorter, stockier.

If they did share a characteristic, Newton noted, it was their eyes: blue, almost hypnotic.

'When you've finished with these,' the younger Milliner said, making a sweeping gesture over the weapons, 'we want them back, right? And don't fucking damage them.'

'You bastards know how to use them, I hope,' Stephen interjected.

Newton and his colleagues nodded.

Morrissey chuckled.

'What's so fucking funny?' Ian wanted to know.

The former soldier shook his head. 'Nothing.' He smiled. 'What do you recommend?'

Ian Milliner regarded him balefully for a second, then reached for an automatic pistol. 'Zastava, Model 70,' he said, passing it to Morrissey. 'Eight-round clip. They do it as a .32 as well as a 9mm. It's Yugoslavian. With all that shit that's been happening out there, we get hold of their old army and police gear without any trouble.'

'What about this?' Gorman enquired. He was pointing at a fearsome-looking pump-action shotgun.

Stephen passed it to him and Gorman felt the weight.

'Spas Model 12,' the elder Milliner informed him. 'Twelve gauge. Takes five rounds. With the butt folded, you can hook this bit over your shoulder – ' he indicated a curved piece of tubular metal that extended from the base of the stock ' – and fire with one hand. But you'd better hang on because it kicks like fuck.'

'Same as the Ithaca?' Morrissey asked, indicating another slide-action shotgun with a pistol grip and no stock.

'Yeah,' Ian told him. 'That holds eight rounds. You could blow a hole in a wall with both of those.'

Newton picked up a sub-machine-gun and hefted it, surprised at its lightness.

'That's a beautiful little gun,' the younger Milliner observed. 'Heckler & Koch MP5. Nine mill again. Takes a fifteen- or thirty-round mag. Fires over six hundred and fifty rounds a minute. The Kraut police use them. So do the SAS. You can fit it in a shoulder holster it's so small.'

'We've got our own gear too,' Newton told the brothers.

'What you got?' Stephen demanded.

'Automatics.'

'What kind?'

'Berettas. Smith and Wessons. We've got a couple of Leland 210s.'

'Sawn off?' the elder Milliner asked, a smirk on his face.

Newton nodded.

'Fuck that,' Stephen said dismissively. 'That's amateur. If you're going to use shotguns, use the Spas and the Ithaca. The shot doesn't spread. It hits in one fucking great lump.' He punched his palm with his other fist. 'Sawn-offs are OK for frightening old ladies in building societies. But then, you never got further than that, did you, Frank?' He and his brother laughed.

Newton eyed the men impassively and blew a stream of smoke in their direction.

Stephen fished in his jacket pocket and pulled out four sets of car keys. He tossed them onto the table one at a time.

'The motors are all stone cold,' he said. 'If you get caught in them, they can't be traced back to us. Same with the guns.'

'What made me think you were going to say that?' Newton chided and it was the turn of the others to laugh.

'You'd better make sure you *don't* get caught,' the elder Milliner rasped. 'Not until the job's done. Billy wants that black cunt Codling dead and it's down to you. If you fuck it up, you'd better hope *they* kill you, because you *know* we will.'

Newton picked up the Ithaca, worked the slide and pulled the shotgun into his shoulder, aiming it at Stephen Milliner. He pulled the trigger and the hammer slammed down on an empty chamber. 'Bang,' he mouthed.

Milliner glared at him. 'You wouldn't have the guts, Frank,' he snarled.

Try me, you cunt. Just you fucking try me.

Newton allowed the shotgun to swing down.

'When you go after Codling and his boys, load all your pistols and sub-guns with these,' Ian Milliner said, placing a handful of bullets on the table. 'We've got boxes of them outside.'

Morrissey picked up one of the rounds and turned it between his fingers. 'Hollow points,' he murmured.

'That's right. They spread on impact,' the younger Milliner observed. 'If you *really* want to make sure, you can always try rubbing garlic on them too. If you don't kill the bastards outright, they'll die of blood poisoning anyway.' He grinned crookedly. 'The geezers who did the St Valentine's Day Massacre did that.'

The two brothers turned and headed for the door of the lock-up.

'Thanks for the history lesson,' Newton mused, still cradling the shotgun.

'Fucking pricks,' muttered Gorman under his breath.

Stephen Milliner paused at the door and turned, looking at each of the men, his gaze finally coming to rest on Newton. 'There's one more thing,' the elder Milliner said, quietly. 'When all this is over, Billy wants proof that Codling's dead.'

'What kind of proof?' Newton asked.

Milliner grinned. 'His head.'

81

Detective Inspector John Ridley saw the fax as he entered his office. It lay on his desk like an invitation.

He crossed to it, rubbing his eyes, wondering whether or not he should get a coffee from the vending machine at the end of the corridor before he read it. He hadn't slept well the night before. He needed more caffeine; the hurried cup of Maxwell House he'd downed at home earlier in the morning hadn't been enough.

He felt in his pocket for change to feed the machine, then noticed the heading on the cover sheet: ROYAL JAMAICA CONSTABULARY.

He looked at the date and time in the top right-hand corner of the first page. The fax had arrived about three hours ago.

Fuck it, the coffee could wait.

He sat down and shuffled the fax into a semblance of order.

There were eighteen pages.

He leafed through them quickly at first, aware that his heart was beating that little bit quicker.

Arrest reports.

Statements.

Prison records.

Photographs.

Even preliminary photo-fits.

Jesus Christ, he'd struck the motherlode.

Without taking his eyes off the first page, Ridley reached for his phone, jabbed an internal number and waited.

It was ringing.

He continued flicking through the flimsy sheets, the phone wedged between his ear and shoulder.

Still no answer.

He slammed the phone back onto the cradle and turned his full attention to the material before him.

The three photo-fits he separated and laid out side by side on the desktop beside the pictures of the three men. For a moment he marvelled at how alike the photo-fits and the actual photos were.

Beneath each one he arranged the corresponding arrest reports and, where applicable, prison records.

It was like assembling a huge jigsaw. The only difference being, he had absolutely no idea of what the finished picture was going to look like.

Beneath the arrest reports and prison records he placed the three sets of fingerprints, then he studied each face individually.

One was broad featured, almost jowly. The second was thinner faced with heavily lidded eyes.

The third glared back at him defiantly; a hint of a smile at the corners of his wide mouth.

There were copies of articles from the *Daily Gleaner*, Jamaica's leading broadsheet. More pictures accompanying the text.

Pictures of two men lying dead in a rubbish-strewn street in Kingston's Denham Town.

He scanned the articles, reaching for the phone once more and stabbing the same digits he'd pressed before.

Ringing.

Come on.

'DS Brown,' the voice at the other end answered.

'It's Ridley.' All the time he spoke his eyes never left the sheets of fax paper. 'Come up to my office now. There's something I want you to see.'

82

Ridley sat back in his chair as he watched Brown reading one of the arrest reports. The DI wore the smug grin of a gambler who has just turned over his cards to reveal a winning hand.

He himself was tapping almost unconsciously at the photo of the third man, the one with the hint of a smile on his lips.

Ernest Malcolm Codling; aka Papa Ernie.

'And the prints match?' Brown asked, still skimming through the scattered pieces of paper.

'All three sets,' Ridley attested.

'It's a good job we got in touch with the Jamaican police,' the DS observed, regarding Ridley over the top of one sheet.

The older man nodded almost imperceptibly, virtually ignoring the statement. 'We'd have found them eventually,' he said dismissively.

Brown eyed him angrily.

Just an acknowledgement of the wisdom of the idea was all he required.

No pats on the back. No bloody medals.

Ridley met his gaze and held it.

Would one word of praise be too much to ask? Or, God forbid, a thank you? A 'well done'?

'There's no doubt Codling's the leader,' Ridley observed, returning to the information before him. 'The brains behind it.'

'He was wanted for six murders in Jamaica, but they could never find enough evidence to convict him. All the witnesses either disappeared or just refused to give evidence in court.'

'Same old story,' Ridley mused.

'Vassell and Gardner have both done time,' the DS read. 'Lawrence Vassell, aka Skeng. A three-stretch for possession and six months for threatening behaviour. Warren Gardner, aka Toad. Four years for armed robbery. Knifed a prisoner, thought to be a member of a rival posse, while inside and they added another year to his sentence. Both served their terms in Kingston General Penitentiary.'

'But no one could nail Codling. The Jamaican police knew he was mixed up in everything from murder to gun-running, but they couldn't make anything stick.'

These newspaper articles talk about gang war in Kingston. Do you reckon Codling was *pushed* out by a more powerful faction?'

Ridley shrugged. 'Difficult to say,' he murmured. 'And not really our problem. *Our* problem is that he's *here* now.'

'They think he entered the UK on a false passport about six months ago.'

'That wouldn't be hard, would it? Enough of the fucking things get stolen over there every year.'

'Vassell and Gardner came in the same way. On stolen or forged passports.'

'And they set up here,' Ridley said flatly.

'Codling must have had contacts over here.'

Ridley shrugged. 'Perhaps Vassell and Gardner came over first, checked things out. Got the lay of the land,' he offered.

'Well, he must be well connected somewhere. How else would he have got access to the sort of firepower he used against Wendell Hadfield?'

'Like I said, he's the brains. He knows what he's doing.'

'If the Jamaican police wanted him that badly, how the hell did he ever get out of the country?'

'Private plane? Boat? It depends how good his contacts were.'

'So now we have to find him,' Brown mused.

Ridley tapped the photo of Codling, staring into those piercing eyes glaring back at him. 'We'll get him,' said the DI, an air of conviction in his voice. 'Him *and* his boys. Now at least we know who we're looking for.' He traced the outline of Codling's lips with one index finger. 'Let's see if you're still smiling when we catch you, you piece of shit.'

83

'HOW'D YOU GET this number?' Billy Parker sat forward at his desk in the office above 'Sensations'.

He could hear laughter at the other end of the line.

Below him, the squeal of a high-powered sander reverberated around the still-unfinished club. The sound was punctuated every now and then by the slightly less shrill note of a drill and the occasional thud of a nail-gun.

Paul Palmer looked across at his employer and shrugged as he nodded towards the phone.

'Codling,' Parker said. 'I asked how you got this number.'

'Does it matter?' the Jamaican wanted to know. 'I needed to talk to you, Mr Parker.'

'What about?'

'I got the times of the flights for tomorrow into Heathrow. The ones carrying the couriers.'

'What the fuck are you telling *me* for? You're doing the job with Newton. Phone *him*.'

'I thought you might want to know.'

Parker gripped the phone more tightly, the knot of muscles at the side of his jaw pulsing angrily.

'And I can't find Newton's number,' Codling continued. 'I thought you might pass the information on for me.'

More laughter.

'What am I? A fucking messenger service?' Parker snarled.

'Just listen carefully, Mr Parker,' Codling chided, his voice mocking. 'Listen to Papa Ernie.'

Frank Newton nodded as he wrote.

Flight numbers.

Arrival times.

He scribbled them all on the small pad next to the phone.

'Got that?' Parker asked finally.

'Yeah.'

'Good. Don't fuck it up.'

'Billy,' Newton said quickly, before the other man could hang up.

'What now?'

'When the job's done, do you want us to bring the drugs straight to you?'

'No. I want you to stand on street corners giving them away to anyone who fucking asks for them.'

'I mean, do you want us to sort out the coke before we take care of Codling?'

'Frank, I couldn't give a fuck *when* you kill that bastard. Just make sure that, by midnight tomorrow, he's as dead as fucking Elvis. Got it?'

'There's one more thing, Billy.'

'I'm a busy man, Frank.'

'One of the Milliner boys said you wanted proof Codling was dead.'

'Is that a problem?'

'He said you wanted his head.'

It was Parker's turn to chuckle. 'You ever seen a film called *Bring Me the Head of Alfredo Garcia*, Frank?'

'No.'

'It's a great film. You'd like it. It's about this rich Mexican geezer whose daughter's been knocked up by this other spic. And he wants him dead. So he pays men to find Alfredo Garcia, the guy who's shagged his daughter, and he offers a reward for his head. He wants the head as proof that Garcia's dead.' His tone grew darker. 'And the funny thing is, it's some right loser who ends up getting the head and bringing it to him.' There was venom in the words by now. 'A loser just like you, Frank.'

He hung up.

84

Ridley watched in silence as Police Commissioner Noel Pritchard leafed slowly through the fax communication.

His face was expressionless. Occasionally he stroked at one cheek with his index finger, but other than that he sat at his desk scanning the material with an air of indifference.

Ridley felt like a student awaiting a judgement on a piece of work he'd produced.

Say something, for Christ's sake.

The silence was beginning to irritate him, punctuated, as it was, only by the gentle rustle of turning pages.

Pritchard continued reading. It seemed to the DI that his superior had already scanned the pages more than once.

What was he trying to do? Memorize the fucking things?

'It seems fairly conclusive,' the commissioner said finally, his eyes still riveted to the fax.

Hallelujah!

'I did tell you when we spoke before, sir, that I thought the Yardies were extending their powerbase,'

Ridley reminded him. 'That was why I wanted the extra men. This confirms it.'

'I'm still not prepared to commit more men to this investigation, John,' the Scot announced.

'Why not? What more do you need?'

'I appreciate the work you've done on this, but as I told you before, if we flood the streets of predominantly black areas of London with uniformed men then we have a lot more than a bloody gang war to contend with. And I am *not* prepared to do that.'

'Even if it means catching Codling and closing the Yardies down?'

Pritchard met his angry stare and held it. 'Removing Codling isn't going to get rid of the Yardies. You know that.'

'But it'll take away the leader of the most powerful black criminal faction in the city. With him gone they'll lose their figurehead.'

'They'll find another.'

'Not as powerful as Codling.'

'According to this, he entered the country on a fake passport. If *he* can do it, so can others. If he *was* chased out of Jamaica, then whoever chased him might just fancy their *own* chances over here.'

'The reports are inconclusive on that, sir. Codling was a powerful man out there. I don't think anyone *forced* him to leave. He came to England because he knew he wouldn't have any bother taking over here. There was no serious opposition for him. What there was, he's wiped out by now.' Ridley lit a cigarette and drew on it. 'Before he arrived,' the DI said, 'the Yardies weren't that well organized. It took a man like Codling to sort them out. These small-time pushers and pimps that have been turning up dead, they were the dregs. He's been cleaning house. Getting rid of his competitors, but streamlining the bastards too. If he's going to be stopped, sir, I *need* more men.'

The commissioner jabbed a button on the console on his desk and leaned forward. 'Could you send in Mr Young, please,' he said, then sat back, fingertips pressed together.

Ridley turned as he heard the office door open.

The man who entered was tall and narrow shouldered. A year or two older than Ridley, he had short, jet-black hair with a very pronounced widow's peak. As he walked past, the DI noticed that the newcomer had used rather too much aftershave that morning. It was a cloying smell that hung in the air.

'This is Assistant Commissioner Andrew Young,' Pritchard announced, gesturing to the other man.

Ridley stood, shook his hand

(*powerful handshake*)

and sat down again once the introductions were complete.

'Assistant Commissioner Young is jointly in command of the Violent and Racial Crimes Task Force,' the Scot said. 'He is also a Senior Officer at SO11, Criminal Intelligence Branch.'

Ridley looked upon the man seated across from him with a sudden wariness.

SO11.

He shifted in his seat.

'SO11,' the DI murmured. 'That's Top Secret?'

Young smiled a disarmingly warm smile. 'You make us sound like refugees from a James Bond film,' he said with a lightness of tone not normally reserved for men in positions of such power. 'But yes, you're right, Detective Inspector, the business of SO11 *is* highly confidential.'

'If you don't mind me asking, sir,' Ridley began, looking from one man to the other, 'what have SO11 got to do with this case?'

'I read the communication from the Jamaican police,' Young told him. 'It merely confirms what *we* already knew about Codling.'

'You've heard of him then, sir?'

Young nodded. 'We've been monitoring his movements for the last fifteen months,' he said. 'Here *and* in Jamaica.'

'Then you know what kind of man he is, sir.'

'Very much so.'

'Then perhaps *you* could explain to Commissioner Pritchard why I need more men to ensure that Codling's found and arrested.' There was a note of angry frustration in the DI's voice.

'That's where we have a problem, Detective Inspector,' Young said flatly.

Ridley looked puzzled.

'SO11 don't *want* Codling arrested,' Young informed him.

'Why?' the DI demanded.

Young looked at him evenly. 'Because, for the last ten months, Papa Ernie Codling has been working for *us*.'

85

Ridley felt as if someone had punched him in the stomach.

He opened his mouth to speak, but no words would come; they formed inside his head, but he seemed incapable of forcing them past his lips.

What the fuck are you talking about?

That would have been a good one to start with, he thought, his mind still reeling, the muscles in his gut still balled like a fist.

Questions spun in his mind – questions he wanted, *needed*, answers to.

'I realize this must be something of a shock to you,' Young said.

Fucking right it is.

'You could say that, sir,' he murmured at last. 'I don't understand what's going on.'

'It's fairly simple, Detective Inspector,' Young persisted. 'As I said, Codling works for us.'

'For SO11?'

Young inclined his head slightly. 'And the Violent and Racial Crimes task force,' he informed the DI.

'Although precisely whose payroll he's on necessitates the kind of grey area I'm sure you'll appreciate.'

Young and Pritchard exchanged a glance.

'Of course there are other agencies involved with an undertaking such as this,' Young continued.

Ridley looked on with interest.

'Both the Immigration Service *and* the Home Office collaborated in Codling's resettlement,' said Young. 'Once he arrived in England he applied for political asylum. That's where the Home Office comes in.'

'But he entered the country on a stolen or fake passport,' Ridley protested.

'Supplied by us,' Young announced.

'Jesus Christ,' Ridley breathed, sitting back in his seat. 'Why? The guy's wanted for six murders in Jamaica and—'

Young cut him short. 'That's one of the reasons we got him out when we did,' said the older man.

Ridley was shaking his head.

'You have to understand, John,' Pritchard interjected, 'none of us *like* this situation. But we have no choice. As you know, the Yardies have grown in power steadily during the last ten years in this country.'

'As with any ethnic criminal organization like the Yardies or the Triads,' Young added, 'anyone attempting to infiltrate their ranks would be spotted immediately. It's difficult enough with conventional criminals. But if we sent Chinese policemen to work undercover among the Triads or black officers to the Yardies, we'd be sending those men to certain death. The only way to gather information about gangs like that is to recruit from within. That's what was done with Codling.'

'What about the two who came over with him?' Ridley asked.

'Vassell and Gardner,' Young said, shaking his head. 'They have no idea Codling's working for us.'

'This doesn't make any sense.' Ridley sighed, looking from one man to the other.

'It isn't the ideal option, I'll grant you that,' Young conceded. 'But currently it's the most effective. We pay him, he supplies us with information about the Yardies from the *inside*.'

'So, Codling goes about his business and we're all supposed to look the other way?' Ridley said angrily. 'In the last three months he's been responsible for at least seven murders that we *know* of and Christ knows how many more we *don't*.'

'And the murders you know of, Detective Inspector,' Young said, fixing the DI in an unblinking stare, 'were of pimps, small-time drug dealers, other Yardie members. Precisely the kind of people Codling was brought here to deal with.'

'You said you paid him for information,' Ridley snapped. 'Do the killings come as part of the deal?'

'He knew the right people to hit,' Young told the DI.

Ridley exhaled raggedly. 'So what happens now?' he wanted to know.

'Codling remains on our payroll. He continues to

supply us with information about current and future Yardie operations. When we have enough from him, he'll be arrested.'

'Does he know *that's* part of the deal?'

Young remained silent.

'What the hell am I supposed to tell my men?' Ridley rasped.

'You tell them nothing, John,' Pritchard informed him, leaning forward in his seat. 'What's been said in this office remains highly confidential.'

'Any breach of that confidentiality could have serious repercussions, Detective Inspector,' Young promised. There was a threat in the older man's tone, emphasized by his piercing gaze.

'I've got a team working on Codling, sir.'

'Let them carry on,' Young added. 'I just don't want him arrested yet. Especially not until his latest venture is completed.'

'Is *that* subject to confidentiality too?' Ridley asked acidly.

Young and Pritchard looked at each other and the DI saw something unspoken pass between them.

'It doesn't leave this room, Detective Inspector,' Young told him, his voice even.

Ridley nodded and sat forward in his chair, anxious not to miss a word that was about to be said to him.

86

THE SOUND OF the hammer slamming onto an empty chamber reverberated inside the lock-up.

Jeff Hobbs jerked his head round at the sound. He saw Ray Gorman holding the Spas automatic shotgun before him, the barrel yawning.

Hobbs watched his younger companion for a moment, then returned to his own task. He cleaned the first of the MP5s with a rag, checking the firing mechanisms before wiping the frames. He set each of the sub-machine-guns aside, noting how the fluorescents gleamed coldly on the weapons.

'Do you want to give me a hand?' he asked without looking at Gorman. 'Or are you going to play cowboys and Indians all day?'

Gorman worked the slide of the Spas, aimed it at Hobbs's back and squeezed the trigger again. 'Bang.' He chuckled.

'If you're going to fuck about, then at least make me a cup of tea, will you?' Hobbs insisted.

Gorman laid the Spas down and retreated to the far corner of the lock-up, where he filled the kettle, milked and sugared two mugs and stood with his arms crossed, leaning against the Formica.

He watched as Hobbs stripped the Zastava 9mm, cleaned each of the parts, then slotted it back together, working the slide to ensure the parts moved with requisite ease.

'Jeff,' Gorman said quietly.

Hobbs continued working, didn't look round at his companion.

'Are you scared?' Gorman continued.

'Of what?' Hobbs wanted to know.

'We could get killed tomorrow, couldn't we?'

'We could get killed crossing the street.'

'You know what I mean. This business with Codling. If we don't kill him, he'll kill *us* for sure, won't he? Him or Billy Parker.'

Hobbs nodded. He stopped cleaning and sat upright, still with his back to his companion.

'I don't want to die,' Gorman murmured quietly.

Hobbs finally turned to face him. 'Me neither, Ray,' he said softly. 'So let's make sure we don't.'

Gorman smiled.

'Make the tea,' Hobbs added.

Peter Morrissey counted the money twice.

Twenty thousand pounds; two piles of ten grand each, two hundred notes in each pile.

That done, he folded the piece of paper around them,

then pushed the whole package into a white A5 envelope.

He wrote one word on the front: JULIE.

Three times Frank Newton tried the mobile number.

Engaged.

At his fourth attempt, a metallic voice told him that there was a fault on the line, could he please try again.

How can there be a fault? It was engaged before. The bastard's talking to someone.

He jammed the receiver back onto its cradle and fished with his index finger in the 'Returned Change' slot.

No money there.

Newton grunted something under his breath, then dug in his pocket for more coins.

As he did he glanced across in the direction of the coffee shop opposite the payphones.

James Carson sat sipping his coffee and chewing disinterestedly on a Danish pastry. He glanced around at the ebb and flow of travellers who littered the concourse of Euston station – commuters; those travelling to see loved ones; shoppers; day trippers.

He wondered where all these people had come from and, indeed, where they were all going.

A young woman headed towards the table next to him, struggling with a holdall, a suitcase and a cappuccino. The wheels on the case were broken and she was dragging it, the piece of recalcitrant luggage making a sound like a wheezing lung.

As she almost overbalanced, Carson got to his feet and took the case from her, lifting it towards the table for her.

It was extremely heavy.

She thanked him and sat down, looking up gratefully into his face.

Beautiful smile.

Carson returned to his own coffee, sipped it, and took another bite of the Danish.

Newton smiled to himself as he watched.

He fed more coins into the phone and dialled again.

This time it was ringing.

He waited.

87

'I DON'T BELIEVE it.' Ridley shook his head and looked first at Pritchard, then Young.

'Believe what you like,' Young said flatly. 'It's true.'

'Billy Parker working with a bunch of jungle bunnies? It'd never happen,' Ridley insisted.

'For thirty million it would,' Young assured him.

'For thirty million, it *will*,' Pritchard echoed.

'How do you know all this?' the DI demanded.

'Codling,' Young explained. 'He told us that Parker was in on the deal.'

'You know that we haven't ever been able to give Parker a bloody speeding ticket before now,' the commissioner interjected. 'His involvement in a drugs deal of this size will allow us to put him away for life. He could buy the most expensive lawyers in the world, but no one would be able to get him off *this* time.'

'Two birds with one stone,' Young offered, smiling.

'So the real target has been Parker all along?' Ridley asked.

'No. The object of bringing Codling to London was to gather information on the Yardies,' Young said. 'His involvement with Parker is merely a fortuitous coincidence. As I said, two birds with one stone.'

'How did Codling find out about the drug couriers?' Ridley asked.

'Information supplied by us,' Young told him.

'Did you send him to Parker with the deal?'

'No. That was his own decision.'

'What if he double-crosses you?'

'He's going down eventually. If he decides to keep the drugs and do a runner we'll have him for that as well as everything else,' Pritchard announced.

'But then you miss out on Parker.'

Young shrugged. 'Parker was a bonus,' he mused. 'Codling and the Yardies are the prize. They always have been.'

'And once he's got the drugs, what then?'

'If he tries to sell them abroad we'll arrest his contacts,' Young said. 'The Jamaican police and the DEA are aware of what's going on too.'

'It's imperative that the job is carried out with no hitches, or at any rate, no interference from us,' Pritchard observed. 'Codling *must* be allowed to take the drugs from the couriers. He *must* be allowed to deliver them to Billy Parker.'

'If Codling's *own* boys find out he's working for you, *they'll* kill him,' Ridley said, looking at Young.

'There's no reason for them to be suspicious of him. Vassell and Gardner particularly. They've known him for years. Worked with him in Jamaica.'

'What made him turn?' Ridley wanted to know.

Young smiled. 'Money, Detective Inspector,' said the older man. 'It's as simple as that.'

'No wonder this is a top-secret operation. I don't think the taxpayers would be too happy to find out their money was going straight into the pocket of a known murderer.'

'The taxpayers would tolerate anything if it meant a crime-free environment,' Young proclaimed.

'So, you pay a criminal to help stop crime. That makes a lot of sense,' the DI observed.

'You must have paid informers in your time. What's the difference? This is just on a bigger scale. It's a dirty game, but a necessary one.'

'No promise of immunity?'

Young shook his head. 'When he's ceased to be of use to us he'll be arrested,' the older man said.

'It might not be that easy,' Ridley protested.

'You'd better hope it is, John,' Pritchard interjected. 'It's *your* case. It's down to you.'

Ridley massaged the bridge of his nose between his thumb and forefinger. 'And Parker's got his own boys working with Codling on this drugs job?' the DI mused.

Young nodded. 'Five of them, as far as we know,' he said. 'Led by a man called Frank Newton. We don't know the others, but they must be members of Parker's organization.'

Ridley felt the hairs rise on the back of his neck. 'Newton,' he murmured, trying to disguise his shock.

Frank fucking Newton.

'Do you know him?' Young enquired.

'Our paths have crossed once or twice,' Ridley said, lowering his gaze.

Frank fucking Newton.

He reached for another cigarette.

What had Gary Carson said about his father and Newton being involved in some kind of job?

He was aware of his two superiors looking at him.

'If there's nothing else, John . . .?' Pritchard said, raising his hands to show the palms.

Ridley understood.

'I'll keep this,' the Scot added, tapping the fax with one index finger.

Ridley got to his feet and headed for the door.

'Remember,' Young called, 'keep away from Codling, Parker *and* his men until this job is over.'

Ridley nodded and left the office.

He stood in the corridor, his breathing harsh, the muscles at the side of his jaw pulsing angrily. His mind still reeling from what he'd heard inside the office.

Newton.

He clenched one fist.

After all this time.

He took a final quick drag on his cigarette, then dropped it on the floor outside the commissioner's office.

'Keep away from them,' he muttered under his breath, glaring at the closed door. 'Fuck you.'

He spun on his heel and stalked off down the corridor, every muscle as rigid as steel.

There was someone he had to see.

88

HE AWOKE IN pain.

Jeff Hobbs sat up quickly, touching his left eye, blinking hard to restore vision already clouded by sleep.

It swam into sharpness, then blurred again.

The old injury.

Sometimes it gave him pain.

Tonight was one of those times.

He lay back and tried to sleep, but found that it now eluded him.

The house was silent, as usual.

He'd opened a window to let in some cool air, but it was tainted by the smell from the gasworks and he closed it again.

The pain in his left eye was subsiding gradually.

Hobbs swung himself out of bed and made his way downstairs to the kitchen, making himself a milky drink before retiring to the living room, flicking on the TV.

His vision had returned completely by now. The pain was gone.

Jeff Hobbs sat alone in his living room sipping at the drink.

After half an hour he returned to bed.

James Carson heard the crash outside in the street and peered through the living-room curtains.

He saw two slender shapes dashing away from the door of the house opposite, saw the broken milk bottles on the doorstep and the path.

The door of the house opposite opened and someone emerged swathed in a dressing gown. The man ventured to the end of his path, shaking a fist at the fleeing figures, careful not to tread on the shattered glass.

Carson stepped back from the window.

The street was dark; only one of the sodium lamps was in operation. The others had either been damaged or simply blown, the council not bothering to replace the bulbs. Probably wouldn't, Carson thought.

'It's some kids,' he called as he reached the hallway.

From upstairs, his wife mumbled something sleepily.

Carson began to climb the stairs. They groaned beneath his weight.

Peter Morrissey felt the hand on his chest, sliding lower across his belly.

Julie Cope had one slender leg across his thigh. He could feel her warmth against his flesh.

'If I'm not here tomorrow night, use your key to get

in,' he whispered, stroking her cheek with one powerful hand.

'Where are you going to be, Pete?' she wanted to know.

He ignored the question. 'You'll find an envelope on the kitchen table when you get here,' he continued. 'The note inside explains everything.'

She propped herself up on one elbow and looked down at him. 'Are you finishing with me?' Julie asked hurriedly. 'Pete, I—'

He shook his head and raised a hand to silence her. 'There's a job I've got to do,' he said quietly.

'What kind of job?'

'Just look in the envelope tomorrow, right?'

He pulled her to him, stifling her protestations with a kiss.

'Do you trust me?' he asked as they parted.

She nodded.

'Then trust me on *this*.'

Again he kissed her.

Ray Gorman listened to the laboured breaths. They seemed to fill the darkness of the bedroom.

He sat beside his father's bed, looking at the dark shape beneath the sheet, and listening to the asthmatic breathing.

He wasn't sure how long he'd been sitting there.

Thirty minutes.

An hour.

Perhaps longer.

He heard liquid voiding into the catheter, then a rumbling.

A low hiss.

A familiar stench.

He touched his father's hand gently, then got to his feet and headed for the bedroom door. Gorman paused there, looking back at the shape as a parent might study a sleeping child.

He closed the door.

The suitcases and other pieces of luggage were piled high in one corner of the living room. Others were in the hall.

'Are you sure this is what you want, Frank?'

Paula looked at Newton for long moments.

He finally nodded. 'We've got to get out, Paula,' he told her. 'We haven't got any choice once the job's done.'

The insistent buzz from the monitor filled the room. Through it, they could hear gentle breathing.

Their daughter.

'For *our* sake,' he murmured. 'And for Danielle.'

She thought about asking him to promise her he'd come back.

Promise he wouldn't get killed.

She wiped her eye, not wanting him to see the tears forming.

'By this time tomorrow night, it'll all be over,' he said flatly. 'One way or another.'

'And if you . . .' She couldn't finish the sentence.

'Take the money,' Newton interrupted, knowing only too well where her thoughts were leading her. 'You can pick up the rest from Billy Parker. Take it and go.'

Still she fought to hold back the tears.

'You've got to, Paula,' he insisted. 'If it comes to that.'

'And will it?' she said, her voice cracking. 'Am I going to lose you, Frank?'

He had no answer.

89

'WHY DIDN'T YOU tell me, you little bastard?' As he shouted the words, Detective Inspector John Ridley slammed Gary Carson against the wall. 'Why?' he snarled, not taking his hands from the younger man's sweatshirt.

'I didn't know,' Carson protested, seeing the fury in the policeman's eyes.

'Fucking liar,' the DI rasped and drove Gary backwards with even greater force, lifting him bodily off the ground.

He groaned as his head smacked against the bricks and, for fleeting seconds, he thought he was losing consciousness.

The incessant thunderous bass rhythm from inside the club sounded like a fevered heartbeat.

Like his own.

'Look, I didn't know what was going on,' Gary gasped.

'I told you to keep your eyes and ears open. Let me know if your old man was involved in any jobs. You didn't tell me.'

He hurled Gary to one side, watching as he collided

with several empty cardboard boxes piled up in the alleyway behind the club.

His face hit the concrete hard. His bottom lip split. He stifled a shout of pain as he felt his teeth cut through his tongue.

Ridley advanced on him as he struggled upright.

'I *told* you he had a job lined up,' Gary protested, wiping blood from the corner of his mouth. He looked at the dark fluid on his hand, then wiped it on his jeans.

The DI stood over him, like a carnivore that had cornered its prey.

'I said that Newton geezer had been to the house,' Gary continued, struggling to his feet. 'I gave you the information you wanted. All I had.'

His breath was coming in gasps.

He could taste the coppery taste of blood in his mouth.

Ridley heard movement behind him, turned and saw two youths peering into the alley.

They looked at him, then at Gary.

Saw the blood around the younger man's mouth.

'What the fuck are *you* looking at?' Ridley said through clenched teeth.

The two youths hesitated a moment.

'Go on, piss off,' the detective urged. 'Unless you want some too.'

They retreated into the street.

Ridley turned back to face Gary, who took a couple of steps back.

'Don't even think about running,' the DI warned him. 'There's nowhere you can hide now.'

'Look, I told you what I knew, that was the deal.'

'You'll do five, I'll make sure of that.'

'I didn't know what the fucking job was! What was I going to do, *ask* him? "By the way, Dad, what kind of job are you pulling with Frank Newton? Only there's some fucking copper on my back wanting me to find out." Is that what I was supposed to say?'

They regarded each other warily in the darkness of the alley, the walls on both sides closing in like a clenched fist.

'What *is* the job?' Gary said finally. 'What's so important? What could my fucking old man and Frank Newton be working on that could possibly interest *you*?'

Ridley turned, preparing to leave the alleyway. 'I'm going to nail Newton *and* your old man,' he said quietly. 'Then I'm coming back for you.'

Gary sucked in a deep breath, hawked and spat blood.

When he wiped his mouth, his hand was shaking.

90

IT WAS A madhouse.

The sound inside Heathrow Airport's Terminal Three was like a whirlwind, sweeping around Frank Newton. There was a cacophony of voices raised in a dozen different languages: laughter; shouts; angry exchanges. Above it all the metallic tones that announced flight arrivals and departures over the airport's tannoy system.

Every so often the automatic doors would open to admit different noises: the droning of engines; the occasional blast of car horns; the ever-present roar of aircraft coming in to land or take off. The sound split the sky and tore rents in the low-lying cloud.

Newton wandered amongst the crowds of passengers, weaving among those struggling with cases and holdalls, or those laden down with gifts they had brought back from holidays. He dodged between two young men, both with huge bulging rucksacks strapped to their backs.

Ahead of him a large man with a red face was carrying a suitcase in one hand while he gripped the hand of a small child with the other. Beside him his wife was carrying a baby while a third child trailed along between them. The baby was crying.

He passed a MacDonald's, and saw two young women seated on battered suitcases eating hamburgers and drinking milkshakes. French fries had been scattered across the floor nearby.

He slipped past a group of people huddled together, looking up at one of the departure screens.

Flight times and numbers flashed on the screen.

Newton bumped into a man carrying a large holdall and a Burberry's carrier bag. The man muttered something, but Newton walked on, sliding one hand inside his jacket, ensuring the man hadn't displaced the mobile phone he'd hooked onto his belt.

He checked it, looked at the glowing digits for a second, then replaced it.

People wandered around apparently aimlessly, some searching for check-in desks.

CATHAY PACIFIC

AIR CANADA

QANTAS

SINGAPORE AIRLINES

EMIRATES

The list seemed endless.

Others searched for familiar faces.

He almost collided with a heavily laden luggage trolley being pushed by a man wearing a baseball cap and a Nike T-shirt. The man was sweating profusely. He raised a hand in apology when he realized how close he'd come to ramming Newton.

Newton met his gaze for a second, then moved on through the crowd.

He saw Codling up ahead.

The Jamaican was sipping at a can of Sprite, seemingly oblivious to the pandemonium around him. His large eyes were fixed on the screen above, scanning the arrivals.

'Anything?' Newton wanted to know, also glancing up at the blue screen.

Codling merely shook his dreadlocked head and took another sip from the can.

'They be here soon,' he said softly, without taking his eyes from the screen.

'You'd better be right,' Newton insisted.

'Everyone ready?'

'I'm just going to check.'

Newton pulled the Nokia from his belt and jabbed out the first number.

91

THEY BOTH REACHED for the phone when it rang.

Ray Gorman looked across at Toad and snatched up the mobile.

'Yeah, Frank,' he said.

Newton wanted to know where they were.

'Parked outside Terminal Three,' Gorman told him. 'We can see everything from here.'

He glanced at the orange Disabled badge stuck on the front windscreen of the Toyota.

Newton told him there was no sign of the couriers yet.

'We're ready to move when you give us a shout,' Gorman told him.

Newton terminated the call.

'I hope your fucking boss's information is right,' Gorman said, looking at his companion.

Toad said nothing.

Newton was forced to cup one hand to his ear to mask the noise around him.

Two travellers were arguing loudly about their position

in the queue leading towards the check-in desk of Britannia Airways.

'I didn't hear you, Jim,' Newton snapped.

James Carson told his companion that he and Aston Thomas were in the short-stay car park opposite Terminal Three.

'Can you get out of there quick if you have to, Jim?' Newton wanted to know.

The older man assured him it would be no trouble.

He added that Thomas had nipped off to take a piss.

'Jim, listen to me,' Newton said. 'If he's not back when you have to go, then leave the cunt behind, got it?'

Carson said he understood.

Jeff Hobbs was out of the car when the phone rang.

Dudley Smith picked it up and handed it to him as he slid back into the passenger seat.

Newton wanted to know where he'd been.

'Stretching my legs, we've been in this bloody car park for over an hour,' Hobbs told him.

Newton wanted confirmation of which car park.

'The one outside the Ramada Hotel,' Hobbs continued. 'The one we're *supposed* to be in.'

Newton wanted to know if they'd have any trouble getting to the M4 when the time came.

'Everything's set,' Hobbs told him.

Newton told him to wait until he was contacted again.

'What else am I going to do, Frank?' Hobbs asked.

*

'Say that again, you're breaking up,' Newton snapped.

'. . . said . . . just coming out . . . a tunnel,' Peter Morrissey told him.

'Where are you?'

'Driving around. Coming past Terminal One. I told Skeng to park . . . up . . . minute . . .'

Static.

'I can't hear you, Pete,' Newton said loudly.

More static.

'Pete,' he said again.

No reply.

Just a high pitched buzzing in Newton's ear.

He shook the phone angrily and then pressed it to his ear again.

'. . . hear that . . .'

He heard Morrissey's voice.

'Pete, can you hear me?' Newton wanted to know.

'Yeah, I can now. I lost the signal for a minute,' Morrissey informed him.

Another burst of static.

'For fuck's sake,' snarled Newton at the phone.

'It's OK, I'm still here,' Morrissey said. 'We're heading round now.'

Codling nudged Newton and pointed to the Arrivals screen.

Flight AA213 was about to arrive from Chicago.

'The first courier,' the Jamaican said. 'He coming in now.'

92

Newton wanted a cigarette.

He badly wanted a fucking cigarette.

Everywhere the signs forbade it.

Chance sparking up? Just once? Just a couple of drags?

And draw attention to yourself when some bastard asks you to put it out?

He knew it wasn't worth it.

'How much fucking longer?' he muttered as he and Codling stood watching the sliding doors that separated the baggage-collection area and customs from the main Arrivals area.

There were hundreds of expectant faces lined up along the barriers, all peering in the direction of the figures they knew would soon be emerging.

Drivers held pieces of card with names scrawled on them.

Excited families laughed in anticipation.

Small children were lifted up so that they too would be able to catch sight of those they sought.

Newton checked his watch. 'He's been in there for nearly half an hour,' he said under his breath.

'He got bags to collect, man,' the Jamaican said, his eyes never leaving the sliding doors.

'And what if the customs have already collared him?'

Codling didn't answer.

The doors slid open. The first of the arriving passengers began to make their way out.

Some were pushing trolleys.

Others only carried hand baggage.

Newton saw a man holding a briefcase in one hand and a huge cellophane-wrapped teddy bear in the other.

There was an excited shriek from close by and he saw a small child waving her arms excitedly at the man.

More travellers spilled through the doors.

Codling watched intently.

So many faces.

Newton looked on, not even knowing who he sought.

He glanced at Codling, trying to catch any hint of concern in the big Jamaican's expression.

Still the passengers came.

Sometimes in groups.

Sometimes alone.

Some smartly dressed (lots of suits). Others in jogging bottoms, sweatshirts, trainers.

They pushed, carried and struggled with their luggage as they sought faces in the crowd or merely headed for the exits.

Codling was still watching.

'How was he travelling?' Newton wanted to know. 'First Class?'

The Jamaican nodded.

'Then he should have been off first,' Newton hissed.

Codling spoke without looking at Newton. 'You ever fly First Class?' he mused. 'How you know that?'

His large eyes moved back and forth like scopes.

Newton could feel his heart thudding more rapidly against his ribs.

The woman next to him shouted something and waved frantically in the direction of two young people who had just emerged from the sliding doors. They rushed towards her, the three of them embracing, almost knocking Newton aside.

He stepped irritably away from the reunion.

'Where is he, Codling?' he murmured.

Then he saw the smile spread across the Jamaican's face. 'Coming through now,' Codling told him.

A tall man with glasses and thin features emerged, carrying a black leather briefcase.

He walked purposefully, but unhurriedly, weaving his way through the crowd with feline grace.

Newton studied the figure for a moment. 'You're sure that's him?' he muttered.

Codling merely nodded.

Newton stabbed the number he wanted into the Nokia, watching the tall courier constantly.

Ray Gorman answered on the third ring.

'The courier's coming out,' Newton told him. 'Tall geezer. Glasses. Brown hair. He's wearing a dark blue jacket, a grey polo-neck under it. Black trousers and shoes. Carrying a black leather briefcase. Got that?'

Gorman said he had.

Newton kept the phone pressed to his ear.

The courier was virtually at the exit now.

Seconds passed.

Through the earpiece he could hear muttering. The sound of cars. Raised voices.

Come on.

He looked at his watch.

The courier had left the building.

Then finally, Gorman on the line: 'I can see him, Frank.'

Newton exhaled audibly.

'He's getting in the queue for a taxi,' Gorman continued.

'Don't lose him,' Newton said and switched off.

Codling was already walking away.

'Where the hell are *you* going?' Newton wanted to know.

Codling smiled. 'Next flight doesn't arrive for three hours,' the Jamaican told him. 'I want a drink. Join me.' It sounded like a request.

Newton nodded. 'Why not?' he said under his breath.

93

NEWTON SCREWED A JPS between his lips and lit up. The smoke rose, joining the grey curtain already hanging thickly in the air.

The smoking section of Shakespeare's Ale House in Terminal Three was almost full. Smokers, soon to board, were puffing away frantically, knowing they'd be denied that pleasure once airborne.

Elsewhere in the bar people were picking at food, sipping at drinks or just talking.

There was a baby crying somewhere.

Beer had been spilled on the worn red carpet nearby. Newton watched as a woman in a white overall mopped it up as best she could.

She glanced occasionally at the two men seated at the table nearest her, noticing that each was staring straight ahead, as if each was anxious to avoid eye contact with his companion.

Once or twice Newton looked at the Jamaican, but only for fleeting seconds.

You'll see him clearly enough when you kill him.

He had no idea how long they'd been sitting in the

bar. There were a couple of empty glasses before him, but if they were marking time with drinks then Newton guessed less than half an hour.

He finished his cigarette, then wandered over to the bar and got himself an orange juice.

'How long before the next courier gets in?' he asked when he returned to their table.

'I already told you,' Codling answered.

'So tell me *again*,' Newton hissed.

'You scared they not coming. Scared to tell Mr Billy Parker his big deal fell through.'

'I just asked. I'm sick of sitting around here wasting fucking time.'

'How long you work for Parker?' Codling asked.

'I've known him for years,' Newton said. 'Most people in London *do* if they're in the business.'

'I didn't ask you how long you known him.'

'Why does it matter?' Newton reached for another cigarette.

Codling shrugged. 'Is he a good man to work for?' the Jamaican wanted to know.

'He's wonderful,' Newton said mockingly. 'The sun shines out of his arsehole. Is that enough for you?'

'He's an old man. Older than you. Everyone who work for him is old. They had their time. Parker had *his* time.'

Newton regarded the Jamaican through a haze of smoke.

'He belong in the past,' Codling continued, a smile flickering at the corners of his mouth. 'Like the dinosaurs. And when *he* extinct something newer, something better will take over.'

'Like you?'

Codling grinned.

'You'll get old too,' Newton continued. 'And then what? Someone else, someone younger'll replace *you*.'

'I got plenty time.'

Newton drew on his cigarette and looked fixedly at Codling.

You've got until I pull a fucking trigger on you.

'*You* ever think about getting out of this business, Newton?' Codling said. 'You no young man anymore.' He smiled.

'I think about it all the time. Make one big score and back off.'

'Back off to what?'

Newton took another drag on the JPS. 'A *proper* life,' he said flatly.

'You got family?'

'Wife and kid.'

'Girl or boy?'

'Little girl. Danielle.'

'Pretty name.'

'She's a pretty kid.'

'Get her looks from her mother then.' Codling grinned.

Newton found himself smiling too.

What are you doing? You're going to kill this bastard and you're sitting here talking to him about your fucking family?

His smile faded. 'I'm going for a wander round,' he

said, turning away from the Jamaican. He got to his feet. 'I'll call the others. Check everything's all right.'

'You worry too much, Newton.'

'It happens when you get older,' he said without looking back. Then he was heading for the exit.

Codling watched him go.

94

'GOING SOMEWHERE?'

As Detective Inspector John Ridley stood on the doorstep of the house in Campdale Road, he peered into the hallway. He could see beyond Paula Newton to the suitcases and other pieces of luggage stacked in the small vestibule.

'You look as if you're moving,' Ridley continued, nodding towards the baggage.

'We are,' she explained.

'Or running?' he said flatly.

As she looked at him in bewilderment, he flipped open the slim leather wallet containing his ID.

'Is your husband in?' he asked.

Paula shook her head.

'Where is he?' Ridley wanted to know.

'He's working.'

'I bet he is,' the policeman murmured, his eyes narrowing.

Paula found his gaze unsettling. 'Would you mind telling me what this is about?'

'I want to talk to your husband.'

'What about?'

'I need some information from him.'

Paula felt her heart beating a little faster.

Was it the Securicor job after all this time?

Ridley held her gaze, watching for any telltale signs of nervousness. He could spot it like predators spot the weaklings in a herd.

Lies always showed around the eyes.

From the living room he heard a baby crying.

Paula hesitated. 'I've got to see to my daughter,' she told him, preparing to push the front door shut.

Ridley blocked it with one hand. 'I'll just step inside while you do,' he told her, following her in. It was he who closed the door.

Paula retreated into the living room and crossed to the Moses basket, peering in at Danielle, lifting her gently into her arms. As she turned, she saw Ridley enter the room and look around, taking in every detail.

'How old is she?' he asked, nodding towards the little girl.

'Just over a week.'

'Easy delivery?'

Paula nodded.

'When did you get home from hospital?' he persisted.

'A day or two ago.'

The lies were coming with surprising ease.

'And you're already thinking of moving? That's a lot of upheaval so soon afterwards, isn't it?'

Paula held the crying baby tightly to her, patting its back rhythmically.

'You got your figure back quickly,' he observed.

She tried to swallow, but couldn't.

Did he know? Was there any way in the world he could know?

Ridley watched her intently.

Danielle continued to cry.

'You can see my husband isn't here,' Paula said, trying to control the anxiety in her voice. 'And there's nothing I can help you with so . . .' She allowed the sentence to trail off.

'You're good at this, Paula,' the DI told her. 'But then again you've had plenty of practice, haven't you?'

'I don't know what you're talking about.'

'The old lag's wife,' he sneered. 'Protective. Always prepared to give her bloke an alibi.'

'Frank's done nothing wrong.'

'Never done time? Never pulled jobs?'

'He's working.'

'For Billy Parker. I know.'

'I don't know what you're talking about.'

'You know he'll go down for life this time, don't you?'

Paula held his gaze now.

'He'll never see his kid grow up,' Ridley continued. 'Other than during visits. He'll be a fucking stranger to her.'

'This could look like harrassment if I reported it.'

'It would do if he's done nothing. But we both know you won't be calling *anyone* about this visit, don't we?'

'I'd like to see to my daughter, please, Detective

Inspector,' she said defiantly. 'If there's nothing else, I'd appreciate it if you left.'

'Tell him I called,' the policeman said, taking a step towards her. 'Detective Inspector John Ridley. Don't forget. It's important he knows I was here. You can tell him I'll catch up with him another time.' He smiled crookedly, then wrinkled his nose. 'I think she needs changing.'

Paula held Danielle tightly as Ridley turned and left the room.

She heard the front door open, then close behind him.

Only then did she let out an almost painful breath.

Her heart was hammering so hard against her ribs she feared it would burst.

Danielle continued to cry.

95

Newton watched as the 747 rose into the air, shafts of watery sunlight arrowing off its gleaming hull.

He wondered where it was going.

Bermuda? Grand Cayman? Was someone else fulfilling a dream while he stood here and helplessly looked on?

The sheer volume of planes arriving and leaving Heathrow was staggering. He was amazed there weren't mid-air collisions all the time.

Others stood watching the constant stream of passengers through the wide plate-glass windows that looked out over part of the runway.

Were they waiting for loved ones to arrive or lost in thought in the wake of their departure?

Did it matter?

He checked his watch. It seemed as if he'd been wandering the airport for hours. More than once he'd stepped outside for a cigarette. Three or four times he'd rung the cars to check on their positions.

Perhaps he should call Billy Parker, let him know how things were going.

Finally, he wandered back towards Shakespeare's Ale

House where he had left Codling. The United Airlines flight they were waiting for was due in from Washington DC any time now.

The bar was still packed with travellers.

Of Codling there was no sign.

Newton looked around the sea of faces, then checked the figures standing at the bar.

The man he sought was nowhere to be seen.

Fucking great. Get separated in a place like this. Talk about needle in a sodding haystack.

He left the bar, eyes scanning the milling crowds. A man of Codling's size and appearance shouldn't be too difficult to spot, he reasoned. Why the hell couldn't he have just sat and waited?

Perhaps he got as bored as you.

Newton himself had the numbers and times of the arrivals carrying the next two couriers, but, most crucially, not the vaguest idea what they looked like.

He wondered if Codling was trying to stiff him, but knew that was impossible. Morrissey, Gorman, Hobbs and Carson were all sharing cars with Codling's men. Even if Codling himself tried to knock over one of the couriers and leg it with the drugs, his boys would have to get away *with* him.

Or would they?

Newton had one brief moment of what he could only describe as panic.

What if Codling intended double-crossing his own boys too? The couriers were carrying one hundred kilos of cocaine each. Knocking over even one of them would be worth it to him.

Newton shook his head.

And if Codling got away, what then? He was the one Billy Parker wanted dead. He was the one that mattered. If they lost Codling they were all fucking history.

Newton pushed past a group of teenagers, who were gathered in a huddle poring over a copy of *Men Only*, cheering delightedly as each new girl was exposed by a turn of a page.

They barely seemed to notice him as he barged through.

Newton's eyes flicked back and forth frantically now, his mind spinning.

What if Codling *had* fucked off with the second load of drugs?

What if he escaped?

What if . . .?

The big Jamaican was standing below an Arrivals screen.

'Where you been?' he asked as Newton sidled up beside him.

'Where have *I* been? You were the one who left the fucking bar—'

Codling cut him short. 'The flight from Washington has just landed,' he said flatly.

96

'MID-THIRTIES. ABOUT five-ten. Short black hair. Moustache. He's wearing a grey suit, white shirt and no tie.' Newton spoke rapidly, the mobile pressed against his ear, his eyes never leaving the second courier as the man side-stepped and dodged his way through the horde of people spilling from the Arrivals area.

'He's carrying a brown leather overnight case on a strap over his shoulder,' Newton continued.

'Got it, Frank,' Peter Morrissey told him.

'He should be coming out about . . . now.'

Newton watched the courier disappear outside.

Silence on the other end of the line.

'Pete, can you see him?' Newton persisted.

'Not yet,' he replied.

Newton looked at Codling, who merely shrugged.

Through the earpiece of the Nokia he could hear talking from inside the car, could hear Skeng muttering something.

'Fuck this,' Newton hissed and set off through the crowd in pursuit of the courier, the phone still pressed to his ear.

He scurried quickly through the crowd, eyes never leaving the grey suit and leather bag.

'There's so many fucking people out here,' Morrissey complained.

'I'll point him out,' Newton said, closing on the courier.

Slow down. Take it easy. Don't draw attention to yourself.

He slowed his pace as he reached the large revolving door that spewed passengers out onto the pavement.

Looking both ways he feared for a moment that he too had lost sight of the courier, but then spotted the man heading for the taxi rank.

'Can you see him now?' Newton wanted to know.

'I can see *you*,' the former soldier said.

'Look to *my* left. Grey suit. White shirt . . .'

'Brown leather bag,' Morrissey added. 'Got him.'

'You stick to him like shit to a blanket,' Newton urged and terminated the call.

Breathing heavily, he turned and wandered back inside the terminal. His heart was thudding hard. Beads of sweat had formed on his forehead.

It's your age.

He smiled to himself.

The phone rang.

'Frank, it's Ray.'

He'd recognized Gorman's voice anyway.

'Where are you?' Newton asked.

'Parked outside the Holiday Inn, Mayfair,' Gorman told him. 'The first courier's checked in there. What do you want us to do?'

'Nothing until I tell you. Just watch the place. If he goes out, follow him. Do you know which room he's in?'

'Not yet.'

'Then find out. I want him taken *inside* the hotel, not on the street.'

'How the fuck do I find out which room he's in?'

'You'll think of something, Ray. Call me back in an hour.'

He jabbed the 'End' button and slid the mobile back onto his belt.

Codling was waiting, a smile hovering as usual. 'Any problems?'

Newton shook his head. 'Number one's already at his hotel, the second one's on his way. He's covered.'

Codling nodded. 'Good.' He looked up at the Arrivals board. 'One left.'

97

'How the fuck are we going to do this?'

Ray Gorman's words hung in the air like stale cigarette smoke.

He was gazing through the side window of the car, his eyes fixed on the large plate-glass window that formed part of the foyer of the Holiday Inn, Mayfair. The concierge's desk and reception were clearly visible through the glass, as were the two lifts that led up to the guest floors.

There were two people sitting on the leather sofas in the foyer. One of them reading a newspaper, the other glancing in the direction of the bar, occasionally checking his watch.

'We don't know his name,' Gorman continued. 'We don't know which fucking room he's in.'

Toad, seated behind the wheel, looked on silently. Every now and then he would glance at Gorman, seeing the agitation on his face.

'Maybe he'll come out,' Toad murmured.

'And what if he doesn't?'

Toad shrugged.

'You're a big fucking help, aren't you?' Gorman hissed.

He looked at the hotel. The flags jutting out from the parapet above the main entrance fluttered gently in the breeze.

There was a doorman in a long black overcoat standing close to the revolving doors that led into the foyer. He paced back and forth every now and then like a soldier on sentry duty. A couple left the building and he nodded and said something. Gorman could see his lips moving, but from where they sat he couldn't hear what the man said.

Come on, think. What are you going to do?

'Your fucking boss was supposed to have all the information,' he snapped, without looking at Toad. 'How come he doesn't know the couriers' names?'

'Even if he did, what are you going to do?' Toad demanded. 'Walk over there and say to the receptionist, "I'm supposed to be stealing some drugs from one of your guests. Can you give me his room number, please?"'

'Funny cunt,' Gorman rasped, shooting the driver an angry glance.

He returned to gazing at the hotel.

Toad reached for a cigarette and lit up.

Gorman looked at him, watching the yellow flame of the lighter.

He suddenly swung himself out of the car.

'What are you doing?' Toad wanted to know, but Gorman was already heading across the street towards the uniformed doorman.

The man nodded a greeting and pulled open the door for him.

Gorman raised a hand almost in salute and walked through into the foyer.

His heart was thudding hard against his ribs.

Get a fucking grip.

The bar was straight ahead of him. The concierge's desk was to his immediate left, but no one was there. Reception was also to his left, just ahead. There was a young woman with shoulder-length black hair standing behind the desk, watching as a computer spewed out paper. Another young woman with short brown hair rose into view and looked in Gorman's direction. Both wore green jackets and white blouses.

The two people seated on the leather sofas also looked at him.

Don't lose your fucking bottle now.

The woman with the short brown hair smiled at him.

He smiled back, then, without breaking stride, moved towards the lifts and hit the 'Call' button.

Waiting.

One was on five. The other on four.

Descending.

Slowly.

Gorman felt as if every eye in the place was boring into him.

He checked his reflection in the polished steel of the lift doors. Ran a hand through his hair.

His heart was banging like a jackhammer.

Come on.

The two women behind the reception desk were chatting quietly; he couldn't hear what they were saying. The blonde looked in his direction.

She's probably realized you're not staying here. She's going to ask to see your key or your card or whatever the fuck they ask for in places like this.

A phone rang on the concierge's desk.

No one to answer it.

Lifts still descending.

One on three.

One on two.

The phone still ringing on the concierge's desk.

What if they know you're not a guest here? The hotel might be quiet at the moment. They might remember every face. They're good at things like that, aren't they?

The concierge emerged from a small vestibule and reached for the phone.

Gorman felt another set of eyes upon him.

The first of the lifts arrived.

The doors slid open and he stepped in, jabbed the '1' button and waited for the car to rise.

Outside he heard footsteps hurrying into the foyer.

Hurrying for the lift?

Fuck that.

Gorman pressed the 'Door Close' button. He heard a voice beyond raised in frustration.

A smile spread across his face as the lift rose.

When it stopped he stepped out into the corridor, looking to his left and right.

412

Oak doors. All tightly sealed.
No one in sight.
Was the courier on this floor?
One way to find out.

98

'Just coming through Chiswick, Frank,' said Peter Morrissey. 'The traffic's been bad all the way from Heathrow. I don't think we've got over thirty more than five or six times. Some silly cunt wrapped themselves round the central reservation according to the radio. That's what's caused the hold-up.'

'Just stay with him,' Frank Newton instructed.

'If the second courier *knows* he's being followed he hasn't done anything about it yet.'

Newton listened intently as he stood outside the main entrance to Terminal Three.

'It looks as if he's heading into central London too,' Morrissey continued. 'Though Christ knows how much longer it's going to take.'

'Have you got Jeff in sight?' Newton asked.

A moment's silence.

'About six cars back,' Morrissey told him. 'We'll let him take over as the mirror car in five minutes. We've been switching all the way from the airport. Even if he was a professional driver he wouldn't have sussed.'

'Any reason to think the courier knows you're tailing him?' Newton asked.

A hiss of static.

'None at all.'

'You call me again when he reaches his hotel,' Newton said, then switched off.

He dug in his pocket for his cigarettes and found he was out. How many had he smoked during the wait at the airport? Forty? Sixty?

He headed back inside, bought another packet and a bottle of Lucozade.

Codling was leaning against one of the concrete pillars sipping from a can of Dr Pepper. He rolled the cool tin over his forehead leaving a wet smear.

Newton also drank. The heat had steadily intensified as the day drew on. Now, with the approach of early evening, the air both inside and outside the terminal felt oppressive.

Still the never-ending tide of travellers continued; arriving and leaving. It had barely abated all through the long afternoon. A sea of faces. To Newton, they were all beginning to look the same.

'The plane was due in from New York an hour ago,' he said to the big Jamaican.

'I know that,' Codling said. 'I can't do anything about the delay. Just chill. She be here.'

He drained what was left in the can, crushed it in one large hand and dropped the crumpled aluminium into a nearby bin.

Newton glared at the Jamaican for a moment.

Then you'll kill her.

Codling caught Newton's prolongd gaze out of his eye corner. 'Something on your mind?' he wanted to know.

'How do they do it?'

'Do what?'

'You reckon that the couriers are carrying one hundred kilos each. Where? In their luggage? They'd never get it through customs.'

'They got it, that all that matters,' Codling said flatly.

'But a hundred kilos?' Newton persisted. 'That's a lot of fucking weight to be carrying.'

'When the last one get here, I show you.'

He looked up at the screen above his head.

VS004 was illuminated in yellow.

DELAYED flashed beside it.

99

THE SOUND OF the fire alarm jolted Toad from his vigil. He sat up behind the steering wheel, trying to locate the source of the ringing.

As he spotted Ray Gorman walking unhurriedly back towards the car he realized it was coming from the Holiday Inn.

'What did you do?' Toad asked as Gorman slid into the passenger seat.

'What does it fucking sound like?' Gorman intoned, tapping one ear as the sound of the alarm continued to fill the early evening air. 'They'll have to evacuate the hotel, make sure all the guests are safe. When they're all out, I'll join them. Find our man. When the hotel realize it's a false alarm they'll let the guests back in. I'll follow the courier and see which room he's in.'

'What about the fire brigade?'

'What about them? They'll have a wasted trip because there's nothing wrong except a smashed fire alarm on the first floor.'

Already guests and members of staff were beginning to spill onto the pavement outside the hotel. Both

Gorman and Toad peered intently at each figure that appeared to swell the concerned ranks.

Dark-uniformed porters, the concierge and the door-man were trying to usher the guests further away from the hotel entrance.

Somewhere in the distance, they heard a siren.

Gorman and Toad watched.

And waited.

As they turned into Park Lane, Morrissey lost the signal. He banged the Nokia against the flat of his hand, but there was still nothing when he pressed it to his ear once more.

'Fuck,' he snarled, looking ahead in the direction of the taxi carrying the second courier.

He didn't know what had caused the break in recep-tion; too much neon, perhaps. The hotels that lined the bottom end of the expensive thoroughfare were bril-liantly lit.

Perhaps the battery on the phone itself was running down.

Whatever the case, he couldn't contact Newton; couldn't tell him that the taxi was heading up towards Marble Arch, then swinging round to join the one-way system travelling back down the opposite carriageway.

He glanced out of the back window and saw the car driven by Dudley Smith close behind.

Jeff Hobbs was pointing, gesturing first at the driver, then at the cab.

They got stuck at a red light.

'Keep going,' Morrissey told Skeng, who skilfully guided the car along Park Lane behind the taxi.

The black vehicle turned into the forecourt of the Dorchester.

'Drive past,' the former soldier instructed. 'Take the first left.'

Through the back window, Morrissey watched the second courier paying the cab driver.

Skeng looked across anxiously as his companion pushed open the passenger door and, with the car still moving slowly, jumped out.

The red light seemed to be taking an eternity.

Dudley Smith shifted uneasily in his seat. He wiped sweat from his forehead.

'Take it easy,' Hobbs said, without looking at him.

'We fucking lost him now,' Smith snapped.

'The others are with him. They'll call us.'

The lights turned amber.

Smith stepped hard on the accelerator, almost collided with a Mazda. The other driver hit his horn.

'Calm down,' Hobbs snarled contemptuously. 'If you hit something . . .' He allowed the sentence to trail off.

'You want to drive?' Smith snapped, taking both hands off the wheel momentarily.

Hobbs eyed him furiously. He reached for the mobile and, as he did so, his hand brushed the Beretta 92F nestled in its shoulder holster.

Smith hawked and spat out of the open driver's window.

'Prick,' Hobbs hissed under his breath.

They turned back into Park Lane.

Hobbs dialled.

100

'THAT'S HIM.' RAY Gorman pointed towards the tall, dark-haired man in the white T-shirt and black jogging bottoms who had just emerged from the main entrance of the Holiday Inn.

Unlike the other evacuated guests, who carried expressions ranging from bemusement to anxiety, he looked irritated by the entire scenario. He moved dutifully away from the hotel when directed by the porters.

A fire engine was parked outside the building, blue lights turning silently. The courier regarded the red engine impassively, then glanced around at the other guests, waiting, like himself, to be allowed back inside.

Gorman swung himself out of the car and walked slowly in the direction of the hotel.

A number of passers-by had stopped to watch the little tableau, mingling with guests. Members of staff were standing talking to each other or to residents; some were even laughing and joking.

It was fairly obvious to everyone by now that the alarm had been unwarranted. There was no fire. The firemen or hotel staff would find the alarm that he'd smashed, Gorman thought, but who gave a toss?

He stood smoking on the edge of the pavement close to the courier, never letting the man out of his sight.

A grey-haired man in a pin-striped suit appeared at the door and raised his arms. 'You may all come back in now, ladies and gentlemen,' he announced. 'I apologize for the inconvenience.'

Muttering, laughing or cursing, the guests began to file back inside.

Gorman stepped in behind the courier as he began walking.

As he hurried across the forecourt of the Dorchester, Peter Morrissey pulled his wallet from his pocket.

The taxi that had deposited the second courier outside the towering edifice of the hotel was about to pull away.

The courier himself was already inside the reception area.

Morrissey chose his moment carefully, bending down and appearing to scoop up something from the tarmac.

Carrying his own wallet, he slowed his pace slightly, even nodded at the doorman, who returned the gesture and opened one of the main doors for him.

Morrissey could hear the sound of a piano playing softly, the mellifluous tone a pleasant contrast to the roar of engines on Park Lane.

The courier had finished registering and was heading for the lifts.

Morrissey approached the desk and was met with a practised smile from the receptionist. 'I think that gentleman dropped this as he was getting out of his taxi,' he said, nodding towards the courier. He put the wallet on the desk, keeping his hand over it.

The receptionist leaned forward.

'Excuse me,' she called. 'Mr Thornton.'

The courier turned.

Morrissey looked straight at him.

Welcome to London, Mr Thornton.

'Did you drop your wallet outside?' Morrissey asked him.

The courier dug in his jacket pocket. 'No, I got it. Thank you,' he replied.

American accent.

The former soldier looked at the overnight case the courier carried.

Mr Harold Thornton turned and headed for the lifts.

'Ah, well.' Morrissey shrugged, taking the wallet back.

The receptionist watched him as he turned and headed into the bar.

Mr Thornton.

Morrissey stood at the bar, watching as a man in a white waistcoat finished serving a customer and headed towards him.

'Yes, sir?' he said with a smile.

Morrissey ordered a mineral water. 'Where are the

toilets, please?' he asked, as the barman poured the Perrier.

'Turn left out of here, they're on your right, sir.'

Morrissey nodded and wandered out.

The receptionist was busy this time. She didn't see him.

He found the toilets, passed by and saw a white house phone on the wall beyond. Without hesitating, he picked it up and flicked the cradle.

'Hello, reception,' said the voice at the other end.

'I've got a room-service order for Thornton,' Morrissey lied. 'But they've given me the wrong room number.'

'He's in 319,' the voice told him.

He hung up.

'Jesus fucking Christ, how much longer?' Frank Newton hissed.

He looked first at his watch, then at the screen above him.

VS004 from New York.

DELAYED.

101

THERE WERE HALF a dozen people ahead of Ray Gorman, a small huddle of guests who were waiting for the lifts to take them back to their rooms.

One woman, in her late thirties, was wearing just a white towelling bathrobe and slippers. Gorman might have sniggered if he hadn't had more important things on his mind.

He was standing close to the courier, aware now of the smell of the man's aftershave. It was probably expensive, he thought. If the bastard had the money to stay here, he obviously wasn't short of cash. But then, transporting drugs around the world probably carried enough financial rewards to counterbalance the threat of capture.

The lift descended once more and more people stepped in.

For a fleeting second, the courier looked as if he was going to push his way into the crowded car.

Has he sussed?

He stepped back when he saw the other lift doors opening.

Both he and Gorman took their place, followed by three other guests.

The portly American standing near the doors looked at each of the other occupants in turn. 'Which floor?' he asked cheerfully, finger poised over the numbered circles.

Gorman swallowed hard.

Fuck it. What now?

He lowered his head slightly.

Voices all around him.

'Three.'

'Six.'

'Four, please.'

And next to him: 'Six. Thank you,' said the courier.

'Six,' Gorman echoed.

The lift rose.

102

FRANK NEWTON SPUN the tap and scooped water into his hands. He splashed his face, enjoying the feel of the cool liquid against his hot skin.

When he straightened up he looked at the reflection staring back at him from the mirror: red-rimmed eyes; unkempt hair; skin the colour of sour milk.

Jesus. You look like shit.

He looked older than his forty-two years. He *felt* older. Much older.

The fluorescents in the ceiling cast their blinding white light over the bathroom. They were so powerful they made him wince.

There was someone in one of the cubicles. Newton could hear a low grunting.

Pre-flight nerves?

Another man, in his late twenties, finished at the urinals and crossed to the row of sinks to wash his hands. He glanced sideways at Newton and the older man saw the look in the mirror.

He eyed the newcomer momentarily, then crossed to

the paper-towel dispenser, tore three free and wiped his face and hands.

There was a screen suspended from the ceiling and he looked up towards it.

VS004, where the fuck are you?

The younger man finished washing his hands and walked out.

Newton paused a moment longer, brushing his hair back with both hands.

He glanced once again at the screen.

The lift bumped to a halt at the sixth floor and Ray Gorman waited a moment, allowing the courier to step out. He also ushered the other occupant into the corridor beyond before wandering out with as much nonchalance as he could muster.

The third man turned to the left.

The courier to the right.

Gorman followed at a respectful distance, heart thudding hard, his footsteps muted by the thick carpet.

The courier slowed his pace, fumbled in his jogging bottoms for his plastic key-card and inserted it in the lock.

Gorman walked past, seeing the green light on the lock flare.

He smiled to himself.

The courier closed the door of room 623.

Gorman headed back towards the lift.

*

Something had gone wrong – James Carson was convinced of it.

The plane should have been here by now.

He wouldn't have been left sitting in this stinking car park all day and most of the evening if everything was running according to plan.

Would he?

His hands were wet on the wheel and more than once he had wiped the palms on his trousers.

Aston Thomas, seated in the passenger seat inspecting the contents of one nostril on the end of his index finger, seemed less concerned.

They had spoken barely two dozen words all day.

No chit-chat.

No sense in getting to know a man you've got to kill, is there?

Carson felt a sudden shiver run along his spine despite the heat inside the car.

He looked at Thomas, who was apparently unaware of his gaze.

Carson was hungry. He'd eaten only bars of chocolate during the entire time they'd been sitting waiting.

Thomas had hurried off midway through the afternoon and returned with a hamburger and chips, but the smell had only made Carson feel sick, despite his need for food.

With the windows down, the stench of oil and petrol filled the car. With them up, the heat was almost intolerable. It had grown worse as day had stretched into evening.

As Carson moved he could feel his shirt sticking to his back.

The phone rang. He snatched it up and pressed it to his ear.

He recognized Newton's voice, heard the urgency in his tone.

'Got it, Frank,' he said, starting the engine, looking ahead at all times, never making eye contact with his passenger.

Thomas peered at him questioningly.

'The New York flight's just landed,' Carson told him.

103

'DON'T LOSE HER.' Codling's voice sounded loud inside the Vectra.

'I'm not going to,' Carson said calmly as he guided the car through the traffic heading into London. 'I know what I'm doing.'

The amount of vehicles had diminished slightly. The Vectra cruised along at a steady sixty in pursuit of the black cab ahead.

From his position in the rear seat, Newton could see the back of the third courier's head.

She'd been one of the first to emerge from the delayed flight: a petite woman in her early thirties with shoulder-length brown hair and smartly dressed in a cream jacket and skirt. She'd looked like any other businesswoman heading purposefully through the crowd, carrying her Gucci briefcase and Versace handbag.

More than once Newton had asked Codling if she was the one.

Could there be a mistake?

Codling was adamant. The woman

(*the attractive woman who looked so elegant despite her long flight*)

was the third courier.

'Don't let her get too far in front,' Thomas added, watching as a mini-coach pulled in behind the taxi.

'Just shut up and let him drive,' Newton snapped.

The car smelled of sweat. Newton could feel it beading on his forehead.

When he sucked in a breath it was stale; acrid, of unwashed bodies.

A hint of gun oil.

And fear?

It wasn't pleasant.

But it was somehow familiar. It belonged to this day. If Newton lived beyond it, he convinced himself he would never forget the smell.

Carson braked hard as a motorbike swerved in front of him.

The other three men were jolted in their seats.

'Be careful,' Thomas snapped.

'I told you once to shut it,' Newton rasped, shoving Thomas with the flat of his hand.

The other man turned in his seat and glared at him.

Codling leaned forward, grabbed Newton's wrist.

'Get your fucking hands off me,' Newton snarled, shaking free of the big Jamaican's grip.

The two men fixed stares for a second.

Inside the car the temperature rose another few degrees.

'Just drop it, all of you,' Carson called, eyes never leaving the taxi.

Codling and Newton were still glaring at each other.

As Newton moved he felt the Smith and Wesson .459 in the shoulder holster against his left side.

So easy to pull it now. Put one in the back of Thomas's head. Another in Codling. Right in the fucking face.

He wiped sweat from his forehead.

Signposts were beginning to display the words CENTRAL LONDON in bigger letters now.

They sped on.

104

'STAY IN THE car.' Newton spoke the words without even looking at Codling.

He never let his gaze stray from the figure of the smartly dressed woman in the cream suit who had just stepped from the taxi.

The vehicle had drawn up outside the main entrance to the Grosvenor Hotel next to Victoria station. Newton chanced a swift look at the building before his eyes returned to the woman once more.

Codling, also watching the courier, attempted to swing himself from the back of the car.

'I said stay there,' Newton hissed.

'Fuck you, man,' the Jamaican snapped. 'I coming in with you.'

'I'll call you when I've got her room number,' Newton said, taking a pace away from the car.

'Frank, she's going inside,' Carson said, watching as the courier made her way up the short flight of stone steps to the main doors of the hotel.

'You try and pull anything without me, Newton,' Codling hissed, 'I kill you.'

'Just shut up and sit tight,' Newton told him, hurrying across Buckingham Palace Road. He was no more than twenty seconds behind the courier.

'This is bullshit,' Aston Thomas complained, turning to look at Codling. 'How do we know what he's doing in there?'

Carson watched his companion climb the steps, almost colliding with an elderly couple who were leaving.

'He better not fuck this up,' Thomas continued.

'He knows what he's doing,' Carson murmured.

Newton slowed his pace as he entered the high-ceilinged foyer. There were a number of guests standing around. To his right, a group of men in their thirties were chatting animatedly, their raucous laughter filling the foyer.

To his left was reception. He could see the courier standing patiently, waiting to check in.

Newton walked slowly towards her and stood close behind.

He could smell her perfume.

Something expensive?

There were two receptionists on duty, but, fortunately for Newton, the second was busy with a Japanese couple who were also checking in. They didn't speak very good English and she was having problems.

Thank Christ. It suited him to have her occupied.

The courier moved forward and was greeted by a smile.

'You should have a room in the name of Wood,' the

smartly dressed woman announced in an American accent.

'First name, madame?' the receptionist wanted to know.

'Ally,' the courier told her. 'It's probably down as Alison.'

The receptionist smiled again and pushed a registration form across the marble counter towards her.

'Can I help you, sir?' the receptionist then asked Newton.

Come on. Buy some time. Wait until you've heard the courier's room number.

'I'm looking for a Mr Bishop,' he lied. 'I'm supposed to meet him here.'

'Which room is he in, sir?' the receptionist asked.

The courier was still filling in details.

'I don't know,' Newton said, using his most impressive fake smile.

'What's the initial? I'll check for you.'

'It's P,' he told her.

The receptionist tapped her keyboard, glanced at the screen before her.

The courier finished filling in the registration form and pushed it back across the counter.

'Just a minute, please, sir,' the receptionist said.

She took the form, scribbled something on it, then tore the bottom portion away, handing it back to the courier with a plastic key-card.

'Room 215 on the second floor,' she announced. 'The lifts are over to your left.'

Bingo.

Newton stepped aside to let the courier pass.

Again he smelled that expensive perfume.

'I can't find a Mr P. Bishop, sir,' the receptionist mused, still scanning names.

'It's OK,' Newton said, already turning away.

The receptionist raised a hand as if to halt him, but he was halfway across reception on his way to the main doors.

105

Why didn't the phone ring?

Ray Gorman gazed at the mobile lying on the parcel shelf, almost willing it to burst into life.

He looked at his watch: 10.06 p.m.

He'd heard nothing from Newton for over an hour.

The other two couriers had been successfully tailed; all three of them were in their rooms.

Gorman shifted in his seat.

What the fuck was Frank waiting for?

Toad glanced across at him and saw the anxiety in his expression.

'When we get word,' Gorman said, '*I'll* go in.'

'Just make sure you come out again with the drugs,' Toad told him.

Gorman reached inside his jacket and touched the Beretta.

Even the gun metal felt warm.

He continued to stare at the phone.

'What if something goes wrong?'

Jeff Hobbs's words hung ominously in the air.

'Like what?' Peter Morrissey wanted to know.

'What if the courier's armed?' Hobbs offered. 'What if he knows we're coming?'

'He doesn't know we're coming,' Skeng said dismissively.

'How can you be so sure?' Hobbs demanded.

'He's going down anyway,' Dudley Smith interjected. 'Who fucking cares? Either way, he's a dead man.'

'Then you can be first through the door, bigshot,' Morrissey said.

Smith scratched at his cheek. 'You think I'm scared?' he said.

'I haven't thought about it,' he replied, reaching for his cigarettes. He offered one to Hobbs, who declined. 'To be honest, I couldn't give a fuck either way. Just do your job when the time comes.'

'You're sure you don't want me to come with you?' Hobbs asked.

Morrissey shook his head. 'If we all go walking in, it'll look like a fucking school reunion,' he said. 'Me and Skeng'll go. Straight in. Get the drugs. Straight out.'

'If anyone gets in the way we take them out too,' Skeng added.

Morrissey drew hard on his cigarette.

'Frank should be ringing soon,' Hobbs observed, looking at his watch.

'I'm fed up of waiting. Let's do it,' Aston Thomas said, looking round at Frank Newton, perspiration beading on his forehead.

Newton ignored him, glancing alternately at his watch and the front of the Grosvenor.

He wondered what the courier was doing now.

Having a shower? Eating supper? Sleeping?

Does it matter?

He managed to swallow, despite the fact his throat was so dry. 'Codling. You come in twenty seconds after me. Straight up to the second floor,' Newton said to the big Jamaican. 'Room 215. Twenty seconds, right? No sooner. No later.'

'Making your big plans,' Thomas sneered.

'Shut up, you cunt, or I'll fucking kill *you*,' hissed Newton. He allowed his hand to slip inside his jacket, brushing against the .459.

Codling himself slapped the back of Thomas's head. 'Shut your mouth,' he snapped.

Thomas returned to staring at the hotel.

Codling smiled. 'You scared, Newton?' he said.

'Scared of what? That I might blow your mate's head off before we've got the drugs?' He nodded towards Thomas.

'Scared because you got to kill a woman.'

Newton held his gaze.

'I told you,' the Jamaican continued. 'Don't worry about it. I'll be there.'

'I know you will,' Newton muttered.

Again he looked at his watch: 10.15.

He reached for the mobile phone and dialled the first number.

106

'YOU KEEP THAT fucking engine running.' Ray Gorman tapped the bonnet of the car as he walked away.

Toad watched him make his way towards the main entrance of the Holiday Inn and disappear inside. Through the wide plate-glass windows, he could see him moving towards the lifts.

As he waited in the foyer, Gorman dug his hands in his pockets. He was aware of the concierge looking in his direction, but he didn't turn to meet the man's gaze.

A couple emerged from the bar.

Gorman looked round.

I don't want you fuckers in this lift with me.

The woman disappeared into the toilets. Her companion wandered across to glance at the framed menu on the wall opposite.

The lift doors slid open and Gorman stepped in. He jabbed the '6' button and the lift began to rise.

As it did he pulled the Beretta 9mm from its shoulder holster and worked the slide, chambering a round. He slid the automatic back into the holster and glanced up at the numbers above the doors as each one glowed.

The lift continued to climb.

Peter Morrissey checked his watch as he paused outside the door of Room 319 in the Dorchester.

Skeng continued walking, heading for the fire exit at the end of the corridor.

The sound of a television drifted from one of the nearby rooms.

He looked around quickly, then pressed hard against the lever that opened the fire door. It moved with an annoyingly loud shriek, the metal grating against concrete floor beneath.

Skeng cursed under his breath and left the door slightly ajar. Then he made his way back towards where Morrissey was standing.

There was a room-service breakfast card hanging on the door handle, carefully filled in and signed.

Morrissey was gazing down at it, as if trying to read what the courier had ordered.

Whatever it was, he'd never get the chance to eat it.

He looked at Skeng, who nodded.

As Frank Newton stepped out of the lift he looked at the sign before him. Arrows indicated the direction he should take for bedrooms 201–225.

He set off down the narrow corridor of the Grosvenor.

As he rounded a corner, a well-dressed man in a dark jacket and trousers passed him and nodded a greeting. Newton returned the gesture and walked on, conscious of the floorboards creaking beneath his feet.

He looked at each door number.

207.

209.

211.

His heart was thudding hard now.

He heard footsteps behind him; heavy and purposeful.

As he glanced back he saw the large shape of Codling loom into view.

As the big Jamaican drew level with him he pointed at the door of Room 215 and Newton nodded.

Codling slid a hand inside his jacket and pulled out a long, wickedly sharp knife. The point was serrated.

Newton eyed the savage weapon warily.

'Gun too noisy,' Codling told him.

Newton checked his watch: 10.30.

He knocked gently on the door of Room 215.

107

THE SILENCER WAS a length of steel tube about seven inches long. As Ray Gorman screwed it into the barrel of the Beretta he knew that the device would aid him a little in his task, absorbing most of the muzzle flash and a fair bit of the retort when he fired the pistol. The term 'silencer' was something of a misnomer in reality as there would still be a considerable bang when the weapon was fired – not the conveniently muffled thud heard so often in films. But it was enough for his purposes.

Enough to give him time.

He knocked on the door and waited.

His heart was hammering against his ribs, the blood rushing in his ears.

He waited a moment or two, then knocked again.

Come on. Come on.

Movement on the other side of the door.

Inside, the first courier would be pressing his eye to the spyhole, anxious to see who was knocking.

Gorman swung the pistol up, jammed the gaping end of the silencer against the peep-hole and fired once.

Travelling at a speed in excess of 1,500 feet per

second, the heavy-grain bullet exploded from the gun, stove in the spyhole and a portion of the door and powered through.

It caught the courier in the left eye, burst the bulging orb and exploded from the back of his head, carrying a flux of brain, blood and pulverized bone with it.

Gorman put his weight against the door and pushed.

It wouldn't open.

The body had fallen against it.

'Room service,' Peter Morrissey called, his hand inside his jacket. He was standing away from the door of Room 319, pressed against the frame on one side.

Skeng was in a similar position on the other side.

He knocked once more. 'Room service,' he called again.

'I didn't order anything.'

The voice from the other side was sudden and startled him.

'I've got an order for Room 319, sir,' he replied, his voice cracking. 'Mr Thornton?'

Silence from inside.

'That's the name I've got on the order,' Morrissey persisted.

Skeng drew the .357 Desert Eagle from its shoulder holster and hefted it before him.

Morrissey shook his head when he saw the weapon. 'Could you just check the order, please, sir?' he persisted.

Silence from inside 319.

He's not going to open the fucking door, is he?

Further down the corridor, another door was opening.

'Mr Thornton?' Morrissey said, as calmly as he could.

They could hear the chink of expensive crockery and crystal as the room-service tray further down the corridor was pushed out for collection.

There was laughter.

A woman stuck her head around the door frame and looked out at them. For interminable seconds they locked stares, then she disappeared back inside the room, wondering who these men were and what they wanted.

She could be calling down for help even now.

'Mr Thornton,' Morrissey called.

He heard the sound of the lock being released.

The second courier opened the door and looked out.

'Step back inside the room,' the former soldier told him, the Zastava 9mm levelled at the courier's stomach. 'And don't make a sound or I'll fucking blow you in half.'

Newton heard the sound of running water as they entered the room.

Despite the electronic lock, he and Codling had found little difficulty gaining entry to Room 215 in the Grosvenor.

The knife, jammed into the slot that normally accepted the key-card, had triggered the device and they had slipped inside.

There was no sign of the courier.

Clothes were laid out on the bed. The cream suit she had worn from the airport was hanging in the half-open wardrobe.

The television was on, the volume low.

Again Newton heard running water and nodded towards the bathroom.

The Gucci briefcase was on the desk near the window, the Versace handbag on the chair nearby.

He moved towards it, preparing to flip it open, when the water stopped running.

They both heard movement from inside the bathroom and now just a steady drip from the shower head.

Codling ducked behind the door.

Newton stepped towards the bottom of the bed, the .459 gripped in his fist.

The courier emerged from the bathroom drying her face, another towel wrapped around her wet hair. The white towelling robe she wore looked several sizes too big and Newton thought, for fleeting seconds, how small and petite the woman was.

As she looked up, she saw him and opened her mouth as if to scream or speak.

He raised a hand to silence her, the moment stretching into an eternity like the frozen frame of a film.

They merely stood looking at each other.

This attractive, petite woman in the towelling robe and the man with the 9mm automatic.

Then, the film began to run again.

Codling stepped forward from behind the bathroom door, grabbed the woman by her wet, dark hair, yanked her head backwards and, with one swift movement, ran the knife across her throat.

Newton saw her eyes bulge madly in the sockets, more in surprise than pain. Then the wound in her neck opened like some yawning mouth, severed arteries spewing their crimson contents into the air, her eyes rolling upwards in the sockets.

Codling kept hold of her, careful that none of her spurting blood should stain his own clothes. It soaked into the towelling robe like ink into blotting paper. Newton could see her body twitching uncontrollably.

The big Jamaican let go, allowing the body to drop at his feet. Blood began to spread in a rapidly widening pool around the courier.

Newton looked at Codling for a moment and saw the faintest trace of a smile on his lips.

'Get the drugs,' the Jamaican said.

He began pulling drawers open in the sideboard.

Newton grabbed the briefcase and up-ended it, the contents falling out like bizarre confetti: air tickets; receipts; pens; a notepad; a map of London.

Codling was still tearing his way through the sideboard. 'Here,' he said, pulling two of the drawers free.

Newton stepped across to join him, careful not to step in the blood that had already soaked into the carpet. The air in the room smelled coppery.

There were several bags of white powder in each of the drawers, perhaps ten at first glance. Codling slit one with the tip of the knife, moistened his finger and tasted the white powder.

It felt cold on his tongue.

'There isn't a hundred kilos there,' Newton snapped. 'What the fuck's going on? Where's the rest of it?'

He raised the Smith and Wesson slightly.

He's done you up, hasn't he? The fucker's double-crossed you!

'Where's the rest of it?' Newton repeated.

'This is it,' Codling told him. 'Fifteen, twenty keys.'

Kill him now.

Newton thumbed back the hammer on the .459 and raised it so that the barrel was aimed at Codling's face.

'You don't understand, do you?' the Jamaican said, grinning.

'No, I don't. And if you don't *make* me understand by the time I count to three, you're a fucking dead man.'

108

Ray Gorman was moments from panic.

He put all his weight against the door of room 623, but it wouldn't budge. The dead weight of the courier had wedged it shut as surely as if it had been barricaded.

He stepped back and thought about trying to kick it down.

Great idea. No one will hear you booting it off the fucking hinges, will they?

Gorman sucked in a deep breath. A matter of thirty seconds had passed since he'd fired.

No one had come yet – no inquisitive heads had poked from the other bedrooms.

Not yet.

He knew that he had to get into the room as quickly as possible; get the drugs and get out.

He stared at the lock.

'Fuck it,' Gorman snarled.

He drew the Beretta once more, aimed at the lock and fired, the silencer again absorbing a good deal of the muzzle retort. There was a dull thud as the shell struck, blasting the surrounding wood into a dozen pieces.

Immediately, he threw his weight against the door and felt it open a fraction.

Through the gap he could see a rigored hand.

As he shoved harder the door opened further.

He saw blood on the wall.

Then he was inside and standing over the dead courier.

No time to lose now.

He went straight to the man's briefcase and shook it; four plastic bags, each sealed with cellotape, fell at his feet.

Gorman snatched them up and placed them on the bed, then he crossed to the bedside cabinets and pulled out the drawers.

Empty.

So was the wardrobe.

He gripped one of the four bags.

Four, lousy, stinking, fucking bags. Just four.

'You fucking cunt,' he hissed, his words directed at the body of the dead courier.

It was then that he heard the knock on the door.

'Where are the drugs?' Peter Morrissey still had the Zastava aimed at the second courier.

The man was sitting on the edge of the bed. His face was milk-white, his gaze darting back and forth between the former soldier and Skeng who was standing with his back against the door.

Morrissey thumbed back the hammer on the automatic and lifted it so that the barrel was inches from the courier's forehead.

'You're going to kill me anyway,' said Thornton flatly. 'Why not get it over with?'

'The drugs,' Morrissey repeated.

The courier pointed to the mahogany chest of drawers on the far side of the room.

Skeng hurried across to them, pulling them open. He held up three bags of white powder.

'Five more in here,' he said, then began stuffing them into his pockets. 'That's it.' He stepped away from the drawers.

Morrissey moved fast. He grabbed a pillow from behind the courier, rammed it into his face and pushed him back onto the bed, forcing the barrel of the automatic against the material.

He fired once, the blast absorbed by the pillow.

The courier's body twitched three times and as Morrissey stepped back he could smell the unmistakeable odour of excrement rising from the corpse as the sphincter muscle relaxed.

A thin plume of smoke drifted from the black hole in the pillow, the stench of burned cotton mingling with the more pungent scent of cordite.

Blood was beginning to soak into the sheets and pillowcase.

'Move it,' he said to Skeng. Then he bent and retrieved the single spent shell case.

109

FRANK NEWTON STILL had the .459 pointed at
Codling's head as the big Jamaican smeared more
cocaine on his fingertip.

'I'm listening,' Newton snapped. 'What's so special
about this stuff?'

'It's pink flake, man.' Codling grinned. 'It don't come
no better than this.'

'What the fuck are you talking about?'

'This gear. It's A1. Top grade. Very rare. Very
expensive.'

Newton lowered the barrel slightly.

'When coke comes into this country, it usually comes
in slightly moist. Almost like a paste,' the Jamaican
explained. 'The good stuff, maybe only twenty or thirty
per cent diluted, it tastes a little of petrol. Make your
tongue and gums go numb quick. This – ' he raised a bag
of the powder ' – this is better.'

Newton reached for some of the coke himself and
squinted at it in the subdued light of the room. He could
indeed see tiny pink dots in amongst the almost phosphorescent brilliance of the powder.

'Pink flake so rare, it usually been cut with pink champagne.'

'What the fuck is that?'

'Speed.'

'So how do you know this batch hasn't?'

Codling smeared more on his gums. 'I've already tasted it once,' he reminded Newton. 'If this was cut with speed, I'd be chewing my cheeks by now.' He grinned.

'You said it was expensive. *How* expensive?'

'Most coke sells for fifty pounds a gram. You looking at two hundred a gram for this. After it's been cut, maybe a hundred.' He licked more from his finger. 'It bites, though. One and a half grams of this pink flake will kill you. Too pure.'

Newton regarded the Jamaican evenly.

'Your Mr Parker should be pleased with this,' Codling said.

'Perhaps it's time we found out,' Newton told him. 'Let's get out of here.'

First the knock on the door. Then, as Ray Gorman watched, the handle was pushed down.

Someone was trying to get in, but the body of the courier was still blocking the entrance, causing enough of an obstruction to hamper the intruder's progress.

Gorman's mind was spinning.

Hotel staff? Had someone heard the shots? Police even?

He raised the Beretta and aimed.

Whoever came through that door wasn't going out again. He'd already gone too far. There was no turning back now.

The movement outside stopped abruptly.

Gorman took a step closer.

He heard someone shuffling from one foot to the other, then an index finger poked through the hole in the door where the spyhole had once been.

Again the handle was depressed.

The door began to swing open this time, the pressure causing the corpse to roll over.

Come on then.

He rested his finger on the trigger and prepared to fire.

Whoever was outside gave one more hard shove and the door opened.

Toad stepped into the room, almost tripping over the dead courier.

'Jesus Christ,' hissed Gorman, lowering the automatic.

'What the fuck are you doing?' Toad asked, looking first at the body, then at the ravaged room. 'You've been up here long enough.'

'That's all there is,' Gorman told him, motioning to the four bags of cocaine on the bed. 'Looks like your fucking boss was wrong.'

Toad pushed past him and picked up one of the plastic bags. 'There must be more than this,' he said.

'Then you *find* it.' He studied Toad's broad back for a second. 'Or, on second thoughts, don't bother.'

Toad half turned, aware that Gorman was raising the 9mm.

The Beretta bucked in his fist as he fired.

One hollow-tip bullet powered into the base of Toad's skull. It snapped his head forward, erupting from the roof of his cranium and sending a fountain of crimson into the air.

The impact threw him forward onto the bed where he bounced once, blood spraying over the mattress. He slid back onto his knees, his bullet-blasted head resting on the counterpane.

He looked as if he was praying.

The second shot was hardly necessary.

Nor the third.

Gorman snatched up the cocaine, stepped over the dead courier and hurried out into the corridor.

As he headed for the lift he wiped two spots of blood from his jacket with the moistened end of his handkerchief.

110

THE FIRST CALL came through at 10.43 p.m.

Frank Newton reached for the Motorola and pressed it to his ear. He recognized the voice immediately.

'We've got it, Frank,' Peter Morrissey told him. 'But not as much as you said there'd be.'

'We had the same problem,' he replied. 'Where are you now?'

Morrissey said they were approaching their car, parked close to the Dorchester.

'What about Jeff?'

He told him that Hobbs was waiting with Dudley Smith.

'Use one car, Pete,' Newton urgd.

There was a moment's silence on the other end of the line.

'Understand?' Newton persisted.

Morrissey said that he did, then switched off.

No more than a few seconds passed and the high-pitched ringing sounded again.

'That'd better be you, Ray,' Newton said.

Gorman told him he was in the car. He had the drugs.

'Any problems?' Newton asked.

Gorman told him everything was under control. He waited a moment, then added that he was alone.

'Good,' Newton said flatly. 'See you soon.'

He hung up.

'The couriers are dead,' he muttered, gazing straight ahead. 'We've got the drugs.'

James Carson caught his reflection briefly in the rear-view mirror.

'Now you ring Parker,' Codling said, smiling. 'Tell him we can do business. Tell him he owes me some money.'

'We're due to meet him at his Mayfair casino at half-past eleven,' Newton informed the Jamaican. 'And that's what we're going to do.' He reached into his pocket for a cigarette and, as he did, his hand brushed against the butt of the .459.

Do it. Just fucking do it.

He glanced briefly at Codling, then ahead once again.

Carson guided the car into Park Lane, then swung right into Stanhope Gate.

Just as they'd planned.

'Nearly there,' Newton said, his words apparently directed at empty air.

Behind the wheel, Carson understood.

Peter Morrissey had no idea how long it would be before the body of the second courier was found. He hadn't given it much thought since he and Skeng had success-fully slipped out of the Dorchester.

He had other things on his mind now.

The two men walked unhurriedly across the main forecourt of the hotel, Morrissey even nodding at the doorman on the way out.

'What the fuck are you doing?' Skeng hissed.

The former soldier didn't answer.

As he walked, his gaze never wavered. He could see the car with Jeff Hobbs and Dudley Smith about two hundred yards away, parked in a dimly lit thoroughfare just off Reeves Mews.

As they drew nearer, Hobbs looked disinterestedly in their direction, reached inside his jacket and took out a packet of Rothmans.

The cigarette was the signal.

They were twenty yards from the car now.

Hobbs was searching for his lighter.

Fifteen yards.

Morrissey could feel the Zastava against his left side. He took a step closer to the black man, making sure that Skeng was no more than a foot from him.

He may only get one chance – he didn't want to miss.

Ten yards.

Hobbs had found his lighter. He lit up, the flame from the Zippo like a beacon inside the gloomy car.

Morrissey pulled the automatic free of its holster and pressed it against Skeng's back.

As he did he fired twice, bullets tearing through the man's kidneys and liver, ripping through his stomach as they exited.

He doubled up, legs giving way beneath him.

Inside the car, Smith shouted something.

Hobbs struck with his right hand; a blow so powerful it shattered Smith's nose and snapped his head backwards against the headrest.

Hobbs turned in his seat and hit him again, breaking his bottom jaw, then grabbed Smith by the back of the head and slammed his forehead into the steering wheel.

Once, twice, three times.

Smith lolled back in the driver's seat, eyes already rolling in their sockets. Hobbs drove two more punches into his throat, rupturing his larynx, driving bone fragments back into his windpipe. Smith let out a liquid gurgle and slid sideways against the window, blood smearing the glass.

Moving quickly, Hobbs clambered out of the passenger seat, scurried around and wrenched open the driver's door, allowing Smith's body to fall into the road where it lay motionless.

On the pavement, Morrissey knelt beside Skeng and put one more bullet into the back of his head. Portions of skull and brain spattered the concrete.

The ex-army man jumped into the passenger seat as Hobbs started the engine.

'Is he dead?' Morrissey demanded, nodding in Smith's direction.

Hobbs stuck the car in reverse, the rear wheel crushing Smith's skull like an egg.

'He is now,' Hobbs murmured.

The car moved off.

111

Frank Newton was gazing out of the side window as they drove.

What's wrong? Can't look at him? Scared you won't be able to pull the trigger?

'How do I know I'll get my money?'

Codling's question startled him from his meditations.

'What?' Newton mused.

'I don't trust Parker.'

'You've got no choice.'

'We could take the drugs for ourselves,' Aston Thomas said from the front seat.

'He'd kill you,' Newton said flatly.

'We might kill *him*,' Thomas offered.

'You ring him now,' Codling urged. 'Tell him we coming.'

'He won't be at the casino until half eleven, I told you that.'

'Then fuck him,' hissed the Jamaican. 'We got the drugs. I say if he not there now, then the deal is off.'

Newton could feel his heart thumping harder.

It's time. No more stalling. Get it done.

He looked ahead once again, saw Carson's eyes in the rear-view mirror; saw the realization.

Do it. Do it now.

The older man turned the wheel sharply, enough to send the other occupants of the vehicle tumbling. With his right hand he reached inside his jacket, his fingers gripping the butt of the .38 he carried.

In the rear of the car, Newton dragged the .459 free and pressed it against Codling's chest, firing twice.

Codling jerked in his seat, blood spattering up the inside of the door panel.

Empty shell cases flew from the weapon as it slammed back against the heel of his hand. Newton kept his finger on the trigger. He pumped three more shots into the big Jamaican, the retort deafening inside the close confines of the car. Blood, cordite and excrement combined to form a noxious odour.

In the passenger seat, Aston Thomas froze, eyes bulging wide.

'Shoot him, Jim!' roared Newton.

Thomas grabbed for the .38 as Carson's finger tightened on the trigger and succeeded in knocking the weapon upwards, the bullet exploding through the roof.

The car skidded slightly, threatening to spin. Carson regained control and drove on.

Newton pressed the .459 to the back of the passenger seat and pumped the trigger. Bullets tore through the upholstery and ripped into Thomas. Some exited, blasting fist-sized holes in his chest and stomach. At least two ploughed on and punched through the windscreen.

His body jerked madly with each impact; blood sprayed the windscreen and dashboard.

The slide finally flew back on the .459, signalling that the weapon was empty.

Newton slumped back in his seat, the effort of drilling the remaining nine shots in the magazine into Thomas making him gasp.

Both he and Carson were deaf, Newton virtually blinded by the searing muzzle flashes.

The entire car was like a mobile slaughterhouse.

There was an underground car park up ahead. The entrance was well lit, but the rest in semi-darkness.

Just as they'd planned.

Carson swung the vehicle into it, only too happy for it to be swallowed by the subterranean gloom.

He parked in a bay furthest from the entrance and switched off the engine and the lights.

In the new-found silence, they heard the first of the sirens.

112

'COME ON, JIM, for Christ's sake,' Newton urged, watching as Carson sat motionless behind the wheel. 'Let's go.'

The older man looked at Newton wearily, then at the bullet-blasted bodies of Thomas and Codling.

The stench inside the car was overpowering.

'Jim,' Newton snapped. 'Come on.'

The sirens were growing louder.

Carson sucked in a lungful of reeking air, nodded almost imperceptibly, then finally scrambled out of the car.

The smell of death was replaced by the stink of oil and petrol inside the underground car park.

He hurried towards the exit behind Newton and the two of them climbed the stone steps to street level. They continued walking, Newton pulling his jacket more tightly around him to hide the bloodstains on his shirt.

He retrieved the Nokia from inside the jacket and dialled.

It rang once, twice.

As they walked, he looked across at Carson who was gazing ahead blankly. His eyes held all the dynamism of a lobotomy patient. He was moving stiffly, as if the simple act of putting one foot in front of the other was a task of incredible complexity that he was still learning.

Newton recognized the voice that finally answered the phone.

'Pete, where are you?' he asked.

'Audley Street,' Morrissey told him.

'Come and pick us up. Corner of Tilney Street and Audley Square.'

'What about Codling?'

'Dead. Did *you* have any trouble?'

'No. The job's done. We're OK. We'll be with you in a couple of minutes.'

Newton switched off the phone and turned to Carson. 'Jim, this is nearly over,' he whispered.

'No it's not, Frank. And you know it.'

'We drop the drugs off at Billy Parker's casino, pick up the money and we're done.'

'That easy,' Carson said, smiling humourlessly.

'If we do it right, yeah. Don't fall apart on me now, Jim.'

'What about the police?'

'Fuck the police. We'll make it.'

'I wish I was as sure as you, Frank.'

'Trust me.' He put one arm around the older man's shoulder and held him for a moment.

There was a car approaching. It was flashing its lights.

Newton smiled as he caught sight of Hobbs behind the wheel.

'Another hour and it's over for good, Jim,' Newton said.

They both climbed into the waiting car.

Ray Gorman parked the car at the junction of Red Lion Yard and Hays Mews. He sat for a moment listening to the radio, then switched it off.

He'd call Frank Newton in a minute, tell him where he was. Ask where they were to meet.

But it could wait a moment longer.

He slid the Beretta from its shoulder holster, pressed the magazine-release button and began feeding 9mm shells into the slim metal clip.

He had two spare clips in his pocket as well as some loose ammunition: over forty-five rounds.

Then he reached for the mobile.

He was ready.

113

'ARE YOU *SURE*?' Detective Inspector John Ridley glared at his companion, the vein at his temple throbbing.

The younger man nodded. 'Positive ID on both bodies,' DS Darren Brown told him. 'The men in the car were Aston Thomas and Ernie Codling.'

'Who called in the report?'

'The security guard who works at the car park found the bodies. A mobile unit checked it out. There's no mistake.'

'And the others?'

'Positive ID on those too,' the DS continued. 'Lawrence Vassell and Dudley Smith.'

'Codling and three of his men killed in one night.'

'And within half a mile of each other.'

'It's got to be Billy Parker's boys. Codling must have pushed too hard this time and we *know* he was doing a job with Parker. It's too much of a coincidence.'

'What do you want to do, guv?'

'How long ago were the bodies found?'

'Ten, fifteen minutes tops.'

Ridley rubbed his cheek with the flat of one hand. 'I

want mobile units to check *all* Parker's places within a mile of where the bodies were found,' the DI instructed.

'They'll need warrants if they're going to search them.'

'Fuck the warrants. Get them to say there's been a security alert. I don't care what they do, but I want uniforms inside his buildings within the hour.'

'What do you think they're going to find? Even if Parker *did* have Codling and his men killed, there's no way we'll be able to prove it.'

'It might unsettle him enough to make him careless. If he thinks we can tie him to these killings he might make a mistake.'

'I doubt it. He—'

'It's all we've got,' Ridley snarled, cutting his companion short. 'We know Frank Newton and some of Parker's boys were pulling a job with Codling. It's just a matter of time before we run down some prints.'

Frank Newton. At last.

'And what if the mobile units *do* find something?'

'I want to know straight away.'

'Parker's not going to let it happen.'

'Just do it,' Ridley snapped. 'And one more thing. I want Armed Response Units on standby.'

114

THE WARMTH OF the day had given way to an unexpectedly cold night. Frank Newton pulled up the collar of
his jacket and shivered slightly. He wasn't completely
sure that the chill was due to the powerful breeze
blowing down Hill Street.

There were lights on in a number of the windows
along the thoroughfare, illuminating expensive edifices
built in the Georgian style. Some were offices, others the
homes of those blessed with more money than people
like Newton could ever imagine.

And then there was the casino.

Towards the Berkeley Square end of the street, it was,
like so many properties on either side, of white stone. A
set of pointed, black-painted metal railings stood on
either side of the three stone steps that led up to the
front door.

There was a curious absence of light and movement
inside the building.

Across the street, builders' rubbish was piled high in
a skip due to the fact a number of the buildings were

undergoing renovation. By the look of it, so was the casino.

Newton took a drag on his cigarette. That was why there were no punters in, he reasoned. The place was being refurbished.

It suited him to think that.

'Are we *all* going in?' Jeff Hobbs asked.

Newton took a final drag, then dropped the butt on the ground.

'I think we should,' Morrissey added.

'Well, Frank?' Gorman added.

Newton shook his head. 'I'll go,' he said quietly.

'I don't trust him, Frank,' Carson murmured.

'We've done what he asked. We kept up our end of the deal. Don't sweat it. I'll take him the drugs, pick up the money and we can get out of here.'

'Be careful,' Morrissey urged.

Newton set off across the street towards the casino, the briefcase gripped in his left hand.

The security camera above the door whirred into action, its cyclopean eye fixing him in an unblinking stare.

He pressed a button on the intercom panel beside the front door and a buzzer sounded inside.

The door opened and Newton stepped into the darkened hall.

There was another intercom unit just inside the door.

'Come up,' said a voice he recognized as belonging to Billy Parker.

Straight ahead were the stairs. To the right and left gaming tables marked with roulette grids, backgammon boards and blackjack stood sentinel. Several doors led off from the central area, the rooms beyond no doubt allowing for poker and other games to be played.

There was a large cloakroom to the left. Beyond it the bar.

The plushly carpeted staircase rose to a marble balcony where there was another bar and more gaming tables.

Paintings in gilt frames hung all the way up the wall that flanked the staircase.

It was towards these steps Newton walked, the carpet muffling his footfalls.

The silence was oppressive.

Halfway up, he heard sounds of movement ahead, then, above him, two figures appeared.

Then two more.

Newton recognized one of them as Adam Rawlings. The other three he'd never seen before.

Another man emerged from the oak-panelled door at the top of the stairs. Newton didn't recognize him either.

'Billy's in there,' Rawlings said, nodding towards a room across the spacious landing.

'Nice to see he's laid on a welcoming committee,' Newton said, attempting a smile.

Rawlings ignored the comment.

There were more men in the area outside Parker's office; more faces he didn't recognize.

One of them knocked on the office door.

It was opened by the younger of the Milliner brothers, who stepped back to allow him entry.

Billy Parker was sitting behind his desk, a Lalique whiskey tumbler in his hand. He looked at Newton, then tapped the face of his Rolex.

'You're late, Frank,' he said flatly. 'I've been waiting.'

115

NEWTON STOOD BEFORE the antique wooden desk and felt three sets of eyes boring into him.

It was the kind of feeling he'd had before – just before sentencing, usually.

The room was as he'd remembered it: the cabinets full of expensive crystal; the antique leather sofas; the fabulous paintings hung on the oak-panelled walls.

The antique swords in a lethal fan-shape behind the desk.

'Why all the new faces, Billy?' Newton asked, attempting a smile. 'Are you throwing a party for us?'

'Is Codling dead?' Parker asked.

'Him and all his boys,' Newton said. 'Just like you said.'

'Where's his head, Frank? I told you to bring me his head.'

Newton shifted from one foot to the other. 'There wasn't time, Billy,' he said quietly.

Parker cracked out laughing. 'I was joking, Frank,' he chuckled. 'I just wanted to see if you'd do it or not.'

The Milliner brothers were laughing too.

'I told the boys – ' Parker nodded at each brother in turn ' – we'd wind you up a bit.'

'Yeah, very funny, Billy,' Newton said without a trace of a smile.

'Would you have done it?' asked Parker.

'I suppose so,' the younger man told him.

'Did you have any trouble getting the drugs?'

Newton shook his head. 'We had to kill the couriers,' he said.

'I thought you would. Show me what you got.' He pointed at the briefcase.

Newton prepared to lay it on the desktop.

'Gently, this furniture wasn't cheap,' Parker said.

Newton laid it down carefully, then stepped back.

There was a loud snap as Parker opened it. 'What the fuck is this?' he said, gazing into the case.

Newton swallowed hard.

Parker turned the case to show him the contents. 'Where's the rest of it, Frank?' he demanded.

'I asked Codling the same thing. That's all there was, Billy.'

'That black cunt told me there'd be three hundred kilos. Where is it?'

'Billy, think about it. If I'd ripped you off, would I have walked in here tonight? I'd have taken the fucking lot and legged it. That's all there is. I swear on my kid's life.'

Parker laughed once again. 'On *what*, Frank?' he sniggered. 'On *your* kid's life?'

Newton clenched his fists by his sides, aware of the grins on the faces of the men standing either side of Parker too.

'You've only got a kid because you bought it, Frank,' Parker reminded him. 'Ten grand. Because your old woman's tubes were fucked or something. And you only got the chance to buy it because of *me*. So, if you're going to swear, then I'd be a bit more choosy about what you swear *on*.'

'The cocaine in that case is pure,' Newton said, trying to control his breathing. 'Codling said it was the purest you could get.'

'And you believed him?' Parker chided.

'Look at it, Billy. Those pink dots in it, they're—'

'Fuck the drugs,' Parker sneered. 'Codling's dead. That's all that matters to me. I don't need this shit.' He closed the briefcase. 'I never did.'

'What does that mean?' Newton wanted to know.

'It means the job's done, Frank.'

'What about our money, Billy?'

Again Parker laughed. 'It's staying in my safe,' he replied, hooking a finger over his shoulder.

'We had a deal.'

'Did you honestly believe I was going to pay you and those fucking losers you work with to do *anything* for me?' snapped Parker. 'You stole from me, Frank. Three hundred and twenty-six thousand pounds to be exact and you thought I'd give you another two million for wiping out a few niggers? You're a bigger cunt than I took you for.' He raised his glass in salute. 'I'll tell you the deal, Frank. You're still alive. Now piss off. If I was you, I'd walk while you still can.'

Newton glared at the gang boss, then at the grinning men on either side of him.

'Go now,' Parker persisted.

Newton stood for a second longer, then turned and headed for the door.

Stephen Milliner walked with him. 'Those weapons we brought you,' he said, leaning close to Newton. 'Bring them back tomorrow. Got it?' He opened the office door.

'Say hello to the kid for me when you get home, Frank.' Parker chuckled.

Milliner closed the door behind him.

From inside the room, Newton could hear mocking laughter.

It cut like a knife.

He made his way across the landing and down the stairs, watched every inch of the way by the other men inside the casino.

Even when he reached the bottom of the steps, there was still laughter ringing in his ears.

116

RAY GORMAN WAS the first to see Newton emerge from the casino. He watched as his companion trudged slowly back across the street, hands dug in his pockets.

'What did he say?' Gorman demanded.

For a moment, Newton couldn't speak.

'Where's the money, Frank?' Gorman persisted.

'There *is* no money,' Newton hissed. 'He set us up. He was never going to pay us.'

'That fucking cunt,' Gorman snarled, taking a step into the street, glaring in the direction of the casino.

'You told him we killed the Yardies?' Carson asked, his voice low.

'I told him everything, Jim.'

'So that's it?' Morrissey asked.

Newton didn't answer.

'We risked our fucking lives,' snarled Gorman. 'Killed eight people and Parker won't pay?'

Newton sat on the bonnet of the car and lit a cigarette.

'We got something out of it,' Carson interjected.

'The money from the Securicor job?' rasped Morrissey. 'What the fuck was that?'

'He promised us two million, didn't he?' Gorman added.

Newton drew on the cigarette, eyes fixed on the casino. He could still hear the laughter inside his head.

Mocking.

'What do we do, Frank?' Hobbs wanted to know.

'What *can* we do?' Carson murmured wearily. 'It's over.'

'Frank.' It was Hobbs who spoke his name and laid a hand gently on his shoulder.

Newton took another drag on his cigarette, allowing the smoke to burn its way down to his lungs. 'One of the Milliner boys said they wanted the weapons back,' he said finally.

Hobbs looked puzzled.

'The guns they gave us to kill Codling and his men,' Newton continued.

'What the fuck are you going on about, Frank?' rasped Gorman. 'Two million quid that we *earned* is sitting up there with Billy Parker and all you can think about is guns?'

Newton looked straight into the younger man's eyes. 'They want them back,' he repeated slowly. 'I think we should deliver them.' He took a final drag on his cigarette and ground it out beneath his feet.

Hobbs nodded almost imperceptibly.

Gorman smiled.

Morrissey was already moving towards the boot of the vehicle.

Only Carson remained motionless, staring at his companion.

'Is it worth it, Frank?' he said softly.

'It is to *me*, Jim.'

'And if I decide not to go with you?'

'Then I'd understand. But what's left, Jim? What's left for any of us?' He walked round to the boot of the car and looked in at the vast array of weapons.

Hobbs worked the slide of the Taurus 9mm and then slid the pistol back into its shoulder holster. He cradled the HK MP5 in his hand, slammed in a thirty-round magazine and chambered a round.

Morrissey lifted the Ithaca from the boot and began thumbing cartridges into the breach. Every now and then he worked the slide until all eight of the lethal projectiles were loaded. He scooped up several spare handfuls from a box and shoved them into his pockets.

Gorman jammed a .357 revolver into his belt, then checked that the Beretta 9mm was loaded and ready. He reached for the Spas, extending the collapsible stock and hooking the loop of metal over his shoulder. He worked the slide with one hand and stepped back.

With the .459 already in its shoulder holster, Newton reached for another of the MP5s. He was about to pick up one of the Leland 210s, but another hand closed around the sawn-off shotgun.

'I'll take that,' said James Carson.

He broke it, thumbed in two cartridges, then snapped the weapon shut again. As Newton watched, he also retrieved another of the MP5s, the sub-machine-gun compact enough to fit in his jacket pocket.

Morrissey slammed the boot shut.

'Ready?' Newton asked, glancing at his four companions.

They were.

'Let's go.'

117

FRANK NEWTON GUESSED that the range of the security camera above the door of the casino was small. Nevertheless, he took no chances.

He stood beneath it for a moment, gazing at the polished lens, then with one swift movement he used the butt of the .459 like a club. He struck twice, enough to tear the surveillance camera from its perch. As it fell at his feet he kicked it aside.

Watching, are you?

He pressed the buzzer and waited.

And waited.

'Who is it?' a voice finally enquired.

'Tell Billy Parker I've got something for him,' Newton hissed.

'What is it?' the voice persisted.

'Open the door,' Newton rasped.

'Fuck off.'

Newton nodded towards the lock and Morrissey stepped forward.

He shouldered the Ithaca in one smooth movement and squeezed off two shots. The thunderous retorts blasted the lock to atoms and Newton kicked hard against the door. It swung back on its hinges and he and his companions ran inside.

Newton could feel his heart hammering as he scurried into the darkened casino, but he told himself it was the adrenalin rushing through his veins that caused the acceleration. This was not fear. It was exultation.

Two figures appeared halfway down the stairs.

Hobbs, Carson and Newton all opened fire and the staccato rattle of sub-machine-guns filled the air.

Bullets drilled into the gaming tables and raked the staircase. They blasted holes in the paintings on the walls. Several struck the nearest man and he toppled forward, blood spilling from wounds in his chest and stomach.

His companion managed to pull a pistol free and get off two shots.

One parted the air inches from Newton's head. The other buried itself in a roulette table.

Carson fired both barrels of the 210.

There was a deafening roar as the shot exploded in a wide arc, peppering the gunman on the stairs. He went down, bleeding from several small wounds in the legs.

Carson jammed two fresh cartridges into the weapon.

Morrissey upended two of the tables, the large structures crashing over onto their sides. They would afford a little cover at least.

The wounded man was trying to crawl back up the stairs, but Hobbs ran across to him and from point-blank range fired a burst from the MP5 into his back. Blood, pieces of cloth and torn flesh flew into the air with each impact.

Hobbs continued up the stairs, aware of movement from the darkened landing.

He saw two figures up there.

The muzzle flash from one of their guns was blinding.

It was all he saw.

He didn't even hear the bang as the bullet cut through the air, ripped through his left shoulder, then exited, shattering his scapula. Hobbs staggered back, tumbling the last few steps.

Morrissey swung the Ithaca up and worked the slide, firing the lethal blasts at the newcomers.

Newton ran across to Hobbs and dragged him beneath one of the gaming tables, gazing down at the ragged wound in his shoulder.

'My fucking arm's gone numb,' hissed Hobbs, panting for breath, clapping a hand to the hole. He felt broken bone inside the wound. 'Jesus.'

The thunderous roar of the Ithaca still deafened them as Morrissey blasted away. Each shot slammed the shotgun back against his shoulder with the force of a steam-hammer, but he continued to pump the trigger.

Several lumps of wood were blasted away from the bannister balustrade as the shot scythed easily through it.

When the hammer finally hit an empty chamber, he grabbed a handful of spare shells from his pocket and began pushing them into the magazine. The metal of the Ithaca was already hot.

'Ray, watch it!' roared Newton.
Gorman heard his name, but turned slowly.
One of the doors to their right was opening.
The man who stood there was holding a pistol.

118

THE MAN GOT off three rounds: the first sliced off the lobe of Gorman's right ear; the second parted air, then blasted away a portion of a blackjack table; the third did the damage.

It struck Gorman in the right thigh, cut easily through muscle and shattered the femur. He screamed in pain and went down like a felled tree.

'*Cunt!*' he roared and began firing the Spas.

The savage rounds pulverized everything they hit. Two gaming tables were blown in half by the impacts. Several huge holes were blasted into the wall panelling. Nothing hit the gunman, who ducked back inside the room.

Gorman pushed the empty Spas away and grabbed at his bloody thigh with both hands. The blood was flowing steadily but slowly. He could at least be thankful the bullet had missed the femoral artery.

He dragged himself up against the bar, pain enveloping his leg and lower body.

From above, bullets were spattering the ground, fired by the men who had appeared on the upper level.

'We'll never get up those fucking stairs,' grunted Morrissey, sweat already gleaming on his forehead. He ducked low and scuttled across towards the door from which the man who'd shot Gorman had emerged.

He knew he wouldn't have long.

'Frank!' he shouted and Newton understood.

Holding an MP5 in each hand, Newton suddenly stood up and squeezed both triggers simultaneously. The barrels flamed as over sixty rounds of 9mm ammunition were spewed forth in short bursts.

It was enough to send the men above diving for cover – enough to give Morrissey the chance he wanted.

He lowered the Ithaca to waist height and began firing, blowing holes in the door, advancing upon it until he could kick it open.

Still firing, he stepped into the room.

The first discharge caught the man in the stomach and doubled him up.

The second dissolved his features into a crimson mask.

The former soldier retrieved the dead man's Browning Hi-power and stuffed it into his belt.

As he ran back into the main hall the air was filled with smoke, cordite and tiny particles of ash. It stung his eyes and caught in his throat.

Gorman tried to move, but, as he did, Carson could hear the shattered ends of bone grating together.

'Strap it,' Gorman snarled, his face contorted with pain and rage.

Morrissey dragged off his belt, looped it around the bloodstained thigh and pulled tightly.

Gorman was undoing his shirt, pulling it off. 'Use that too,' he instructed.

'You'll never be able to walk on it,' Morrissey told him.

'Just fucking do it, will you?' Gorman gasped. 'Help me up.'

Carson and Morrissey dragged him to his feet, ignoring his agonized groans.

As they began to haul him towards the overturned gaming table that Newton and Hobbs sheltered behind, a fresh salvo of gunfire came from above.

It was one of those bullets that hit Carson.

119

IT STRUCK HIM in the hand; smashed carpal bones and blew his middle finger off.

As he swung the 210 with one hand, another shot caught him in the side. It stove in ribs, burst his left lung and he dropped like a stone.

There was surprisingly little blood.

Morrissey managed to keep going, dragging Gorman with him until he could deposit his injured companion on the blood-spattered carpet close to Newton.

Carson wasn't moving.

Ducked low behind the overturned gaming tables, the four men sucked in breath that was tinged with the smell of gunpowder and blood.

'There's at least six of them up there,' Newton said, nodding towards the landing. 'Including Parker.'

'Any other way out?' Morrissey wanted to know.

'Not as far as I know.'

Newton looked across at Carson once again.

He was still motionless.

'He's dead, isn't he?' Newton said breathlessly.

'Hard to tell,' Morrissey replied. 'But he must be

unconscious. Wounded blokes move about a lot. I can remember *that* much from the army.'

'Take these,' Newton said to Hobbs and Gorman, handing them the sub-machine-guns.

'Where the fuck are *you* going?' Gorman asked.

'Up those stairs,' Newton told him. 'Keep the bastards up there pinned down.'

Newton scrambled across to the body of the man lying at the foot of the staircase. His bullet-riddled corpse was soaked with blood, some of it leaking onto Newton as he slid one arm around the chest of the dead man and lifted it, using the body as a shield.

He began to climb. The weight was almost unbearable, but he drove himself on.

From beneath him, bullets exploded from the sub-machine-guns.

Above, those who dared to raise their heads, fired back.

A slug cut through the dead man's cheek and narrowly missed Newton's head. Another thudded into the chest of the corpse.

Newton guessed he had nine or ten more steps to go until he reached the upper level.

Then what?

Five steps.

More gunfire. From above and below.

His shirt and trousers were drenched in blood from the body he supported.

He fired blindly with the .459, the recoil numbing the heel of his hand.

Two steps.

He pushed the body away from him and dived for the floor, rolling over, not knowing where the next shot was coming from.

And, behind him, Morrissey appeared, the Ithaca roaring in his grasp as he fired.

Newton saw one man go down, his stomach ripped open by a blast from the shotgun. He dropped to his knees and struggled to hold in his intestines.

Another turned to flee, to find shelter somewhere.

Morrissey shot him in the back. The blast severed his spine and propelled him several feet forward. He slammed into the wall, then slid down it, leaving a thick crimson slick behind him.

Newton was on his feet now, turning to see Adam Rawlings emerge from a door away to the right.

He saw him raise the .357 ... saw him fire ... saw the first round catch Morrissey in the back.

DS Darren Brown didn't bother to knock as he burst into the office.

'A mobile unit reports shots fired at number nine Hill Street,' he said.

'That's Parker's casino, isn't it?' DI Ridley muttered. He was already on his feet. 'Get that ARU there now!' he snapped. 'Hurry!'

120

Frank Newton saw Morrissey hit the ground, then he turned, swinging the .459 up, pumping the trigger.

He got off three rounds.

The first went wild, but the second struck Adam Rawlings in the shoulder, tore through and left an exit hole big enough to get a hand in.

The third caught him in the chest.

It didn't, however, prevent him from returning fire.

Newton felt as if he'd been hit in the side by a red-hot hammer. The impact winded him, sent him sprawling backwards, blood pouring from the wound.

His teeth began chattering.

He hauled himself upright and dashed after Rawlings, who was heading for the door that led into the toilets.

Newton fired again, the bullet slicing through the wooden door, before he crashed into the room itself, expecting a dazzling whiteness. But it wasn't a pure white.

It was a charnel-house; the tiles were spattered all over with blood. There was sputum too and some vomit.

And, as he stood there, his own life-fluid dripped down to form fresh puddles.

Rawlings was leaning against the urinals, bleeding heavily from both wounds.

The .357 hung limply in his grip and, for fleeting seconds, he just stared at Newton, his face as white as the tiles behind him.

Newton shot him in the stomach.

The explosion of sound inside the room was incredible.

Newton felt his left eardrum burst. More warm fluid dribbled from his ear.

Rawlings dropped to his knees, the gun skidding across the tiles.

Newton put another hollow tip in the back of his head, then staggered back towards the door.

From his vantage point, he could see that Morrissey was crawling across the floor towards the Ithaca he'd dropped. Once his shaking hand had closed around it, he lay still again.

An unearthly silence had descended over the building, a marked contrast to the seemingly incessant gunfire that had been raging for

(*an hour? It felt like an eternity*)

Christ knew how long.

Newton glanced at his watch. Jesus. The first shot had been fired just six minutes ago.

He could barely hear.

His throat felt as if someone had filled it with chalk and every time he inhaled he smelled blood.

He coughed, tasted a coppery tang on his tongue and, when he spat, the mucous was tinged red.

Below him he heard movement.

Newton took a step forward.

He saw Hobbs scuttling up the stairs, one of the MP5s gripped in his fist.

In the darkness, Newton spotted a thin shaft of light cut like a rapier across the wide landing.

One of the doors opposite was opening.

He swung the .459 up, drew a bead on the figure emerging.

It was Stephen Milliner.

He was carrying an Uzi 9mm sub-machine-gun.

He too had heard Hobbs coming.

Newton smiled thinly as he aimed, the sight trained on Milliner's head.

Hobbs was at the top of the stairs now. But he still couldn't see Milliner who had levelled the Uzi, ready to fire.

Newton pulled the trigger.

Nothing happened.

The gun was jammed.

121

NEWTON FRANTICALLY WORKED the slide and tried again.

Still nothing.

He shook the pistol, raised it, squeezed the trigger.

Gunfire.

But it was coming from the Uzi that Stephen Milliner was holding.

He fired two short bursts at the advancing figure of Hobbs.

Hobbs staggered back as each bullet struck him.

One hit him in the chest, tore through his lung and erupted from his back carrying gobbets of pinkish-red tissue with it.

Another drilled into his stomach, ricocheted inside and cracked his pelvis.

He threw out his arms as the other slugs powered into him.

One blasted a hole in his other shoulder; another punctured the palm of his hand.

He toppled sideways, over the shattered balustrade.

For precious seconds he clutched at empty air, then

plummeted to the ground where he landed with a loud thud.

Newton tossed the .459 aside and pulled the MP5 from inside his jacket, squeezing the trigger.

As he did, he heard a thunderous roar from across the landing. Muzzle flash illuminated the room.

Morrissey had fired the shotgun.

Milliner screamed in agony as the savage discharge caught him between the legs. It blasted away both testicles and most of his penis, practically severed one leg at the groin and sent him toppling backwards, his bowels and lower intestine spilling from the huge hole. Laying on his back with his legs open, he looked as if he had given birth to his own pulverized internal organs.

Newton scurried across to where Morrissey was lying, dragging the former soldier towards a door and throwing all his weight against it. The two of them tumbled through, relieved the room was unoccupied.

The bullet that had floored Morrissey had powered into his back in the lumbar region, macerated a kidney and lodged there. Dark blood was still pumping from the wound and he looked deathly pale. There were ribbons of blood running from both his nostrils and one corner of his mouth.

'They killed Jeff,' said Newton, catching his breath.

Morrissey nodded. 'Get me up, Frank,' he croaked, more blood bubbling over his lips.

Newton hesitated.

'I can feel my legs,' Morrissey insisted. 'I'll be able to walk.'

Supported by Newton, Morrissey struggled upright, still gripping the shotgun. The effort brought fresh pain and he coughed, more blood spraying from his mouth. But when Newton moved to help him he waved him away.

He held up a hand, as if to keep his companion at bay, then took two faltering steps. With each one, the wound wept crimson. But he stayed upright and nodded at Newton.

'Three left including Parker,' Newton said, trying to suck in a deep breath. The wound in his side was throbbing mightily. The front of his shirt and trousers were sodden with blood. His own and others. 'They're in his office,' he continued.

'What've you got left?' Morrissey wanted to know, thumbing fresh cartridges into the Ithaca.

Newton held up the MP5. 'This and one spare mag,' he said.

Morrissey handed him the Browning automatic he'd taken from the man downstairs.

Newton slid the magazine free and counted nine rounds, then he slammed the clip back into the butt, worked the slide and chambered a round.

The two men looked at each other.

Morrissey was the first onto the landing.

The first of the four vehicles carrying the men of the Armed Response Unit roared along Piccadilly, lights flashing, sirens blaring.

Inside each one, the men dressed in dark blue overalls, helmets and protected by Kevlar body armour checked their weapons.

All carried HK81 rifles and many of the men inspected the thirty-round magazines as the convoy sped along the thoroughfare, scattering traffic before it.

They all carried at least two spare magazines.

Detective Inspector John Ridley rode in the leading vehicle.

122

The door of Billy Parker's office was tightly closed.

As Newton and Morrissey edged their way towards it, their eyes never left the oak partition. They expected it to fly open at any moment and their advance to be met by a hail of bullets.

They were less than fifteen feet from the door.

Newton stepped over the body of Stephen Milliner and looked down to see that the dead man's eyes were still open.

They edged nearer.

Morrissey slowed his pace slightly, pain racking his features. He gripped the shotgun so tightly his knuckles turned white – but not as white as his face.

Much of the damage he'd suffered was internal. Bleeding from the nose and mouth was a sure sign of that. He knew it himself.

It felt as if the entire lower part of his body was on fire.

The pain was incredible, but he moved on.

Ten feet.

Newton wiped the perspiration from his face with the

back of one bloodstained hand. It left a red smear on the skin.

Six feet to the door now.

He levelled the MP5; held the Browning at arm's length.

Come on, you bastards. Step out now.

They were within touching distance of the door.

Newton pressed himself against one side of the frame, Morrissey the other.

With infinite slowness, Newton reached out a hand and closed it around the handle.

His palm was slippery with sweat and blood and slid uselessly on the brass fitting.

He gritted his teeth and tried again. The handle wouldn't budge.

He looked across at Morrissey, pointed first at the shotgun, then at the handle.

The former soldier understood. He raised the Ithaca and fired twice.

The handle was blasted off, the door itself swung open.

Both men dashed in, fingers jerking hard on triggers.

The rattle of machine-gun fire mingled with the thunder of shotgun blasts and the shouts of men to form one incredible cacophony.

Newton felt a bullet cut through his forearm; another hit him in the chest, punching through bone and muscle. Blood sprayed into the air.

He fired back, blinded by the muzzle flashes.

Morrissey worked the slide of the Ithaca, the thunderous blasts ripping through whatever they hit.

They heard the sound of breaking glass, of splintering wood.

Then they were inside the room: still firing, still being shot at.

Newton was hit again in the shoulder.

Morrissey took one in the chest, his elbow splintered by a round.

He dropped the shotgun and collapsed in a rapidly spreading pool of his own blood.

And before him Newton saw Paul Palmer slump forward, his body drilled with over a dozen rounds.

Beside him, Ian Milliner was standing with his back to the far wall, bulletholes in his chest, stomach and face. One eye socket had been blasted empty by a stray shot. Most of the left side of his head was missing, splattered across the wall.

Smoke hung in the air like a shroud.

Newton could barely hear anything. His head was spinning. Pain enveloped him like a heated glove and it squeezed until he moaned with the sheer effort of remaining upright.

And, in the middle of it all, panting like a dog, was Billy Parker, his body punctured by half a dozen bullets including one that had torn away part of his bottom jaw. There were several of his teeth lying on the desk before him.

He was holding an automatic in his right hand, but the slide was back. The weapon was empty.

Newton took a step towards him and, as he did, he heard the sucking sound coming from one of Parker's ruptured lungs. The air whistled loudly in the hole every time he tried to draw breath. A rasping noise like bellows filled with mucous.

Another few minutes and the lungs would cease working completely.

Newton walked around him, aware that Parker hardly had the strength to move. All he could do was stand motionless as Newton pulled at something on the wall behind him.

He realized it was one of the antique swords.

Newton hefted the samurai blade in both hands, amazed at the lightness of the lethal steel. 'What did you say about the Yardies, Billy?' Newton gasped. 'No honour? What the fuck do you know about honour?'

He swung the blade.

It cut effortlessly through Parker's neck, severing the head just below the chin. An enormous gout of blood erupted from the stump, spraying into the air like a crimson fountain.

The head itself fell onto the desktop, then rolled off.

The body toppled sideways, blood still ejaculating from the neck.

Newton dropped the blade, his body shaking now.

He felt cold.

So cold.

He fell backwards, slumped upright against the wall.

As he heard the first sirens, he closed his eyes.

123

THE NIGHT ITSELF seemed to be ablaze.

Everywhere Detective Inspector John Ridley looked there were emergency vehicles blocking Hill Street, their red lights blazing.

Ambulances. Fire engines. Police cars.

The men of the Armed Response Unit advanced towards the door of the casino. But there was no urgency now.

Elsewhere, uniformed officers were clearing the thoroughfare of passers-by. Some of the houses were even being evacuated.

Ridley joined the second wave of armed policemen, moving slowly into the gaming club that had become a slaughterhouse. Paramedics also scurried in and out amongst the armed men.

'Jesus Christ,' he murmured, surveying the carnage.

There were bodies everywhere.

He recognized one: James Carson was being lifted onto a stretcher.

Ridley watched as the plastic body bag was zipped up around him.

'This one's still alive,' shouted a paramedic.

Ridley hurried across to where the man was hunched over Ray Gorman. He was about to slide a hypodermic needle into the injured man's arm: a sedative – a painkiller. Something to put him out.

Ridley stopped him. 'Where's Newton?' the DI asked.

'Upstairs,' Gorman murmured. 'But I think you're a bit late.'

The paramedic pumped 25cc of Thorazine into him and Gorman slipped into the welcoming arms of unconsciousness.

Ridley climbed the stairs, past more bodies.

He reached the landing.

There was blood everywhere: on the walls, the carpets, the balustrade.

He saw more corpses, stepped over that of Stephen Milliner.

He paused as he entered Parker's office.

More blood. More bodies.

As he took a step forward his foot brushed against something and he looked down.

Billy Parker's severed head rolled over.

Ridley stepped away quickly.

He saw Newton over by the window, chin resting on his chest.

Frank fucking Newton.

Ridley stood over the body wanting to feel something. Hate. Anger. Satisfaction.

He felt nothing except perhaps a little sadness.

In death, Newton looked so old. So vulnerable.

Ridley knew that feeling well.

He knelt beside the body and looked down at the hands. At the wedding ring.

It came free with surprising ease and the DI slipped it into his pocket and straightened up just as two paramedics entered.

'No need to rush,' he said flatly.

He turned and walked out of the office, down the stairs and into the street. Out of the reeking air, away from the stink of cordite and blood.

He leant on the bonnet of a car and lit a cigarette.

'Looks like they've done us a favour,' said DS Brown, joining him. 'Killing each other. First the Yardies, now Parker. All gone.' He smiled. 'Makes you wonder what'll come next, doesn't it?'

More bodies were being brought out now, carried on stretchers to ambulances that would ferry them to morgues for identification.

'Things are changing,' Brown remarked.

Ridley wondered if he might wait for Newton's body to be brought out, but, finally, he decided against it.

'I said things are changing,' the DS repeated.

Ridley nodded. 'I think I liked them better the way they used to be,' he murmured. He took a drag on his cigarette, dug his hands in his pockets and set off down Hill Street towards Berkeley Square. He could feel the wedding ring in his hand.

'Guv, where are you going?' the DS wanted to know.

Ridley kept walking.

He didn't look back.

124

PAULA NEWTON HADN'T cried as much as she'd expected to.

The policewoman who had called at the house in Campdale Road had been unusually compassionate, even putting her arm around Paula at one stage.

Perhaps, she told herself, her lack of tears were because she had felt an awful inevitability about this particular knock on the door. This uniformed constable telling her that her husband had been killed.

There was, she'd been told, no need for her to visit the morgue. Formal identification had already been made.

Paula was grateful for that, especially when she learned *how* he had died.

Also, who would she get to look after Danielle while she visited his body? While she stood over him and said her final goodbye.

Over an hour had passed when she heard another knock.

For a moment she considered ignoring it, then, finally, she trudged through the hall and opened the front door.

Detective Inspector John Ridley nodded a greeting.

'What do *you* want?' she snapped.

'Could I come in, please?' he asked, his tone soft, almost reverential.

'You know Frank's dead?'

'That's why I'm here.'

'What do you want to do? Search the house?'

'I just want to talk.'

'I've got nothing to say to you.'

'*I've* got something to say to *you*.'

Paula stepped back and allowed him in.

The hall was still filled with suitcases and holdalls.

He wandered through into the living room.

'Where's your little girl?' Ridley asked.

'She's asleep and I'd appreciate it if you didn't disturb her. Say what you've come to say and go.'

'Seventeen years ago your husband was involved in a wages snatch. I swore then that I'd catch him. He caused the death of my brother. It ate away at me. I was obsessed with finding him, putting him away.'

Paula watched him impassively.

'You see, when my brother died *he* left behind a wife and daughter too. So I know how you must be feeling.'

'You have absolutely *no* idea how I'm feeling,' she rasped.

'I spent enough time with my sister-in-law after my brother's death to know. Believe me.'

'If you've come here to offer your sympathy, I don't need it.' She wiped her eyes quickly, as if anxious he shouldn't see the tears.

'I know now that no matter what I could have done to your husband, it wouldn't have helped bring my brother back. I don't even think I was doing it for *him*. With your husband gone, it's like a part of me is gone too. I hated him for so long that was all I had. Now he's not there, nor is that hate, that need for revenge. I don't know what *is* left for me now.'

'This change of character doesn't suit you, Detective Inspector,' she said, sniffing back tears. 'Please go. I really don't care what *you're* feeling. I don't care what's missing from *your* life. I've lost my husband, the man I loved. That's all that matters to me.'

He dug in his pocket and pulled out the ring. 'I thought you might want this,' he told her, pressing the ring into her hand.

As she stared at the gold band, tears beginning to flow freely, Ridley made his way to the front door. When she heard the door open she hurried into the hall, wiping the tears away.

'Thank you,' she said, clutching the ring to her chest.

Ridley nodded and closed the door behind him as he left.

Paula stood motionless in the hall for a moment, then she uncurled her hand and looked at the ring lying on her palm.

She began to cry, great racking sobs that shook her entire body. She felt she would never be able to stop.

Then, from upstairs, she heard a softer, smaller cry.

Danielle.

Paula took a deep breath, fought to control herself.

She kissed the ring and pushed it into the pocket of her jeans. Then, slowly, she made her way up the stairs.

'I'm coming, darling,' she called softly as she climbed.

She even managed a smile.

Her daughter was waiting.